B. P. Pratten

The Scottish Antiquary

Northern notes & queries. Vol. XII

B. P. Pratten

The Scottish Antiquary
Northern notes & queries. Vol. XII

ISBN/EAN: 9783337239282

Printed in Europe, USA, Canada, Australia, Japan

Cover: Foto ©Andreas Hilbeck / pixelio.de

More available books at **www.hansebooks.com**

THE
SCOTTISH ANTIQUARY

or
Northern Notes & Queries

EDITED BY

J. H. STEVENSON, M.A., F.S.A. SCOT.,

ADVOCATE

ESTABLISHED 1886

VOL. XII

EDINBURGH
GEORGE P. JOHNSTON, 33 GEORGE STREET
MDCCCXCVIII

Edinburgh: T. and A. CONSTABLE, Printers to Her Majesty

CONTENTS

No. 45—JULY 1897.

No. 46—OCTOBER 1897.

No. 47—JANUARY 1898.

No. 48—APRIL 1898.

LIST OF ILLUSTRATIONS

ANNUAL SUBSCRIPTION, 4s., payable in advance. Postage 6d. extra
Subscribers' Names to be sent to the PUBLISHER, 33 GEORGE STREET,
EDINBURGH, from whom back numbers may also be got.

CONTENTS

BINDING

THE PUBLISHER has arranged to bind the Volumes of *The
Scottish Antiquary* uniformly in a strong, durable, and tasteful
binding of best English morocco and cloth sides, with gilt tops, at
4s. 6d. per Volume. Two volumes may be bound in one.

33 GEORGE STREET, EDINBURGH.

The Scottish Antiquary

OR

Northern Notes and Queries

VOL. XII. JULY 1897. No. 45.

ROBERT STEWART, BISHOP OF CAITHNESS, AND THE DATE OF LINDSAY OF PITSCOTTIE'S CHRONICLE.

ROBERT STEWART, Bishop of Caithness, to whom the dedicatory verses prefixed to several MSS. of the Chronicle of Scotland by Robert Lindsay of Pitscottie. a name so well known to students of Scottish history and of the Scottish prose dialect, were addressed, was a man of minor importance in himself, but of considerable consequence as a representative of the curious career led by some Scottish nobles in the transitional and revolutionary period called the Reformation. Lord Lindsay in his *Lives of the Lindsays* has expressed doubt whether the verses were really written or sent by Pitscottie. They are poor poetry of which no one could be proud, but there is no reason to suppose Pitscottie was a poet. Picturesque prose was his forte as a writer. His age was not one which produced original poetry, and the verses are only an indifferent specimen of the kind then in vogue, and which almost any one who used the pen could write. When examined in the light of the Bishop's life, and in relation to his position and connections, it will be seen that Pitscottie has good claim to be, as he claims to be, their author. They help us to understand the origin and purpose of his *History*, which was like so many of the works of this period. a pamphlet in the war of the Reformation. They also enable us to fix approximately the date of its composition, which has been hitherto an unsolved problem.

Robert Stewart, Bishop of Caithness, must not be confounded, as he is by a slip in the index of Laing's edition of the *Works of John Knox* and by Gordon in his *Monasticon* (i. p. 88), with Lord Robert Stewart, the bastard of James V., who became Abbot of Holyrood and Bishop of Orkney. He was the second son of the third Earl of Lennox, and younger brother of Matthew, fourth Earl, the father of Darnley, and Regent of Scotland. His mother was Lady Anne Stewart, daughter of John, Earl of Athole, brother-uterine of James II. He was born in 1523. While yet a youth he became Provost of Dumbarton College, and in 1541 or 1542 was granted the 'administration of the Cathedral of Caithness' and designated to the Bishopric by Paul III., 'having nothing of the sacred character except the tonsure,' to use the singular but probably very appropriate expression of the letter by the Regent Arran to that Pope in December 1544. The object of this letter was to induce the Pope to deprive him of these offices and their emoluments in consequence of his having taken part with his brother the Earl in the rebellion against Arran. After its failure he fled with Lennox to England. On 17th May 1543 he had signed a contract between the Earl of Glencairn, Lennox, and Henry VIII. at Carlisle by which the two Earls promised to aid Henry against Scotland, and Henry in return engaged to give his niece, the Lady Margaret Douglas, in marriage to Lennox and to make him Governor of Scotland. The Bishop-Elect of Caithness was to remain as a hostage in England while his brother made an expedition against Scotland.[1]

Hertford's raid on the east coast in 1544, and one by Lennox on the west in the following year, resulted in nothing but pillage, and on 1st October 1545 the Bishop of Caithness was impeached for treason before the Parliament which met in Edinburgh on 2nd September of that year. Cardinal Beaton protested that as a Bishop-Elect he was subject to his jurisdiction as his Ordinary and not to that of Parliament. The summons for treason was deserted at the adjourned Parliament of Linlithgow on 1st October 1545.[2] Lennox, who had also been impeached, was forfeited on 9th October 1545.

To such a height had the privilege of clergy risen at the eve of the Reformation that the treason of a clerk, who had nothing of the clerical character but the tonsure, could only be tried in the Ecclesiastical Court to the exclusion of Parliament.

The Bishop of Caithness appears to have lived several years chiefly in England, but not without making occasional visits to Scotland. While on one of these visits we find him in contact with a curious character well known to those who have wandered in the by-paths of Scottish history, John Elder. Elder was the author of the letter written in 1542 to Henry VIII. advocating union with England, in which the often-quoted description of the Highlanders as 'rough-footed Scots' occurs.[3] In 1555 he published in London a letter sent into Scotland and addressed to 'The ryghte reverende and his very especial good lord Robert Stuarde, Bishop of Catheness and provost of Dumbritane Colledge in Scotlande, John Elder, his humble oratour, wisheth health and prosperous felicitie.' The letter bears to be written for New Year's Day 1555, and its most interesting part contains an account of the arrival and marriage of Philip of Spain to Queen Mary, and the legation of Cardinal Pole. The writer appears in complete sympathy with Cardinal Pole and the restoration of the Roman Catholic Church, and confesses his repentance for his lapse from it during the last twenty years, though curiously enough he absolves himself from 'association with hereticks,' while he accuses himself of

Keith, *History*, i. p. 87.   [2] *Act. Parl.* ii. pp. 452, 454-456.
[3] Appendix to Camden Society, *Chronicle of Queen Mary* (Vol. for 1855).

'voluptuous living.' Whether he thought the Bishop shared his senti-
ments is not made quite clear, but he would hardly have written to him
in such terms otherwise. He encloses certain verses and adages written
by Darnley, the Bishop's nephew, at Temple Newsome, then only a boy
of nine, and praises his 'towerdness in the Latin tongue and the French
and in sundrye other virtuous qualities whom also God and Nature hath
endowed with a good wit, gentilness, beautie, and favour.' The parents
of Darnley he calls his 'singular good patrons,' and the Bishop had
evidently befriended him, though how or why this New Year letter, as he
styles it, got into print is not clear. It was a fortunate accident, for it
contains the only full account of King Philip's marriage to Mary Tudor,
and the earliest description of the young Darnley.

In 1563 the Bishop finally returned to Scotland, where he became a
supporter of the Reformers, though the date when he turned Protestant
does not seem certain. When the death of the Regent Moray in 1570
opened that office to Lennox, his brother shared the spoils, and became
Commendator of the Priory of St. Andrews, still continuing, however, to
hold the designation of Bishop of Caithness and to draw the revenues
without discharging any of the duties of the See. Almost the solitary
Episcopal act with which he is credited was that in 1571 he joined with
John Spottiswoode, the Superintendent of Lothian, and David Lindsay,
Minister of Leith, afterwards Tulchan Bishop of Ross, in the consecration
of John Douglas, Morton's Tulchan Archbishop of St. Andrews.

The death of his brother the Regent and of his nephew Charles, Earl
of Lennox, without issue in 1576 made the bishop next lawful heir, after
the young king himself, to the title of Lennox, which was recognised by
a charter of confirmation in his favour, dated 16th June, 1578, and ratified
in Parliament by the Acts 1579, c. 39 and 40. But James VI., by an act,
which shows the arbitrary power of the Scottish king in dealing with titles,
revoked the infeftment in favour of the Bishop and bestowed the title and
estates on his then favourite James Stewart, Lord of Aubigny. Some
sort of compromise had been arranged with the Bishop, who received in
exchange the title of Earl of March, and James availed himself of the right
of revocation on attaining his fourteenth year by revoking the grant of the
Lennox Earldom to the Bishop of Caithness. An attempt seems to have
been made about the same time to get the Bishop to surrender the Com-
mendatorship of the Priory of St. Andrews in favour of another royal
favourite, Captain James Stewart, afterwards Earl of Arran, and a Procuratory of Resignation in James Stewart's favour was executed, but the
Bishop revoked it on 9th June 1580.[1]

It was not wonderful, for this was the very time when the scandalous
process of nullity of marriage was in progress at the instance of the
Bishop's wife in order that she might marry Arran. This lady, Elizabeth
Stewart, a daughter of John, fourth Duke of Athole, is described by Spottis-
woode as 'a woman intolerable in all the imperfections incident to that
sex.' When very young she had been married to Hugh, seventh Lord
Lovat, and after his death, 1st January 1576, she became the wife of the
Bishop of Caithness on 5th January 1578-9. They separated in
November 1579, and she raised her action of nullity before the Com-
missaries on 22nd March 1580, in which, after very singular pleadings,

[1] *Reg. Priv. Council*, iii. p. 293; and see Professor Masson's preface to this volume.
p. xxx., as to the whole history of the proceedings relative to the Lennox Earldom.

narrated by Riddel,[1] she obtained final decree on 19th May 1581. On 6th July following she married Arran, with whom she had been carrying on a criminal intrigue.

It has been said that the Bishop of Caithness lived a retired life at St. Andrews, which seems to have been his chief residence in Scotland after his return. He probably lived in the Prior's house. But in fact he took a considerable though not a leading part in public business. In 1578 he was a commissioner for visiting the Universities of Glasgow and St. Andrews, and he signed the visitors' report in 1579. He attended Parliament and the Privy Council, acted as Auditor of Accounts, and was more than once on the Committee of the Articles. He is one of the somewhat numerous body of persons who are mentioned as having seen John Knox on his deathbed, and he acted as one of the curators of Elizabeth Stewart, daughter of the Regent Moray. One of his last acts was signing in 1585 a league with England against the Catholic powers, and entitled ' Band anent the Trew Religioun or Act of Estates for a League offensive and defensive with England,'[2] which had been negotiated through the skilful diplomacy of Sir Henry Wotton.

On 2nd July 1583, when James VI. visited Falkland, it is mentioned that he supped with his great-uncle. The Bishop died at St. Andrews in 1586 at the age of sixty-three, and was buried in the Chapel of St. Leonard's, the college which took the side of the reformers. In its roofless aisle a tablet to his memory may yet be seen with the lines on the architrave

> ' In portu Fluctusque omnes classemque relinquo,
> Me spectans mundumque omnem fascesque relinquo.'

As the Bishop is described in the lines prefixed to Pitscottie as Bishop of Caithness and Commendator of the Priory of St. Andrews, and neither as Earl of Lennox nor Earl of March, it appears certain that they must have been written before he attained either of these dignities. Although his nephew Charles, Earl of Lennox, died in 1576, his nearest heir was King James himself, and the Bishop of Caithness did not hold the title till it was conferred upon him by the Charter of 16th June 1578. John, the fourth Duke of Athole, who is referred to in the verses, and who was father-in-law of the Bishop by the marriage of his daughter to him on 5th January 1578-9, died on 24th April 1579 at Stirling, and as the verses request the MS. of Pitscottie to be sent on to Athole after the Bishop had perused it, they cannot have been written after his death.

We may therefore conclude that both the verses and the accompanying MS. of Pitscottie, which brings the History of Scotland from the death of James I. down to the year 1575, as having been written, or at least completed, between 1575 and 16th June 1578, the date of the Charter of the Earldom of Lennox in favour of the Bishop of Caithness. The latter date very nearly corresponds with the period of his closest intimacy with Athole, who became his father-in-law on 5th January 1578-9.

Æ. M.

[1] Riddel, *Peerage Law*, i. pp. 532 *et seq.*
[2] *Reg. of Privy Council*, iii. p. 760, and *Acts of Parliament*, iii. 811, and iv. 212 : C. Howard, *History*, iv. 373.

THE POEMS OF DAVID RATE, CONFESSOR OF KING JAMES THE FIRST OF SCOTLAND.

WITH the exception of the Register of the Great Seal, Scottish records do not appear to contribute anything towards a biography of David Rate. What is more remarkable, however, is the omission of all mention of him in *Scriptores Ordinis Praedicatorum* by Quetif and Echard, the historians of the Order. To them his very name appears to have been unknown. The fact of the silence of that work regarding the Confessor of King James the First of Scotland was first communicated to me by the Very Reverend John Placid Conway of Hawkesyard Priory, Rugeley, to whom also I am indebted for a suggestion which has led me into a field that otherwise might have been wholly unexplored. To the question—Do the English archives of the Dominicans preserve any information about David Rate? Frater Conway replied in the negative. But having read the proof-sheets of my previous article,[1] he pointed me to a memoir in Quetif and Echard's work, and asked if there might not be some strange confusing of Ralph Strode with David Rate. The memoir in question is as follows:—'Frater Ralph Strode, a Scot, an alumnus of the House of Dryburgh in Teviotdale, having read at home the usual philosophy and theology, was sent to Saint James's, the seminary established at Paris for the English Province. He is said to have travelled not only in France, but also in Germany and Italy, and indeed to have gone beyond sea into Syria and the Holy Land. On coming home he was entrusted with the planting and establishing of new Houses in the kingdom, as Dempster relates on the authority of Gilbert Brown, a Scot, in his *Foundations of Monasteries in Scotland.*

'In the vernacular speech of the Scots he was eminently skilful, and spoke it elegantly. He also cultivated vernacular poetry, and so excelled in that kind of writing as to be reckoned by Geoffrey Chaucer among the chief poets of his country and of the age. He flourished 1370. He wrote many things in Latin and in the vernacular which may be thus classified:—

'Charming tales in verse.

'Several panegyrics in vernacular verse.

'Summulae logicales, Formulae Consequentiarum et Sophismatum strophae.

'Ralph's Fancies.

'An Itinerary to the Holy Land.

'Positions and xviii. arguments against John Wiclif, etc.[2]

'Dempster mentions a certain place where, in a Scottish MS. awaiting editing, they possess and even show his writings. The well-known Simler and Possevin mention this writer only as a monk: our notice has been made on the testimony of Dempster.'

---

[1] *Scottish Antiquary*, vol. xi., April 1897, page 145.

[2] 1370. F. Radulphus Strodus Scotus domus Dryburgensis in Trevalia alumnus post jam lectas apud suos de more philosophiam et theologiam, Parisios ad gymnasium San-jacobeum pro rata Provinciae Angliae missus est. At non Galliam modo sed et Germaniam et Italiam lustrâsse dicitur, quin et in Syriam et in Terram Sanctam transfretasse. Unde ad suos reversus, novis in patria erigendis instituendisque domibus praepositus est, uti Dempsterus refert ex Gilberto Bruno gentili Scoto in Monasteriorum Scotiae Fundationibus. Vernaculam Scotorum linguam egregie calluit, eaque loquebatur elegantissime. Poeticen etiam vernaculam coluit, eoque scribendi genere sic emicuit, ut inter praecipuos

Four authorities for that biographical sketch are cited, namely, Dempster, Brown, Simler, and Possevin, Dempster being the principal. Simler and Possevin, we are expressly informed, do not mention Strode as an author, but only as a monk, Gilbert Brown, it will be observed, being merely named as the authority followed by Dempster. It is therefore to Dempster's *History*,[1] *voce* Radulphus Strodus, that one naturally turns first. 'Ralph Strode,' it tells us, 'studied at Oxford, but earlier received his education in the monastery of Dryburgh in Teviotdale, as Gilbert Brown mentions in his *Foundations of Monasteries*. Subsequently he so excelled in the English tongue that Geoffrey Chaucer ranked him among the chief poets of his age. Many of his works, not seen by Englishmen, are extant in the library of the beforementioned monastery. It is supposed that he travelled in Italy, Germany, and France; also that he visited the Holy Land, and returned hither to end his days.' Dempster's catalogue of works agrees with the one in *Scriptores Ordinis Praedicatorum*.

We shall direct attention immediately to the slight points of divergence between these two versions, but before doing so it will be better to note what is said concerning Strode in earlier writers.

He has been regarded by Chaucerian editors as the person addressed, along with Gower, in the well-known passage of *Troilus and Criseyde*, Book v. st. 266 and 267 :—

> O moral Gower, this book I directe
> To thee, and to the philosophical Strode
> To vouchen sauf, ther nede is, to corecte,
> Of your benignitees and zeles gode.
> And to that sothfast Crist, that starf on rode,
> With al myn herte of mercy ever I preye ;
> And to the lord right thus I speke and seye :

---

patriae seculique sui poetas apud Galfredum Chaucerum annumeretur. Claruit ad annum MDCCCLXX. Scripsit Latine et vernacule plura, quae sic recensentur.

Fabulae lepidae versu.

Panegyrici plures versu patrio et vernaculo.

Summulae logicales, Formulae Consequentiarum et Sophismatum Strophae.

Phantasmata Radulphi.

Itinerarium Terrae Sanctae.

Positiones et XVIII. argumenta contra Joannem Wikliff haereticum ea aetate in Anglia furentem.

Sic refert Dempsterus illa autem ubi habeantur saltem ms. docebant qui catalogo codd. Ms. Scotiae edendo dicuntur incumbere. Hujus scriptoris meminerunt Simlerus et Possivenus monachum solum praestantes, nostrum ex fide Dempsteri non exhibere non potuimus. *Scriptores Ordinis Praedicatorum*, Sec. xiv. p. 666, ed. by Quetif and Echard (*c.* 1700).

[1] Radulphus Strode eadem lege qua superior Oxoniae studuit, sed prius in Dryburgensi Tevidaliae coenobio diu bonis literis incubuerat, ut in Monasteriorum Fundationibus Gilbertus Brunus docet: postea Anglorum linguam et elegantias sic didicit, ut Galfredus Chaucerus inter praecipuos sui seculi poetas eum reposuerit. Extalant multa ejus opera, non visa ab Anglis, in bibliotheca dicti coenobii. Putatur Italiam Germaniam et Gallias lustrasse, tum Terram Sanctam visitasse, ac domum rediisse illique supremum diem obiisse. Scripsit Fabulas lepidas versu, lib. i. Consequentiarum Formulas, lib. i. Sophismatum Strophas, lib. i. Itinerarium Terrae Sanctae, lib. i. Panegyricos versu patrio, lib. i. Summulas logicales, lib. i. Phantasma Radulphi, lib. i. Positiones et xviii. argumenta contra Wiclessum, Haereticum, lib. i. Quaesuborum lib. i. quae falso nuper prodierunt sub nomine Radulphi Feriburgi. Claruit anno MCCCLXX. *Historia Ecclesiastica Gentis Scotorum*, *voce* Radulphus Strodus (Bann. Club. 1829), vol. ii. p. 596.

Thou oon and two and three eterne on-lyve
That regnest ay in three and two and oon
Uncircumscript and al mayst circumscryve,
Us from Visible and invisible foon
Defende : and to thy mercy everichoon
So make us, Jesus, for thy grace digne
For love of mayde and moder thyn benigne ! Amen.

In his *Collectanea*, John Leland tells us that he found in a book of Merton College at Oxford the name Ralph Strode in a list of Fellows of that House.[1] The entry as he gives it, under the year 1370, is as follows :—'Radulphus Stroode nobilis poeta fuit, et versificavit librum elegiacum, vocatum Phantasma Radulphi.' In the *Commentaries concerning British Writers*, by the same learned antiquary, Strode is noticed as a distinguished Mertonian, who had ardently wooed the Muses. The poem mentioned in the catalogue of Merton Fellows, we are told, was from its theme, called *Phantasma*.[2]

In John Bale's *Britanniæ Scriptores*, printed in 1548, Strode is mentioned as 'an Englishman, the same who is named by John Major in his *History of the Scots.*' Nothing is said about his having written poetry ; only his philosophical and controversial works are catalogued. In the edition of 1557, however, the biography is amplified, two works being added, one the *Phantasma Radulphi*, the other an *Itinerary to the Holy Land*. In that second edition Strode is identified as the friend of Chaucer named in *Troilus*.[3]

In the *Relationes Historicæ* of John Pits, published in 1619, we find Strode described as 'an Englishman, a poet-laureate, who studied at Oxford, and was of Merton College, where he wrote his works in polished and correct Latin, in poetry greatly excelling.'[4]

---

[1] *Collectanea*, vol. iii. p. 54.

[2] Radulphus Strodaeus Maridunensi choro ornamento vel maximo fuit. Coluit enim flagrantissimo amore eloquentiam et Musas canoras. Illae rursus cultorem usque adeo reclamabant suum, ut veneres, gratias et lepores in ejus abunde instillarent osculum. Vates autem, tantis donatus muneribus cantionem elegiacum voce sonora liquida arguta cecinit : cui et *Phantasma* nomen à re inditum teste catalogo illustreis Maridunensis societatis viros percelebrante. *Commentarii de Scriptoribus Britannicis*, Joanne Lelando ; ex autographo Lelandino nunc primus editit, Antonius Hall, Oxford 1709.

[3] The text of the 1548 edition is as follows :—'Strodus Anglus, eodem in Scotorum gestis Joanne Majore et illo ipso in libro teste, ab Oxonio quoque prodiit sophista subtillissimus, omni enim impostri-ce doctrina armatus pro Antichristi regno advers. Wicleum, tumentes attolebat cristas, Octodecim argumentis sophisticis, et aliis positionibus iniquis, veritatem nitebat supprimere, sed a gloria majestatis illius oppressus, in fovea cecidit quâ paraverat. Ita quod posthac nec cleri dotatione dominium celibatum, missas, horas, caeremonias, nec simile qoodpiam sulcire poterat, argutiis frivolas. Evomuit tamen ad posteritatis corruptelam

Consequentiarum formulas
Sophi-matum strophas
Summulas logicales
Positiones contra Wicleaum.

Et alias adhuc persimiles tenebricosi putei feces Paganicae temeritatis flagitium esse tunc dicelant, etc.' In the 1557 edition the Memoir begins :—'Radulphus Strodus, Martonensis collegii apud Oxoniensis alumnus, dialecticorum gravissimus author ab Italorum et Gallorum sophistis appellatur. Iuvenis flagrantissimo desiderio eloquentiâ quaerebat musasq. et lepores colebat : unde laureolum poeticam meruit tandem. Ab Italia reversus postea superbas contra Vuicleum, etc. . . . Anglicum poetam Chaucerus hunc vocat in fine sui Troili,' etc.

[4] Radulphus Strodus Poeta laureatus Anglus, Oxonii diu studuit fuitque è societate Collegi Mertonensis, ubi omnem sermonis Latini politiorem elegantiam accurate dedicit et in poesi maxime excelluit. Postea Gallinam peragravit et Italiam magnamque in

Later writers who have had occasion to mention Strode have generally accepted without question Dempster's statement about the Scottish origin of the man and his connection with the Dominican Order. George Mackenzie, author of *The Lives and Characters of the most Eminent Writers of the Scots Nation*, simply translated Dempster's memoir, adding, as his custom was, a few quite worthless embellishments of his own. Rashdall in *The Universities of Europe in the Middle Ages*, has a note, ' Ralph Strode is said to have been a Scotch Fellow of Merton.' It was left to Dr. Horstman, some six years ago, to awaken new interest in Chaucer's philosophical friend. From him came the suggestion that Strode's poetry is to be identified in certain well-known and highly meritorious alliterative pieces in the British Museum MS. Cotton. Nero A. x.—a suggestion almost immediately accepted and strenuously maintained by Mr. Israel Gollancz in the Introduction to his delightful edition of *Pearl*, published in 1891. Mr. Gollancz is of opinion that Ralph Strode wrote not only *Pearl*, but also *Gawain and the Grene Knight, Clanness, and Pacyence.* ' One must not despair,' he says, ' of solving the most complex problem of the poet's personality. Indeed of one fourteenth-century writer, whose name and Latin writings are preserved, it is recorded that during his youth and early manhood he was an ardent wooer of the muses, and that his fame rested on a poem described as an elegy and a vision. Our knowledge of this writer is mainly due to the happy chance that Chaucer was his friend and admirer, and dedicated to him no less important a poem than his *Troilus and Criseyde.* . . . The antiquary Leland was the first to inquire concerning the second of the two names held in such esteem by Chaucer. In an old catalogue of worthies of Merton College, drawn up in the early years of the fifteenth century, and still preserved in the College muniment-room, he discovered the following most valuable reference :— " Radulphus Strode nobilis poeta fuit et versificavit librum elegiacum vocatum Phantasma Radulphi." This Ralph Strode is identical with the famous philosopher of that name whose philosophical works hold an important place in the history of mediæval logic. He was also famous in his time as a controversialist with Wiclif and from Wiclif MSS. still unprinted it is possible to gain some insight into Strode's religious views. But neither his theology nor his philosophy help us in any way to identify the writer with the poems in the Cottonian collection. The evidence such as it is, tending to connect Strode and the writer of *Pearl*, is derived from the following considerations :—The Merton description of the lost poem does not apply to any known poem in the English language so well as to the *Pearl*. Again, the peculiar force of the Chaucerian dedication has, I think, never been properly understood. Chaucer felt that his *Troilus and Criseyde* was open, and justly so, to the charge of being somewhat too free ; wherefore, in a spirit of banter he dedicated it to two fellow-poets whose poetry aimed primarily at enforcing moral virtue. Now if asked to name the very antithesis to *Troilus*, a student of fourteenth-century literature could choose no better instance than the romance of *Gawain*. Further, there is a tradition that Strode left his native land and

..... regione cum doctissimis quibusque viris contraxit amicitiam et familiaritatem. Erat ...... vir urbanus et acuti lepidique ingenii quique sales jocosos in omni familiari ...... gratiose miscere potuit et saepenumero consuevit. Hunc Galfredus Chaucerus in ...... Troili honoris causa ita nominat quasi inter praecipuos Anglice gentis poetas ...... licet,' etc.—*Relationum Historiarum*, Paris, 1619. The catalogue of works is ... in Bale.

journeyed through France, Germany, and Italy, and visited Syria and the Holy Land. An *Itinerary to the Holy Land* by this writer seems to have been known to Nicholas Brigham,[1] the enthusiastic devotee of Chaucer, to whom we owe his monument in Westminster Abbey.' It remains to be seen whether this chaplet so recently brought to light is an ancient one now being restored to Strode, or only one made partly in Germany partly in England in the last decade of the nineteenth century.

Taking the early writers in their chronological sequence, they stand as follows:—Chaucer, Leland, Bale, Pits, Dempster, Quetif, and Echard, and in that order we propose now to examine them.

Chaucer's friend is, in *Troilus and Criseyde*, simply 'the philosophical Strode'; his Christian name is not given. John Bale, writing more than one hundred and fifty years after Chaucer's time, is, as we have seen, the first to identify Ralph Strode as the person honoured by the great poet. The note in Leland's *Collectanea*,[2] which describes Strode as 'a noble poet who wrote a book in elegiac verse, entitled Ralph's *Phantasma*,'[3] loses much of its value when we are told that the *Vetus Catalogus* in which it occurs, still preserved at Merton, and written not earlier than 1420, originally set forth only the surnames of the Fellows,—the Christian names and short biographical notes appended being in a late fifteenth-century hand.[4] The editor of *Memorials of Merton College* states that several cases of palpable error in these biographical notices have at various times been discovered. Both the Christian name of the Merton Fellow and his authorship of the unknown book of elegies must, therefore, for the present be received with caution.

To Bale, the immediate successor of Leland, the Christian name of the Oxford scholar appears to have been unknown in 1548. In the first edition of *Scriptores* we find simply 'Strodus Anglus.' and it is noteworthy that in John Major's *History* also, cited by Bale, the surname alone is given. It is as a philosopher and controversialist that Strode finds a place among distinguished Englishmen; his poetical gifts are never mentioned. The second edition of *Scriptores* was enlarged, as Francis Thynne long ago quite truly remarked, 'for the most parte from the Collections of Lelande.' It shows few signs of original research anywhere; certainly in the case of the Strode memoir there is manifest copying. All that is truly Bale's own is demonstrably wrong in fact, namely, the statement that Chaucer at the end of *Troilus* styles Strode an English poet.

When we reach Pits and Dempster we have to do with seventeenth century writers. At this point, however, we must speak of a book now unfortunately lost, which, if we possessed it, might clear up the enigma we are about to discuss. We refer to the *Collectanea*[5] of Gilbert Brown, Abbot of Sweetheart. It is cited by Dempster frequently, as is also another work by the same author, the *Foundations of Monasteries*. Brown, we know, after fighting valiantly for the old Faith for more than forty years, quitted Scotland and settled in Paris, where he died in 1612. It is

---

[1] Mr. Gollancz adds this note:—'Bale ascribed an Itinerarium Terrae Sanctae to Strode on the authority of a statement by Brigham in his lost work *De Venatione rerum memorabilium*; see Selden Ms. 64, f. 170.'

[2] The notice of Strode in Leland's *Commentaries* is manifestly founded solely on the *Vetus Catalogus*.

[3] I purposely do not translate *Phantasma*.

[4] *Memorials of Merton College*, by the Hon. George C. Brodrick (Oxf. Hist. Socy., 1885), preface, pp. viii. xi. etc.

[5] *Bruni Collectanea sive Historiam labentis in Scotia Religionis Catholicae.*

certainly probable that MSS. which he had diligently compiled during a
lifetime were not left behind in Scotland. If Pits—who wrote in France—
did not see Brown's collections, one is at a loss to understand where he
derived so much new matter for Strode's biography; and the same remark
applies, although in a less degree, to Quetif and Echard. We shall see
the reason for this observation immediately. Pits gave the Christian name
Ralph as in the edited *Vetus Catalogus* of Merton : *poeta laureatus* is his
rendering of *nobilis poeta* in the same document : *Phantasma Radulphi* is
also included in the list of works. It does not require express mention
of Strode's connection with Merton College to let us see that one and the
same person is referred to by Leland, Bale, and Pits—*Phantasma Radulphi*
is sufficient. But none of these writers, be it observed, ever alludes to
vernacular poetry : Pits, indeed, expressly praises a correct and polished
writer of Latin. From him we learn for the first time of Strode's friend-
ships with foreign scholars, of his urbanity and lively wit. In other particulars there is agreement with Bale, making allowance for the Protestant
and Catholic standpoint of the two biographers.

Dempster's contribution to a biography is chiefly remarkable for the
statement that Strode was bred in the monastery of Dryburgh. He is the
first to hint at his Scottish origin; to mention vernacular verse; to speak
of works in MSS. preserved in the library of Dryburgh monastery; to tell
about the visit to the Holy Land. Dempster, however, must be regarded
as a partial witness. The preposterous nationalism of the man which led
him 'to sweep in the whole flock of Irish saints, make a general raid on
the Bollandists, and carry off all the names that suited his fancy,' is properly
characterised by Dr. Hill-Burton as insolent mendacity, and by Mr. Henry
Bradley as extraordinary dishonesty.[1] Finding in Pits that Strode's name
was associated with Merton, it was in strict accordance with Dempster's
own method of writing literary history to claim the Oxford scholar as a
Scot, by selecting Dryburgh in the parish of Mertoun as the place where
he received his early education.[2] One may doubt if in Gilbert Brown's
History there was anything more than the statement that Strode studied
at Oxford. Quetif and Echards' narrative, it will be remarked, considerably amplifies Dempster's. From these writers we learn that Strode completed his studies at Saint James's, Paris, and that after foreign travel, he
was entrusted with the erection and regulation of monasteries in the
English provinces. Greater stress is also laid upon his works written in
the vernacular.

There are questions suggested by a collation of these writers of special
interest to editors of Chaucer, which however cannot at present be dis-
cussed at large,—for example the identity of Chaucer's friend with the Oxford
scholar, and the Christian name of that worthy. It may be quite reasonable to identify 'the philosophical Strode' as the Oxford scholar. That
there was at that university a distinguished philosopher and theologian
named Strode, *c.* 1370, supposed by some to have been of Merton, is not
in the least doubtful. Some of his MSS. are extant; and the author is
mentioned by his surname by other writers.[3] But no poetry of his, either
in Latin or vernacular, is known in the present day. His Scottish origin,

[1] *Vide Scot Abroad,* and *Dict. of Nat. Biog.*
[2] I arrived at this opinion independently of Mr. Gollancz, who gives a similar explanation in his edition of *Pearl.* For references to Mertoun and the church of Dryburgh,
vide Dryburgh Chartulary, Bann. Club publications.
[3] *Vide* David Cranstoun's *Tractatus,* cited in Major's *Hist. Appendix* (Scot. Hist.
Socy. edition).

resting as it really does on Dempster alone, is not tenable, neither does there appear to be any sufficient ground for believing him to have been a Dominican. The fellowship of Merton College, if admitted, would almost of itself be enough to negative that belief, for scholars of that house, it is well known, were expressly forbidden to take religious vows. In the region of pure conjecture—as Chaucer has bequeathed his text to us we can only conjecture—it seems most reasonable to suppose that he was Magister N. Strode, who is named at the end of part ii. § 40 of the *Treatise on the Astrolabe*: 'explicit tractatus de conclusionibus Astrolabii compilatus per Galfridum Chauciers ad Filium suum Lodewicum scolarem tunc temporis Oxonie, ac sub tutela illius nobilissimi philosophi Magistri N. Strode,' etc. Have Chaucerian editors who favour *Ralph* Strode sufficiently taken into account the uncertainty concerning his Christian name and the curious evolution of his poetical reputation? It certainly is not from the text of *Troilus and Criseyde* that they derive information that 'the philosophical Strode' was a poet.

Of Mr. Gollancz's conjecture concerning the authorship of *Pearl*, can it be said, when early writers are fairly examined, that it is even a plausible surmise? 'A book in elegiac verse called Ralph's *Phantasma*' by itself is a description far too vague to found anything on. As designating *Pearl*, it is besides extremely infelicitous. Neither is it easy to understand what is meant by 'the peculiar force of Chaucer's dedication' of *Troilus and Criseyde* to Gower and Strode. Banter is nowhere else so hard to discover in Chaucer, nor, let me add, so seemingly out of place, as in stanzas 266-267, book v. of that poem—if banter there be in these stanzas. Again, 'the tradition that Strode left his native land and journeyed through France, Germany, and Italy, and visited Syria and the Holy Land,' is of late and exogenous growth. Leland was the first to tell of journeyings in France and Italy; Dempster added Germany and the Holy Land; Quetif and Echard, Syria. Even could it be shown that Strode the philosopher and theologian had written an *Itinerary to the Holy Land*, it would not prove that he had himself travelled thither. Adamnan of Iona[1] wrote a similar work from the narrative of a shipwrecked monk. Many churchmen who had never been out of their own country attempted a like theme.

It may be only a coincidence, but a strange coincidence it certainly is, that the biography of Ralph Strode—so much of it as is apochryphal—assumes the appearance of fact when transferred to David Rate, confessor of King James the First of Scotland. He was a Scot, a Dominican, and vicar of the order within Scotland. If it cannot be affirmed that he was educated in France, the works ascribed to him in the Ashmole MS. 61 at any rate prove to a demonstration his intimate knowledge of French literature, while another of his poems in the Scottish MS. kk. 1. 5, preserved in University College, Cambridge, is known to have been derived from an Italian original. He cultivated vernacular poetry, and in the speech of the Scots was eminently skilful. His poems evidence his urbanity, his nimble and merry wit, his worldly wisdom heightened throughout by sly humour. As a vicar of his order he would, no doubt, be zealous for the planting and establishing of new houses within the northern bounds of the English province.

[1] The Columban monk was also the author of a *Vision* (Fis Adhamhain), a religious discourse on Psalm cxlvi. 5, 6, telling of 'his soul being carried to heaven to behold the angels there, and to hell to behold the wretched hosts.'—*Saint Columba*, by Reeves (Scot. Historians, vol. vi. clii and clvii pref.).

When the *opera omnia* of Ralph Strode are examined, we have no difficulty in rendering to the Oxford philosopher and theologian the professional items. These unquestionably are his own, namely *Summulae logicales, Formulae consequentiarum, Sophismatum strophae, Positiones et argumenta contra Wiclif.* But there are in the lists of Pits and later biographers works attributed to Ralph Strode, for which there is not in the present day a tittle of evidence. These are the *Fabulae, Panegyrici, Phantasmata,* and *Itinerarium.* Here, again, David Rate steps forward as a claimant. *Fabulae lepidae versu* exactly describes at least four poems ascribed to him in Ashmole 61—namely, *The Romance of Ysombras, The Romance of the Erle of Tolous, The Romance Lybenus Dyconius,* and *A quarrel among the Carpenter's tools. Panegyrici versu patrio,* which is Dempster's entry, describes poems found in both the Ashmole and Camb. MSS. like *A Father's instructions to his Son, A Mother's instructions to her Daughter, The Thewis of Wysmen, The Thewis of Gud Women.* These, as I pointed out in a previous article, were in all probability written by David Rate as a preceptor of 'bele babees, merchants' sons, and goodwives' daughters,' and intended for recital on festival, or, as we would say nowadays, at public examination of his younkers. Dempster's phrase is expanded in Quetif and Echard to *Panegyrici plures versu patrio et vernaculo,* and the change is rather remarkable, leading one to ask what it was Dempster meant to convey by his adjective *patrius.* It might of course be read as meaning panegyrics in 'native verse,' but it might also be read as panegyrics in verse 'pertaining to a Father,' or 'relating to the Home,' and if that is a legitimate rendering then we have a perfect description and even designation of the poems I have just referred to. Quetif and Echard's *et vernaculo* is not then redundant but only a further and quite accurate statement of fact. Next there is *Itinerarium Terrae Sanctae,* and again we have a poem by David Rate in Ashmole 61, *The Stasyons of Jerusalem.* That the author of that poem himself visited the places he describes is not doubtful. He says he was there : tells us of the places he visited and those he saw only from a distance. His voyage began at Venice. From that city he journeyed *viâ* 'Curfe Modyne and Candy,' 'Sypres,' 'Famagoste,' and Jaffa to Jerusalem. He visited Bethlehem, 'Jeryco,' and other places, even going north into Galilee : and he wrote his poem, he tells us, for the edification of the Faithful at home as well as for future voyagers to the Holy Land. With *Phantasma Radulphi* or *Phantasmata Radulphi* as we find it written in Quetif and Echard, there is more difficulty. For a vernacular poem called *Ralph's Raving, Phantasma Radulphi* would be a tolerably good rendering in Latin : if the anonymous editor of the *Vetus Catalogus* of Merton,—who fell into errors in his biographical notices other than Ralph Strode's,—read *Ratis Raving* as *Rafs Raving* his *Phantasma Radulphi* would be explained. The error, if error there was in the beginning, is most likely past finding out now. All that can be said about *Phantasma Radulphi* is that it is unidentifiable as a genuine and extant work of Strode, and in its present guise it certainly cannot be claimed for David Rate.

A coincidence such as I have pointed out may perhaps yield little or nothing for a serious study of David Rate's works; its chief interest appears at present to be the clear call it gives to students to investigate anew the sources for the biography of Strode, the friend of Chaucer.

J. T. T. BROWN.

SCOTTISH OFFICES AND OFFICERS UNDER THE CROWN IN 1741.

At this time, when so much attention is turned to the period of the great attempt of Prince Charles Edward, and to ascertain who were 'Out in the '45,' it seems appropriate to print the names of the holders of Scottish Offices of either position or pay under the dynasty which the Prince then came to overturn.

The following List, which is substantially that of 1745, was found among the papers of the Office of the Sheriff-Clerk of Argyll. ANDREW ROSS.

Marchmont Herald.

A List of Places and Offices in Scotland, at the Gift and Disposal of the Crown, 1741.

Offices.	Officers.	Life or Pleasure.	Sallary.
Lord Keeper of the Great Seal	Earl of Islay	Pleasure	£3000.
Lord Keeper of the Privy Seal	Duke of Athol	Pleasure	£2000.
Keepers of the Signet	{ Duke of Newcastle Lord Harrington }	Pleasure	No Sallary. Their perquisites about £1400.
Lord Register	Marquis of Lothian	Pleasure	£1200. Perquisites about £400.
Vice Admiral	Earl of Morton	Pleasure	£1000.
Judge Admiral	Mr. James Graham	Life	No Sallary. His perquisites are about £200.
Admiral Clerk	Mr. Archibald Inglis	Life	No Sallary. Perquisites £200.
King's Advocat	Charles Erskin, Esq.	Pleasure	£1000.
King's Sollicitor	Mr. William Grant	Pleasure	£400.
Lyon King of Arms	Alexander Brodie	Life	£300.
	The Lyon names the heraulds and pursivants.		
Lyon Clerk	David Erskin	Life	No Sallary. Perquisites £40.
Knight Marischal	Earl of Kintore	Pleasure	£400.
Master of Works	Sir John Anstruther	Pleasure	£400.
Clerk of the Stores under the Master of Works	William Adam	Pleasure	£30.
Post Master	James Colquhoun, Esq.	Pleasure	£300.
	Note.—The whole Sallarys belonging to the Post Office here amounts to £552.		
Receiver General of the Land Rents	Allan Whitefoord, Esq.	Pleasure	For self and Clerk £650.
Director of the Chancery	Robert Kerr, Esq.	Life	£25. N.B.—His perquisites are about £400.
Conservator of the Scots Priviledges in the Netherlands	Archibald M'Aulay	Pleasure	£200.
King's Limner	James Abercromby	Life	£100.
Deput Keeper of the Signet	Alexander M'Millan	Pleasure	£100. His perquisites are about £150.
	This Commission is from the Secretarys of State.		
Writer to the Privy Seall	Thomas Goldie	Life	Perquisites £160.
King's Writer	Andrew Marjorybanks	Life	£50.
King's First Physician	Dr. Andrew Sinclair	Pleasure	£100.
King's Second Physician	Dr. James Lidderdale	Pleasure	£50.
King's Appothecary	George Cunningham	Pleasure	£40.
King's Botanist	Doctor Charles Alstone	Pleasure	£50.
Surgeon to the Castle of Edinburgh.	John Lauder, dead	. .	£50.

Offices.	Officers.	Life or Pleasure.	Sallary.
King's Printers	John Basket and Agnes Campbell	The assigneys of. For 41 years	No Sallary.
King's Stationers	{ George Ridpath Joseph Watson Andrew Bell }	40 years	No Sallary.
Library Keeper in Holyrood-house and Historyographer	Mr. David Simson had his death. The Library Keeper had £80, and the Historyographer £40.	both these places, and now sunk by	
Inspector of the King's Palaces and Castles	.	. . .	.
Under Keeper of the Palace of Holyrood-house	. Porterfield	{ Both named by the Duke of Hamilton, but paid by the Crown }	£50.
Porter of the Palace	Walter Mitchel		£37, 15s. 6d.
Inspector of the Invalids	Captain Walter Lockhart	Pleasure	10/- per diem.
King's Under Falconer	Sir Gilbert Kennedy	Pleasure	£50 per annum.
Master of the Revells	Vacant	. . .	No Sallary. His perquisites a triffle.
Fencing Master	.	.	No Sallary.
King's Taylor	David Campbell	.	No Sallary. Perquisites £40 per annum.
King's Wright Slater Coupar Glazier Smith Dyer Glover Plumber Armourer Masson	Robert Moubray James Syme Robert Provan Alexander Barton James Wilson James Chrystie Patrick Campbell John Simson James Mack	. . Pleasure	No Sallary. No Sallarys.
	Their Commissions from the Board of Ordnance.		
Mr. Baker Bower Coachmaker Hatter Landress Saidler Gardener Goldsmith Hozier Barber Cloakmaker Shoemaker	All vacant and in disuse since the Union.		
King's Trumpeters who attend the Circuit Courts	James Marine James Gordon Charles Erskin John Yeats Thomas Weir John Menzies	Life They have for going the Circuits	Sallary £16, 13s. 4d. £10 each.
The Judges of the Court of Session	Duncan Forbes of Culloden, Esquire, President	. .	£1000.
	Andrew Fletcher of Milltown, Lord Justice Clerk	. .	£500.

Offices.	Officers.	Life or Pleasure.	Sallary
The Judges of the Court of Session	Sir James Mackenzie of Roystoun Mr. David Erskin of Dun James, Lord Balmerino Sir Gilbert Elliot of Minto Mr. Hugh Dalrymple of Drumore Mr. Patrick Campbell of Monzie Mr. John Pringle of Haining Mr. Alexander Fraser of Strichen Mr. Pat. Grant of Elchies Mr. John Sinclair of Murkle Alexander, Earl of Leven Sir James Fergusson of Kilkerran	All for Life	Sallary £500 each.
The Six Principal Clerks of Session	Sir John Dalrymple Mr. William Hall Mr. John Murray Mr. Thomas Gibson Mr. James Justice Mr. William Kilpatrick	All for Life	No Sallary. Their perquisites are about £300 per annum each.

The Six under clerks who have just the half of the perquisites of the principal clerks and all the Extractors depend upon the principal clerks. Their Commissions are for life.

The two principal clerks to the Bills	Sir Philip Anstruther Mr. David Anstruther	Life	No Sallary. Perquisites £30 per annum each.
Keeper of the Minute Book	Thomas Butter, dead	Life	No Sallary. His perquisites are about £100 per annum.
Clerk and Keeper of the Register of Hornings	William Douglas of Cavers	Life	£20. His perquisites about £200.
Keeper of the Register of Sasines	Mr. William Kilpatrick	Life	No Sallary. Perquisites £10.
Clerk to the King's Processes before the Court of Session	Sir John Dalrymple	Life	£40.

He names the under clerk and Extractor who have £10 each.

Clerk to the Admission of Nottars	Mr. Robert Naismith	Life	No Sallary. Perquisites £100.
Court of Police— President	Earl of Lauderdale	Pleasure	£1200.
	Earl of Sutherland		£800.
	Earl of Hyndford		£800.
	Lord Torphichen	Pleasure	£800.
	Lord Alexander Hay		£400.
	Charles Erskin, Esq.		£400.
	Mungo Halden, Esq.		£400.
Secretary	Mr. George Kerr, Advocate	Life	£200.

There is also a Deput Secretary, Doorkeeper, and Messenger.

Offices.	Officers.	Life or Pleasure.	Sallary.
Court of Justiciary—			
Lord Justice General	Earl of Ilay	Life	£2000.
Lord Justice Clerk	Mr. Andrew Fletcher of Miltoun		£400.
	Sir James Mackenzie of Roystoun		£400.
	Mr. David Erskin of Dun		
	Sir Gilbert Elliot of Minto	Life	£100 each, and as much for going the Circuits.
	Mr. Alexander Frazer of Strichen		
	Mr. Pat. Grant of Elchies		
Clerks of Justiciary—			
Principal Clerk	Mr. John Davidson	Life	£100.
Depute Clerk	Mr. Leith	Life	£40.
	They have each £30 for going the Circuits.		
Macers of Justiciary	Thomas Leslie		
	Robert Brisbane	Life	£20 each.
	Murdoch		
Doorkeepers of Justiciary	Archibald M'Kewn		each £8, 6s. 8d.
	Kenneth M'Kenzie		
Dempster	John Dalgleish		£5.
Officers of the Wardrobe—			
First Keeper	Mr. Thomas Hamilton	Pleasure	£55, 11s. 4d.
First Under Keeper	Thomas Oliphant	Pleasure	£40.
Second Under Keeper	Patrick Lindsay	Pleasure	£20.
Clerk to the Wardrobe	James Baird	Pleasure	£30.
Court of Exchequer—			
Lord Chief Baron	Matthew Lant, Esq.	Life	£1000.
	He has a Privy Seal for £500.		
The Judges of the Court of Exchequer	Sir John Clerk of Pennycook, Bart.		
	George Dalrymple of Dalmahoy, Esq.	Life	each £500.
	Edward Edlin, Esq.		
	Baron Edlin has a Privy Seal for £300 more.		
Keeper of the Exchequer Seal	Anthony Norman, Esq.		£100.
King's Remembrancers	William Stewart, Esq.	Life	£400.
	John Tarver, Esq.		£200.
Auditors of Excise	George and Christopher Tolsons	Life	£310.
Examiner of Excise	David Anderson	Depends on the Court	£50.
Clerk of the Port Bonds	William Kelso	Depends on the Court	£40.
Presenter of Signatures	John Dundas, W.S.	Life	£52, 15s.
	His perquisites are £100 good.		
Keeper of the Register of Resignations in Exchequer	Wescomb	Life	£40.
Doorkeepers	Clement Porter	They depend on the Court	£15 to each.
	George Baron		
Messenger of Exchequer	George Ross	Depends on the Court. Life	£6, 13s. 4d.
Macers of Exchequer	Thomas Park		
	John Herriot	Life	£50 to each.
	John Chalmers		

Offices.	Officers.	Life or Pleasure.	Sallary
Macers before the Court of Session	Thomas Graham Francis Gibb Francis Gibson Alexander Mitchel	Life	Each £10 per (annum?). Perquisites £80 each.
Macers to the Commission of Teinds	Thomas Park John Herriot One vacant	Life	No Sallary. But perquisites £10 to each.
Commissariot Courts—			
Commissars of Edinburgh	Mr. George Smollett, Advocate Andrew Marjorybanks, W.S. Mr. James Lesly, Advocate Mr. Robert Clerk, Advocate	Life	No Sallary. Perquisites about £80 each.
Principal Clerks	Sir William Nairn Mr. Alexander Nairn	Life	Perquisites £200 to each.
	They name a deput who has about £100 per annum.		
Procurator Fiscal	Alexander Stevenson	Life	Perquisites £100 per annum.
Commissar of the Isles	Dougald Clerk		
Aberdeen	Robert Paterson		
Hamilton and Campsie	. . . .		
Inverness	John Stewart		
Dunkeld	Alexander Pitcairn		
Lanerk	William Hamilton		
Dumfries	Mr. John Alves		
St. Andrews	David Bethune George Lindsay		
Lauder	James Hume		
Kirkcudbright	Mr. John Hamilton		
Wigtown	Mr. Robert Wallace		
Dunblain	John Finlayson	All for Life	No Sailarys.
Stirling	Alexander Munro		
Glasgow	Charles Madland, Advocate		Perquisites, some more and some less, according to their different dioceses. Glasgow and Peebles are £100 per annum. Others not £30.
Caithness	Alexander Gunn		
Murray	Alexander Ross		
Ross	Duncan Munro		
Brechin	John Spence		
Orkney and Zetland	William Lidel		
Peebles	John Rutherfoord		
Argyll	Heritable in the family of Argyll		

Shires.	Sheriffs.	Shires.	Sheriffs.
Edinburgh	Earl of Lauderdale.	Bamff	Earl of Findlater.
Hadingtoun	Lord Belhaven.	Air	Earl of Loudoun.
Inverness	Earl of Murray.	Linlithgow	Earl of Hoptoun.
Ross	Lord Ross.	Kincardin	Earl of Kintore.
Berwick	Earl of Home.	Aberdeen	Alexander Grant of Grantsfield.
Lanerk	Earl of Hyndfoord.		
Stirling	Gabriel Napier, Esq.	Forfar	Earl of Northesk, dead.
Perth	Duke of Athol.	Caithness	Sinclair of Ulbster.

Shires.	Sheriffs.	Shires.	Sheriffs.
Cromarty	Earl of Cromarty.	Argyll	Duke of Argyll.
Murray	Earl of Murray.	Fife	Earl of Rothes.
Roxburgh	Douglas of Cavers,	Stewartry of Kirkcud-	Marquis of Annandale.
Selkirk	Murray of Philiphaugh.	bright	
Peebles	Earl of March.	Sutherland	Earl of Sutherland.
Dumfries	Duke of Queensberry.	Stewartry of Orkney	Earl of Mortown.
Wigtoun	Sir James Agnew.	and Zetland	
Dumbarton	Duke of Montrose.	Clackmannan	Colonell William
Bute	Earl of Bute.		Dalrymple.
Renfrew	Earl of Eglintown.	Kinross	Sir John Bruce.
Nairn	Campbell of Calder.		

Lieutenancies.	Lieutenants.	Lieutenancies.	Lieutenants.
Orkney and Zetland	Earl of Mortoun.	Aberdeen, Fife, and	Earl of Rothes, *dead.*
Clydsdale	Earl of Hyndfoord.	Kinross	
Berwick	Earl of Marchmont.	Haddingtoun	Vacant.
Dumbarton	Duke of Montrose.	Stirling and Clack-	Earl of Buchan.
Perth	Earl of Breadalbin.	mannan	
Inverness	Lord Lovat.	Air	Vacant.
Dumfries and Kirk-	Duke of Queensberry.	Galloway	Earl of Stair.
cudbright		Bute	Vacant.
Twedale	Vacant by the death of	Angus	Duke of Douglas.
	the Earl of March.	Roxburgh	Duke of Roxburgh.
Ross, Cromarty,		Linlithgow	Earl of Hoptoun.
Murray, Nairn,	Earl of Sutherland,	All during pleasure.	
Caithness, and	*dead.*	Selkirk	No Commission appears
Sutherland			for this County.
Midlothian	Earl of Lauderdale.	Argyll	Heritable in the family
			of Argyll.

CHURCH AND UNIVERSITY PREFERMENTS.

Offices.	Officers.	Life or Pleasure.	Sallary.
Deans of the Chappel Royal	Mr. Neill Campbell Mr. William Gusthard Mr. John Goldie	Pleasure	Each £60 besides considerable perquisites.
Bishop of the Chappel Royal	Alexander Hope	Life	£20.
Almoner	Mr. Neill M'Viccar	Pleasure	£45.
Chaplains	Mr. Robert Bell Mr. John Lumsden Mr. John Mathison	Pleasure	£50 each.
... for the Church	Mr. William Grant.		
Colledge of Glasgow—			
Principall	Mr. Neill Campbell	Life	£166. 13s. 4d.
Professor of Church History	Mr. William Anderson	Life	£100.
Professor of Botany and A...	Dr. Brisbane	Life	£30.

N.B. The rest are named by the Faculty.

Offices.	Officers.	Life or Pleasure.	Sallary.
Colledge of St. Andrews—			
Principall of St. Leonards	Mr. James Heidels	Life	
Principall of St. Salvators	Mr. William Young	Life	
Principall of St. Mungos	Mr. John Drew	Life	
Professor of Hebrew	Mr. Thomas Craigy	Life	
Professor of Ecclesiastick History and Divinity	Mr. Archibald Campbell	Life	
Professor of Divinity	Mr. Thomas Tullidelph		
Professor of Mathematicks	Mr. Charles Gregory		
Colledge of Edinburgh—			
Professor of Law	Mr. Charles Erskin	Life	£150.
Professor of Church History	Mr. Pat. Cumming	Life	£100.
Colledge of Aberdeen—			
Principall of the New Colledge	Mr. Osburn	Life	
Professor of Greek			
Professor of Medicine			
Three Professors of Philosophy			
Professor of Oriental Languages in the New Colledge	Mr. George Gordon	Life	£66, 13s. 4d.

Collectors of the Bishops Rents in Scotland—

Robert Urquhart, Esq., Collector of the Rents of the Bishopricks of St. Andrews, Edinburgh, Galloway, Brechin, Dumblain, Dunkeld, Aberdeen, Murray, and Caithness. His sallary for himself and deputes is per annum . . . . . . £400.
The Principal and Professors of the University of Glasgow are Tacksmen of the Rents of the Archbishoprick of Glasgow.
James Fraser, Esq., Collector of the Rents of the Bishoprick of Ross.
Sallary per annum £83. 6s. 8d.
John Hay of Balbethen, Tacksman of the Rents of the Bishoprick of Orkney. The Tackduty gifted to Lord Aberdeen is per annum . . . . . £200.
The Bishops Rents of Argyll and the Isles were gifted to the Synod by Queen Ann.

Castles.	Governours.	Sallarys.
Edinburgh	Major-General Campbell	
Stirling		
Dumbarton	Earl of Cassils	
Fort William		
Fort George	General George Wade	
Fort Augustus		
Blackness	William Kerr, Esq.	
Inverness	Colonell Kennedy	

Chamberlains of Crown Rents in Scotland—

David Ross, Chamberlain of the Crown Rents of Ross. His sallary per annum £83, 6s. 8d.
John, Earl of Wigtoun, Chamberlain of Fife and Strathern. His sallary is per annum £300.
John Mackie, Chamberlain of Galloway. Sallary . . . . £18.
John Davidson, Chamberlain of Lindores. Sallary . . £5. 11s. 1½d.
David Rutherfoord, Chamberlain of Ettrick Forrest . . . £8, 6s. 8d.
Robert Ewing, Chamberlain of Orkney and Zetland. He holds it for the Earl of Mortown. His sallary is . . . . . . £500 per annum.
Discoverer of Conceal'd Rents, Vacant sallary, etc., . . . £100.

THE FIRST UNIFORM TARTAN.

Much has been said on the origin of tartan, using that word as meaning a checkered cloth ; but it is probably not known to most Highlanders that the first reliable account we have of its adoption as a uniform was by the Royal Company of Archers, now the Queen's Bodyguard for Scotland, which has its headquarters still in Edinburgh. The history of this Company commences in August 1677, when the 'Council of Archers' took into consideration 'former acts' as to their manner of shooting. The first regulations of the Company are subscribed by the Marquis of Atholl. Whether they had a uniform or not at that date we have no information ; but on the 15th of June 1713 an 'overture' was brought in for considering 'a proper habite and uniform garb for the Company,' and on the 27th of July Messrs. George Drummond, Robert Freebairn, and Alex. Murray were appointed, 'to get swatches for the Archer garb and to make an estimate of the price, and to receive overtures for that effect, . . . and likewise to consider the fashion, . . . and report.'

By the 19th of October 'the Council having seen and considered a piece of tartan laid before them by Alex. Murray, merchant, they approved the same as being proper to be used for their habit.'

On the 22nd of March 1714, the Council ordered the Treasurer 'to wait on the Captain-General in his habite to have his Lordship's opinion yr upon.' The Captain-General was the Earl of Wemyss. On the 14th of June 1714, the Company did 'march, handsomely drest in their proper garb with their bows unbent in their right hands, and a pair of arrows on the left side under a white bow-case.'

The roll of the Company from 1704, at which date it got a charter from Queen Anne, to the date of the march out, shows 341 members, proving that the body was a considerable one.

The choice of a habit distinctively Scottish was not unnatural, and parti-coloured clothing could be so described.

In 1633, but forty-four years before the Council of Archers were considering 'former acts,' Lord Kinnoul wrote the Laird of Glenurquhe to send to Perth to meet the king (Charles i.) in July of the same year, a number of his friends, followers, and dependers 'in their best array and equipage with trews, bowes, dorloches, and other thair ordinarie weapouns and furniture' in order that the king might see a 'mustour mad of Hielandmen, in their cuntrie habite and best order.' Scottish archers, where they existed, were at this time Highlanders, and in 1627 it is on record that Charles i. raised 200 Highland bowmen for service in his war with France ; because 'the persones in those high countries are ordinarilie good bow-men' (*Black Book of Taymouth*, p. 437). That this practice of archery was maintained in the Western Islands till the very end of the 1600's we know from Martin, who says that in the Island of Lewis the inhabitants are very dexterous in the exercises of swimming, *archery*, vaulting, or leaping.

That tartan was fashionable after 1622 is not to be wondered at, when we remember that Charles ii. at his marriage on the 20th May had tartan ribbons on his coat, a coat which is still preserved. These ribbons, says the author of the *Records of Argyll*, were Royal Stuart tartan. The writer's recollection of them is that the pattern required the whole breadth of the ribbon to show it.

So much for the choice of a tartan; as to the fashion of a garb. In 1651 the Earl of Argyll raised a regiment which became the Scots Foot Guards of Charles II. (*Records of Argyll*, p. 408). 'Above the door of Dunstaffnage House is a coat of arms, carved, having for supporters two privates of Argyll's Regiment 1692; so say the Dunstaffnages. Their head-dress is a Scotch round flat bonnet, such as is now worn. The long coat and deep sleeves of the period of William Third's reign, reaching to a little above the knee; knee-breeches and stockings—the garter being concealed by the knee-breeches, and tied below the knee; shoes and buckles. Collar of shirt, showing also cravat; sword slung behind—not the broad-sword, but regulation English sword.'

'This description of the dress is taken from a steel engraving lent by Dunstaffnage, which was done from the stone carving over his door.'

'The only *National* part of the dress granted to these men appears to have been the blue bonnet. In all the other particulars the dress is that of well-equipped musketeers of William's reign.'

There can be little doubt that the above description is accurate. It almost exactly corresponds with the private's uniform of the Royal Company in 1714. The description of the relation of the breeches to the stocking is not suitable in the case of the Royal Company; there, the stocking was drawn up over the knee of the breeches and tied below the knee with a narrow garter. The Archer's coat was slashed in the upper arm, all the rest of the description, to the flat bonnet, is quite correct.

It is possible to speak thus with certainty because the authority in the case of the Archer's dress is unimpeachable. (1) A picture painted and signed 'Rich. Waitt, pinxit 1715,' which picture is now at New Hall, Carlops, near Edinburgh. It is supposed to be Archibald Grant, younger of Cullen (according to Mr. D. W. Stewart, *Scottish Antiquary*, vol. vii. p. 100), and this gentleman undoubtedly joined the Company on the 4th of October 1714. On the back of the picture is written, but in a late hand, 'The Old Pretender': this is an evident mistake. (2) A uniform coat and breeches of the same period, now at Archer's Hall, Edinburgh.

Comparing the coat and Waitt's picture, the latter, though dim with age, corresponds most accurately in regard to the cut of the coat, the lines of braiding, and fringing, and the make of the sleeve. The uniform is hung in a wooden case with the front and sides of glass, the right side of the coat next the spectator and well displayed, and the breeches hung below it showing the part from the knee up to about mid thigh. All visible is in excellent preservation, though there are one or two small patches in the coat.

Now as to the set of the tartan, the author of the *History of the Royal Company* says (p. 52), 'they ultimately fixed upon a Stuart tartan for the coat.' On inquiry, Mr. Balfour Paul was unable to call to memory the reason for ascribing this tartan to the Stuarts, though he repeated his conviction that it was so. It will have been seen from the extracts from the minutes given above, which contain the whole information, that the Minute Book of the Company makes no such statement.

From the lines of braiding and the folds as the coat hangs, and the complexity of the pattern, which is great, the set is difficult to follow. After consideration, however, and speaking as one who is not expert in weaving, the conclusion reached is, that the set required the whole breadth of the web to show it. If the cloth were very narrow it might possibly, to make both sides of the pattern the same, have required to be joined up the middle like an old Highland plaid or blanket. As no join in the side of the skirt, however, is recognisable, it seems as if the web had been made like a ribbon. There is a special stripe close to the selvage where the skirt opens in front, and the same stripe is recognisable close to the opening of the back of the skirt, and the pattern seems to run towards the centre from these two points. The tartan may be called a red tartan. The colours used in addition being blue, yellow, and white. No single colour is anywhere broader than half an inch. The cloth is a fine hard tartan.

It will give an idea of the complexity of the pattern if the following, written down in the attempt to follow one line of the colouring, is considered.

Greyish yellow and red, bright yellow and red, red and blue, yellow and red, red and blue, yellow and red, red and blue, bright yellow and red, greyish yellow and red, red, white, red, white, red, yellow and red, blue and red, yellow and red, blue and red, yellow and red, blue and red, yellow, blue, red, blue, red, white, blue, white, red. This commences near the edge of the cloth, and what has been mentioned as the stripe near the selvage, is described between the two stripes 'greyish yellow and red.'

This by no means brings us to what could be determined as the centre of the pattern. Many of the stripes are only the breadth of a thread or two, and those described as of two colours are those where the differently coloured threads can be distinguished crossing one another in a slanting direction to the general pattern.

The small clothes, from what is seen of them in the uniform itself, and in Waitt's picture, give the impression of being 'knickerbockers' cut a good deal like the loose riding breeches now usually worn, confined below the knee by a narrow band fastened with a single small buckle. The set is quite different from the coat. The colours used are the same, but the pattern is more simple, though from the fact that in the length of cloth shown one cannot be certain that you see fully one half of the pattern, it may be surmised that in this also the whole breadth of the cloth was necessary to show a pattern with two corresponding sides.

Having the coat and breeches of two different tartans seems to have been the ordinary arrangement in the first half of the eighteenth century. If the coat was Stuart tartan, perhaps the breeches were MacNassau? As a matter of fact there seems not the least reason for it being called any other tartan than that of the Royal Company of Archers. Seeing that the Company owed its charter to Queen Anne, and received it but ten years before the adoption of this uniform, it is improbable that so pronounced a Jacobitism should prevail in it that they should flout the giver of their charter by choosing deliberately a Stuart tartan if they knew of such a thing at all. One thing is certain, the Royal Company tartans have no resemblance to the Stuart tartans of the *Vestiarium Scoticum.*

The Royal Company long stuck to tartan in their uniform. In 1789, when a change was next made, we find that while the 'common uniform' of all ranks was a green coat, the shooting coat was ordered to be of 'the tartan, same pattern as the 42nd regiment.' Of this tartan we have excellent representations on subjects painted life-size, and it is not the least the same set as the present 42nd tartan. It is a green tartan but could not be described characteristically as dark (Gaelic *du*, black). If it was not thread for thread the same as that worn at the moment by the Black Watch, the orders are distinct as to what the pattern should be, and the representation of it is there to speak for itself. Its *lightness* goes some distance to support the general opinion of Gaelic-speaking Highlanders, that the 'Black' Watch was so characterised not on account of its uniform but on account of its duties, which did not make it specially acceptable, at first, to its own countrymen. At the date of the adoption of this tartan the Captain-General was the Duke of Buccleuch, and there is not a Campbell among the officers named at that time, and but seven Campbells among the members who could possibly be of an age to shoot.

Everything goes to prove that the patterns chosen were so chosen because they were satisfactory to the Council and its Committee and the Captain-General of the Company.

It is true, that it has been contended that uniform patterns had been made before 1714. Seeing the persistence with which the Company stuck to tartan—it still wore a tartan in 1823—it is by no means improbable that it had a tartan uniform as its first garb, which was superseded by the one we have attempted to describe.

In the Regality of Grant Court Book we are informed that in a Court holden at Delny, 27th July 1704, David Blair, Notar and Clerk, the Bailie, 'ordains and inactis that the haill tenantes, cottars, malenders, tradesmen, and servantes within the said lands of Skeraidtone, Pulchine, and Calender, that are fencible men, shall provyde and have in rediness against the eighth day of August nixt, ilk ane of them, Haighland coates, trewes, and short hose of tartane of red and greine sett, broad springed, and also with gun, sword, pistoll, and durk : and with these present themselves to an rendesvouze, when called, upon forty-eight hours advertisement.'

The tartan here is evidently a plain broad red and green check, and was the young laird of Grant's idea of a suitable livery for his 'tail.' It is undoubtedly a Grant tartan, for the reason that it was invented by a Grant; probably for no other. There is but one other attempt to establish a claim to a uniform tartan previous to the two above mentioned. It is to be found in the so-called *Red and White Book of Menzies*. Any person desirous of seeing the tartan worn by 'Sir John the Menzies' and 'eight nobles, his knights, companions and clansmen,' in 1405, will find a large coloured illustration of it facing page 84 in that book. It is unnecessary to refute this in detail as the authority quoted, 'P. Bill, de Privato Sigillo,' is not comprehensible or get-at-able except by the *Red and White Book*'s author. R. C. MACLAGAN, M.D.

A HISTORY OF THE FAMILY OF SETON DURING EIGHT CENTURIES. By GEORGE SETON, Advocate, M.A. 2 Vols. Privately Printed, 1897.

No more magnificent family history has ever, we should imagine, been produced than the two volumes now before us. To give any adequate or detailed idea of their contents would require a much more lengthy notice than our limits will allow, but when we say that they are fully worthy of the reputation of the accomplished author of *The Law and Practice of*

Heraldry in Scotland we have said enough to show that his task has been accomplished in an able and graceful manner. A delightful introduction, written with all that charm of style and wealth of allusion which is so characteristic of the author, leads us to the main line of the family, treated of in the tripartite division of the ten lairds or knight, the seven barons (the exact number is doubtful, but Mr. Seton naturally takes the benefit of the doubt), and the five earls. Then the cadet branches with certain allied families are described in detail, the most conspicuous of these being the Huntly and Eglinton lines. Then follows a list of the architectural achievements of the Seton Family: they seem to have been distinguished builders, and Seton Church and Palace, the Houses of Winton and Pinkie, and the Castles of Niddrie and Fyvie, all commemorate their enterprise in this direction: why, however, should Greenknowe Tower have been left out in this connection and relegated to a comparatively obscure place in the Appendix? Pleasant pages then discuss such various topics as the armorial bearings of the family, their stature, their portraits, charters, and letters, ending with a list of their literary productions, though the last are not, considering the size of the clan, of very great extent. The 'Miscellanies' occupy about a hundred pages, and forms a rich-feast of 'confused feeding.'

We have used the word 'magnificent' in connection with this work, and when we consider the manner in which it has been got up, the epithet does not seem extravagant. The binding, typography, and illustrations (with an exception to which allusion will be made) are alike excellent, and testify to the care and taste displayed in the get-up of the volumes. The full-page illustrations of the different places and residences mentioned in the text are admirable etchings, and the portraits scattered throughout the book are produced in a warm brown tint, which gives very satisfactory results. There are also many black-and-white illustrations indented in the pages which add a great charm to the letterpress.

What will probably attract most readers, however, are the illuminated coats of arms which are distributed with a profuse hand throughout the pages. They are executed in metal and colours on Japanese paper and affixed to the page: they make a very brave show, and are for purposes of reference most interesting. But truth to say they are the least satisfactory part of the book: in the large number of coats it would be surprising if a few mistakes did not occur, and too much importance need not be attached to the substitution of *or* for *argent* (blazoned correctly in the letterpress) in the Kingston coat on p. 721, that of *vert* for *azure* in the fleur-de-lys in the chief of the Hunter coat on p. 612, or the occurrence of other errors which we need not specify in detail. The draughtsmanship of the coats-of-arms leaves much to be desired: it is weak and wanting in spirit, though, perhaps, not below the general average of its class. If our heraldic designers wish to do good work they must go for their inspiration to the fountainhead, and study the heraldic work of the fourteenth and fifteenth centuries. It seems ungracious when so much pains have evidently been taken with the matter to criticise adversely the system adopted of emblazoning the arms in metal and colour instead of adopting the old plan of indicating gold by yellow and silver by leaving the paper untouched. The latter is far more artistic, and what is of still more importance, it is far more distinct, and the essence of blazon is distinctness: its function is to challenge the eye. The use of metals almost debars the study of the coats by artificial light when gold and silver and sable shimmer and twinkle in a most perplexing manner. We have mentioned sable because the artist has indicated that tincture by a sooty grey, evidently thinking that in those days of subdued colours coats of arms, like men's coats, should be modest in their hues. How different from the old masters of the art who were distinct and vivid in their representation of arms, while the distinctness was not gained at the cost of good taste. The reader can judge for himself of the truth of the above remarks by comparing the arms of Lord Seton as reproduced from Lindsay on p. xxxv. with the other arms in the book, though it is not a very favourable specimen of the treatment in question.

Having liberated our mind on the subject of the arms we have little but praise for the rest of the book. We have said it was sumptuous, but it is more than that, it is a sound and well-done bit of historical work, and forms a fitting crown to the writer's career as an author. He is far too accomplished a genealogist to make many slips in his narrative, and he is one of the pleasantest of companions as he guides the reader along the many branching mazes of the family pedigree. With the blue blood of the Setons he possesses that courtesy and geniality which comes to him from a long line of illustrious ancestors. They are qualities which are eminently displayed in these pages, and he has woven together an interesting story of the race. Sometimes indeed he has hardly done himself justice in the utilisation of all the matter which he had accumulated, as when he states on p. 98 that the second Lord Seton is said to have died in 1441, when at the same time he prints on p. 944 an extract taken by Mr. Riddell from the Exchequer Rolls, which shows that in 1436 Sir John Seton of that ilk (he is not termed Lord) was dead and his lands in ward.

But we must now take leave of this work: enough has been said to show that it is one of which—notwithstanding some minor blemishes—its author may well be proud; and not less proud may be the fortunate possessors of the 212 copies which form the extremely limited edition.

EDINBURGH TREASURER'S ACCOUNTS, 1734-1735.

The Accounts given below are extracted from the Municipal accounts kept by Thomas Young, Treasurer of the City of Edinburgh in 1734 and 1735. The extracts are sufficiently numerous to give a fair impression of the whole, and they indicate a diversity of duties performed which the Town Council of to-day can scarcely claim to equal. Such duties ranged from attendance at a hanging to examining candidates for the Mastership of the High School, from patronage of the Leith Races to the care of the lantern at the pier end, and from anxious consultations with the Lord Advocate to advertisements about the Vagrants 'that feigned themselves Dumb.' Several points of interest occur—the references to 'the Head Court at Potterraw,' to the City Waits (a single survivor of this band, a clarionet player, is still living), to the numerous whippings, to the fees to Advocates' servants,—which appear to have been on much the same scale as those paid to Advocates' clerks now. The occurrence of items including $\frac{1}{4}$ or $\frac{3}{4}$ of a penny, indicates the recency of the change from the Scots standard of money. Throughout the accounts the frequent payments at Sloash's, Cassie's, 'Mrs' Johnstone's, and other houses of good cheer, show that the strain of city affairs was not without its relaxations. The Rev. Thomas Pitcairn, whose presentation to the West Kirk is mentioned, was the colleague of the Rev. Neil MacVicar, well remembered for his prayer on behalf of 'that young man who is come among us seeking an earthly crown.'　　　　　　　　　　　　　　　　　W. B. W.

Debursements by Thomas Young, City Treasurer, allowed by the Council.

1734

		Sterling.		
Dec. 12. Paid Mathew Duning, Merch¹ for 40½ yrd sacking to be tarred for covering the roof of the Reservoir where tirred by Accompt discharged,		£1	1	11½
Paid Ditto for Black Orkney Stuff for the Assessor's gown,		0	8	5
21. Paid John Hyslop Incidents at the races at Leith by Accompt discharged,		1	11	3½
More incidents at the Races,		0	2	6
Paid John Johnstone, Coachman, for Coaches to the Councill at the Races by Accompt discharged,		5	10	0
To his servants,		0	3	0
.. 30. Paid fraught cartage & to workman for 2 casks of glasses for the lamps,		0	14	0
Spent with tacksman & others about the touns affairs at sundry times,		0	8	0
Gave to my Lord Provosts servant the evening his Lordship entertained the Councill before his going for London,		0	2	6
Paid for wax cloth & tape to wrap up some papers thought proper to be sent to London by my Lord Provost on the Citys Accompt,		0	2	0

1735

Jan. 2 Paid consulting Mess. Rob¹ Craigie & Hugh Forbes Advocats in the cause of Henderson against the Shoar Master of Leith & the Good Toun of Edinb¹ for some pretended damage done to his Ship in the harbour and to their servants,		6	1	0
Paid Mr. David Daes for Ropes for the Posts at the Races of Leith,		0	13	9
3. Paid for Seven firelocks with Baygonets		3	11	0
Spent in Mirs Thoms with the Magistrats about the vagrants that did pretend the Loss of their tongues,		0	8	1
22. Spent with the Stent Masters in Mushets at their closing the Annuity Books,		5	9	8
31. Spent in Robert Clarks with the Auditors at the auditing of Mr. Blackwood late City Treasurers Accompts.		4	5	5
Feb. 5. Paid charges of Canongate Head Court to Serjeant, 5s., and to officers, 5s.,		0	10	0
Spent w¹ Tacksmen of the Impost on Wines,		2	2	6

Feb. 10. Paid for a new pewther Standage for Ink to the Lords of Session, 4s., and for a sand glass, 6d.., £0 4 6

  „ 12. Spent w^t the Committee of Council and Examinators after examining the candidates for Master of the High School, ... 5 11 7

Paid John Dalgleish, Lockman, for whiping 2 women, ... 0 6 8

  „ 17. Spent in Sloashes with the Auditors of Dean of Gilds acc^{ts}, ... 3 16 0

March 1. Paid for silverising, cleaning, and for more mercury to the weather glass in Council Chamber, ... 0 5 0

  „ 21. Paid Mr. Walter Rudiman for advertisements inserted in the Mercury about the Vagrants that feigned themselves Dumb, and the vacancy of the High School p^r acc^t, ... 1 1 6

  „ 29. Paid Bill in Mirs Nicolsons at Admission of Mr. Taylor, Minister of Edinburgh. . . . 12 7 2½

Aprile 3. Paid John Dalgleish for whiping a man, . . 0 3 4

  „ 5. Paid toun officers their dues for whiping three persons, ... 0 15 0

  „ 18. Paid John Fergusson, Candlemaker, for candle furnished to the Pier End of Leith in October 1729, 1730, and 1731, ... 3 12 5

May 9. Paid John Dalgleish, for whiping a woman, . . 0 3 4

Paid Walter Rudiman for the Caledonian Mercury from 10 Aprile 1734 to 10 Aprile 1735, . . 1 0 0

  „ 24. Paid for cleaning ¼ of the toun for 2½ weeks not sett, ... 0 3 9

  „ 26. Paid John Dalgleish for whiping a woman, . . 0 3 4

June 2. Spent with the Magistrats at Installing Mr. Lees, Rector, and Mr. Creich, Master, of the High School, ... 0 5 2

Paid Hugh Barclay, Watchmaker, for helping the Tron Kirk cloak, per accompt, . . . 1 3 6

  „ 16. Paid consulting Mr. Robert Craigie to Draw an Information agst Colonel M'Douals Reduction of the Dean of Gild's Decreet concerning the Bottle of Rum, and to Servants, . . . 3 11 6

  „ 17. Paid consulting Lord Advocat Mr. Rob. Dundas, The Solicitor, Mr. Craigie, Sir James Elphinstoun, and Mr. Midleton, Advocats in the cause against the Tradesmen of Leith, and James Johnstone's Reduction of the Few of the Milns, ... 21 0 0

And to Servants, ... 3 2 6

  „ 18. Paid William Mathison for Candle to the Lanthorn at the End of the Pier, from Sept. 1734 to Aprile 1735, and his salary for Lightning them, 2 16 6

July 2. Paid Toun Officers their fees for 3 whipings, 0 15 0

  „ 10. Spent in Robert Biggers w^t My Lord Provost, Magistrats and Conveener, after the moderating a Call for a Minister to the West Kirk, . 2 18 1

July 22. Paid Thomas Moore, for Ham, Tongues, Chickens, Wine, etc., furnished to the Burrow Room when his Grace the Duke of Buccleugh was made Burgess, ... £14 10 11½

Paid City Waits for attending with Musick at the making the Duke of Bucleugh Burgess, . 1 0 0

26. Paid consulting Lord Advocat, Solicitor, Mr. Patrick and Mr. Clark, Advocats, to plead the cause of extending the Shirrifship before the Barons of Exchequer, . . 14 14 0

To their servants, ... 1 12 6

Aug. 4. Paid John Dalgleish his ffees for whipping a woman, ... 0 3 4

6. Paid William Bruce, late Tacksman of Sheep Flecks charges of poynding William Ross his lambs for the custome, ... 0 8 4

Spent with ditto when paid up his arrear, . 0 12 0

9. Paid Toun Officers their ffees for two whippings, 0 10 0

Paid for cords and snares to City drums, . 0 5 1

11. Spent with the Magistrates ye first Race, . 1 19 3

With Ditto at 2nd Race, ... 0 2 0

With Ditto in Patrick Grants the 3rd Race, . 4 12 6

Paid Drink money to the City Guard during ye Races, ... 1 1 0

Paid John Hyslop Incidents at ye Races pr Accompt, ... 2 5 5

Paid Mirs Johnstone for Coaches to the 3 Races, 7 13 0

To her Servants Drink Money, . . . 0 5 0

Paid for a Coach more to bring some of the Council from Leith, ... 0 3 6

17. Paid Chyrurgeons officer Drink Money when Dined in yr Hall, ... 0 10 6

Spent in Cassies with Magistrats and Stent Masters, ... 6 14 6

Spent with tacksmen of Weighouses, . . 0 8 6

Paid Mirs Moffat for 10 dozen of Flambeaus, . 1 5 0

Paid Walter Rudiman for advertisements in the Mercury about the Races, etc., . . 2 19 0

26. Paid three trumpets attending the Duke of Buccleugh being made Burgess, . . 1 10 0

Sept. 10. Paid officers their fees for a whipping, . 0 5 0

Paid Ditto their fees for hanging James Brown, . 0 6 8

Paid the Lockman his fees for two whippings, 0 6 8

Paid Ditto for hanging James Broun at Galalee, . 1 2 2¾

Paid Ditto for ropes, ... 0 5 0

Paid Ditto for a Barrel Salt, etc., . . 0 2 0

Paid Tronmen for carrying the Ladder, . 1 1 0

Paid Wrights Servants, ... 0 11 8

Paid Smiths Servants, ... 0 5 0

Paid Mirs Johnstone for a Coach and 4 horses to attend the Magistrats at the Execution, . 0 6 0

Spent with the Magistrats in Cassies, . . 1 0 10

Sept. 10. Paid John Hyslop small disbursements by accompt, £0 9 2¾
Paid Ditto for emptying the conveniences and
the City's Water Says for 1 year to Michaelmas
1735, ... 1 4 0

,, 22. Paid fees of a presentation from the Crown to
the Reverend Mr. Pitcairn to be
Minister of West Kirk, ... 10 19 9

,, 23. Paid Bill in Mirs Clarks the Evening before
Chusing the Merchant and Trade Counsellors, 7 17 0
Paid Toun Officers their fees for the head court
at Potterraw, ... 0 5 0

,, 25. Paid Bill in Mushet's the night before Leeting,
and also on Munday yᵉ 29 Septᵣ, wᵗ the Conveener and his Brethren, ... 13 17 9

,, 30. Paid Bill in Mirs Nicolsons the evening before
the Election, ... 8 19 11
Paid Bill in Charles Straitons the Saturday before
the Election. 8 2 1
Paid Bill in John Jollies on the Election Day, . 24 11 4
Paid Bill in George Fenwicks said day, . . 4 1 8
Paid Drink Money to the City Guard for firing
when Duke of Buccleugh was made Burges, . 0 10 0
Paid Mirs Johnstone for 8 coaches to the Magis-
trats to go to Leith on the Election Day, . 2 9 0

SIXTY YEARS' RETROSPECT, 1837-1897.

IN these days of retrospects, the antiquary naturally scans the discoveries
in his own departments in the last sixty years and enumerates the
facilities of study afforded to the student of ancient things, in 1897
which were denied to the inquirer of 1837. The first of these subjects
is beyond the limits of this article and the powers of this pen : even a
rough enumeration of some of the facilities for study gained in Queen
Victoria's reign is a considerable task. Very important contributions to
archæology had been made before the Queen's accession, but nevertheless,
during the subsequent period which we have now completed, the Imperial
Government, local authorities, scientific and historical societies, and individuals have contributed in an unprecedented degree to lay open to
view the relics and records of the past, and the stores of learning on these
things which have been already amassed.

As the Joint-Stock Company laid the foundation of much of Scotland's
financial prosperity, so the literary combinations known as the Book Clubs,
though perhaps not invented north of the Tweed, took a foremost part in
Scotland in the excavation and preservation of early records, state papers,
and general literature, and have flourished here in a manner unapproached
in any other country. Of the publications of these Clubs, the greater
number belong to the present reign. More than half the Bannatyne
Club and Maitland Club volumes, which are about 200 in all, and almost
all those of the Abbotsford Club—about 25 out of 31, were issued after the
Queen's accession. The Spalding Club, and the New Spalding Club
belong to this reign entirely, so do the Grampian Club, Wodrow Society,

the Spottiswoode Society, the Iona Club, the Scottish Burgh Records Society, the Ayr and Wigtown Archæological Society, the Scottish Text Society, the Scottish History Society, etc. All the Proceedings, and the greater part of the large 4to Transactions, ultimately called Archæologia, of the Society of Scottish Antiquaries, founded in 1792, belong to the reign. There are also the Transactions of the Glasgow Archæological Society, the Aberdeen Ecclesiological Society, and the Archæological Papers in the Transactions of the Berwickshire, Dumfriesshire, and other similar local Clubs and Societies.

It is plainly impossible in a short article to even enumerate the contents of these Club-books and Transactions, which have shed light on every department of Scottish History, military, political, social, and religious. Almost every existing chartulary or Register of our ancient ecclesiastical houses, has been printed through the agency of the Clubs, along with great numbers of early treatises, contemporary accounts of historical transactions, original documents, and papers of all kinds, and a mass of early text of linguistic value in prose and poetry.

In June 1864, Sir William Gibson Craig, Lord Clerk Register, represented to Government the propriety of making the National Records which were under his charge in the Register House in Edinburgh, accessible to the world of letters, by printing a Scottish series of Calendars of State Papers, and a Scottish series of Chronicles and Memorials, uniform with the English series. The result of this representation, backed by opinions from the most eminent Scottish Historical Lawyers of the day, was the establishment in the following year of the present Historical Department of the Register House, under the direction of the former Superintendent of the Antiquarian and Literary Department, Joseph Roberton, with the new title of Curator. A grant of £1000 a year was made to meet the cost of editing such Records as might subsequently be selected, but the reconstruction of the Department was scarcely effected, before the great record scholar who had been appointed head of it, died, and the burden of inaugurating the work of editing the prints of the Records fell on his successor Dr. Thomas Dickson.

Previous to the beginning of the reign, the Record Edition in great folios of the Acts of the Scottish Parliament had been begun under the editorship of Thomas Thomson. It consisted at first of eleven volumes, two of which (5 and 6), so far as they contained the proceedings of the parliament for the period 1639-50, were not printed, like the rest, from the original record, but from such authentic materials as were at the time available. The original record was known to have been removed in 1651 to the Tower, but had not been sent back to Scotland when the national records were restored after the Restoration, and had been quite lost sight of. It was, however, discovered in the State Paper Office in 1826, and was printed to take the place of the old volumes (5 and 6) as the first instalment of the work undertaken under the new grant for record publications in 1865.

The publications of the Record Commission were for Scotland :—

Acts of the Parliaments of Scotland. 11 vols. (*Pub.* i. 1844, ii.-x. 1814-24.)

Abridgment of the Retours of Services of Heirs, to 1700. 3 vols. (1811-16), and now continued to the present time.

Acta Dominorum Concilii, 1478-95. 1 vol. (1839.)

Acta Dominorum Auditorum, 1466-94.   1 vol.   (1839.)
Registrum Magni Sigilli Regum Scotorum, 1306-1424.   1 vol. (1814.)

Those issued under the present grant are :—
Acts of Parliament, vols. v., vi., and General Index.
Facsimiles of National MSS.   3 vols.
Chronicles of the Picts and Scots.
Halyburton's Ledger.
Historical Documents relating to Scotland, 1286-1306.   2 vols.
Register of the Great Seal, 1424-1651.   8 vols.
Register of the Privy Council, 1545-1625.   13 vols.
Exchequer Rolls, 1264-1529.   15 vols.
Lord Treasurer's Accounts, 1473-98.   1 vol.
Calendar of Documents relating to Scotland, preserved in the
     Public Record Office, London, 1108-1509.   4 vols.
The Hamilton Papers, 1532-90.   2 vols.
The Border Papers, 1560-1603.   2 vols.

The index to the Acts which has been mentioned above is in reality three indices :—one of Persons, one of Places, and one of Matters.   It is a work of great merit, and certainly one of the most valuable of the publications, as making for the first time thoroughly available the great mass of unassorted information contained in the Acts.

While these Government publications have been issuing from the Register House, Calendars of State Papers, and other such publications containing documents of interest to Scotland, have issued in England. As an instance—one of the latest of these is a volume of Papal Petitions, a calendar of records which are lying in the library of the Vatican.   The volume relates to a period when there was a schism in the western church on the question of which of two claimants was the true Pope.   The Petitions which have been preserved, and are now calendared, happen to be those which were presented to the Pope whose side was taken by the church in Scotland—a happy accident for the history of many Scottish families, as the petitions which the volume contains for dispensations to marry within the prohibited degrees, go necessarily into much genealogical detail.

Next to these publications may be mentioned the Reports of the Historical Manuscripts Commission.   Of the charter rooms on which the Commission have reported, the contents of those of Scottish families have naturally been richest in the additions they have made to our knowledge of Scots history.   But as is seen in the recent discovery of De Foe's letters among the Harley Papers, the stately halls of England may be found occasionally to contain documents which illuminate just what is left darkest after our northern authorities are exhausted.

Two works which might have been issued by Government have been executed by Government officials—the Scottish Armorial, by the present Lyon King, and the volumes of Scottish Arms by the late Lyon Clerk, the Heraldic MS. of Sir David Lindesay of the Mount reproduced there by Stodart had been previously printed by David Laing.

Scotland may well be proud of the unique spirit of her burgh corporations and their officials shewn in the printing of civic records under their charge.   To them we are indebted for the volumes of Records of the Convention of Royal Burghs dating from 1295 onwards, the Scottish

Burgh Records Society volumes, the Edinburgh Charters, Glasgow Commissariot and Protocol Books, etc., etc.

A Scottish branch of the British Index Society has lately been founded, and it is understood that a provost of a Scottish burgh, who is also a Scottish peer, is engaged at the present moment on an extensive and erudite work on Burgh Seals.

Of general Scottish histories Tytler's, which is Victorian in virtue of the third edition of it having been printed as late as 1848, and Burton's are the principal. The names of Thomas Thomson, George Chalmers, John Lee, Stuart, Grub, Joseph Robertson, Cosmo Innes, Skene, Fraser, Cochran-Patrick, and many others occur to the mind as those who contributed from their special departments to the elucidation of Scottish history in general.

It is remarkable that the country which can boast of the Old and New Statistical Accounts is still so far behind in parish and county histories. Much doubtless has been written specially on the history of the smaller localities, and some has been done admirably. Messrs. Blackwood are making at the present time a notable attempt to make up some of our lee-way by providing a complete county history of Scotland.

When Tytler's history appeared, his friends, and probably he himself to some extent, believed that the last word on Scottish history had been said. Ever since, the work of collecting the materials of history has been proceeding. In 1897 the History of Scotland has still to be written—and withal the time is not yet.

Meantime some of the keenest intellects in Scotland have been turned to the study of the early Scots language and the problems of the nationality of early literature. Folk-lore, place-names, the coinage, architecture ecclesiastical and domestic, legal and social and other antiquities have been and are being studied with systematic and scientific methods unpractised and results unattained before.

The multiplication of libraries and museums is another feature of the reign. The printing of library catalogues, both of MSS. and printed books, has been of incalculable service. A most notable delinquent, however, in this respect is the Edinburgh University.

Cataloguing has not been confined to permanent libraries. There are the catalogues issued by dealers in 'Second-hand'—in truth sometimes nearer twenty-second-hand—books, and the catalogues of auction sales of books, or of things of art and ornament, and some of them are of more than temporary value. The rightly managed museum, as we now know it—with its wealth of contents, their classification and catalogues, and the Loan Exhibition of all sorts, with catalogue memorial illustrated, are all Victorian.

Not least among the labours of the Victorian era is that of the conservation and restoration of ancient buildings, and not least as an evidence of the better instruction of the latter part of the reign is the difference between the restorations of to-day and those of sixty years ago. Between, the one hand, the 'restoration' of the outside of St. Giles's Church, Edinburgh, little more than sixty years ago, 1833, and on the other hand, that of the interior of this same church in 1883, there is a wide gulf fixed. The study of the traces of Roman, Saxon, British, and early Celtic occupation has kept pace with that of monuments of later date, as the transactions and museum of the Society of Scottish Antiquaries amply testify. In the matter of the preservation of ancient monuments, as in other things, Scotland has not been equitably treated by Government. But the last Sixty Years has shown how much, with very little help, Scotland has been able to do for herself.

JOHN GRAHAM OF KILBRIDE (*See* vol. xi. p. 108).

A POINT fatal to 'B.'s' argument, and which he entirely overlooks, is that the Earl of Menteith would not have had a legitimate son called or christened John about 1478 if John of Kilbride, a previous son, had been alive in that year. The younger John was under age in 1494, but of age in 1499. 'B.' also does not take into consideration that the Earl had a natural son John. He has not established any ground for believing that the entry in the *Acta Dom. Concil.* stating the elder John to be son *and heir* of his father on 7th April 1469 is unreliable. To acquiesce in his suggestion, therefore, would be to reduce public records to the level of a mere farce. Until he can prove that it is unreliable there confronts him the fact that Patrick Graham of Gartrenich or Auchmore is twice styled son *and heir* of his father, the first time on 19th April 1471, the second occasion being 19th October 1478, and which completely shatters the idea 'B.' entertains that the said John was alive in 1480 and received a charter of lands about Kippen. The John Graham who received these lands, if son of Earl Malise, was the illegitimate one of that name of whom it is nothing remarkable to presume that he got a lease of Kilbride after the decease of his lawfully born namesake: hence the appearance of a John Graham of Kilbride at the infeftment of the earl's then heir, Patrick, in the lands of Gartrenich in 1478. The latter John would also be the person referred to in the *Exchequer Rolls* as quoted by 'B.' In those days there was little difference between legitimate and illegitimate sons, both often shared the paternal domicile, only of course the illegal ones could not be heirs of succession to heritable property or titles of honour.

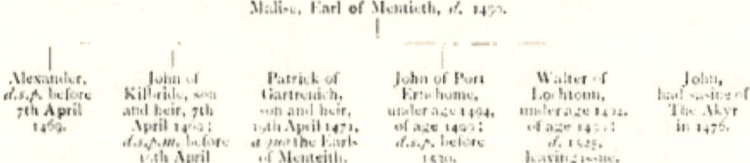

Malise, Earl of Menteith, d. 1490.

| Alexander, d.s.p. before 7th April 1469. | John of Kilbride, son and heir, 7th April 1469: d.s.p.m. before 12th April 1471. | Patrick of Gartrenich, son and heir, 19th April 1471, at *pro* the Earl of Menteith. | John of Port Errehome, under age 1494, of age 1499: d.s.p. before 1530. | Walter of Lochtoun, under age 1494, of age 1495: d. 1525, leaving issue. | John, had seisine of The Akyr in 1476. |

WALTER M. GRAHAM EASTON.

THE PIRATES OF BARBARY IN SCOTTISH RECORDS.

DR. CRAMOND'S paper on the above in *The Scottish Antiquary* for April is full of interest, and illustrates the subject from various points of view. Dr. Cramond supplies a large number of entries from Kirk-Session Records. I came on one not given in his paper in the Rev. Adam Philip's *Parish of Longforgan* (p. 188). It occurs in a list of Longforgan charities aptly described by Mr. Philip as 'cosmopolitan':— '"Given to a Grecian priest named Mercurie Sascurie." "To ane Irish Protestant." "To a persecuted Polonian." "To a distress'd Irishman."

" To a professour of Tongues fled from France." "To a Sea-man newly plundered by y⁴ French." And in 1695 an Act was read for a collection " for y⁴ relief of 7 captive Christians in Barbary." '

J. M. M., Glasgow.

OLD SCOTS BANK-NOTES.

(*Continued from vol. xi. p. 185.*)

Five Shilling and Ten Shilling Notes.

The issue of Guinea Notes was not the only measure taken by the Scots Banks to meet the difficulties created by the scarcity of coin, nor would it have been at all adequate to the crisis which was slowly but surely approaching. As early as 1750 the British Linen Company, as has been seen, had issued notes for the value of ten shillings. It issued similar notes—in 1754, 1759, and 1762—of which last note a proof copy is affixed to the Bank's minute authorising its issue. The Bank of Scotland issued similar notes for the first and last time in 1760. The copper plates (two) for the notes are still in that bank's repositories. They are dated 15th May 1760, but the minute authorising their issue was not passed till 25th June. If the recognised Banks followed here the example of the British Linen Company, they had, as their rivals in it, mercantile houses which had much less title to call themselves banks. Thus, in 1764, the Glasgow house of George Keller & Co. issued notes for the value of 'Ten shillings

sterling for value received in goods.' Blacklaws, Wedderspoon & Co. of Perth, issued notes of '£3 Scots,' or 'Five shillings sterling in cash, or, in our option, Edinburgh notes, value received.' In this year, however, Parliament stepped in, and, whether at the time its reasoning was good or bad, passed an Act prohibiting the issue of notes of smaller denomination than 20s. sterling.

But of the silver, which was 'diminished of late and scarce' in 1758, there was a 'great demand and scarcity' in 1772, and such a dearth in 1796, that people, to provide substitutes for it, were tearing their twenty-shilling notes into halves and quarters. Whatever may be supposed now to have been causes contributing to produce this dearth of coinage, it was believed by sagacious bankers at the time to have been mainly due to hoarding, which was prompted by the feeling of insecurity aroused by the expectation of French invasion. The public was familiar with the results of bank failure ; during a panic in 1793, an Edinburgh and a Glasgow bank had come down, and in the provinces of England bank failures had been numerous. At last, in February 1797, only a few weeks after the unsuccessful descent of the French on Bantry Bay, a fresh rumour of invasion produced an unprecedented run on all the banks. In Edinburgh, the resolutions passed by a meeting of the County of Midlothian, called to concert measures for the defence of that part of the country, accentuated the panic. On 1st March, while the run was still at its height. a mounted express arrived to inform the management of the Bank of Scotland that on the 26th of February the Bank of England, instructed by the Privy Council, had suspended payment in specie. The presence of a common danger immediately quelled the rivalries of the Edinburgh bankers. The news was communicated to the other banks. Mr. Fraser, manager of the Bank of Scotland, and Mr. Simpson, manager, and Mr. James, Deputy-Governor of the Royal Bank, repaired for conference to the private bank of Sir William Forbes. There they found Sir William and all his partners in attendance, and the counting-room 'crowded as usual with people demanding gold.' The bankers then sent for Mr. Hog, Manager of the British Linen Company, 'for,' says Forbes in his *Memoir* (p. 83), 'all ceremony or etiquette of public or private banks was now out of the question, when it had become necessary to think of what was to be done for our joint preservation on such an emergency.' They then adjourned to meet the Directors of the Bank of Scotland, and, backed up by the Lord Provost and business men of the town, resolved on imitating the action of the Bank of England, and sent expresses to Glasgow, Greenock, Paisley, Ayr, Perth, Dundee, and Aberdeen, to inform the banks in these places of what they had done. 'The instant,' says Forbes, 'that this resolution of paying no more specie was known in the street, a scene of confusion and uproar took place. of which it is utterly impossible for those who did not witness it to form an idea. Our counting-house, and indeed the offices of all the banks, were instantly crowded to the door with people clamorously demanding payment in gold of their interest receipts, and vociferating for silver in change of our circulating paper . . . their noise and the bustle they made was intolerable ; which may be readily believed when it is considered that they were mostly of the lowest and most ignorant classes, such as fishwomen. carmen, street-porters, and butcher's men, all bawling out at once for change, and jostling one another in their endeavours who should get nearest the table, behind which were the cashier and ourselves endeavouring to pacify them as well as we could.'

No attempt seems to have been made on the part of any one to compel the banks to rescind their most illegal but inevitable resolution. The first effect of it was that the gold and silver currency in the hands of the public was hoarded, and immediately disappeared from circulation. Partial and temporary relief was found by the Government minting some Quarterguineas and putting into circulation a great quantity of Spanish dollars, with a Government stamp on them to give them currency. The Government then turned to paper-money. On 27th March, an Act of Parliament legalised the issue of notes for any sum under Twenty shillings till 15th May (which period was afterwards extended to 5th July 1799) by banks which had been in the habit of issuing notes prior to 1st March 1797. The Act contained also an indemnity in favour of such banks as had issued notes for fractional sums previously to its passing. 'Of this permission,' says Forbes, 'the Royal Bank and several country banks availed themselves; and I have no doubt they were considerable profiters by the measure. For as these notes mostly passed into places of the lowest traffic, they soon became so torn and ragged that they would scarcely hang together; and many of them must doubtless have been entirely destroyed, so as never to return for payment on the issuers. We did not issue any notes of that description; being convinced that there was no real scarcity of specie in the country, and that it would again make its appearance when the panic should wear off, as actually proved to be the case.'

The consensus of banking opinion was in favour of notes for Five shillings.

By 31st March the British Linen Company Five-shilling note was out.

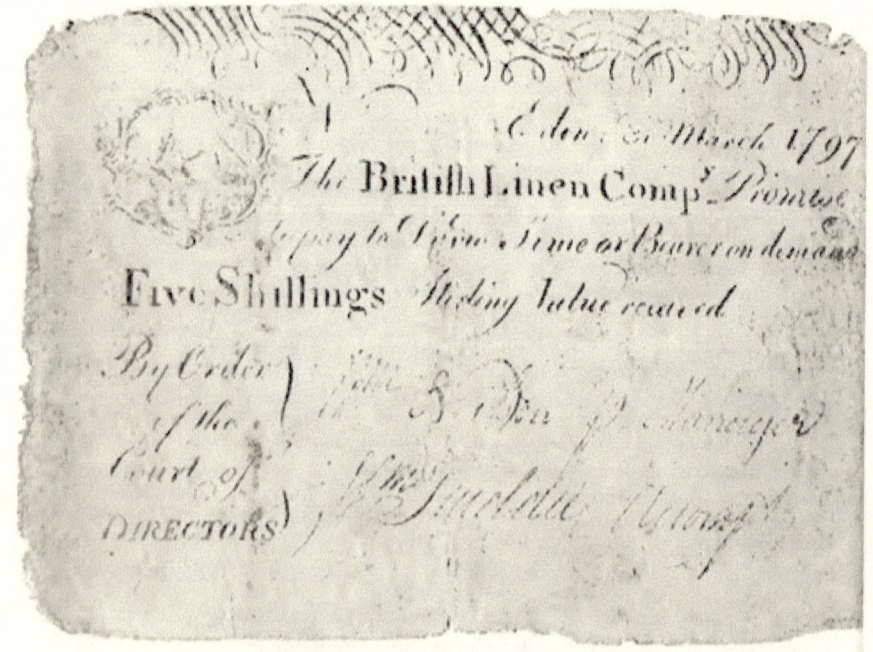

The Royal Bank followed on 3rd April. The Falkirk Bank issued a note on 6th April. The Perth Banking Company on 1st January 1798. The extension of the statutory permission to issue these notes is said to have ended on 5th June 1799, but we find the Banking Company in Aberdeen issuing a note dated 2nd September 1799. The Merchant Banking Company of Stirling issued one on 1st January 1800 : Belch & Co., of Stirling, another, dated 28th December 1804. The terms of this note are that John Belch & Company promise 'one twenty-shillings Bank note for four of this description.'　　　　　　　　　　　　　　　　　　　　J. H. S.

(To be continued.)

THE COMMISSARIOT REGISTER OF SHETLAND.

(Continued from vol. xi. *p.* 135.)

2nd September 1628.

436. Andrew Erasmusson in Middale, Walls.

437. Garthrow Mansdochter, spouse of Henry Thomasson in Boxsetter, Delting.

438. Andrew Coghill in Papa Stour, died January 1625. Helen Bruce his relict, and Margaret his daughter.

439. Margaret Irving, spouse to Edward Manson in North Hammersland, Tingwall, died April 1628. Nicol, William, and David her children.

440. Jean Erasmusson in Easterfiord, Delting.

20th September 1628.

441. Robert Hunter in Isbuster, Whalsay, died March 1628. James his only son.

442. Marion Christophersdochter, spouse to Thomas Erasmusson in Setter, Weisdale.

27th September 1628.

443. Mans Manson in Nesting, died February 1628. Ann Gariock his relict, William, Manss, Margaret, and Christian his children.

444. Helen Nicolsdochter, spouse of William Mansone in Effirth, Sandsting.

11th October 1628.

445. Mans Johnson in Oeraquoy, Dunrossness.

446. Katherine Erasmusdochter, spouse of Mans Williamson in Neep, Nesting.

447. Marion Thomasdochter, relict of William Tait in Tronafirth, Tingwall.

448. Erasmus Johnsone in Oeraquoy, Dunrossness.

28th October 1628.

449. Andrew Manssone in Bigsetter, Aithsting.

450. John Wirk in Scalloway-banks, died January 1628. Barbara Bie his relict, Patrick, Lilias, and Elspeth her children.

451. John Androsson in Wester Quarff, within the isle of Burray.

452. Manss Laurenceson in Dowane, Nesting.

453. Thomas Cheyne of Valay, Walls, died June 1626. Agnes Strang, his relict, and Laurence and James his children.

454. Manse Manson in Viggor, Unst.

455. Henry Wardlaw in Clousta, Aithsting, died March 1628. Margaret Buchanan his relict.

456. Robert Tulloch in Northbister, Burra, died December 1627. Arthur and Grissel his children.

11th August 1629.

457. Marion Alexandersdochter in Southland, Unst.

458. William Magnusson in Mailland, Unst.

459. Breta Jamesdochter, spouse of Erasmus Olasone in Collasetter, Unst.

460. James Hay, in Houll, Unst, died February 1629.

461. Sinevo Matchesdochter, relict of —— Marenssone in Collasetter, Unst.

462. Agnes Antounsdochter in Collasetter, Unst.

463. Isabel Aickla, spouse of John Olasone in Ronan, Unst.

464. Schewart Johnsone in Bewd, Unst.

465. Andro Androison in Cliff, Unst, died March 1629. Ingagarth Androisdochter, his relict, and Sinnevo and Agnes his children.

466. Andrew Stewartson in Bigton, Unst.

15th August 1629.

467. Peter Hallowson, Yell.

18th August 1629.

468. Margaret Magnusdochter, spouse to Magnus Tullan in Eshness, North maven.

19th August 1629.

469. John Mathewson in Wester Sterd, Delting.

26th August 1629.

470. Marion Olasdochter, spouse to Nicol Manson, Aithsting.
471. Alexander Isbister in Cardwell, Delting.
472. Robert Anderson in Elvista, Walls.

10th September 1629.

473. William Manson in Neep, Nesting.

12th September 1629.

474. Margaret Williamsdochter, spouse of William Dempster, in Skewingsta, Unst.
475. Marion Graham, spouse of Andrew Tailzeor in Stromness, Whiteness, died March 1628. Magnus and William her children.
476. Barbara Olasdochter, spouse of Erasmus Thomson in Cudabister, Weisdale.

17th July 1630.

477. Barbara Olasdochter, spouse of Edmond Smyth in Scrawald, Unst.
478. Katherine Hay, spouse of Laurence Anderson in Houll, Unst.
479. Margaret Erasmusdochter, spouse of John Mathewson in Uphouse, Unst.
480. Gairthrow Petersdochter, relict of Shewart Henrieson in Clisbo, Unst.
481. Isobel Laurencedochter, spouse of Thomas Couttie in Hundagarth, Unst.
482. Marion Ferquair, relict of Henry Coupland of Skae, Unst, died December 1629. David Ferquhair her brother and Katherine her sister.
483. Marion Johnsdochter, spouse of Nicol Johnissone in Watquhy, Unst.
484. Magdalen Fowler and Andrew Thomasson, spouses in Gairdiegarth, Unst.
485. Christian Strang in Voesgarth, Unst, died February 1630. James Strang of Voesgarth, her father's brother.
486. Claus Johnson in Langhouse, Unst.
487. Margaret Antoniusdochter, spouse of Nicol Williamson in Ska, Unst.
488. Henry Coupland in Ska, Unst, died December 1629. Ann Coupland his sister.
489. Christian Mansdochter in Scotland, Unst.
490. Marion Olasdochter, relict of Walter Manson in Langaschall, Unst.
491. Magnus Matchisone in Westhouse, Unst.
492. Agnes Hay in Wailzie, Unst, died May 1629. Andrew Hay her brother's son.
493. James Erasmusson in Under Hammer, Unst.

Fetlar, 22nd July 1630.

494. Thomas Nicolson in Urie.
495. Magnus Olasone in South Dail.
496. Daniel Forrester, died July 1629. Alexander Forrester his brother.
497. George Strang in Gord. Jean Arthur his relict, Martha and Marian his children.
498. Patrick Peterson.

Yell, 23rd July 1630.

499. Dorothie Johnsdochter, spouse of William Moolson in Nether Houll.

Northmaven, 26th July 1630.

500. Erasmus Laurenson in Glus.
501. James Christophersone in Tangwick.
502. Symon Manssone in Glus.
503. Marion Olausdochter in Housset.
504. William Ollasone in Nibon.
505. Thomas Olasone in Frangord.

31st July 1630.

506. Helen Wishart, spouse to James Christopherson in Madsetter, Isle of Papa, died February 1629. Andrew, Patrick, Arthur, James, Christopher, Elspeth, Breta, and Jean her children.
507. Magnus Ellinson in Fofragarth, in Sandness.

4th August 1630.

508. Elspeth Androsdochter, spouse to Henry Thomasson in Twat, Aithsting.

7th August 1630.

509. Magnus Nicolsone in Gulberwick.
510. Marion Smyth, spouse of Gabriel Erasmusson in Kergord, Weisdale.
511. Ola Jameson in Sett, Papa.
512. Andrew Straughen in Bigton, Papa.
513. Ola Gregoriusson in Instifer, Bressay.
514. Mathew and Bothwell Erasmussons in Wairavo Northmaven.
515. John Olason in Enaflirth, Northmaven.
516. Arthur Erasmusson in Gunyesetter, Northmaven.
517. Gairthrow Erasmusdochter, spouse of Erasmus Stephanson in Urie, Fetlar.
518. Marion Thomasdochter, spouse of Andrew Porter in Hewgoland, Northmaven.
519. Iver Laurenceson in Burravoe, Northmaven.
520. Magnus Fressar in Setter, Walls.
521. Elspeth Matchesdochter, spouse of Zeanes Peterson in Coppasetter, Yell.
522. Magnus Giffort, spouse of Andrew Robertson, in Setter, in Bressay,

died October 1629. Laurence, Andrew, Alexander, Gilbert, Robert, John, Elspeth, Marie, Katherine, Jean, Doratie, Janet, Helen, Christian, and Isabel her brothers and sisters.

523. Katherine Sinclair, spouse to Bartelmo Hawick of Nischeam, Delting, died March 1622. Janet, Elspeth, and Agnes Hawicks her children.

524. Peter Manson in Setter, Yell.

13th August 1630.

525. Margaret Coghill, daughter of Andrew Coghill in Olagarth, Papa Stour.

526. Marote Bruntska, spouse of James Johnson in Scalloway.

14th August 1630.

527. Mallie Whyte in Hewgoland, in Whiteness, died November 1629.

23rd August 1630.

528. Ingagarth Davidsdochter, spouse of Bartelmo Antoninsone in Isbister, in Whalsay.

529. Marion Williamsdaughter, relict of Arthur Simpson in Lie, in Whalsay.

Dunrossness, 27th August 1630.

531. Christopher Garthson in Clumlie.

532. Gayn Gadie in Clumlie, died October 1629. Judith Mowat relict, Mans, John, and Oliver his children.

533. Magnus McFerssone, spouse to David Bruce in Wilsness, died June 1630. Henry and Marion her children.

534. Elspeth Copland, spouse to Gilbert Leisk in Soutries (? Scatness), died February 1627. Henry, Laurence, Marione, and Marion her children.

30th August 1630.

535. Andrew Tailzeor in Stromness, Whalsay, died October 1629. William his son.

536. Margaret Sinclair his relict, died October 1629. James, eldest son, William and Janet her children.

537. William Thomassone in Quarff.

538. Lilias Mansdochter, spouse of Erasmus Androisson in Hagrasetter, Northmaven.

539. William Johnsone in Tingon, Northmaven.

540. Ola Patersone in Liewith, Dunrossness.

54 Katherine Christopher-dochter, spouse to Alexander Drevar in Fitch, Tingwall.

542. Alexander Drevar in Fitch, Tingwall, died October 1629. Margaret, Marion, and Christian his brother's bairns.

543. Nicoll Androisson in Holland, Tingwall.

Unst, 4th July 1631.

544. Christianus Copland, alias Willamson, in Row.

545. Erasmus Ollasome in Collaster.

546. Nicol Fressir in Scae, died February, 1630. Katherine his relict, Agnes his daughter.

547. Andrew Peterson in Ordaill.

9th July 1631.

548. Agnus Marensdochter, spouse of Nicoll Molotsone in Hildigarth, Yell.

549. Bessie Lewis, relict of Magnus Henryson in Rosbuster, Fetlar.

550. Ola Nicolsone in Setter, Yell.

551. Nicoll Mansson in Cloudaun, Fetlar.

552. Magnus Davisone in Heull, Yell.

11th July 1631.

553. Magnus Christopherson in Uyea, Northmaven.

14th July 1631.

554. James Smith in Daill, Delting.

18th July 1631.

555. Elizabeth Androisdochter, spouse of Peter Jamieson in Foulla.

556. Bartian Reid in Kettinsetter, Walls.

20th July 1631.

557. Magnus Nicolson in Skeld, Sandsting.

558. Katherine Reid, spouse of Mathew Manson in Westerskeld, Sandsting.

559. Allan Dewar in Voe, Walls.

560. Laurence Manson in Uyeasound, Aithsting.

27th July 1631.

561. James Manson in Glaitness, Nesting.

31st July 1631.

562. William Peace in Channerwick, Dunrossness.

10th August 1631.

563. Jerom Christopherson in Kirkabister, Bressay.

564. Bothwell Erasmussone in Northmaven.

565. Marie Strang, spouse of Mr. Thomas Hendrie, minister of Walls, died February 1629. Gilbert, James, and Janet her children.

566. David Paterson in Daill, Walls.

567. Jenat Gudlet, spouse to Jerome Sclaiter in Lie, Walls.

568. Agnes Henricsdochter, spouse to Thomas Galt in Setter, Yell.

569. Magnus Ollasone in Voy, Dunrossness.

570. Jerome Nicolson in Caseliff, Tingwall.
571. Marion Edwardsdochter, spouse to William Jacobson in Setter. Yell.
572. Breta Nicolsdochter, spouse of Thomas Manson in Scalloway.

2nd July 1632.

573. Ola Sinclair in Norbie, Sandness, died April 1632. Henry, Arthur, Robert, Daniel, and Jerome his bairns.

4th July 1632.

574. Erasmus Gregoriusone in Isbuster, Northmaven.
575. Magnus Nicolson in Burravoe, Northmaven.

10th July 1632.

576. Ingagarth Magnusdochter, spouse to Walter Corisone in Frangord, Unst.
577. Andrew Shewartson in Maill, Unst.
578. Breta Symonsdochter, relict of Robert Williamson in Hamer, Unst.
579. Henry Williamson of Bowanes, died May 1632. Elspeth Mudie his relict, Manss, Andrew, William, Gilbert, James, and Robert his children.
580. Ingagarth Mansdochter, spouse to Nicole Polson in Funzie, Fetlar.
581. Marion Olasdochter, relict of John Mansone in Westerhouss.
582. Marion Androisdochter, spouse to Christopher Williamson in Aith, Fetlar.
583. Ingagarth Nicoldochter, spouse of Laurence Manson in Bith, Fetlar.

20th July 1632.

584. Nicol Olasone in Gruting, Delting.

24th July 1632.

585. John Robertson in Howland, Northmaven.
586. Syne Thomasdochter, relict of Finla Donaldson in Burraland, Northmaven.
587. Marion Spence, spouse to Arthur Fresar in Setter, Yell, died June 1632. Andrew her son.
588. Sinnevo Symondisdochter, spouse to Simon Manson in Little Setter, Yell.

28th August 1633.

589. Janet Magnusdochter, spouse to Christopher Olasone in Glaitness, Unst.
590. Helen Antoninsdochter, spouse of Edward Sinclair in Ska, Whalsay.

Unst, 29th August 1633.

591. Jonas Strang of Voesgarth.

592. Mr. Magnus Norsk, minister of Unst, died May 1632. Doratie Thomsdochter his relict, Thomas, Patrick, Robert, Olaf, and Magnus his children.
593. Magnus Baltisone, Isle of Newhouse.
594. Margaret Williamsdochter, spouse of Robert Duncan in Midlehouse.

2nd September 1633.

595. George Sinclair in Aith, Fetlar, died August 1632.

6th September 1633.

596. Margaret Robertsdochter, spouse to Nicol Smyth in Geldisbak.

20th September 1633.

597. Magnus Mitchaelson in Duafirth, Northmaven.

21st September 1633.

598. Ola Harieson in Setter.

22nd September 1633.

599. Magnus Matcheson in Isle of Papa Stour.
600. Manson Giffart, spouse of Berald Mowat in Reafirth, Northmaven, died May 1632. Laurence and Malcolm her children.
601. Andrew Person in Gonfirth, Delting.

10th October 1633.

602. Janet Ingsetter, spouse of Laurence Sinclair in Nisbister, died January 1632. Laurence, Robert, Adam, and Marion her children.

25th October 1633.

603. Katherine Halero, spouse of Walter Leisk in Voe, Dunrossness, died May 1632. James, Laurence, Patrick, Grissil, Marjorie, and Elspeth her children.

26th August 1634.

604. Turvold Polson in Glaitness.
605. Bartelmo Gilbertson in Newing, Nesting.
606. Katherine Robertsdochter in Kirkabister, Sandsting.
607. Sara Williamsdochter, spouse to Malcolm Gilbertsone in Hamnasetter, Whalsay.

Unst, 29th August 1634.

608. Magnus Nicolson in Uzeasound.
609. Nicol Jonson in Sandvoe.
610. Matches Olasone in Uphouse.
611. James Olasone in Gairdie.
612. Andrew Strang in Burreswick, died October 1633. Magdalen his relict, Sinnevo Androsdochter his daughter.

(*To be continued.*)

QUERIES.

SIR JOHN COPE.—Does any portrait, or even caricature, exist of Sir John Cope who fought at Prestonpans? And does any one know where and when Sir John was born? J.

TRINITY FRIARS.—Dr. Cramond in his paper in April (vol. xi. p. 173) refers to the hospitals in Scotland of the Trinity Friars, an order of monks founded for the special purpose of redeeming Christian captives from Turkish slavery. He remarks:—'They had six monasteries in Scotland in 1209. At the Reformation they had thirteen houses—in Aberdeen, Dundee, Brechin, etc.' Where can one see a complete list of these foundations? J. M. M., GLASGOW.

See below—REPLY—TRINITY FRIARS. ED.

CRAIGBRACK CLADDICH.—What do these words mean? They occur as follows in the reddendo clause in a charter which forms part of the titles of the island of Ulva. ZETA.

'Giving therefor yearly the said Francis William Clark and his foresaids to the said Duke . . . one penny Scots . . . in name of blench farm if asked only, along with one pressand as often as it shall happen any strangers to visit the said Duke within the parts or bounds of Mull, and that at the will and discretion of the said F. W. C. and his foresaids, and that exaction called Craigbrack Claddich when and as often as the other Inhabitants of the proper lands of the said duke in Mull shall pay.'

THE MACKIRDY FAMILY.—I am preparing for publication the genealogy, history, and traditions of the MacKirdy Family, including a complete genealogical classification and pedigree-charts of all the MacKirdys, as far as possible, in Scotland, Ireland, and America. In this work I have the co-operation of the eminent historical writers, Mrs. Evelyn MacCurdy Salisbury, only child of the late Hon. Charles J. MacCurdy, LL.D. (Yale), Judge of the Supreme Court and U.S. Minister to Austria, and her husband Professor Edward E. Salisbury, LL.D. (Harvard and Yale), formerly of the Faculty of Yale; and of General Thomas MacCurdy Vincent, a distinguished officer of the U.S. Army. We would be very thankful for any information, or suggestions as to sources of information, upon the following queries:—

1. A statement has reached America from the north of Ireland in regard to the Scotch-Irish MacCurdys, that about 1666 five brothers of the name of MacKirdy, driven by religious persecution from Scotland, took an open boat and crossed from Bute to the north of Ireland, landed near the Giant's Causeway, and settled at Ballintoy, County Antrim, where some of their descendants have remained ever since. It is stated that Pethric MacKirdy (= Patrick M'Curdy in Ireland), who seems to have been the most prominent brother, was in the siege of Derry, and was an officer in the Battle of the Boyne.

We would be glad to have additional data relative to the above statements, and information about the ancestry of these five MacKirdy brothers.

2. It is further stated that Pethric MacKirdy, who came from Scotland to Ireland about 1666, married Margaret Stewart, a descendant of Robert

II., King of Scotland, and that whenever a new sovereign ascends to the throne of Great Britain, a payment of 'crown money' is made to their descendants. It is said that when Queen Victoria came to the throne, officers of the crown went to Ballintoy in Ireland, traced the descendants of Margaret Stewart in the MacCurdy line, and paid 'crown money' to a Patrick MacCurdy and his four brothers and a sister, each payment being about £100. If this is so, the ancestry of Patrick MacCurdy must be recorded in some public office.

We would be grateful for further particulars in reference to these statements, suggestions as to how we may obtain a confirmation of the facts, and information about the ancestry of Margaret Stewart. It is not 'crown money' that we are after, but simply genealogical facts.

3. We have the statement that John MacCurdy, son of Pethric MacKirdy, who came from Scotland to Ireland about 1666, married a MacQuillan, of Dunluce Castle in Ireland, and that she descended from the great De Burgh family.

Can any person throw additional light on this subject? Any information in reference to these queries, or about the MacKirdy genealogy, history, and traditions, will be much appreciated. We are making these inquiries solely for genealogical purposes.

IRWIN POUNDS MacCURDY.
SOUTH-WESTERN PRESBYTERIAN CHURCH,
PHILADELPHIA, U.S. AMERICA.

FAMILY OF ANDREW OR ANDREWS.—Any information would be gladly received about a family of Andrew (or Andrews) who went from Ayrshire or neighbouring counties (tradition says Ayrshire) to the north of Ireland, settling in County Down. They went at the same time as a family of Agnew, who were relatives. The earliest members of the family in Ireland of whom there are records were :—

William Andrew, ...	born 1636 (or 1640), died	1720
John Andera, ...	„ 1652	„ 1718
James Andrew, ...	„ 1663	„ 1728
Margret M'Artney, wife of John Andera,	„ 1671	„ 1726
Hugh Andrew, ...	„ 1689	„ 1774

As no doubt some of these were born in Scotland, perhaps some of your readers can give information as to where records of their births or marriages might be found, or of any Scotch family of Andrew from whom they might be descended. Burke's *General Armoury* mentions the families of Andrew of Clockmilne and Andrew of Nethertarvit. Can any one give information as to where these places were, or where information about these families can be found? G. M. A.

WILLIAM FERGUSSON, STRAITON.—Can any one tell who were the parents of William Fergusson who married Margaret Goudie, and who was parish schoolmaster in the village of Straiton, County of Ayr, from 1788 till 1818?

An answer will be gratefully received by Alex. C. Fergusson, 3305 Arch Street, Philadelphia, Penn., U.S.A.

1. HOUSTON OF CREICH, SUTHERLAND.—I shall be indebted to any reader who can give me the genealogy of this branch of the family of Houston of Houston from 1650 to 1750.

2. STEUART OF WEYLAND.—I am obliged to 'A.F.S.' for his reply to
my query. Can any one supplement his information by giving me the
parentage of William Steuart (b. 1686), Secretary to the Prince of Wales
and Remembrancer of the Exchequer of Scotland, and that of his cousin-
german Charles Steuart, Stewart Clerk of Orkney?

3. NEIL M'VICAR.—In a seizin dated 1732, I find a Neil M'Vicar,
Notary, designed as 'Clerk of Edinburgh.' As he does not appear to
have been Town Clerk, any information concerning him and the office
he held will oblige. About the same time there was a Rev. Neil M'Vicar,
minister of St. Cuthbert's, Edinburgh. Were they related?—if so, how?

4. FORBES OF UGSTON.—Who was Alexander Forbes of Ugston
(Haddingtonshire?), writer in Edinburgh? He was alive in 1714.

SPERNIT HUMUM.

WHEYMAN, etc.—I am anxious to obtain information, armorial and
genealogical, relating to the familes of Wheyman, Weyman, Wayman,
Allan, Allen, Allyn, Merrill, Murrill, Byllynge, Billing, Washington, Warner.

(MRS.) MARY E. RATH-MERRILL.

ST. ALBAN'S INSTITUTE,
COLUMBUS, OHIO, U.S.A.

REPLY.

TRINITY FRIARS.—Keith in his *Account of Religious Houses in Scotland*,
appended to his *Catalogue of Bishops*, devotes chapter iv. to the order
known as the Red Friars, Trinity Friars, etc. He mentions friaries of the
order which were established at Aberdeen, Dunbar, Howston, Scotland-
well, Failefurd, Peebles, Dornock, Berwick-on-Tweed, Dundee, Cromarty
or Crenach, Loch-Feal, Brechin, and Luffness. ED.

NOTICES OF BOOKS.

The History of Scotland from Agricola's Invasion to the extinction of the
last Jacobite Insurrection, by John Hill Burton. New edition in
eight volumes. (Blackwood and Sons, 1897.) 8vo, vol. i. pp. xiv+448;
vol. ii. pp. xii+435; vol. iii. pp. xii+451; price 3s. 6d. each.

IT is just thirty years since the original edition of these volumes first
appeared, and to any one who has noticed the thumbed condition of the
copies of the work which belong to our lending libraries it is manifest
that the time has come for a large re-issue. In a historian we ask for
three things, and one thing more—knowledge, judgment, and impartiality,
and the fourth is style. For all these qualifications Hill Burton's credit
still stands well. If his knowledge of original documents was inferior to
Joseph Robertson's, and his statements sometimes less laboriously vouched
for than Tytler's, he is still pre-eminent among Scots historians in his
acquaintance with printed literature, and in the common-sense of the
man of the world. He had the advantage of coming after Tytler, and
he is free from some of Tytler's prejudice. If he was not a record
scholar himself, he was the intimate of Joseph Robertson, Stuart, Cosmo
Innes, and others who were. His chapters on the social condition and
progress of the nation show the influence of the new historical method

which the record scholar has introduced, and which the excavations of the record scholar have made possible. All the materials of Scottish history are not even yet available, nor the nature of them even known; when they are, Hill Burton may be superseded: but he will not be superseded, till there appears a writer who unites to deeper and wider knowledge Burton's narrative power and his discrimination both of facts and opinions. When this writer does appear, he will owe much to John Hill Burton, not only to his history, but to his representations to the authorities, which at least contributed to the unlocking of the records, and the establishment of the present Historical Department of the Register House.

The reception of this new edition of Burton's history will prove the high position which this work still holds in the estimation of the public. Might it not then be fitting at this time that some few of the thousands who have derived hours of pleasure and instruction from his pages should unite and ask leave to express the public gratitude to his memory by rearing a monument in the churchyard of Dalmeny over his nameless grave?

Historical Notes on Peeblesshire Localities, by Robert Renwick, author of *Gleanings from Peebles Records;* editor of *Stirling Records, Lanark Records,* and *Glasgow Protocols.* (Peebles, Watson and Smyth, 1897.) 8vo, pp. xix+630, and folding map, price 7s. 6d. net.

In this book — unpretentious to the borders of severity — we have a repository whose contents remind us of Joseph Robertson's four Spalding Club quartos of *Illustrations of the Topography and Antiquities of the Shires of Aberdeen and Banff.* Believing that the valuable but little-known information concerning Peeblesshire printed by the old book clubs, etc., might be interesting to Peeblesshire people, Mr. Renwick offered a series of archæological and historical articles to the editor of the *Peeblesshire Advertiser.* They were cordially welcomed, and subsequently appeared in that newspaper. They have been collected and revised, and now constitute a most valuable record, unique in the south of Scotland. The book before us is no mere reprint of charters, though charters do here and there appear in all their quaint and instructive phraseology. All the sources of local and personal information, charter-rooms, chartularies, registers, reports of trials, etc. etc., have been ransacked, and ancient kings, knights, ladies, churchmen, get up and walk and talk again. The work is a most important addition to Scottish historical literature. It contains the results of infinite research in matters both ancient and modern. A full index, and a reprint of the map of the ancient Deanery of Peebles, from the *Origines Parochiales,* enhance the value of the book.

The County Histories of Scotland: A History of Moray and Nairn by Charles Rampini, sheriff-substitute of these Counties. (William Blackwood and Sons, 1896.) 8vo, pp. xii+438, price 7s. 6d. net.

The writer of a history of Moray, which is to form a volume of a series of county histories, is brought face to face at the outset with a question of some difficulty. The territory known by the name Moray has been a varying quantity. To-day it is the shire of Elgin, but it began in history as a province consisting of the counties of both Elgin and Nairn, the County of Cromarty, Inverness-shire from the Spey to Glengarry and Ben Attow, and a great part of Ross. When in the thirteenth century this ancient province was absorbed into Scotland and broken up into smaller fiefs, the name remained as the name of the see of the bishop of these parts. The boundaries of the bishopric of Moray did not, however, exactly coincide with those of the province. The bishopric included the southern and eastern parts of the province, but no part of Ross and Cromarty. It extended, however, on the other hand, as far east as Huntly and Keith ; thence south to Ben Avon, and down the Grampians as far as Lochaber. The earldom again, though it preserved the boundaries of the bishopric on the north and south, shrank back to pretty much the line of the province on the east, and included new territory on the south-west where it touched Loch Linnhe, Loch Eil, Loch Nevis, and the Sound of Sleat. The first and most obvious alternative open to the county historian was to write the history of the Moray of to-day, leaving the ancient history of those parts which are now in the shires of Inverness, Ross, etc., to the historians of these shires. But to attempt the history of the capitals of at least the earldom and the bishopric, Darnaway Castle and Elgin Cathedral, which are both in the present county, without giving the history of the earldom and the bishopric, would be unprofitable if it were possible. The alternative, which the learned sheriff has adopted, of treating both province, bishopric, and earldom has its manifest propriety. Whether the treatment of the greater Morays in this the first northern volume of the series will lead to overlapping and repetitions in the future volumes of Inverness, Ross, etc., remains to be seen. In the meantime it adds largely to the importance and interest of the volume before us, and, at the same time, makes the story of the present counties of Elgin and Nairn the easier to tell.

After tracing separately the general history of the province, the bishopric and the earldom, the author sketches the history of the principal families, the Calders and Campbells, Roses of Kilravock, the Gordons, Duffs, Brodies, etc. He devotes chapters to the towns, the land and its people, and distinguished men : among them is a sketch of that strange character Roualeyne George Gordon Cumming, the lion-hunter, which will be new to most people. A miscellany of topography, geology, customs, superstitions, etc., composes another chapter of great interest.

The historical parts of the volume are carefully and well done. The author has spent much pains over the genealogical and biographical chapters, and there and elsewhere he exhibits a thorough understanding of the character of the northern men whom he has resided amongst and known both privately and officially. The Morayshire legends and superstitious and other customs are by no means few, and some of the latter are decidedly peculiar. The learned sheriff devotes a very adequate space to them, for which the folklorist and general reader will thank him. One of his quaintest tales is of the election of St. Giles as Provost of Elgin in 1547.

Within the four hundred odd pages of the volume the learned sheriff takes his readers over a surprising amount of ground and sometimes at a great rate, but he chooses his line and varies his pace with great judgment, and halts a breathing-space when the position calls for it. He has constructed a delightful book.

The book is enriched like the others of the series with a bibliography of books concerning Morayshire, and with maps ancient and modern which, in this case, consist of Blaeu's map of the province (1654), the Ordnance Survey map of the present counties, a plan of Elgin Cathedral and its precincts, and a map of Scotland showing the boundaries of province, bishopric, earldom and counties.

Eminent Arbroathians, being Sketches Historical, Genealogical, and Biographical, 1178-1894, by J. M. M'Bain, F.S.A. Scot. (Arbroath, Brodie and Salmond, 1897.) Fcap. 4to, 452 pp., price to subscribers, 10s. 6d. ARBROATH and the territory about it have several claims to immortality : they contain the site of a remarkable and historical abbey, and constitute the scenery of a famous novel ; they are also the birthplace, or are intimately connected with the career, of many of Scotland's celebrities. If Arbroath were famous for nothing else than as the birthplace of James Chalmers, the inventor of the adhesive postage-stamp, it would still be a place of pride to Scotsmen, and of interest to the world ; but the list of historic personages born in or connected with that district is most notable—Cardinal Beton, on the one side, Walter Myln and James Melville, on the other : Sir Peter Young, preceptor and librarian to James VI. ; William Aikman, the portrait-painter ; Principal M'Cosh, of Princetown ; the Rev. D. Bell, inventor of the reaping-machine ; Alexander Kirk, inventor of the triple-expansion engine—are but a few of them. Nor is Arbroath exhausted by its past, as the list of eminent personages at home and abroad, who are still living, testifies.

To Arbroath in history and fiction Mr. M'Bain devotes a short and interesting sketch ; but the bulk of his book is devoted to the short sketches, biographical and genealogical, which the title of the book announces. To say that the result is interesting and gratifying chiefly to natives of Arbroath would be no disparagement. But the volume is a valuable contribution to general Scottish biography and genealogy ; it evinces very extensive acquaintance with the sources of information, and is ably and pleasantly written.

The book is well got up, with superior paper and type, and is bound in dark-blue cloth, not unlike that of the Scottish History Society's series.

Fletcher of Saltoun, by G. W. T. Omond. 'Famous Scots Series.' (Oliphant, Anderson and Ferrier, 1897.) Pp. 160, price 1s. 6d.
MR. OMOND'S *Life of Andrew Fletcher of Saltoun* is so full of exciting incident, reckless daring, and desperate endeavour, that one reads it more as a charming romance than a piece of serious history. Mr. Omond's style is direct, concise, and vigorous, and his view impartial ; while enlisting the keenest sympathies of the reader on behalf of his hero, he does not deny the fact that his somewhat hasty temper did from time to time cause some indiscreet person to lose his life ; while his own life and liberty, and the cause he had most at heart, were continually endangered.

Born in the year 1653, and educated either at home or in the parish school of Saltoun, Andrew Fletcher shared the common fate of genius. He was immeasurably ahead of his generation : the extraordinary daring and originality of his statesmanship was regarded by his friends as the Utopian dreaming of a visionary, and by his enemies as the dangerous madness of a fanatic. It has much more in common with that of the present day than with any preceding. Fletcher was also a man of literature and wide culture. A large number of books collected by him are still preserved at Saltoun Hall, a monument to the largeness of grasp of the man who was at once a keen soldier, an ardent politician, a distinguished man of letters and a devoted patriot.

The Blackwood Group, by Sir George Douglas. 'Famous Scots Series.'
(Oliphant, Anderson, and Ferrier, 1897.) 8vo, price 1s. 6d.
IT would no doubt have been impossible to deal in a satisfactory
manner with the whole of the 'Blackwood' Group in a single volume of this
series. Still an account of that group with the Ettrick Shepherd and
John Gibson Lockhart left out is suggestive of the proverbial comparison
from Shakespeare's play. In a prefatory note it is explained that these
two striking members of the Group are to be the subjects of forthcoming
volumes. Even with their omission, however, the volume before us forms
an interesting addition to the series. It gives a brief but sufficiently
complete account of the lives and works of John Wilson, John Galt,
D. M. Moir ('Delta'), Miss Ferrier, Michael Scott, and Thomas Hamilton,
all of whom, but especially the first-named, contributed largely to the
phenomenal success of 'Maga' in the beginning of the century. The
book will do good service in recalling to this generation a number of
writers who are apt to be forgotten amid the host of moderns, and some
of whose works at least will bear comparison with the best that is written
to-day. It is a little pathetic that 'Christopher North,' unquestionably
the most brilliant of the Group and its most interesting personality should
have left nothing more enduring than the *Noctes*. It is different with
Galt. In spite of incredible carelessness, and lack of steady purpose, he
succeeded in producing the *Annals* and the *Provost*, with which Sir George
Douglas would associate as of equal merit *Ringan Gilhaize*. 'Delta,' has
left in *Mansie Wauch* a book that will be read as long as good Scots is
understood, and frolicsome humour unseasoned with coarseness appreciated. In comparison with these three, Miss Ferrier's contributions to
literature were few, but perhaps more lasting. The interest of her work
depends more on what is simply human and less on local colouring than
Galt's, her only real rival in the Group. Her pen has a wider intellectual
and moral range. Sir George Douglas gives it high praise, but not too
high, when he says of *The Inheritance* that it was 'the superb performance'
of which *Marriage* had been the 'brilliant promise.' To the remaining
two, Michael Scott and Thomas Hamilton, the authors respectively of
Tom Cringle's Log and *Cyril Thornton*, the biographer does full justice.
It only remains to be said that the book is written in an easy, pleasant
style, with an agreeable absence of any attempt at smart writing. If
occasionally a trifle careless and heavy, it succeeds in leaving a very
definite impression of the subjects it deals with.

*The Genealogical Magazine, a Journal of Family History, Heraldry, and
Pedigrees.* (Elliot Stock.) No. I.—May; No. II.—June. 4to, price 1s.
THE new monthly magazine has been started under the charge of an able
editor, and with contributions from well-known writers. It bids fair to
be a valuable addition to the present organs which profess its departments.
In its first number the place of honour is given to an article by Mr. J. H.
Round, on the Surrender of the Isle of Wight, and Mr. Hubert Hall's
editing of the Red Book of Exchequer. The second number contains
Mr. Hall's reply to Mr. Horace Round. Among other articles in the first
number is one on the Sobieski-Stuarts, which, if it doesn't add largely to
our knowledge of the subject, at least tells its story pleasantly. Mr.
Graham-Easton, who is well known to our readers and those of *Notes
and Queries* for his correspondence on the Grahams, Earls of Menteith,
has an article on the subject in the second number. A feature of the
magazine is to be 'The Gazette of the Month.'

L'Archæologia de Paris.—Revue mensuelle des découvertes, des collections, des musées, des sociétés et des publications archéologiques. Dirigée par C. R. Graville, lauréat de l'Académie des Inscriptions et Belles-Lettres.

We have received from Paris two numbers of *L'Archæologia de Paris*, a new antiquarian and historical monthly, started at the beginning of the year under the editorship of M. C. R. Graville, which promises to be a valuable addition to the periodical literature dealing with the past. Each number contains one or more detailed monographs on special subjects, and a comprehensive survey of the archæological discoveries and publications of the day. We note with special interest an article by M. H. Prévost on the Tomb of Mausolus, and the discoveries made by Sir Charles Newton and Sir Robert Murdoch Smith at Halicarnassus ; also an appreciative notice of the Proceedings of the Society of Antiquaries of Scotland. The pages devoted to correspondence and inquiries have been fully taken advantage of, and contain many interesting suggestions. M. Graville is greatly to be congratulated on his illustrations ; we note with special admiration the beautiful drawing, printed in silver, of a chased silver vase found at Alise-Sainte-Reine, which appears in the April number.

The Church of Keith, reprinted from the *Banffshire Herald*, by William Cramond, M.A., LL.D., etc., Schoolmaster of Cullen. (John Mitchell, Keith, [1897].) 8vo, pp. 95, price 6d.

This little book of annals of the ecclesiastical and scholastic affairs of Keith begins with the dedication and appropriation of the church and such notices as exist of the clergy in pre-Reformation times ; the bulk of the matter which follows is mainly composed of extracts from the Records of the post-Reformation Church courts. Dr. Cramond has, with his usual systematic and laborious search, collected from these records a series of interesting and noteworthy passages, and exhibited very fully the miscellaneous cares of the kirk-session in the seventeenth and eighteenth centuries, and its quaint manner of executing its office. In 1742 it melts down the bad copper found in the church collections, and makes the licensed beggars' badges with it. It fixes the days of the week on which alone they are to beg in the various parts of the parish. In 1715 the Earl of Huntly's men seriously annoy the session-clerk on their way south, but on their return—after Sheriffmuir—he has some revenge in chronicling that the Earl passed through Keith 'looking very disheartened like.' It is not always easy to account for the choice of the titles of the sections.

BOOKS, THE NOTICES OF WHICH ARE UNAVOIDABLY HELD OVER.

Diary of a Tour through Great Britain in 1795 by the Rev. William MacRitchie, with introduction and notes by David MacRitchie. (Elliot Stock, 1897.) 8vo, pp. x + 169, price 6s.

Prehistoric Problems, being a selection of Essays on the Evolution of Man, and other controverted problems in Anthropology and Archæology, by Robert Munro, M.A., M.D., etc. (William Blackwood and Sons). 8vo, pp. xix + 371, price 10s. net.

Guide to Grantown and District, by W. Cramond, M.A., LL.D., etc., with Map of District by Messrs. W. and A. K. Johnston. (Dundee, John Leng and Co., 1897.) 30 pp., price 3d.

The Scottish Antiquary

OR

Northern Notes and Queries

VOL. XII.   OCTOBER 1897.   No. 46.

MACBETH AND THE MOVING WOOD.

Messenger. As I did stand my watch upon the hill,
I look'd toward Birnam, and anon, methought,
The wood began to move.
    Macbeth.   Liar and slave !
Messenger. Let me endure your wrath if't be not so ;
Within this three mile may you see it coming ;
I say, a moving grove.
                            Macbeth, Act V., sc. 5.

I.—*The Wood in the Play.*

ALTHOUGH it is known that the events and character of Macbeth's reign
are very far from truly represented in the historical sources used by Shakespeare, and that the resulting picture of the man is therefore entirely false,
the impress of Shakespeare upon his features has been such as to make
him the most real of all our monarchs. Not Robert the Bruce, and
James IV., and Queen Mary themselves, are individualities so conceivable
as Macbeth. Shakespeare's powerful dramatic portraiture explains much,
though not all ; he had admirable material at his command and he added
but little to what he found in it. His imagination was inappreciably required
for his plot ; the matter, already dramatic enough, scarce needed to be
fused anew in his brain : a very little in the way of reshaping was demanded,
perhaps even less than in most of his histories.

The episode of the moving wood, one of the touches he inherited, he
utilised with fine scenic effect. Heavy-laden storm-clouds have gathered
overhead ; the lightning flash may come any moment. Young Malcolm
is at the gates, but the witches have promised fair, and Macbeth welcomes
as a relief from anxious introspections the active duty of generalship. The
Queen's intellect, oppressed by the terrible secret which she had carried
with so much outward coolness and self-control, has given way at last and

her frenzied death is the first thunderclap. The King, however, has supped so full of horrors for years that this great bereavement falls upon him with only slender shock. 'She should have died hereafter,' he says, and turns to the next messenger. The witch had said, 'Fear not till Birnam Wood do come to Dunsinane,' and now the message tells him the wood was come. This the penultimate climax in the play is greater than the final one, which is reached in the disclosure of Macduff's Caesarean birth; it seems to mean far more in the crisis of his fate; it knocks away the mainstay of his soul, shaking beyond recovery his faith in his oracles. Crushed for a moment only by the blow, his manhood rises out of the ruin of his hope. Face to face with the worst he stands at bay, and with a great burst of despairing courage defies both man and fate :—

> Blow wind, come wrack,
> At least we 'll die with harness on our back.

The episode, which in the master's hands thus served as a chief turning-point in a great tragedy, bringing out for the last time a flash of the old spirit in the decadent hero, would on that sole account warrant investigation even had it not been in itself of moment sufficient to make examination worth while. How did it come Shakespeare's way? whence came it into the authorities directly used by him? what are its relations to history, and to those traditions from which the springs of history are fed?

II.—*Shakespeare's sources.*

As everybody knows, Macbeth in the mass is Holinshed transmuted into Shakespeare; that is, of course, leaving aside any suggestion of joint-authorship with, or imitation of, or by, Thomas Middleton. The history in the play is in virtual entirety to be found in Holinshed's account of Duncan and Macbeth, blended with his description of the murder of King Duffe by Donewald. Mr. W. G. Clark and Mr. Aldis Wright have therefore referred to Holinshed's Chronicle as the single authority consulted by Shakespeare for this play. A recent writer, however, Mrs. Charlotte Carmichael Stopes, has in the *Athenæum* (25th July 1896, p. 139) expressed her strong belief that besides Holinshed, Shakespeare made use of William Stewart's *Buik of the Croniclis of Scotland*, a metrical Scots translation of Boece made for James V. in 1535, but scarce heard of either in literature or history until its publication in the Rolls Series in 1858. This opinion is wholly based on the argument that wherever Stewart differs from Holinshed Shakespeare follows Stewart. After having carefully and not without sympathy examined this proposition I cannot help saying that it is certainly not demonstrated by the eight examples adduced, the best of which strikes me as hardly more than a very ordinary coincidence. One of them is that Stewart paints more prominently than Holinshed the shock Macbeth suffers from the moving wood. 'It is Stewart,' Mrs. Stopes says, 'who gives the picture of Macbeth, paralyzed by the sight of the moving forest, refusing to fight, and of his followers deserting him who would not defend himself—a fatalist till the last.' The weight attachable to this interesting view may be best gauged by quoting both Holinshed and Stewart.

'He [Makbeth] had suche confidence in his prophecies that he beleeud he shoulde neuer be vanquished till Byrnane wood were brought to Dunsinnane nor yet to be slaine with anye man that should be or was borne of any woman. Malcolme folowing hastily after Makbeth came the night

before the battaile vnto Byrnan wood, and when his armie had rested a
while there to refreshe them hee commaunded euerye man to get a bough
of some tre or other of that wood in his hande as bigge as he might beare
and to march forth therwith in such wise that on the next morrow they
might come closely and without sight in thys manner within viewe of hys
enimies. On the morow when Makbeth beheld them comming in this
sort hee first marueyled what the matter ment but in the end remembred
himselfe that the prophecie which he had heard long before that time of
the comming of Byrnane wood to Dunsinnane Castell was likely to bee now
fulfilled. Neuerthelesse he brought his men in order of battell and exhorted
them to doe valiantly howbeit his enimies had scarcely cast from them
their boughes when Makbeth perceiuing their numbers betook him streight
to flight whom Makduffe pursued with great hatred' [etc.].

HOLINSHED.

l. 40,381.   This Makcobey illudit wes so daft,
     Sic credence gaif to witchis and thair craft,
     Quhilk gart him trow that he sould never de,
     Quhill Birnane wod, quhairin grew mony tre,
     Onto Dounsenane suddantlie wer brocht ;
     His fals beleif that tyme wes all for nocht.
     This ilk Malcolme, the quhilk that rycht weill knew
     Sic thing of him as Makdufe to him schew,
     With all the power he had with him thoir

l. 40,390.   To Birnane wod passit the nycht befoir
     The da he thocht that the battell sould be,
     And euerie man ane greit branche of a tre,
     Vpone his bak than, other les or mair,
     That samin nycht gart to Dunsenane bair :
     Syne on the morne, sone i e the da wes lycht,
     This Makcobey beheld into his sicht
     So greit ane wod, quhair neuir none sit grew
     Sen he wes borne, ne of sa grene ane hew :
     Traistand it wes ane taikin of his deid,

l. 40,400.   sit neuirtheles restles but ony reid,
     Rayit his men that wapons docht to weild,
     And suddantlie syne gaif this Malcolme feild :
     And, as tha war haith reddie for [to] june,
     Out of the feild he fled awa full sone :
     His men that tyme quhen that tha sa him wend
     That wald nocht fecht him awin self to defend
     Tha thocht folie with sic ane man to stryfe :
     To Malcolme than tha come ilk man belyve.

STEWART, lines 40,381-408.

Noticeable distinctions in these passages are : (1) that 'bough' is the
word in Holinshed, and 'branch' in Stewart, answering to Latin *ramus* in
Boece ; (2) that the Shakespearean motive for carrying these boughs is given
in Holinshed but neither in Stewart nor Boece ; (3) that in Holinshed, as
in Boece, the boughs are cast away when the battle opens, whereas in
Stewart this is not mentioned ; and (4) that in Stewart, as in Boece, there
is a wholesale surrender of Macbeth's men, an important feature which has
no place in Holinshed. Now the play, so far from conforming to Mrs.
Stopes' law of agreement with Stewart, in deviation from Holinshed, does
the express contrary : (1) using the word 'bough'; (2) stating why the
boughs were resorted to, viz. : as cover ; (3) telling how they were thrown
down ; and (4) not mentioning so vital a fact as the general submission.
It only remains to say that the picture of Macbeth's paralysis of courage
at sight of the moving wood appears to be no more distinct in the one

account than in the other. Boece's brief phrase *nova specie territus* being perhaps more emphatic than any word of either, or indeed of any of his translators. It is curious, too, that they all omit his express record of the passage of the Tay.

For the sake of completeness, and to effect some minor contrasts, a passage may be quoted from Bellenden, whose free rendering of Boece was first published in 1536.

'Nochtheles he [Makbeth] had sic confidence in his fretis that he belevit fermely nevir to be vincust quhil the wod of Birnane war brocht to Dunsinnane : na yit to be slane with ony man borne of ane woman. Malcolme following haistely on Makbeth come the nicht afore his victory to the wod of Birnane. And quhen his army had refreschit thame ane schort time he commanded ilk man to tak ane branche of the wod that thay micht come on the nixt morow arrayit in the same maner in his ennimes sicht. Makbeth seing him cum in this gise understude the prophecy was completit, that the wiche shew to him ; nochtheles he arrayit his men. Skarsly had his ennimes cassin fra thame the branches and cumand forthwart in batal quhen Makbeth tuk the flicht.'

BELLENDEN'S *Boece* (ed. 1821), xii. cap. 7.

Boece's own words translated are in effect as follows :—

' But he [Macbeth] was carried away by his prophecies, through which he was persuaded that not before the wood of Birnen was brought thither [to Dunsinnan] could he be conquered, and that not even then would death threaten him, because the soothsayers had foretold that he should not be slain by the hand of any man born.[1] Malcolm very swiftly pursued Macbeth and, the day before he gained the victory, halted with his army at Birnen wood. When they had rested a little there and refreshed themselves he commands them all to go into the wood and each to cut down a branch, the largest he could carry. In the first watch of the night they set out. Then the Tay is crossed, and with branches held aloft they came in sight of the enemy at earliest daybreak. When Macbeth saw them he was terrified at the strange spectacle, but at last interpreted it as concerning himself and his prophecy. However, with a mind boding no good, he led his troops forth to battle. Scarce had the branches been thrown down and the lines met when he by flight deserted his army. The troops seeing this, unwilling to lay down their lives for a coward wretch, all came over to Malcolm's allegiance.'

The rationalised motive for carrying the branches is absent entirely, if indeed it is not actually negatived, by Boece followed by his translators ; Holinshed alone excepted, his words ' that they might come closely and without sight in thys manner within viewe of hys enimes ' being perfectly clear.

III.—*From Boece back to Wyntoun.*

The tale, though commonly considered part of Boece's peculiar ... roidery of previous chronicle, did not originate with him, having been

---

' Non ab homine nati manu necandum' (ed. 1574, p. 254[b]). Possibly *homine* and ... ought to be in the same case here. 'Non ab homine nato interfici' is Boece's phrase ... ... The exemption of the prophecy thus was enlarged by Macbeth's thought ... In the original—' neque unquam hominis manu ex muliere prognati interimendum ' ... ... ' born of woman born ' to ' born man.'

inherited from Wyntoun, in whose page it appears fully developed, although it is neither given by Fordun before him nor by Bower after him. Wyntoun's vigorous passages form the earliest authority for the incident.

l. 2201.　Than wyth thame off Northumbyrland
　　　　This Malcolme enteryd in Scotland
　　　　And past oure Forth, syne strawcht to Tay
　　　　Wp that wattyre the hey way
　　　　To the Brynnane togyddyr haie.
　　　　Thare thay bade and tuk cownsale.
　　　　Syne that [q. thai?] herd that Makbeth aye
　　　　In fantown fretys had gret fay,
　　　　And trowth had in swylk fantassy,

l. 2210.　Be that he trowyd stedfastly
　　　　Nevyre discumfyt for to be
　　　　Quhill wyth hys eyne he suld se
　　　　The wode browcht off Brynnane
　　　　To the hill off Dwnsynane.
　　　　Off that wode than ilka man
　　　　Intill hys hand a busk tuk than :
　　　　Off all hys ost wes na man fre
　　　　Than in his hand a busk bare he :
　　　　And till Dwnsynane alssa fast

l. 2220.　Agayn this Makbeth thai past,
　　　　For thai thowcht wytht swylk a wyle
　　　　This Makbeth for till begyle,
　　　　Swa for to cum in prewate
　　　　On hym or he suld wytryd be.
　　　　Off this quhen he had sene that sycht
　　　　He wes rycht wa and tuk the flycht.
　　　　The flyttand wod thai callyd ay
　　　　That lang tyme eftyrehend that day.
　　　　And owre the Mownth thai chast hym than
　　　　Till the wode off Lunfanan.

　　　　　　　　　　WYNTOUN, vi. 2201-30.

There is much in Wyntoun's story of Macbeth, such as the legend of his being the devil's son, that is not found in Boece. This precludes any too positive statement as to the quarter from which Boece took his information. Wyntoun, it will be noticed (lines 2207-14, which may be compared with Stewart, 40387-8), countenances the view that Malcolm had heard of the Birnam-wood prophecy of which, on that supposition, his famous stratagem was a conscious and designed fulfilment. Boece, however, apparently has no words that would warrant a parallel interpretation : nor, of course, has either Holinshed or Shakespeare. It is a pity that Bower (vol. i. pp. 250-1) has nothing whatever about the moving wood ; he was too patriotically angry with William of Malmesbury (*Gesta Regum*, cap. 13) for giving all the glory of the victory to Siward. It was innate in the English, he said, to praise far too faintly the laudable deeds of the Scots. Macbeth's men, he declares, would never have fled from the battle if Siward alone had been in command. Bower does not help us : Boece's source must remain somewhat uncertain : Wyntoun, writing probably about the year 1423, is the ultimate express authority, behind whom we cannot go except on speculation from analogies.

IV.—*Parallels.*

The moving wood itself, divested of its prophetic associations, is not peculiar to Macbeth's mythical history, but though much less luxuriant in form, occurs in one or two other places. An ancient Greek or Roman army on the march might under some conditions be suggestive of it. The *ro..* carried by the Greek soldiers were pales with many and large branches all round the trunk. Those of the Romans, however, which Polybius commends as preferable to the Greek system, had only two, three, or four branches all on one side of the trunk. Of course, on the other hand, the *ro..* were not of green wood and had no foliage—a vital contrast to the leafy screen in Macbeth. Saxo Grammaticus, writing about the year 1200, tells (bk. v.) that Eric Mal-Spiki, in a marine expedition against the pirate Selavs, sailed up to the enemy with only one ship, the rest of his flotilla being hidden under wooden battlements covered with boughs of trees so as to present the aspect of a leafy wood. The enemy were naturally astounded at beholding a wood turned into a fleet.[1] Again Saxo (bk. vii.) describes the like stratagem on shore made use of by Hakon, son of Hamund, advancing to attack Sigar. His directions to his followers remind one of Malcolm's words in *Macbeth* :—

> Let every soldier hew him down a bough
> And bear 't before him,

said Malcolm to his men. Hakon's order was that boughs should be cut and carried by his : so that when they advanced into the open a woody shade might not be wanting. Macbeth's messenger reported that he saw a moving grove. Sigar's sentinel rushes to his bedside to announce that he saw leaves and shrubs marching in the manner of men.[2] Sigar asks in reply, How far distant is the coming wood? And when he knows that it is at hand he pronounces it a portent of his own death—from which some commentators have concluded that Saxo's words imply a previous oracle, like Macbeth's (see *Saxo*, ed. Stephanius, 1644, pp. 84, 132-3, and Mr. Oliver Elton's capital translation of the first nine books. Nutt, 1894, pp. 185, 286). Although Camden declares that no ancient writer has anything of the legend of Swanscomb Hill, the tale of the 'Kentishmen carrying boughs before them and representing afar off a moving wood' (*Camden*, ed. Gibson, 1695, column 187), it is clear that this is only true if the term 'ancient' be considered very relatively, for the monk William Thorne, praised for his accuracy and diligence by many writers from Leland to Selden, flourished in the second half of the fourteenth century, and in chronicling the episode, which he does in lively and naive phrase, is believed to be following the words of Thomas Sprot, an author who was at work about 1274. The story runs thus : Duke William, the Conqueror, is approaching after the battle of Hastings, and the whole power of Kent has mustered on Swanscomb, each man, horseman and footman alike, carrying a branch. 'The Duke, therefore, in the morning, coming into the open ground near the foresaid place, beholds, not without con-

---

[1] It was not nearly so marvellous as that in Lucian's *True History* (bk. ii.) where the deep sea was seen planted with a large and thick wood of pines and cypresses without root but swimming upright! A less fantastic example occurred at the second siege of Constantinople in 716-18. The attacking fleet of the Arabs was, according to Gibbon (c... 52), metaphorically styled by the Greeks a 'moving forest.'

[2] 'Frondes ac frutices humano more gradientes' : a phrase reversing that of the Vulgate, Mark viii. 24, where the blind man says : 'Video homines velut arbores ambulantes.'
[...] history knows its Przemislas, afterwards Lesko I., and the legend of the stratagem [...] outwitted the Hungarians. With the branches and bark of trees he formed [...] bearing lances, swords, and bucklers, and stationed them on the border [...] opposite the Hungarian camp. The ruse enabled the Poles to decoy their [...] into an ambuscade and thus destroy him.

sternation of mind, the whole country gathered round about it like a
moving wood and approaching him with steady pace. When the leaders
of the Kentishmen see Duke William surrounded in their midst, a horn is
blown as a signal; their banners are raised; they throw their branches down;
and with bent bows, swords unsheathed, and spears and other kinds of arms
outstretched they show themselves prepared for battle. The Duke and
those with him stood stupefied, and no wonder: he who had been under
the belief that he had all Kent in his grasp now vehemently trembled for
his own life' (*Decem Scriptores*, 1786). The voice at once proclaims the
historian a man of Kent. One understands it better when one remembers
that both Sprot and Thorne were monks of Canterbury. How excellent,
so often, are the descriptions of great events which, critics assure us, never
took place! There was, however, in Scottish history one example of a
moving wood which there is no need to brand as mythical. In 1332,
after the battle of Dupplin, in which he had defeated the national party,
Edward Baliol took possession of Perth. Patrick, Earl of March, in an
assault upon that city, went to the wood of Lamberkine

> 1. 3582. And thare ilk man a fagote made
> [Swa] towart Perth held strawcht the way,
> Wyth thai fag attis thai thowcht that thai
> Suld dyt the dykis suddanly,
> And till thare fays pas on playnly.
> Qwhen thai off the town can thame se
> That semyd ane hare wode for to be
> Thay ware abaysyt grettumly.
>
> WYNTOUN. viii. 3582-89.

Bower, who gives the same account, has for 'hare wood' the corresponding
phrase *nemus pruinosum*, which does not make the meaning much
plainer. The townsmen, he says, were greatly afraid when they saw the
wood marching upon them, but putting themselves in a posture of defence
for the protection of the town, they awaited in astonishment the attack of
the woody army—*adventum exercitus nemorosi* (Bower, xiii. 24: *Extracta
ex Cronicis*, 161). It does not seem impossible to conceive that this
scheme of Earl Patrick's for filling up with fascines from the wood of
Lamberkine the ante-mural fosses of Perth may in the ninety years between
Dupplin battle and the writing of Wyntoun's *Cronykil* have contributed
largely to the Perthshire legend of Birnam and Dunsinane.

V.—*A Suggested Evolution.*

We have now seen that whilst the story of Macbeth and the moving
wood in its oldest written form belongs to the fifteenth century, the moving wood is found in parallel Danish and English legends in the thirteenth
and fourteenth centuries. These latter are certainly not sources for Macbeth, their only importance for present purposes being the illustration
they afford of the stratagem itself having in distinct countries and at
different times found place amongst those abundant popular traditions in
which early history takes its rise. Yet it seems by no means a common
story, and the occurrence of two versions in one county of Scotland must
arouse question regarding the relation of the one to the other. Time,
circumstances, and assigned cause unite to favour the reliability of the
record of Earl Patrick's exploit at Perth as true. It stands every test,
including that of geography, for Lamberkine is only some two miles west

of Perth. Macbeth's story, on the other hand, is not only admittedly unhistorical; geography is fatal even to its vraisemblance. Dunsinane, on which stands the oval earthwork known as Macbeth's castle, lies as the crow flies fully fifteen miles south-east of Birnam, and the Tay flows between. One finds it hard to think of Malcolm and Siward's troops bearing their boughs all that distance. The Birnam tale is radically legendary: the Lamberkine incident is almost beyond question historical; but there is in each the rare phenomenon of the moving wood, and the scene is in each case within a few miles of Perth. The query, therefore, grows pertinent—Have we at bottom one tale or two? We have on the one hand a simple historical fact, and on the other a variant with added marvel and *diablerie*. It is perhaps much seldomer than people suppose that problems of origin are capable of definite solution, especially when they are problems of remote origins. Definitive solution is impossible in the present case, yet emphasis deserves to be laid on the recurrence here, as in so many places elsewhere in early history, of a similar story under different names and of different times. The test of duplication applied to other legendary chronicles has been found of great value, and is assuredly very applicable here. It is not on the stage only that eleven buckram men grow out of two; a small fact often swells into a large fiction. There is more helpfulness than hazard in the suggestion that the true incident at Lamberkine in 1332 may have furnished a nucleus for the embellished legend of Birnam, which is not known to have been reduced to writing earlier than 1420. So there would be one historical original and its legendary outgrowth; a simple fact and what it became when magnified and touched with miracle by popular imagination.   GEO. NEILSON.

A JACOBITE PASQUIL.

THE following political pasquil, which I have not seen in print, was obviously penned after the return of the Whigs to power under George I. in 1714, and before the raising of the Stuart standard by the Earl of Mar in 1715.

The MS. which I have of this effusion is written on a folio sheet of paper, in a clerkly hand, of the date of the piece. The omitted parts of verses 7 and 8 are coarse as well as personal.

G. P. J.

THE CHARACTERS

INTRODUCTION

WHEN Israel first provoked the Liveing Lord
God Scourg'd their Sins with famine plague and Sword
They still rebell'd God in his wrath did Sling
No thunder bolts amongst them but a King
A George like King was heaven's severest Rod
The utmost fury of ane incens'd God
God in his wrath sent Saul to punish Jewry
And George to England in a greater fury.
For George in Sin as far Exceeded Saul
As Bishop Burnet did the great Saint Paul.

CHARACTERS

1

Shame fall my Eyn if ever I have seen
   Such a parcell of Rogues in a nation
For the Campbell and the Graham are equaly blame
   Seduc'd by a strong Infatuation
The Squadrone and the Whig are upish and look big
   And designe for to ride us at pleasure
For to lead us by the nose is what they do propose
   And Enhance to themselves all our Treasure.

2

The Dalrymples come in play tho' they've Sold us all away
   And basely betray'd this poor nation
On Justice lay no stress for this Country they'le oppress
   Having no sort of Commiseration
No nation ever had a sett of men so bad
   That feed on its vitals like Vulturs
Bargany and Glenco and the Union doth Show
   That to Country and Crown they are Traitors.

3

Lord Annandale must rule tho' he's but a very tool
   Hath deceiv'd every man that did trust him
To promise he'l not stick and to break will be as quick
   Give him money you cannot disgust him
It happen'd on a day that us Cavaliers did say
   And drink to their health in a Brimmer
But now he's turned his Coat and again he's changed his note
   And acted the part of a Trimmer.

4

Little Rothes now may huff and all the Cadies cuff
   Cowley Black must resolve to knock under
Belhaven has of late found out his father was a Cheat
   And his Speech on the Union a Blunder
And Hadington that Saint may rove roar and rant
   He's a prop to the Kirk in his Station
And Ormeston will hang all the Torries in a bang
   And every man that's against Reformation.

5

Mr. Baillie with his sense and Roxburgh's Eloquence
   Must find out a design'd Assasination
If their Plotts are not well laid Mr. Johnston will them Aid
   He's Expert in that nice Occupation
Tho' David Baillie's dead honest Kersland's in his stead
   His Grace can make use of such Creatures
Can teach them how to Steer 'gainst whom and what to Swear
   And prove whom He will to be Traitors.

6

Can any find a flaw to Sir James Stewart's Skill in Law
  Or doubt of his deep Penetration
His Charming Eloquence is as obvious as his Sence
  His Knowledge comes by Generation
Tho' there's some presums to say that he's but a Lump of Clay
  Yet these are Malignants and Torys
Who to tell us are not Sly that he's much Inclined to Lye
  And famous for Coyning of Storys.

7

Mr. Cockburn with his Airs most Gloriously appears
  Deriding his poor fellow Creatures
And who wou'd not admire a Youth of so much fire
  So much sense and Beautifull ffeatures
Lord Polwarth need not grudge the Resignement of a Judge

  *   *   *   *   *

8

Lord Sutherland may roar and drink as heretofore
  For he's the Bravo of the party
Was ready to Command a Chosen trusty Band
  In Concert with the Bloody Mackartny
Had not Lothian the mishap   *   *   *
  He'd been of great use in his Station
Tho' he's much decay'd in Grace his Son succeeds his place
  A Youth of Great Consideration.

9

Zealous Hary Cunninghame hath acquir'd as much fame
  By the Service he's done to the Godly
A Regiment of horse has been bestowed worse
  Than on him who did serve them so boldly
But in nameing of this Sett we by no means must forgett
  A man of Renoun Captain Monro
Tho' he looks indeed a Squint his head's as hard as flint
  And he well may be reckon'd ane Hero.

10

The Ladys Lauderdale and Forffar's mighty Leal
  Brought their Sons very soon into favour
With grace they did abound the sweet of which they found
  When they for their offspring did Labour
Ther's Tweddale and his Club who have given many a Rub
  To their Honour their Prince and this nation
Next to that heavy Dron good honest Skipness John
  Have Established the best reputation.

11

The Lord Ross's daily food was on martyr's flesh and blood
And He did disturb much devotion
Altho' he did design to oreturn King Willie's reign
Yet he must not want due promotion
Like a Saint Sinceer and true He discovered all he knew
And for more there was then no occasion
Since he made this holy turn his heart with zeal doth burn
For the Kirk and a pure Reformation.

12

In making of this List Lord Isla should be first
A man of ane upright Spirit
He's sinceer in all he says and a double part ne'er plays
His word hee'l not break you may swear it
Drummond Warrender and Smith who have wrought with all
their pith
Claim a valuable Consideration
Give Hyndford his Dragoons hee'l Chastise the Tory Lowns
And Reform every part of the nation.

13

Did ever any Prince his favour thus dispense
On men of no merrit nor Candour
Would any man Confide on such as do deride
All notions of Conscience and honour
Hath any been untold how these this Country Sold
And would sett it againe for more Treasure
Yet Alas these very men are in favour all againe
And will rule us and Ride us at Pleasure.

FINIS.

THE FIRST UNIFORM TARTAN.

BELIEVING that representations of the tartans used in the uniform of the Royal Company of Archers during the first quarter of last century, possibly the first tartan uniform worn, are well worthy of publication and preservation, I have had plates made from photographs taken by permission of the Council of the Company.

It is evident at a glance that the coat and breeches differ entirely in the arrangement of the stripes. The succession of coloured lines already given at page 22, commences near the edge of the cloth at the division behind of the skirt, and ceases a little to the spectator's left of the end of the sixth inch of the affixed scale. The one side of the pattern is, however, only completed at the line on which the commencement of the scale touches. The pattern was therefore fully two feet broad, and apparently the breadth of the web. In the breeches the centre of the pattern seems to be about four inches to the left of the scale. From that point to the

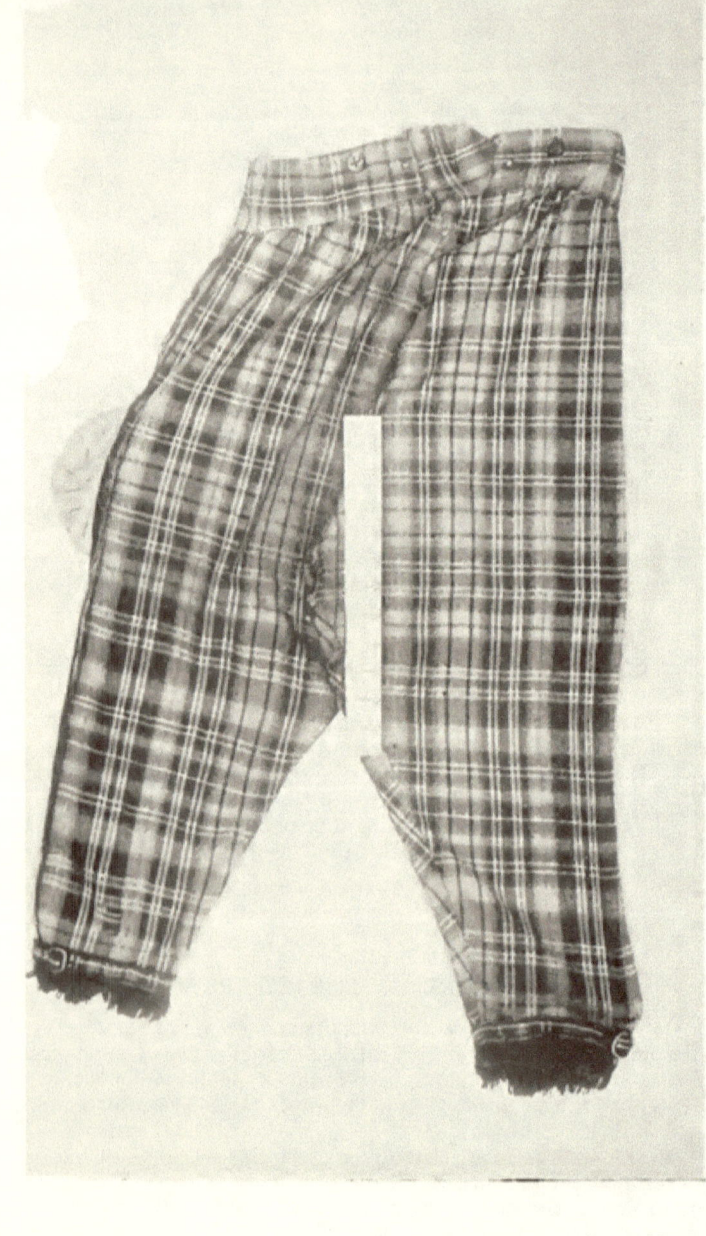

garter strap the breadth is about two feet two inches, so that the completed equal-sided pattern was about four feet four inches long.

These tartans seem to mark a stage in the development of patterns where the breadth of the web was made to contain one equal-sided pattern, while the 'bar blanket' (chequered blanket—*plaideag*, *plaid*) was woven so that two breadths had to be joined to make the centre of the pattern correspond with the centre of the plaid. By reducing the size of such bar blanket patterns so that two or more of them could be in one breadth of cloth the present system of tartans would seem to have originated.

R. C. MACLAGAN.

WILLIAM ERSKINE, ARCHBISHOP OF GLASGOW,
1585-1587.

WILLIAM was certainly a member of the noble house of Erskine, and one of the many of the name who had grants of church lands at the Reformation.

Dr. Cameron Lees, in his account of the Abbey of Paisley, states that besides being Parson of Campsie (by which title he was generally known) he had a grant of the temporalities of the abbey, he is styled 'Parson of Campsie, chamberlain of the Abbey of Paisley,' *Reg. Priv. Con.* 1579, Sep. 24. He caused a well to be sunk in the abbey place which still bears the name 'Balgownie Well,' this points to his being a son of James Erskine of Balgownie, younger brother of John, Lord Erskine (see *Scot. Antiq.* vol. v. p. 98), yet stronger evidence exists in his archiepiscopal seal, for he held for about two years (1585-1587) the revenue and title of the Archiepiscopal See of Glasgow; a good engraving of this seal is given as a frontispiece to the 12th vol. of *The Genealogist* (new series). It is large and handsome, being designed after the style of older Episcopal Seals, though the details show debased sixteenth century work : at the base of the seal his shield of arms is placed, *ar.* on a pale *sa.* a buckle (probably *or*). Now the wife of James Erskine of Balgownie was Catherine Stirling of the house of Keir, and on her tombstone at West Kirk, Culross, the buckles of the arms of Keir form prominent ornaments (see plate *Scot. Antiq.* vol. v. p. 98). The adoption by William Erskine of a buckle as a difference seems to confirm the tradition that he was a son of James Erskine and Catherine Stirling. Keith in his *Scottish Bishops* states that he was never in orders, which seems proved by the fact that in 1582, while he is styled parson of Campsie, John Spehard is styled 'Minister of Campsie' (*Reg. Priv. Con.* 1582, ap. 12). Erskine was in fact what in England is still known as a 'Lay Rector,' he held the tithes or teinds. That he was married is proved by an entry in the Stirling Registers, Oct. 11, 1590, of the marriage of Helen Wilson, 'washer to the persone of Campsies wyf.' It is also certain that he had at least one child, for in 1594 Catherine, daughter to the parson of Campsie, was married at Stirling to John Blaw of Westkirk.[1]

---

[1] For a pedigree of the family of Blaw of Castlehill and Westkirk, see *Scot. Antiq.* vol. vi. p. 64. When it was compiled I did not know of the marriage of John Blaw, nor of the fact (proved by other evidence) that the estate of Westkirk, adjoining Castlehill, was owned by the Blaw family.　　A. W. C. H.

In the highly interesting and most artistic work *Old Stirling*, by J. W. Small, F.S.A. (Scot.), lately issued by Messrs. R. and J. Shearer, Stirling, amongst drawings of old tombstones in Stirling Churchyard (plate 35) is an oblong slab. On the upper part is the inscription 'Heir Lyeth Agnes Leishman who departed the last of Mairch 1633. Hir aig 77.' In the centre of the stone a shield with the arms of her husband, D. Forester, and his initials on either side; below this, on a shield of similar size and shape, the arms borne by William Erskine, parson of Campsie, with the initials M.E. It is possible that M. Erskine may have been D. Forester's first wife, and a daughter of the parson. This seems the only explanation for the presence of these arms on the tomb. Perhaps some reader of the *Scottish Antiquary* can throw light on the family history of the parson and his possible descendants besides the Blaws or Blows, whose pedigree has been already printed.   A. W. CORNELIUS HALLEN.

ANE SIDAN CHIRE, OR HORSE LITTER.

A SEDAN CHAIR was, it is almost unnecessary to state, a covered vehicle for carrying a single person, borne on two poles by usually two men. The name is derived from the town of Sedan, where this species of conveyance is said to have been invented. They were used by persons of rank in England in the reign of James I. Buckingham, the royal favourite, is said to have given general offence by using one, as making his fellow-countrymen to do the work of beasts. In 1674, Sir Saunders Duncombe got letters patent granting him the sole right and privilege, for fourteen years, to let and use for hire, within London and Westminster, covered chairs, to prevent the unnecessary use of coaches. According to Evelyn he got the idea from Naples. In Edinburgh at the close of the eighteenth century, sedan chairs were far more numerous than hackney coaches. They were then almost all in the hands of Highlanders, some of whom are said to have amassed considerable sums of money. They were in great demand about the Parliament Square, most members of the College of Justice having their stated chairmen in attendance. The learned but eccentric Lord Monboddo, though he invariably went home on foot, used to employ a sedan, if it rained, to carry his wig (Kay's *Portraits*). The accompanying drawing (Fig. 1) of a sedan chair and chairman is taken from Kay (ii. 367).

FIG. 1.

Chairs, both private and for hire, continued in use in Edinburgh till past the middle of the present century. The Museum of the Society of

Scottish Antiquaries possesses a good specimen of a private chair, which was in use till 1840 (Fig. 2). This chair belonged first to Professor Alexander Hamilton, M.D., who died in 1802. It then belonged to his son and successor, Professor James Hamilton, M.D., better known as Cocked-hat Hamilton, or even more familiarly as Cocky. He was 'the last gentleman in Edinburgh,' says Sir Robert Christison, 'who adhered to the single-breasted coat, breeches, and black silk stockings, shoes and shoe-buckles, ruffles and wrist-frills, and tri-cocked hat of last century; and a very handsome and picturesque figure he was in this quaint costume' (Christison's *Life*, i. 141). This second Professor Hamilton died in the end of 1840. His successor, Sir J. Y. Simpson, some years subsequently acquired his sedan, and presented it along with its poles to the Museum. The chair in shape is somewhat like a miniature of the body of a hansom cab. It is about five feet four inches in height; under the cornice of the roof its walls measure two feet ten and a half inches along the sides from back to front, and about two feet three inches across from side to side, both in front and at the back. It tapers slightly towards the foot on all sides. The door is in front, and fastens, about the middle of the staple, with a handsome brass catch of the hook-and-eye order. There are windows on each side of the chair, and in the upper part of the door. These open after the manner of the windows of a brougham, but have no appliances to fix them, save when altogether open or shut. The roof is hinged at the back and fastens at the front with a spring-catch on the top of the door. To open the door you raise the hook below, press the button at the top to release the spring-catch, then raise the roof on its hinges a few inches; the door is only then free to be opened, and the procedure must have seemed rather elaborate when, as it is said it sometimes happened, the chairmen turned out to be unsteady of habit, and temporarily so of foot, and the occupant's safety depended on his instant evacuation of the chair.

The roof and back of the chair and the panels of the sides and front are covered with black varnished leather: the ribs of the frame are covered with red leather, over which are ornamental brass mountings.

The inside and the seat which it contains are padded, and covered with red cotton stamped with sprigs of rose and rose-leaves in black. The windows are furnished with red silk curtains, which draw up with rings and red silk cords.

On the back of the chair (outside) there is an oval containing, under the Hamilton crest and motto, a Hamilton coat of arms impaled with another, which we are not acquainted with—viz. *ermine* on a chief sable, three cinquefoils *or* (Dr. A. Hamilton's wife was a Miss Reid of Gorgie). The Hamilton coat is *gules*, between three cinquefoils *argent*, a mullet *or*; on a bordure of the second six fleurs-de-lis alternated with as many crescents *sable* (?). These precise bearings do not appear on the Register of Arms. Dr. Hamilton, however, registered in 1785. The coat he then obtained resembles that on the oval more nearly than any other in the Register, but it has these differences—that the bordure is engrailed and the charges on it are four and four, and are *vert*. If an argument can be founded on the variation between these coats, it may be surmised that Dr. Hamilton painted his arms on his chair before they were regulated by the King of Arms.

As early as the beginning of the eighteenth century it appears that

FIG. 2.

F.

there was in use in Scotland a kind of sedan chair, or litter, which was carried by horses. How long previously to that date the horse litter was used here it would be difficult to say. But the litter, as a mule litter, was widely used in Europe and Asia, in some countries of which latter continent—as Persia—it is still in use. The litter opened from the side, and was in other respects different in construction from the sedans above referred to. I some time ago perused a contract, upon record, entered into between Sir John Shaw of Greenock and Isack Venderplank, coach-builder in Edinburgh, close upon two centuries ago, by which the latter is to build for the former a sedan of the kind last mentioned, and which contract, though drawn up with commendable brevity, is expressed with care and particularity. The following extract from it may interest the readers of *The Scottish Antiquary*, as showing that the Scottish gentry of those days were not unaccustomed to the use of modes of conveyance of a comfortable, and even luxurious kind, and that there were persons in the Scottish capital whose business it was to furnish them with such:—
'The said Isack Venderplank is to make for the use of the said Sir John Shaw ane sidan chire, or horse litter, lyke a little charriot, that it may be gone into when on the horses; the seat of it to be two foott fyve inches within, and a competent breadth, so that there may be room for a man's legs, mounted with brass nails, good leather, and strong in the frames, and yet as light as possible; the frames thereof on each side to be seven foott long, of wydnes betwixt two foot five inches; and lykewyse to furnish two sufficient sadles, two brydles, and the other furnitur necessar for the horses that carryes the said chire: which chire is to be lyned with fyne grey cloath musht about it and waltings, which the said Sir John is to furnish upon his own propper charges and expenses: and lykewise to put in four lozens in each door, with a shutter before, which glasses the said Sir John is to furnish; and the said Isack Venderplank is to delyver the chire to John Cuninghame of Ballendalloch for the use of the said Sir John within a month or fyve weeks at fardest after the date hereof.' On the other hand, Sir John Shaw is 'to pay the said Isack eight pounds sterling, the one-half in hand at signing hereof, and the other upon the delyvery of the said chire.' The contract is dated at Edinburgh, 27th February 1701. Judging from the name, Isack Venderplank must have been a Dutchman, or of Dutch extraction.

Jas. Ronaldson Lyell.

JOHN GRAHAM OF KILBRIDE.

(See vol. xi. p. 108, and vol. xii. p. 33.)

Mr. Easton is peculiarly unfortunate in the objections he takes to the article printed at the first reference. Writing for a learned periodical, I took it for granted that its readers (and especially its contributors) would be aware that there are numerous instances in old Scottish families of two brothers with the same Christian name being alive at the same time. This was more frequently the case where the father had a second or third wife. A friend informs me that in St. Andrews there are at the present time two brothers by one mother who have the same Christian name. This, it is explained, is owing to the fact that the younger son was called after a new minister, and of course is not to be founded on as evidence of custom. I have a note of a well-authenticated case, where the father was twice married, so late as the early part of the seventeenth century, but the practice of duplicating favourite Christian names in families was more in vogue at an earlier period. A few instances may be given from published works with which Mr. Easton may be presumed to have some acquaintance. *The Red Book of Menteith* (vol. i. pp. 7-10) gives an account of two Earls of Menteith who were brothers and both named Maurice, the elder being distinguished as Maurice senior, and his brother as Maurice junior. A competition for the earldom proves that both Maurices were living at the same time. Sir W. Fraser, borrowing from the late Mr. John Riddell, suggests that there may have been a question of legitimacy here, but it is more probable that it was a case of the father having two wives, and calling a son by each by a favourite Christian name. Alexander de Seton, first Earl of Huntly, had by his second wife, Sir Alexander, ancestor of the Setons of Touch and Abercorn, and by his third wife, Sir Alexander, who assumed the name of Gordon, and was ancestor of the Gordons of Abergeldie. Both these Alexanders were alive at the same time (*History of the Family of Seton,* by George Seton, pp. 382-3). Sir Kenneth Mackenzie of Kintail, who died in 1491, had by his first wife Kenneth Og, his heir and successor, and by his second wife, Kenneth, ancestor of the Mackenzies of Ord, etc. (*History of the Mackenzies,* by Alexander Mackenzie. p. 108). Lord Hugh Fraser of Lovat, who was born in 1498, had by his first wife, Hugh, who was killed along with his father in a clan battle in 1554, and by his second wife, Hugh, who died in his eighteenth year, but must of course have been alive at the date of his elder brother's death (*History of the Frasers,* by Alexander Mackenzie, pp. 98 and 99). Duncan Stewart of Glenbucky, who was twice married, had one son named John and another named John Beg, the distinguishing addition 'little' showing that both must have been alive at the same time (Duncan Stewart's *History and Genealogical Account of the Royal Family of Scotland,* p. 132). Other similar instances might be given, but perhaps those cited above will show that the point which Mr. Easton says is fatal to my argument does not exist, and therefore could not have been overlooked by me. Malise Graham, Earl of Menteith, had two wives, and had a family by both, so that there was nothing remarkable in two of his legitimate sons being called John, although they were contemporaries. Mr. Easton's second objection, that I did not take into consideration that Earl Malise had a natural son John, must also fall, because this son will be found mentioned in my article, and duly considered. Mr. Easton holds I have not established any ground for believing that the entry in the *Acta Dom. Concil.,* stating the elder John to be son *and heir* of his father on 7th April 1469, is unreliable, apparently because he has implicit faith in the literal accuracy of our public records. A closer study of the *Acta* will convince Mr. Easton that they are not infallible. There are few records—I have not met with any myself—which are absolutely correct. The accidental insertion of the words 'and heir' in the entry in question is a small mistake in comparison with others in the same register, but I will not take up space with extracts to prove what any one may see for himself. Since writing the article on John Graham of Kilbride. I have observed that Cranfurd in his *Peerage* (p. 331, *Note*) says, 'There is a charter in the custody of Robert Graham of Galangad and Gartmore, granted by Malise, Earl of Menteith, to John Graham, his son, of the lands of Kilbride, on the 7th April 1464.' This is obviously the identical charter referred to in the *Acta Dom. Concil.*, and the absence of the words 'and heir' in Craufurd's *Note* goes to prove the inaccuracy of the reference in the minutes of the Lords of Council, and to confirm my contention that John Graham was at no time heir of his father. It is also highly probable that the year of the charter as given by Craufurd (1464) is the correct one, and that the *Acta* err in making it 1460. As there is no reason to suppose that Earl Malise's eldest son, Alexander, was dead in 1464, the improbability of John (even if he were the Earl's second son) being designed in the missing charter as his father's heir, is raised to an impossibility. Having, as I consider, proved that the *Acta* are not to be relied on in this case, it is unnecessary to notice at any length the other parts of Mr. Easton's criticism. It is precisely the styling of Patrick Graham as heir of Earl Malise in 1471, and again in 1478, which proves that he must have been the Earl's second son, and that John of Kilbride was his younger brother. For one who holds so strongly by the public records, Mr. Easton shows a strange disregard for the *Exchequer Rolls* when he imagines they would year after year from 1464 to 1473 design John Graham as son of Malise, Earl of Menteith, although the legitimate John Graham had died in the interval (as Mr. Easton assumes he had) and the person all along receiving payment of an annual fee was only a natural son of the Earl. It is also a somewhat violent assumption that an illegitimate son received a *lease* of Kilbride and was called John Graham *of* Kilbride, in 1478, in a deed infefting his father's heir in the lands of Craguchty and Auchmore. No such blunder could be made in a document of so much importance. The John Graham of Kilbride who witnessed the deed must have been so in reality, and not a tenant of the lands of Kilbride usurping the title of their owner. On the crucial point of the service of the real John Graham of Kilbride's widow's brief of terce, which proves the existence of her husband long after his brother Patrick was styled the heir of Earl Malise, Mr. Easton is discreetly silent, and it may be regarded as significant that a critic with his knowledge of the Menteith pedigree, and apparent interest in assuming and asserting the position that 'Sir John with the Bright Sword' left no male issue, has been unable to answer the arguments put forward in my previous article to prove that this negative position has not been established. When the claim made to the Earldom of Menteith by Mr. Easton's cousin, Mr. George Marshall Graham, of Toronto, comes up for hearing (if it ever gets so far) there ought to be some interesting information forthcoming for Scottish genealogists, especially if the latest edition of the claimant's pedigree, as published in the *Genealogical Magazine* for June, is to be seriously maintained.

B.

OLD SCOTS BANK-NOTES.

(*Continued from p.* 37.)

Five Shilling and Ten Shilling Notes.

The five-shilling note issued by the Royal Bank on 3rd April 1797 was not dignified with the reigning monarch's portrait, which embellished the

Royal Bank's notes of larger amounts. It bears instead the device of a unicorn apparently leaping out of the ground at the foot of a luxuriant plant of Scots thistle, from behind which arises an imperial crown surrounded by an irradiated halo. Perhaps Scotland, in its efforts to escape from the financial bog, was, with the benign permission of the Government, to find a firm footing on the Five-shilling note.

Merchants' Notes.

The Ten-shilling note issued in 1764 by the Glasgow merchant-house—George Keller and Company—has been mentioned already, but that firm

issued also, in the same year (1764, November 7th), a Twenty-shilling note with an option clause. This clause is not identical in terms with the original option clause invented by the Bank of Scotland—to pay in coin with interest in six months, but to pay 'in an Edinburgh or Glasgow bank-note.' As these bank-notes, however, themselves had option clauses at that date, the holder of Keller's notes was not entitled in any case to immediate cash payment.

The majority of the notes of merchant houses were, so far as can now be judged, for smaller sums than a pound. R. Robertson, merchant, Perth, issued one, dated 4th February 1765, for 'Five shillings for value received in goods.' It has been already noticed that Messrs. Blacklaws, Wedderspoon and Company, of the same town, issued (20th June 1764) a note for '£3 Scots,' or 'Five shillings sterling in cash, or in our option, Edinburgh notes, value received.' We can picture the faces of these pushing traders the first time that some discriminating customer declined payment of such a note when it was tendered in the shape of a Five-shilling note of an Edinburgh bank, and demanding *notes* according to their promise.

The numbers of note-issuing banks and merchants, the insignificance of some of them, and the insignificance of the sums which their notes frequently represented, soon became a laughing-stock, and the merchant whose business might be strengthened by a show of a little humour turned naturally to an issue of more or less mock promissory

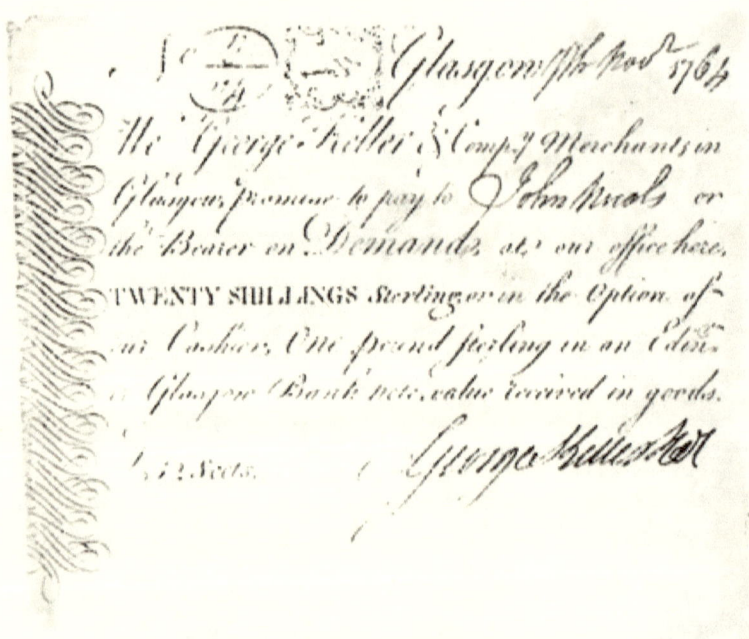

notes—more or less, for it is difficult to say where the business intent ends, and only the joke is left. 'James Smiton, seemingly a coffee-house keeper in Edinburgh, obliges himself "to pay the bearer on demand, in money or drink, two shillings and sixpence sterling." On the backs of his notes, it is stated, are sometimes marked receipts for one or more mugs of porter, or bottles of strong ale, etc.'[1] Peter Williamson, the famous Aberdonian who had been kidnapped in his youth, in his mature years wrote the history of his adventures, started in Edinburgh the first penny post, kept a coffee-house, and issued his own bank-notes. In derision of the option clause, he called himself the 'Ready-Money Bank.' But he too had his option clause. His notes[2] promise to pay 'to Sir

[1] Kerr: Banking, 71.   [2] Kerr: Banking, 71.

John Falstaff or bearer, on demand, in books, coffee, or ready-money, according to the option of the Director, One shilling sterling, value received.'

About the same time notes appeared in Glasgow (16th January 1765) signed by Daniel M'allum and Daniel M'funn. That these Daniels, bitter and humorous, had come to a judgment on the pernicious multiplication of note-issuing estab'ishments there is not much doubt. They date their notes, then procee 1 to the statement 'We swarm.' This has a whole line for itself. The next line is composed of a procession of wasps. The sum named in the note which forms the illustration is 'Three pence sterling,' and the option, which is in due form, is to give the bearer

'nine ballads six days after demand.' In other notes of the same date, signed with the same signatures, the sum is 'One penny,' and the option is 'three ballads six days after demand.' Another penny note with a line of three wasps under the motto, and a border additional composed of eleven, bears to be issued on the same day as the others and to be signed by John Bragg. How far these notes may have been used by—say the itinerant singers and sellers of ballads of the Glasgow of that day, or how far they were jokes the signatures we find attached to them leave it doubtful. But there can scarcely be a doubt of the intention of the note which had appeared in Edinburgh shortly before them—dated 1st October 1764—the 'Mason Barrowman Company's' note for 'One shilling Scots'— a penny sterling. It has been printed from a carefully engraved copper plate, and is of an ordinary size, for a bank-note of the time—6½ by 3½ inches. Unlike the three Glasgow notes last mentioned, which were produced from types and metal blocks in a cheap and simple style, this engraving cannot have left more than a modest profit even to the publisher,

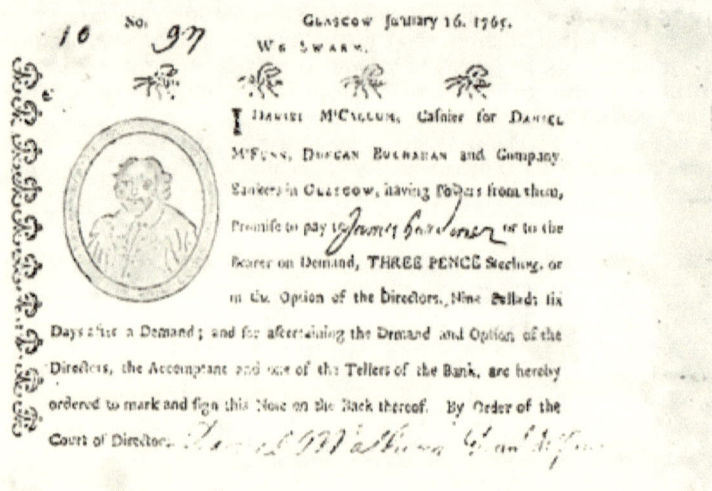

it it was sold at a penny. Several of the Mason Barrowman notes are made payable to Solomon Hod, and one at least is signed 'Tim⁷ Credit,' Accomptant, 'Barcklay Cash,' Teller. The note here reproduced is signed 'William Johnston,' 'George Dunbar.' The 'notes' may have been sold

blank, as some valentines used to be and as some Christmas cards are, the purchaser being left to sign them with his own or another name, according to his humour.[1] In any case they played some part in preparing the public mind for the legislation of 1765.   J. H. S.

(To be continued.)

THE QUARE OF JELUSY.

INTRODUCTORY NOTE.

As a poetical composition the *Quare of Jelusy* has but slight claim to consideration from the lover of poetry. It is distinctly a dull performance —what Henry Weber, editor of the *Metrical Romances*, would probably have called 'a prolix and wire drawn morality and second-hand narration,' its author 'not a poet *virum volitare per ora*, nor one of those whose better fortune it is to live in the hearts of devoted admirers.' That is perhaps rather an unhappy note to strike when seeking to introduce the piece to present-day readers.

On several grounds, however, it may fairly claim attention from students of early Scottish literature.

§ 1. It is an important exemplar of a group of Scottish poems, written in the second half of the fifteenth century, all of which exhibit 'a purely artificial language such as was probably never spoken.' Its relationship to *The Romaunt of the Rose* (Fragment B), *Lancelot of the Lak*, *The Court of Love*, and the *Kingis Quair*, will be evident to every one who studies these poems together. As yet they have only been edited each by itself: they still await the critic who, by careful analysis, will reduce their strange grammatical forms to order and in that way seek to explain the presence of many Midland and Southern inflexions engrafted on poems written by men whose native speech was the dialect of Lowland Scotland.

The relationship of *The Court of Love*, the *Kingis Quair*, and *The Quare of Jelusy* to Lydgate's *Temple of Glas*, and to each other, is another interesting study for the plodding investigator.

§ 2. The use of final *e* as a distinct syllable in Scottish versification has been assumed by some modern editors who have been misled by certain analogies from English poems of the Chaucerian and post-Chaucerian age. By the same line of reasoning, several instances of that highly artificial syllable would be postulated in the case of the *Quare of Jelusy* (*vide* lines 17, 63, 67, 101, 119, 138, 300, 533). When, however, due value is given to the vowel sounds of Lowland Scottish, perfect scansion is obtained without the necessity for the sounding of any final *e*, the simple explanation being that north of the Tweed, words like *nee*, *strong*, *scharp*, *sone*, *hert*, *old*, *nice*, were, and are to this day, often pronounced as dissyllables as indicated by the diaeresis. Innumerable instances of such dissyllabic use of words, seemingly monosyllabic to uninitiated readers of Wyntoun, Barbour, Blind Harry, Henryson and other early Scottish poets, might easily be cited.

§ 3. The *Quare of Jelusy* occurs on folios 221-228 of the well-known Selden MS. B. 24. No other text is known in the present day. It was printed about fifty years ago in the *Bannatyne Miscellany* (vol. ii. p. 161) from a transcription made by the late Dr. David Laing. That printed

---

[1] It ought to be noticed, however, that the Mason Barrowman note is taken seriously by the authors of *The History of Banking in Scotland*, p. 71, and *The One Pound Note*, p. 61.

version has been collated with the manuscript and numerous mistaken readings are now corrected.

The colophon, it will be observed, ascribes the piece to '*Auch*'—the latter portion of the name unfortunately being illegible. Ever since its publication by Dr. Laing the poem has been accepted as a work of James Auchinleck or Afflek, one of the poets mentioned in Dunbar's famous *Lament for the Makars*—

> That scorpion fell has done infek
> Maister Johne Clerk and James Afflek
> Fra ballat making and tragedie
> Timor mortis conturbat me.

Auchinleck again, has been identified with James Auchlek, a licentiate or graduate of Glasgow University, *c.* 1471, who became 'Secretar to the Earl of Rosse.' He is referred to in the Privy Seal Register as dead about September 1497.

The scribes who wrote the manuscript were, however, so reckless in other attributions that their testimony in the case of the *Quare of Jelusy* must needs be received with caution even were it certain that the mutilated surname was originally *Auchinleck*.

From an inspection of the manuscript in the Bodleian Library in August 1896, I am inclined to think that it was originally intended to be a purely Chaucerian collection executed by a Scottish scribe for Henry Lord Sinclair, whose arms are emblazoned at the end of *Troilus* on folio 118. A second scribe begins at folio 192 with a transcription of the *Kingis Quair*, but ends his copy abruptly at stanza 178 of that poem, a third scribe completing the remaining nineteen stanzas. This last mentioned scribe then proceeds as far as folio 228, that is to say, to the end of the Quare of Jelusy, after which scribes two and three divide the remaining portion of the MS. between them.

From a memorandum on folio 120 immediately following the *Troilus* and written in the same hand, it is absolutely certain that the portion of the MS. which we conjecture to have been compiled for Henry Lord Sinclair was written not earlier than 1488 : it may even be considerably later in date. The second and third portions of the MS.—if penmanship can be taken as any guide—may belong either to the end of the fifteenth or to the first half of the sixteenth century.

In the text now printed it has been deemed unnecessary to distinguish by italics the contractions of the manuscript.

J. T. T. B.

THE QUARE OF JELUSY.

(f. 221 v.) Here beginnithe the Quare of Jelusy,
Avise ye Gudely folkis and see.

> This lusty Maii, the quhich all tender flouris
> By Nature nurisith with hir hote schouris,
> The felde oureclad hath with the tender grene
> Quhich all depaynt with diverse hewis bene
> And every thing makith to convert   5
> Agayn the stroke of Winter cold and smert :
> The saym moneth and the sevynt Ide
> The sonne, the quhich that likith not to hyde

His course, ascending in the Orient
From his first gree, and forth his bemys sent   10
Throu quhich he makith every lusty hert
Out of thair sleuth to walkyn and astert
And unto Maii to done thair observaunce:
Tho fell it me in to remembraunce
A thing, the quhich that noyith me full sore   15
That for to rest availith me no more:
Bot walking furth upoun the new grene,
Tho was the ayer sobir and amene,
And solitare allone, without my fere,
Unto a bonk quhare as a small ryvere   20
Makith his course doun by a woddis syde
Quhois levis fair did all the bewis hyde,
I past me furth remembring to and fro
All on this warldis changeing, and his wo,
And namely on the suffrance and the peyne   25
Quhich most hath do my carefull hert constreyne :
The quhich as now me nedith not report,
For thare is non that likith to support
Nor power has, quharefor I will sustene
And to no wicht I will compleyne nor mene :   30
Bot suffering furth, as I have done to fore
Myne hevynes and wo : quhat is thare more ?
Wele long I walkit there, till at the last
Myn eye estward agayne the sonne I cast,
Quhare as I saugh among the levis grene   35
A Lady, quhich that was rycht wele besene
And als fresch in hir beautee and array
As the bricht sonne at rising of the day,
Off coloure was sche lik unto the rose
Boith quhite and red ymeynt ; and I suppose   40
One gudliar that Nature nevir wrocht
Of lustyhede ne lakkit sche rycht nocht.
My spirit coud nocht resemble hir, nor gesse
Bot unto Dyane or sum hie Goddesse ;
And prevely I hid me of entent   45
Among the levis to here quhat sche ment,
And forth a passe sche walkit sobirly
There as I was, and passing cam so ny
That I persavit have upoun hir chere
The cristall teris falling from hir eyne clere   50
It semyt wele that wo hir hert constreynit
Sche sorowit sche sikit sche sore compleynit :
So sobirly sche spak that I no mycht
Not here one word quhat that sche said arycht.
Bot wele I herd sche cursit prevaly   55
The cruell vice of causeless Jelousye !
Sche wepit so a quhile till at the last
With that hir voce and eyne to hevin sche cast
And said 'Goddesse Imeneus thou rewe,
Of me, in to thy dangerouse bound of newe   60

Y-come, allace! quhich be the cause that I
Am turment thus, withoutyn cause or quhy
So sudaynly under youre strong lowe
For it the quhich is unto me unknowe
As als sekirly here in thy presence   65
Geve evirmore I did in suich offence
The scharp deth mote perce me through the hert
So that on fute from hens I nevi[r] astert,
(f. 222 v.) Nor nevirmore it was in myn entent
Thare of I am both hole and innocent   70
And gif I say false, Pluto that is king
Quhich the derk regioun hath in his governyng
Mote me into his fyry cart do ta
As quhilom did he to Proserpina,
And thare my body and my soule also   75
With him ay dwell in torment and in wo.
O Dyane goddesse of fredome and of ese
Under quhom I have bot thraldome and disese,
Litill of treuth of gladness or plesaunce
So helpith me agayn this waryit chaunce.   80
For of this gilt thou knowis wele my part
And Jupiter that knoweth every hart
Wote that I am sakelese me defende
Ne for no want nor for to have commend
Not say I this for here nys non bot ye   85
Of thilk hid thing that knowith the veritee
And sen thou wote that my complaynt is treuth
Off pitee than compassioun have and reuth:
My life to gone mak on ane othir daunce
Or me delyvir of this warldis chaunce: 90
Quhich is to say that efter as I deserve
That I may lyve or sodaynly to sterve.'
And thus apoun the Goddis can sche crye
And evir among sche cursit Jelousye.
With that sche sichit with a rycht pitouse chere   95
Allace, gret reuth hir pleynyng was to here
Hir coloure quhich that was so fair to sene
It changit oft and wexit pale and grene
Hir to behold thare was no gentill hert
Than he schuld have compassioun of hir smert   100
To sene from hir lusty eyne availle
The glettering teris als thik as ony haile
As thai descendet from the ayr abune [1]
Upoun the lusty colourit rose in June
Quhen thai ar fairest on thair stalkis newe   105
So was the teris upoun hir fresch hewe.
Allace hir chere, allace hir countenaunce
For to behald it was a grete pennaunce
And as I was uprising for to go
To confort hir and counsele of hir wo   110

---

[1] The MS. has *aboun*.

So come one othir Lady hir allone
The nerrest way unto hir is sche gone
And one thai tuo y-samyn gan to fare
Bot quhens thai past I can nocht you declare
Bot quhen that thai out of my sicht were gone   115

(f. 223.) And I in wod belevit me allone
My goste hath take in sad remembering
This Ladies chere and wofull compleyning
Quhich to my hert sat full very nere
And to my selfe I thocht in this manere   120
Quhat may this mene? Quhat may this signifye?
I can nocht wit quhat is the cause or quhy
This Lady suffrit this strong adversitee?
For as me think in erde suld no thing be
Possible to ony wicht of wele willing   125
As ony richesse or hertis cherising,
And every thing according to plesaunce
Than sche thare of suld have full suffisaunce
To gladin hir and plesyn with thair chere
Bot deth of lufe or deth of frendis dere   130
Quhich is impossible for to bring ageyn
For thing possible, me think, sche suld nocht pleyne
For sche for fairhede and for suete-having
Mycht wele accorde for ony wicht lyving.
Bot tho it fell into my fantasy   135
How sche so oftsyse cursit Jelousy
Than thouch I thus Gife lyvis ony wicht
Quhich fynd in to his cherlisch hert mycht
Thus for to turment suich one creature
To done hir wo to done hir payne endure?   140
Now wele I wote it is no questioun
Thare lyveth none in to this erth adoun
Bot he [be] cummyn of sum churlisch kynd
For othir wayis forsuth I can nocht fynd
He suich one Lady wold in ony way displese   145
Or harme do to hir honour or hir ese
Be as be may, yit my consate me gevith
This Jelousye the quhich that sche reprevith
Annoyith hir, and so it may wele be
Ofe evill condicioun evirmore is he   150
As the devill ay birnyng in to hate
Full of discorde and full of frese consate.
How evir it stonde, yit for this Ladies sak
Sa mekle occupacioun schall I tak
Furthwith for to syttyn doun and writt   155
Of Jelouse folk sum thing in to despitt
And quho be wroth or quho be blith, here I
Am he the quhich that sett no thing thareby

(f. 223 v.) For Ladyes schall no cause have gif I may
Thame to displese for no thing schall I say   160
And gif I do it is of negligence
And lak of connyng and of eloquence

For it is no thing in to myn entent
To say the thing schall mak thame discontent
Nor yit no faithfull lover to displese   165
Nor schewe no thing in contrare of thaire ese
Nor of no wicht of gude condycioun
Bot of this wickit ymaginacioun
Quhich by his name is clepit Jelousye
That every Lovere hatith of invy.   170
And thouch all suich war wode in thair entent
As Herculese quhen he him selven brent
Or cursit Nero quhen he his perile sawe
Ofe his own hond ymurderit and yslawe
Ne rek I not nor geve I of thame charge   175
Lat thame go saile all in the Devillis barge
And quhethir thay flete or in to hell synk
Yit schall I writen efter as I think.
And ye Loveris that stondith furth in treuth
Menyt eke compassioun have and reuth   180
How Ladies evill demanit ar oftsyse
By this foule wrech go helpith him dispise
And to compleyne thair treuth and innocence
That mekle suffrith throuch thair owin pacience
And of my termes and my rude endite   185
Excusith me sett thai be inperfyte
Beseking you at Lovis hie reverence
Takith gude will in stede of eloquence
For as I can non othir wyse I may
Thus I begyn and on this wise I say.   190

O Tendir Youth, that stant in innocence
Grundid on treuth sadnes and pacience
Wommen I mene all vicis contempnyng
That void I bene of every violens
And full of pitee and benevolence   195
Humble and wise rycht sobir and bening [1]
And full of mercy unto every thing
In suffrance stant of mony grete offense
Full paciently in to this erth lyving.

Under thraldome and mannis subjectioun   200
And mekly suffrith thair correctioun
Allace the wo, allace the sad grevance
In suffering men ofe evill condicioun
(f. 223.) Quhich hath no pitee and lakkith discrecioun
And bene ysett under thair govirnance   205
Youre suffering thare is mony one hard mischance
Youre fairhede goth, your youth is brocht adoun
With weping teris ay full of strong penance.

Loveris compleyne and every gentill wicht
Help for to mene help for to waill arycht   210

---
[1] The MS. has *being*.

Compassioun have and reuth upoun the nede
In helping and supporting at your mycht
Thame quhich that of youre gladnese is the licht
That is to say all lusty Womanhede
Quhich you in lufe and chevalry doth fede   215
But quhom this warldis gladnes from his hicht
Schold sone avale and fallyn out of drede.

In to this erth quhat is our gladnese here
Iff that we lak the presence and the chere
Of thame that bene this worldis hole plesance?   220
Quhat ar we worth gif that thair help ne were?
All vertuouse wommen Salomon holdith dere
And mekle worth of thair govirnance.
Thai ar our ese thai ar oure suffisance
From viciouse women passith my matere   225
Thai most all gone apoun ane othir dance.

Allace the wo quho can it specify
That wommen suffren ay withoutyn quhy
Into this erth in dangere and in vere
And to recist agaynis tyranny   230
Is no defense thai have to pas thareby
Bot weping with the teris of thair chere
With syking wailling pleynyng and prayere
And everich thing sustene thai paciently
Thus livith ay thir sely women here.   235

This mene I all be wickit men oftsyse
That giltles dooth thir ladies to supprise
Withoutyn cause of ony maner thing
And namely by thair varyit tyrannyis
The cruelteis the wikkitnes that lyis   240
In Jelousy and false ymagynyng
Quhich harmyth all this world by his demyng
Of quhom I think sumthing to devise
And schewe to you here eftir my connyng.

(f. 224 v.) Quho schall me help allace for to endite   245
For to bewaill to compleyne and to write
This vice that now so large is and commoun
Quhat sall I say? quhom sall I awite
For hie nor low is non estate to quyte.
Now all hath fele of thilke poysoun   250
Allace this false and wickit condicioun
The lusty hede and every glade delyte
Hath of this world full nere ybrocht adoun.

For in the tyme was of our elderis old
Quhen Jelousy abhominable was hold   255
Quhareof eschamith every noble wy
Than was thir Ladies ever in honour hold
Thair lusty hede quhich causith mony fold

Fredome gentrise disport and chevalry
Thai syng thai dance and makith company   260
Thame to defame was non that durst nor wold
As now thai do wilhoutyn cause or quhy.

And yit I wote thir Ladies bene echone
Als trew and sad as ony tyme aygone
And ar to blame als litill or repreve   265
But now thai mone thame uttirly dispone
To duell as doth the anker in the stone
Yf thot thai think undemyt for to leve
So fast encressyn can this false beleve
That in this world fewe Ladyis ar or none   270
Quhich schall unsclanderit from his tong escheve.

For ife sche makith chere or company
As they were wount he raisith up his cry
And yfe sche loke he jugith of hir thocht
And sett sche loke or speke unto no wy   275
Yet evill he demith in his fantasy
And be sche glad or wele besene in oucht
This tyrane saith It is nat do for nocht
Allace, by him the harm withoutyn ony quhy
Is every day into this world ywrocht.   280

And ife a spouse stant with this vyce I wys
All thing is said all thing is wrocht amys.
In his consate, and gif that ony way
Fro home he goth, his spy he schall nocht mys
That feynith tailis no thing as it is   285
To plesyn him for sum thing mon he say
Than goth all rest than goth all pes away
Farewele of lufe the gladnese and the blis
Fro he cum home, als ferfirth as he may.

And yit to hir is double wo and grame   290
(f. 225.) For thouch that he be gilty in the same
Full mony a lady nothing dare sche say
And yit thir Ladies in Jelousy to blame
Ar nocht as men for men haith now no schame
To be in love als double as thai may   295
Thir Ladies thus full mony a cause have thay
And thouch he speke it hynderit nocht his name
And ife sche loke it harmith hir allway.

This may be clept a wrech intill his mynd
For as we may in old bukis fynd   300
In lak of hert ay stant this maladeye
To him the quhich supposith aye behynd
And verreis to stond in lufis kynd,
For Salamoun saith ane noble hert nor eye
Haith to enquere of ladis nor espye   305
Nor thame misdeme in to thair treuth unkind
As doth this wrech that hot is Jelusye.

Off quhom in to contempnyng and dispite
My will is gude for to declare and write
Suppose of wit I empty be and bare   310
Thou Ecco, quhich of chiding is perfyte
I the beseke thou helpith me to flyte
And Thesiphone, thou lord of wo and care
So helpith me this mater to declare
On Jelousy his malice to acquyte   315
With the supplee of every trewe lufare.

Here efter folowis
The Trety in the Reprefe of Jelousye.

The passing Clerk, the grete philosophoure
Sydrake,[1] enspirit of hevinly influence
Quhich holdyn was into his time the floure
Of clergy, wisedome and intelligence,   320
In to his bukis declarith this sentence
To Bokas King amang his doctrinis sere
Off Jelousy, and saith in this manere.

(f. 225 v.) He clepith it foly of one ignorant
The quhich evill humoris makith to procede   325
As hert corrupt or quho it list to hant
Malancoly it raisith up but drede
That lust of slepe of mete or drink of dede
And wit of man confusith it all plane
With this hote fevir that is cotidiane.   330

And suth it is by resoun as we fynd
That this Suspicioun and this Jelousye
Is and cummith of the veray kynd
Of Herubus the quhich that of Invye
The Fader is and be this resoun quhy   335
For evirmore in rancoure and in ire
As Ethena he birnyth in the fyre.

Thus with the cheyne of sorow is he bound
Furth in this world full of adversitee
His frendschip to no wicht it schall be found   340
Quhy in him self ay at debate is he?
Withoutyn lufe withoutyn cheritee
In his consate and his ymagynyng
Ay to the worst he demith every thing.

That in this erth lyveth thare no wicht   345
Of no condicioun nor of no degree
In his presence that wisedome has nor micht
To reule him self in onywyse than he
Schall deme thareof amys, y-sett he be
Als chaste als trew and reule himself als wele   350
As evir hath do the prophete Daniele.

---

[1] *The Romance of Bertus and Sidrac.* It was translated from the French by Hugh
Campeden: Ms. Laud, G. 57, Bodl. Library.

For every thocht and luke and countenance
Suspect he holdith in to his demyng
And turnyth all to harm and to mischance
This tygir with his false ymagynyng   355
Lith as a devill in to this erth lyving
Contenyng aye in anger and in hate
Both with him self and otheris at debate.

But cheritee thus evirmore he levith
Quhich Crist of wedding clepith the habyte   360
But quhilk of hevin every wicht belevyth
But of the blisse and of the fest is quyte
And Paule thus to the Corinthies doth writ
Off Faith of Hope and eke of Cheritee
The last the most he clepith of the thre.   365

(f. 226.)   And he declarith in the samyn chapture
That thouch men be as Angelis eloquent
Or all thair gudis gyvith to the pure
Or yit for Crist y-suffering suich turment
To be y-slawe, y-marterit or brent   370
Or doth all gude the quhich that may be wrocht
And lakkith cheritee, all it availith nocht.

And every wicht that hath discrecioun wote
That quho thus lyvith in to Jelousye
In ire and malice birnyth ay full hote   375
From worldis joy and hevinly companye
Excludit ar thus throuch thair false invye
And oft thareof cummith [suich] mischaunce
As strife debate slauchter and vengeaunce.

Quhareof I coud ane hundreth samplis tell   380
Of stories olde the quhich I lat oure go
And als that in this tyme present befell
Amongis quhilk we fynd how one of tho
His lady sleuth and syne himself also
In this ilk lond withoutyn ony quhy   385
But onely for his wickit gelousy.

Off quhich full mony ensample may we fynde
Of old y-gone and new experiment
That quho this gilt hauntith in his mynd
It hath bene cause quhy mony one were schent   390
Sum sleuth him self and sum of evill entent
From innocentis bereving oft the lyfe
Sum sleuth his lady and othir sum his wife.

And Jelousye hath evir suich a tong
That from the malice of his hert procedith
By quhich that sclander wyde [all] quhare is rong   395
And Crist he saith 'That quhom of sclander dredith
Wo be to him and more unto him bedith
Away the sclanderouse member for to kerve
Quhich dampnith you eternaly to sterve.   400

And the first verteu as poetis can declare
Is tong with wysedome to restreyne [1] and stere
Quhich unto God is nerest evirmare
And Salamoun saith Fer better that it were
Allone to duell with lyouns than be nere   405
A sclanderouse tong of chiding and of hate
So odiouse he holdith suche debate.

(f. 226 r.)   A poete saith That never more is pes,
Quhare suich a tong hath dominacioun
Nor yit the tong the quhich that can nocht ces   410
Ay schewing his evil ymaginacioun
And hath of langage no more discrecioun
Than he the quhich that talkith in his slepe
Nor unto him aucht no wicht takyn kepe.

Approvit is by resoun and scripture   415
Of Crist and his Apostlis evirilkone
By prophetis doctouris poetis and nature
Off quhom this vice of quhom this gilt is tone
And quhens he cummith and quhider he schall gone
Quhich is to say that Jelousy at schort   420
Commyth of the devill and thedir schall resort.

As onys of one Emperoure we rede [2]
One haly man and clepit was Henry
In prayer fasting and in almouse dede
And for no cause bot for his Jelousye   425
The quhich he caucht and for non othir quhy
Upoun his lufe trew and innocent [3]
Efter his deth he come to Jugement.

And thare as in to revelacioun
Till one of oure Faderis old was sene   430
He had ressavit his owin dampnacioun
For the ilk gilt of Jelusy I mene
Had nocht Laurence the blisfull marter bene
By merci of oure blissfull Salvioure
Suich is the fyne of all this false erroure!   435

And quhareof long it hath bene said or this [   ] [4]
That of hote lufe ay cummith Jelousye
That sentence is interpret to amys
And schortly said, nocht understand the quhy
For it is nocht for to presume tharby   440
That Jelousye, quhich is of vice the ground
Is in to lufe or in a lufare found.

For Jelousy the quhich of lufe that risith
Is clept nothing bot of a simple drede
As quhen thir lufaris remembreth and avisith   445

---

[1] The MS. has *restreyne*.
[2] The Emperor Henry II. who reigned 1002-24. The story of his jealousy is found in the *Mag. Chron. Belgicum.*
[3] Queen Cunigunda.   [4] Illegible word in margin here.

Sum of thair wo and sum apoun thair nede
And sum of gladnese that doth of lufe procede
Throuch quhich thair hertis brynt ar in the fyre
Sum of grete raddoure and sum of hote desire.

(f. 227.)　Than every thing thay dout that may thame make　450
Of lufe the grettest plesance to forgo
Throuch quhich sum lufaris hath suich drede y-take
That it to thame is hevynes and wo
Bot natwithstonding ay thai reule thame so
Thair drede it is to euery wicht unknowe　455
Thame likith not to sclander nor to schowe.

Thir Jelousyis full diverse ar of kynd
The tone it harmith to no creature
Bot secrete dred and symple as we fynd
That lufaris in to lufing most endure　460
That othir bereth all one othir cure
He sclanderith feynyth defamith and furth criyth
And lufe and every lufar he invyith.

O Wofull Wrech and wickit evill consate
O false suspicioun nurist full of hate　465
In hevyn and erth thi harm is boith y-writte
O cruell serpent aye leving in awayte
O sclanderouse tong fy on thy dissayte
Quhare that thou lovith thou feynyth that ypocrite
That thou art jelouse Lufe thou gevith the wyte.　470

Thou leis thareof as that I schall declare
To understand to every trewe lufare.[1]

For every wicht that is with lufe y-bound
And sad and trewe in every faith y-ground
Syne likith nocht to varye nor escheve　475
|Ra]ther suffer schall he the dethis wound
|T]han in to him schall ony thing be found
|T]hat to this Lady may displese or greve
|Or d]o to hir or to hir fame represe
|For h]is desire is althir most to sé　480
|Hir] stand in honoure and in prosperitee.

And contrair this thy cursit violence
Staunt ay : for quhy? thy sclanderouse offense
Harmith thy Lady most of ony wy
Quhich stryvith evir agayn hir innocence　485
That hath no suerd bot suffrance and pacience
For to resist agaynis hir inyury
The quhich thou art and be this resoun quhy
Thou wirketh that quhich may hir most annoye
|T]hat is to say hir worship to distroye.　490

[1] ... ve lines are joined in the MS. with the next stanza by mistake. They
... ... sort of index to the remainder of the poem.

(f. 227 v.) For every Lady of honour and of fame
Lesse settith of hir deth than hir gud name
Oft be experiment previth it is so
Off mony o lady quhich done the same
Rather chesyn can thair deth than blame   495
So lovyn thai thair honoure evirmo,
Fy on the wrech, fy on the lufis fo,
That for to sclander hath no schame nor drede
The innocence and fame of Womanhede.

Quhat helpith the be clepit hir lovare   500
Syne doith all thing that most is hir contrare
Quhat servyth it, quhat vaillith it of ocht
Forgo thy Lady schall thou nevirmare
And set hir corse be thine yit I declare
Hir hert is gone it servyth the of nocht   505
Thare is no lufe quhare that such thing is wrocht
And thouch sche wold it is as thou may fynd
Contrair to lufe to resoun and to kynd.

Thus of thi Lady makis thou thy fo
Quhois hert of resoun most thou nede forgo   510
Be thyne owin gilt may no thing it appese
And every othir lady schall also
Ensample tak to adventure evirmo
Under thine hond thair honour or thair ese
And yfe thai do suppose thai have disese   515
Quho schall thame meve of weping eve and mo[rowe]
Quhich seith to fore syne rynnith on thair sorowe.

To every Lady schortly I declare
That thare thou art beith thare nevirmare
Rest nor quyete treuly to conclude   520
Nor grace nor ese nor lyving in welefare
Bot every thing of gladness in his contra[re]
For barane ay thou art and destitude
Off every thing that soundith unto gude
A lady rather schuld hir deth y-tak   525
Than suich a wrech till have on to hir mak.

Quhare is thi wit or thy discrecioun
Quhich be thine evill ymaginacioun
In sewing thingis the quhich that bene unknewe
Quhat helpith the thy false suspicioun   530
Or quhat availith thy wickit condicioun
To sayne or done that thou most efter rewe
(f. 228.) O nyce foole thine owin harm for to schewe
Drink not the poysoun sene to fore thine eye
Lest thou corrupt and venymyt be thareby.   535

For yf the lestith as thou hath begoune
Of Jelusy to drinkyn of the toune

Thare thy confusioun sene is the before
Thou wo yneuch unto thy self hath woune
Fare wele of lufe thy fortune is y-roune　　　　　540
Tny ladyis dangere hath thou evirmore
For thy condicioun greveth hir so sore
And all thi lufe furth drivyth in pennaunce
With hevynes and suffering grete mischaunce.

For it hath bene and aye schall be also　　　　　545
Thou Jelousy in angir and in wo
Enduryn schall thy wrechit cursit life
Y-fret rycht by the suerd of cruell syte a tuo
Thy stormy thoucht ay walking to and fro
As doth the schip amang the wavis dryve　　　　　550
And not to pas and note quhare to arryve
Bot ay in drede furth sailith eve and morowe
So passith thou thy worldis course in sorowe.

[For] scharp wo doth so thi dredfull goste bete
That a]s the tree is by the wormis frete　　　　　555
[So] art thou here ay wastit and y-brent
[An]d birnyng as the tigir ay in hete
[Qu]ho lyvith nowe that can thy wo repete?
[Bot in] thy selfe thou sufferith such torment
[Le]ving to deth ay in thin owen entent　　　　　560
[Thy]ne owin harm consumith the and annoyith
[And bot]h thi body and thy soule distroyith.

[Bot] sith it is thou failith not one of two
[Th]at is to say in to this erth in wo
[Still] to endure or efter to be schent　　　　　565
[Etern]ally withoutyn ony ho
[And well] accordith it for to be so.
[Quho] is thi Lord? the Fader of haterent
[And] quhens that cummith every evill entent
[Quhois] love thou ay full besyly conservith　　　　　570
[For] thy desert[?] rewardith the and servith

[Thus] may thou fynd that proffit is thare none
[In Jelo]usy tharefore thou the dispone
(f. 228 r.) My counsele is playnly and (thou) for see
This fantasy to leve quhich thou hath tone　　　　　575
And furth among gud falouschip thou gone
Lyving in ese and in prosperitee
And love and eke with Ladies lovit be
Gif so the likith not I can ne more
Thus I conclude schortly as for me　　　　　580
Quho hath the worst I schrew him evirmore.

You loveris all rycht hertly I exhort
This litill Write helpith to support
Excusith it and tak no maner hede
To the endyte for it most bene of nede　　　　　585

Ay simpill wit furth schewith sympilnese
And of unconnyng cummith aye rudnese
Bot sen here ar no termes eloquent
Belevith the dyte and takith the entent
Quhich menyth all in contrair Lusis so   590
And how thir Ladies turment bene in wo,
And suffrith payne and eke gret violence
Into thair treuth and in thair innocence
As daily be experience may be sene
The quhich allace grete harm is to sustene   595
Thus I conclude with pitouse hart and meke
To every God that regnyth I beseke
Above the erth the water or the aire
Or on the fire or yit in wo and care
Or yit in turment slauchter or mischance   600
Or mycht or power hath to done vengeance
In to this erth or wickitnese distroye
That quho thir Ladyis likith to annoye
Or yit thare fame or yit thaire ese engrewe
Mote suffryn here and sallyn grete mischiewe   605
In to this erth syne with the falouschip of hell
In body and soule eternaly mot duell.

Explicit quod Auch.

SCOTTISH DIALECTS.

IT is now some months since Dr. James Colville called attention in
the columns of the daily press—*Scotsman*, 2nd February, to the fact that
in Scotland there is 'a fast-fading vernacular,' which is outside the spheres
of the Scottish Text and Scottish History Societies, and which no society
has been formed to preserve the record of.

This is only too true. The dialects of Scotland are rapidly dying out,
and the process accelerates in speed as time goes on. Dr. Colville points
to the excellent work doing by the English Dialect Society in collecting
'obsolescent material' from Warwick, Northumberland, Derby, Cumberland, etc., and asks—'Has no one ever put such questions as these:—Is
there any call for a similar society here, any field for it, any likely workers?
If dialect work is worth doing, and if we are as capable as the southrons
of working at it, why not take courage, and a leaf out of their book?'

It is to be hoped that Dr. Colville's suggestion will ere long bear
fruit. Might not very material and systematic assistance in the collection of local words, phrases, and idioms be rendered by the officials part
of whose daily work is to keep an eye on them, and is indeed a principal
agent in their obliteration—the Board-School masters and mistresses?

ED.

OLD AGE PENSIONS AND INSURANCES UNDER THE
FEUDAL SYSTEM.

EARLY in the year 1320 the men of Tweeddale had a dispute with their
overlords, the Monks of Dunfermline. The feudal system recognised that

the right of the superior over his vassal entailed a correlative right in the vassal to the superior's protection. But the claims of the men of Tweeddale were large and in part peculiar, and the case was submitted to a jury. In the Abbey Register (*Reg. de Dunfermline.* Ban. Club print, p. 240, No. 354) we find recorded both the claims and the jury's findings, viz. :—

1. To have a bailiff of their own kindred for repledging them to the Abbey Court.

This the jury find they ought to have ; not, however, in virtue of the terms of their feu, but only as custom warranted.

2. To be supported by the Monastery when they are verging on want or broken down with age.

The jury find that the monastery is not bound to do this, save out of kindness as the claimants are the monastery's own men.

3. That any of the claimants coming to the Abbey on account of manslaughter or some other crime, for which he might claim the immunity of the Church, should be supported while there by the Monastery.

To which the jury answer that the Convent would do so for a stranger —much more then for its own vassals.

4. That if any of the claimants should be fined for committing homicide, the Convent should be bound to contribute twelve merks towards payment of the fine.

To which claim all that the jurymen replied was that never in all the days of their lives had they heard the like of it. (Ad quod responderunt requisiti quod nunquam tale quid omnibus diebus vite sue audierint.)

A NEW SCOTTISH ASSOCIATION IN THE NORTH OF LONDON.

WE have received a copy of the objects, rules, etc., of the Northern Suburbs Scottish Association which has lately been formed. Of Scottish Associations in London we are glad to say there are many, yet it has occurred to several prominent Scotsmen that there exists ample room for an association which will have for its prime object the cultivation of the national sentiment by means of lectures on Scottish history, literature and folk-lore, and it is intended to form an attractive syllabus for next winter by arranging with several of the most eminent Scotsmen to deliver lectures on subjects pertaining to the national life and character. It is not to be understood, however, that this is to be exclusively a learned society, for concerts and other social gatherings will be arranged for. Among the vice-presidents appear the names of Dr. Clark, M.P. for Caithness, J. H. Dalziel, Esq., M.P. for Kirkcaldy Burghs, a number of Scottish ministers, and of that fraternity of which London feels justly proud—Scottish medical men. The Chairman of the Executive—Dr. A. Lamont Macphail—is a well-known medical practitioner in Stoke Newington, and is interesting himself to a great extent in the welfare of this Association. The membership is open to ladies as well as gentlemen, and to all persons connected with Scotland, by birth, marriage or descent, the main endeavour of the originators being to bring together every one resident in the northern suburbs of London interested in Scottish matters. An association with such laudable objects in view deserves success, and we recommend our readers to bring it to the notice of their friends, who on communicating with the Hon. Secretary, Mr. William Gray, 201 Albion Road, Stoke Newington, will be furnished with full particulars.

THE COMMISSARIOT REGISTER OF SHETLAND.

(Continued from vol. xii. *p.* 40.)

613. Helgo Magnusdochter in Yow.
614. Ola Spence in Gardie, died May 1634. Breta Androisdochter his spouse, William his son.
615. James Nicolson in Wallie, died April 1634. Elspeth Gray his relict, Edward, Margaret, and another his children.
616. Magnus Coutts in Balzesta.

3rd September 1634.

617. Andrew Strang in Underfaillie, Fetlar, died July 1634. Margaret Linklater his relict, John, Henry, Catherine, and Marion his children.

5th September 1634.

618. Sinevo Nicolsdochter, spouse of Magnus Hermansone in Failzie, Yell.

9th September 1634.

619. William Anderson in Swinesetter, Delting.

18th September 1634.

620. Inga Magnusdochter in Scalloway.
621. Barbara Laurencedochter, spouse of Robert Manson in Gil-breck, Lunnasting.
622. Erasmus Thomasson in Overbister, Weisdale.

27th September 1634.

623. Edward and Nicoll Cloustans in Sandwick, Dunrossness.

8th October 1634.

624. Laurence Sinclair of Houss in Burray, died April 1632. Arthur (eldest), John, George, Laurence, Grissel, Margaret, Barbara, Elizabeth, Helen, and Anna his children.
625. Elizabeth Sinclair, his relict, died February 1634.

23rd October 1634.

626. Marion Henrysdochter, spouse of Malcolm Halcro in Hoswick, died May 1634. Nicoll, James, Henry, Laurence, and Patrick her children.

27th October 1634.

627. Isobel Moir, spouse of Thomas Linklater in Laxfirth, died July 1633. William, Robert, James, Marjorie, Janet, Elspeth, and Bessie her children.
628. Katherine Johnsdochter, spouse of Magnus Swanesone in Gulberwick.

26th August 1635.

629. Katherine Halcro, spouse of Ola Robertson in Kirkasetter, Nesting.
630. Robert Manson in Gilsbreck, Lunnasting.
631. Marion Cattane, spouse of Henry Manson in Skelberrie, Lunnasting.
632. Marion Mansdochter, spouse to William Stewartsone, Lunnasting.
633. John Robertson in Gairdoun, Lunnasting.
634. James Christophersone in Bigsetter, Whalsay.

Unst, 3rd September 1635.

635. Robert Punt in Skeggar, died January 1635. Agnes Strang his relict, David (eldest), William, and Helen his children.
636. Agnes Pount, spouse of Laurence Andersone in Soitland, died February 1635. Marion, Agnes, and Christian her children.
637. Breta Johnsdochter, spouse to Erasmus Nicolson in Daill.
638. William Gray in Clift, died February 1634. Sinnevo Schewartsdochter his relict, Walter, Jerome, Agnes, Catherine, and Magdalen his children.

VOLUME V.

27th May 1648.

662. Magnus Guidlet in North Ler.
663. Barbara, spouse of Laurence Irving in Coule.
664. Ola Sinclair in How, in Whiteness, died April 1645. Laurence, Malcolm, Nicol, James, and Marion his children.

6th June 1648.

665. Edward Manson in South Nesp, Nesting, died May 1647. Magnus his son, Euphan Margaretsdochter his relict.

7th June 1648.

666. John Thomasson in Sound.

14th June 1648.

667. Thomas Sinclair in Lerwick, died August 1645. Christian Sinclair his relict, Laurence, Katherine, and Jane his children.
668. Thomas Duncanson in Lerwick.

23rd June 1648.

668. Andrew Christopherson in Setter, Nesting, died May 1648.
669. Agnes Nicolsdochter, spouse of Andrew Erasmusson in Sound.
671. Sara Fleyming, spouse of Andrew Mansone in Sound, died March 1645.

29th June 1648.

672. Malcolm Sinclair, son to Henry Sinclair in Gathesbark, died 15th April 1645. George, William, Isabel, Martha, Mary, and Margaret his brothers and sisters.
673. William Young in Moo, died 1st April 1648.
674. Mathew Litster in Lerwick, died January 1644.
675. Laurence Sinclair in Norst, died August 1647. Barbara Henriesdochter his relict. John and George his sons.
676. Margaret Billie, spouse to Andrew Mader in Dunrossness, died June 1645.
677. Isobel Murray, spouse to John Mackphune in Dunrossness, died June 1644.
678. Malcolm Leask in Lie, died May

1648. Isobel Anderson his relict, Adam and Margaret his children.
679. Marion Caird, spouse to James Archibald in Lie.
680. Marion Petersone, spouse to Magnus Sinclair in Dunrossness.
681. Beggis Morisone, spouse to David Bruce in Wilsness.
682. Grissel Halcro, spouse to George Graigie in Dunrossness.
673. Robert Bruce of Sumburgh, died March 1636. William his eldest son, Laurence, Andro, Patrick, James, and Mary his children, Isabel and Ola.
684. Henry Leask in Graitness, died June 1643. Isobel Drewer his relict, Patrick, Elspeth, Margaret, Martha, and Katherine his children.
685. Magnus Williamson in Hollwell, died February 1648.
686. Malcolm Sinclair in Gairth, died February 1647. William, Andrew, David, Margaret, and Katherine his children.
687. Margaret Kirkhouse, spouse to John Burniesone in Moo.
688. James Burnieson in Hillwill, died January 1648.
689. Katherine Sinclair, spouse to Henry Strang in Hillwill, died July 1643.

(To be continued.)

TRANSACTIONS OF SOCIETIES.

EDINBURGH BIBLIOGRAPHICAL SOCIETY.—One of the chief results of the past session has been the commencement of a work which is one of the primary objects of the Society, and to which much of the work already done has been leading up. This is the formation of a catalogue of books printed in Scotland before 1700. At the first meeting of the Society for the session it was decided that the scheme should now be taken up in a definite way. What is ultimately aimed at is a full bibliographical catalogue, but as a necessary preliminary a hand-list of short titles is being prepared. It is the intention, as soon as the work has proceeded far enough, to issue a preliminary list with the object of obtaining additions so as to fill in the blanks as far as possible before the hand-list is issued in its final form. The papers read during the session included one by Mr. J. S. Gibb on Andrew Symson, clergyman, author and printer, and one on Peter Williamson and his press by Mr. Wm. Cowan. Mr. J. P. Edmond contributed a particularly interesting paper on the 'Mécométrie de Feymant' of Nautonier, in which he drew attention to a Scottish translation of the book which appears not to have hitherto been noted by bibliographers. Mr. E. Gordon Duff notified the discovery of two books printed at York (c.) 1540 and in 1579, which help to fill in the history of printing in that city. An interesting evening was also spent, under the direction of Mr. W. B. Blaikie, with Grant's, Finlayson's, and other maps of the movements of Prince Charles Stuart. Among the books exhibited at the meetings may be specially noted the '*Edinburgh' Common-place Book or Private Journal of Robert Burns*, begun in Edinburgh on 9th April 1787, and an account of its history and the use made of it by different editors was given by Mr. Wm. Brown. This book, it will be remembered, when sold in London last month, realised £355. and has, it is satisfactory to hear, come back to Scotland.

QUERIES.

OGILVIE OF AUCHIRIES.—Can any one supply me with a pedigree of Ogilvie of Auchiries? Some mention of the family occurs in Burke's *Landed Gentry*, under Irvine of Drum and Crimond, but I wish for more particulars. C. H. MAYO.

LONG BURTON VICARAGE,
SHERBORNE, DORSET.

DALGLEISH OF TINNYGASK IN THE COUNTY OF FIFE.—Can any of your readers give me any information concerning this family? My maternal ancestor, James Moodie of Cocklaw, married at Beath, July 26th, 1755, 'Janet Dalgleish, daughter to Tuniegask in y⁻ parish of Saline,' and I am most anxious to discover the four grand-parents of this lady in order to complete a series of Seize Quartiers for my History of the title of Raineval.

The Registers of Saline are unfortunately not in existence before 1739 so they throw no light on the matter, but from other sources I have collected the following:—

(1) Robert Dalgleish of Fingask, 17th July 1617 (*Indexes to the Commissariot of St. Andrews: Testaments*, 1616-1629).

(2) Robert Dalgleish of Tinnygask to his father Robert Dalgleish of Tinnygask, who died March 1733. Heir special in Tinnygask and Foulford or Dewar's Beath, in the parish of Dunfermline, dated 20th July 1733 (*Decennial Indexes to the Service of Heirs in Scotland* 1730-1739).

(3) 1767, May 29th. Mortcloth money for Robert Dalgleish of Tiny-Gask (*Saline Register of Burials*).

(4) Dalgleish, Robert, of Tunnygask, to his grandfather Robert Dalgleish of Tunnygask who died September 1768. dated 22nd October 1771 (*Decennial Indexes, etc.*, 1770-1779).

(5) Robert Dalgleish of Tunnygask, 648a. £381 (*Scotland: Owners of lands*. 1872-73).

I presume Janet will have been the daughter of the Robert who died September 1768. She herself was buried in the Moodie vault at Beath, April 28th, 1807.

I shall be very greatly obliged for any information on this subject.

RUVIGNY
(MARQUIS DE RUVIGNY AND RAINEVAL)

7 VICTORIA ST., WESTMINSTER, S.W.

ALEC BURNETT, DIED 1787.—Is anything known of Alec Burnett who died 19th April 1787, aged 43? I have a mourning ring with an inscription to this effect, which belonged to the wife of my mother's maternal grandfather, Andrew Smith, born 1783, died before 1830, merchant of Barbadoes (a son of Smith of Balgonie, Fifeshire).

I am trying to discover Mrs. Andrew Smith's maiden name, which in spite of an extensive search through the Scottish and West Indian Registers, I have so far completely failed to do. RUVIGNY.

ST. MARTIN OF BULLION'S DAY.—The date of this festival (July 4th) is known, but there is some uncertainty as to the origin of its name. Chambers, in his *Book of Days* (vol. ii. p. 20), says: 'That the Church of Rome should not only celebrate the day of St. Martin's Death (November 11th), but also that of the transference of his remains from their original humble resting-place to the cathedral of Tours, shows conclusively the veneration in which this soldier-saint was held.

' In Scotland, this used to be called St. Martin of Bullion's Day, and the weather which prevailed upon it was supposed to have a prophetic character. It was a proverb, that if the deer rise dry and lie down dry on Bullion's Day, it was a sign there would be a good gose-harvest—gose being a term for the latter end of summer ; hence gose-harvest was an early harvest.'

In his hand-book of *Weather Folk-Lore*, the Rev. C. Swainson gives some additional information regarding the festival. After quoting the proverb about the deer, he recalls another, viz.—

> Bullion's day, if ye be fair,
> For forty days 'twill rain nae mair.

Mr. Swainson addes : ' In Scotland this day is called St. Martin of Bullion's Day ; for what reason it is uncertain. Du Cange styles it : "Festum Sancti Martini Bullientis, vulgo etiamnum Saint Martin Bouillant," *i.e.* Hot, boiling : perhaps from the heat of the season in which this festival falls.'

And so we find in France :—

> S'il pleut le jour de la Saint Martin bouillant,
> Il pleut six semaines durant.—MAINE.

Can any reader of the *Scottish Antiquary* clear up the point regarding the etymology of *Bullion*? As the cultus of St. Martin came to us from France, it is probable that the name of the fourth of July festival came thence also. J. M. MACKINLAY, F.S.A. (Lond. and Scot.).
GLASGOW.

DUMBARTON PROTOCOL BOOKS.—The Protocol Book of Master Matthew Forsyth, N.P., at date 4th May 1564, and that of Walter Watson, N.P., at date 22nd December 1580, are referred to in *The Stirlings of Keir and their Family Papers* (pp. 131 and 139, *notes*), and are there stated to be then (1858) in the office of the Sheriff-Clerk at Dumbarton. They are not, however, now to be found there, nor are they among the records in the Town-Clerk's office, though in the latter there is an older (1517-1529) Protocol Book of Matthew Forsyth. I have made inquiries at the Register House and at the Advocates' Library, but the above are not among the Protocol Books in either. I will be glad of any information as to where these books may possibly be preserved. A. W. G. B.

ABSALON, ANSELAN.—The name Absalon (or Absolon) is of frequent occurrence among the witnesses to charters granted by Maldoven, 3rd Earl of Lennox, between 1225 and 1270 (see *Cartularium de Levenax*,

Registrum Monasterii de Passlet, and *Registrum Episcopatus Glasguensis*) ; the person or persons referred to being variously described as 'Dominus Absalon de Buchkan,' Absalon clerk to the Earl, Absalon seneschal to the same, 'Absolone de Levenax,' and Absalon, father of Gilbert and Matthew (Matheus). These probably represent two or at the most three individuals, and the last three may be pretty certainly identified with Absalon, son of Macbed, to whom a charter of Clarinch was granted by Earl Maldoven in 1225.

'Filius Absolonis' occurs as the patronymic of the above Gilbert till probably after 1274 ; also 'Macabsolon' as that of a Malcolm, who is probably identical with Malcolm de Bougheannan, who signed the 'Ragman Roll' in 1296.

The name Anselan is given by Buchanan of Auchmar as that of three early lairds of Buchanan, the last being identical with Absalon, son of Macbed. There is also an 'Anslan Macgilespic de Lany' (date probably about 1330) mentioned in the old Genealogical Tree of the Lanys of that Ilk (compiled probably before 1540), of which a reduced facsimile is given in Mr. Guthrie Smith's *Strathendrick.*

I strongly suspect that *Auselan* is the correct form of the name and that *Anselan* is comparatively modern, having arisen from *u* having been mistaken for *n*, these letters being frequently indistinguishable in ancient documents.

Are there any other instances of the above names to be found in early Scottish records? A. W. G. B.

DONOTE (DONATA?).—In the old Stirling Protocol Book, 1469-1484 (fol. 305), there is a Resignation by Thomas Buchanan of Gartincaber, 31st May 1482, in which, 'Donote,' spouse of the said Thomas, is mentioned. Are there any other Scottish instances of the name? Can it be a notarial form of 'Jonat'? A. W. G. B.

FAMILY OF MACAUSELAN.—Buchanan of Auchmar states that MacAuselan was the original patronymic of the Buchanans, and was retained by the eldest cadet when disused by the rest of the clan. Of this branch he mentions four chieftains ('Barons MacAuselan') namely, Malcolm (date about 1296), Macbeth (about 1400), a Baron MacAuselan, two of whose sons having settled in Ireland, were ancestors of the MacAuselans there, and Alexander, 'last Baron MacAuselan,' whose daughter and heiress married one Campbell, and sold her lands to her superior. Sir Humphrey Colquhoun of Luss.

There is still pointed out in Luss Churchyard the tomb of a Baroness MacAuselan whose husband distinguished himself at the siege of Tournay (see Macleod's *Historic Families of the Lennox,* p. 207). The date of this Baron must have been about 1340.

The MacAuselans seem to have held that they were the elder line of the Buchanans and not merely the eldest cadet, though the tradition in one branch was that the Buchanans were a distinct family who had dispossessed the MacAuselans of their lands, and it is curious that in the old Genealogical Tree of the Buchanans, 1602, the first Buchanan mentioned is 'Sir Valtir yat conquest pairt of ye landis frae ye Macauskins' (see reduced facsimile of Tree in Mr. Guthrie Smith's *Strathendrick*).

In the Dennistoun MSS. there is an account of the MacAuselans of

Caldanoch, but I am unable to identify them with the Barons Mac-Auselan. and take it that they were a junior branch.

I will be glad of any information as to the origin and history of this Lennox family.   A. W. G. B.

PELDER.—The hill in East Lothian which is generally known as Traprain Law is known to the fishermen from Cockenzie to Eyemouth as Pelder. What is the meaning of the word? It would be interesting to learn if any others of the natural features of the land are called among the fishermen by names which are not used by the landsmen.   Z.

THE FIRST STEAMBOATS ON THE FORTH.—I am anxious to ascertain whether the *Elizabeth* plied on the Forth between 1812 and 1815, and what were the names of the second and third boats that ran continuously on that firth. The first, I believe, was the original *Comet.*   X.

REPLY.

THE REBELS OF 1715.—A contribution towards a list of these rebels will be given in an early number.   ED.

NOTICES OF BOOKS.

Prehistoric Problems: being a selection of Essays on the Evolution of Man, and other controverted Problems in Anthropology and Archæology, by Robert Munro, M.A., M.D., etc., 1897 (William Blackwood and Sons). 8vo, pp. xix + 371 ; price 10s. nett.

IN reading this interesting volume, there is brought home to us the immense progress that has been made in anthropological and archæo-logical science during the Victorian period ; and how, gradually from the evidence furnished by many isolated discoveries of fragmentary relics of antiquity, it has become possible to tell so much of the story of prehistoric man and his times.

Dr. Munro has brought together in a collected form a number of suggestive essays, some of which have already appeared in scientific periodicals. The first portion of the volume is anthropological, in which he discusses 'The Rise and Progress of Anthropology,' 'The Relation between the Erect Posture and the Physical and Intellectual Develop-ment of Man,' 'Fossil Man,' and 'The Intermediary Links between Man and the Lower Animals.' The second portion of the volume is devoted to studies in comparative archæology, in which Dr. Munro treats of 'Prehistoric Trepanning and Cranial Amulets,' the 'Otter and Beaver Traps of the Lake Dwellers,' 'Bone Skates,' and the evolution of 'Saws and Sickles' from the early forms of flint, collected in Egypt and the Italian terramare to Early Iron Age specimens from La Tène. Dr. Munro has produced a most readable book. His style is clear and vigorous, and he has fully recognised the advantage in such a work of numerous illustra-tions. As in his well-known work on the Lake Dwellings of Europe, he has shown how necessary it is, in dealing with prehistoric problems, to reach for the materials requisite for their solution, in wide archæological areas, and how little such areas coincide with modern geographical divisions.

Old Stirling measured and drawn for the Stone, by John William Small,
architect (Shearer and Son, Stirling, 1897). dbb. cap. fol. (17 × 13
inches), 67 pp.; price 21s.

STIRLING vies with Edinburgh in its historic buildings, and we have now
in our hands a large instalment of drawings, both sketch and scale, which
will facilitate the study of its architectural treasures. Perhaps the most
generally interesting part of this volume is that which treats of those
remarkable specimens of renaissance work of which Stirling is the proud
possessor, viz. :—The palaces of James V. and the Earl of Mar ('Mar's
Wark') and James V.'s Chapel Royal. The book, however, includes
notices also of the remains of the 'Parliament Hall' (1460-88) of James III.,
which is said to have been built by Cochrane, the royal favourite,
whom the nobles afterwards hanged over Lauder Bridge, also of 'Queen
Mary's Palace,' 'Darnley's House,' 'Prince Charlie's Lodging,' 'Cowane's
Hospital,' the Old Mint, the Castle furniture now in the Douglas
Chamber, etc. The volume contains, besides relative descriptive letterpress, fifty full-page lithographed plates of sketches, scale drawings to a
uniform scale of ¾-inch to 10 feet, details on ½-inch scale, and sections of
mouldings ¼ of full size. It is an interesting book to Scotsmen in general,
and an instructive and useful book to the archæologist and architect.
The book is handsomely printed on highly finished cartridge paper.

The History of Scotland, from Agricola's Invasion to the extinction of the
last Jacobite Insurrection, by John Hill Burton, D.C.L. New edition,
in eight volumes (Blackwood and Sons), 1897. 8vo, vols. iv. and v.;
price 3s. 6d. each.

THIS further instalment of the Messrs. Blackwood's reprint of Hill
Burton's History is in all respects equal to the preceding volumes, of
which a notice appeared in our last issue. The period covered by these
volumes extends from the triumph of the Reformation in 1560 to the fall
of Melville and the restoration of Episcopacy under James VI. It includes therefore many of the events of our history around which the
keenest controversy has raged. How Hill Burton treats of these, and
especially of the questions touching Queen Mary and the later Reformers
is well known. Without entering into the merits of the controversy, we
venture to affirm that any one who desires a calm, dispassionate account
of these times cannot do better than consult Hill Burton. The volumes
are handy, well bound, and excellently printed, while the price at which
they are issued must ensure them a wide circulation.

Handbook to St. Andrews and Neighbourhood, by D. Hay Fleming. New
edition, profusely illustrated (J. and G. Innes, St. Andrews *Citizen*
Office), 1897. 8vo, pp. viii + 142, and two folding maps; price 1s.

LOCAL handbooks are often written by local enthusiasts, but St. Andrews
and its district have the advantage of having their Guide written by one
who is a general historian, an archæologist, and a scholar of everything
pertaining to his subject as well. The cathedral, the colleges, and
churches, the harbour and the links, and everything else in St. Andrews
itself, are dealt with. The 'neighbourhood' extends as far as Balmerino,
and Mr. Fleming takes his readers walks and drives through it all, and
points out its beauties and its classic spots, and tells its tales and relates
stories of local character all the while. It is an admirable and most
entertaining guide.

Diary of a Tour through Great Britain in 1795, by the Rev. William MacRitchie, with an introduction and notes by David MacRitchie (London, Elliot Stock), 1897. 8vo, pp. xii + 169, price 6s.

ALTHOUGH it may be a little difficult for some people to see that any very useful purpose was served by the publication of this book, it throws a certain amount of light on the conditions of travel in Great Britain at the end of last century. The author, a worthy Perthshire clergyman, made a journey on horseback to and from London in 1795, and in his chronicle of his experiences shows himself to have been a man of intelligence and of considerable powers of observation. Though not possessed of much originality of mind, he was evidently animated by a sincere love of nature, and is seen at his best in describing places like the Yordas cave and the fine scenery round Chapel-in-the-Dale in Yorkshire. He must have been, moreover, no inconsiderable botanist, and has compiled with care lists of the names of various uncommon plants he noted in the fields and hedgerows. Sooth to say, however, the Rev. Mr. MacRitchie's observations and reflections on men and things are somewhat commonplace, and his journey was throughout marked by an utter absence of exciting or interesting episodes. His architectural taste was thoroughly characteristic of the period in which he lived, and may be measured by the fact that he considered Greenwich Hospital the finest building in Britain. It is curious that at a period when the fame of Burns was so widely spread throughout Scotland he should have noted the well-known lines scratched on the window of Rae's Inn at Moffat, with the initials of the author, and yet these should have had no special meaning or interest for him.

The diary has been carefully edited, and the excellent footnotes by which it is accompanied convey much useful information as to the places and people mentioned.

Sir Walter Scott, by George Saintsbury, 'Famous Scots Series' (Oliphant, Anderson and Ferrier), 1897, pp. 158, price 1s. 6d.

UNDER the above title Prof. Saintsbury has written a highly appreciative and somewhat exhaustive dissertation on the literary works of Scott. If the style is somewhat laboured and obscure, one must admit that no quotation, allusion, or comparison has been omitted, however remote its connection or far-fetched its origin, which might help to reveal the mind of the writer.

The book is full of technicalities. One is tempted from time to time to ask oneself if this is certainly a 'life' through which we are wandering, and not a cross section out of a handbook of English literature.

Guide to Grantown and District, by W. Cramond (John Leng and Co., Dundee), 1897.

BESIDES the usual guide-book information, Dr. Cramond's little book contains notices of a number of matters interesting to the antiquary, such as the sculptured stones of the Grantown district, and the collection of arms and portraits in Castle Grant. The author also gives some account of the historical associations of the neighbourhood, of which, perhaps, the most interesting is the fight in the Haughs of Cromdale, which ended the campaign of the Revolution. There is a spirited ballad descriptive of this affair, which might with advantage be added to a future edition. The map which accompanies the book is on too small a scale to be of much use to the tourist.

The Scottish Antiquary

OR

Northern Notes and Queries

| VOL. XII. | JANUARY 1898. | No. 47. |

UNION TRACTS.

THAT the Union of Scotland with England in 1707 should have been at the time highly unpopular with the Scottish people was only natural. For an ancient and proud-spirited nation it was no easy matter to join hands for common life with 'our auld enemies.' Strange too, and unwelcome, was it for the Scots to think that they must now be under the rule of a parliament sitting in London—a parliament mainly English, and that the land of their fathers was henceforth to be only 'that part of Great Britain called Scotland.' The Darien tragedy also was fresh in men's minds; and all knew and felt keenly the ruin of Scottish trade effected by the persistent enmity of England. Can we wonder then that our forefathers hated the change of government into which their country was being unwillingly forced? It could not have been otherwise. Sir Walter Scott and other writers of the early part of this century have indeed been disposed to blame the opponents of the Union; but was not their opposition justified by the long period of heavy commercial and industrial depression which followed 1707, and by the alien, ungenerous, and blundering administration of Scotland by the authorities in London? Neither the men who fought so hard against the Union nor their sons ever saw the good fruits promised them as the outcome of that measure. One of its most notable effects was to drive many Scotsmen into the arms of the Jacobites. Even its ultimate success is largely due, not to the manner of the Union itself, but to the wisdom and adaptive power of the two nations, and to the *vires medicatrices naturæ* in a free and vigorous race.

The three following papers may not be without interest as specimens of the tracts which the Union proposals brought into being. They state with force and some humour current arguments on the subject which was moving the country. And they have a certain philological interest. We possess few such early examples of writing in our local dialectic forms— forms whose value is only now coming to be fully felt.

The first tract is written with considerable spirit in opposition to the threatened Union. The language is not by any means so careful in its dialect forms as we should now look for in such a work. Its dialect, however, is quite as good as that of much that passes current in our time as dialectic writing. It belongs, moreover, to an age when, as yet, our schoolmasters had made little way in their war of extermination with our local dialects. The writer wears the garb of a westland farmer, a Clydesdale man, perhaps. He speaks in rural fashion as a man of simple knowledge, practical shrewdness, and slight education. As becomes the country life of the time, he is rich in the rural lore of proverbs and quaint, telling adages. For these alone the tract is worth reading. There is old world wisdom in the warning against 'baith skaith and scorn,' and in that which speaks of having 'your bairns to ban your banes.' There is power too in proverbs like these, 'As the fool thinks the bell clinks'; 'Fair heghts maks fools fain'; 'To quit pearls for pebbles'; and so forth. To some it may seem like a modern vulgarism to say that 'the English will surely *gull* us some gate or other, do we our best.' We should like to see other early instances of this use of the word *gull*. A still more vulgar modern phrase is suggested when we read, at the end, 'A' is like to gae to the pot together.' But even 'going to pot' can show an old pedigree.

The second paper is a defence of the Union, to which the writer gives her 'braid benison. She speaks as a poor labouring woman, one of the spinsters or female wool-workers of Aberdeen, the only place in the kingdom which favoured the obnoxious measure. The Aberdonians looked at the question as it concerned their own local trade, and that is the writer's standpoint. The case is well stated, despite the affectation of ignorance which appears in styling ivory, 'iliphan's teeth,' and in speaking of wool as wrought in 'malefactiries.'

Many familiar points of the Aberdeen dialect occur in this early example. The coming change is called an ' eenion.' The northern 'gweeds' are sent to 'far aff quintries.' The *f* for *wh*, which modern ethnologers point to as a shibboleth of the old Pictish remnant, is here in its fulness. The policy of the Phigs (whigs) is alluded to. And we have pha, phan, phar, phat, phil, and phy, for wha, whan, whar, what, quhil, and why. Likewise we have deen (done), tee (two), abeesed (abused), peer (poor), seere (sure), eesed (used), and so forth. It is a quaint statement that the lasses of Aberdeen were longing for the Union as for their bridal day.

The third tract is an early effort in Highland English. It speaks for the fishermen and others of the labouring class in the highlands. Its point of attack is the increased duty on salt proposed as a part of the Union scheme. In the last paragraph an effort is made to strengthen the argument by a droll reference to the prospect of a rise in the price of whisky, which, even in those ale-drinking days, is a thing 'her nane sell cannot well want.'

Evidently these two latter tracts were written to influence other districts than those whose dialects they speak. It was felt that a statement of the Aberdeen case, given in the workers' well-known speech, would tell as a quaint argument in other parts of the country. So, on the other side, the hard times in prospect for the poor highlanders are brought to bear upon lowlanders in somewhat similar circumstances. Even if the highlanders themselves could have read the tract, its burlesque of their broken English would have been sure to give offence. But it would not be easy to find a stronger appeal to those threatened with burdens like their own than is contained in this statement of their grievance in their own uncouth words.

W. T. D.

A

Copy of a LETTER

FROM A

Country Farmer

TO

His Laird, a Member of Parliament.

An't like your Honour,

I Mack bauld to send this Line to your Honour; Necessitie has nae Manners: I grant I'm no Book-learn'd; and therefore ye mannee look for sic well-buked Language, as the Gashgabbed Pamphlet-men set aff their Tales wee. But I hope yee'l tack my honest Meanen in my awn hamelie fasson of Moubanden what I wad say. Sir, there's's mickle dinn in our Countrie-edge, about an Union of our Kingdom of *Scotland* wee *England*; this is a Tale of twa Drinks; I find the maist part of Fock here-awae very sair against it, and sayen wee greeten Faces, They're fly'd at the heart, it'l be a black Bargain for poor *Scotland:* for the *Engleses* are owr auld farren for us, and there's little Ground to think, they'll gee us a seen Vantage wee their will, they neer liked us sae well; and its nae forgotten yet, the foul Plisk they play'd us about our *Caledonia* Business: *Brunt Bairn Fire dreads.* And its strange, that they wha slighted our Commissioners sae meickle nae lang since, whan they were up at *London* upon the sam Errand, and they that by Act of Parliament made us Foreigners about a Year syne, that a' of a sudden they shude seem to change their Mind; *I fear there's a Hook beneath the Bait,* and there's mair Policy nor Reality in their new appearand Kindness: *It's nae a' Goud that glitters.* It's said ye're gane to pit down our Parliaments, and mack us nae mair a Kingdom, and gee us up to be at the *Engleses* reverence, to be ruled and guided in a' things be them: and we may luik wee *New Lords to hae new Laws too.* This will be very odd, for a *Scots* Parliament to do this, or *Scotsmen* to play their own Country sic a Tod's Turn: Fy, fy! whare's the bauld and bra Spirits of our Fore-fathers, wha wad as soon a shoot their Head in the fire, as pit too their hand to onny sic discreditable Bargain, by whilk we'll *Get baith Skaith and Scorn:* Fy shame! what daft unnatural Bairns is they that wad quate with their awn Mother, in hopes of getten a Stap-Mother; I fear, an anes the *Engleses* had us on their Haunch, they'll skult us to purpose, for they hae mair pith to lay on, nor we to Lad aff: and it were well ward, that we were soundly belted for our Daffin. Dear Sir, hae nae hand in sick an ill Turn, as ye wad nae hae your Bairns to ban your Banes when ye're gane: and for ought I hear, an ye gee your Vote the wrang gate, ye need nae look for a blyth Blink frae ony in this Countrv, e'en your awn Friends will turn their back upon ye. I grant I'm nae Politian, but we cannee guess here-awae what Vantage our Land can get be this Bargain; I hear few speaken for't but a wheen Chapmen and

Pedlers, that fancies they'll get *Goud in Goupens.* As the Fool thinks the
Bell clinks: But *Engles* Merchants is better Stocked nor ours, and I doubt
nae, an there be onny Gear gaen, but they wad *Lick the Butter aff our
Cocks Bread.* But let me tell you Sir, that People here-awae are sae far
frae Happen to be made Rich be *England,* that they're fly'd they wad be
herried by this Union: for its little Gear we have, to pay our awn Stents
and Cesses, that we man pay in our awn Fasson, but ilkie Bodie tells us,
we'll be garr'd pay Taxes amaist upon ilkie thing; no our very Reek and
Sinders but will be Stented: By this means we wad soon hae *A cald Coal
to Blaw at.* And mair they say, our Yeal is to be rais'd to twa Groats the
Pint, and our Salt to ten or twal Shillen the Peck, that will be saat Saat
indeed: and a' this it's said, to pay a scare of *England's* Debt, which is
unco great: it seems they crack mair o' their Wealth nor they hae cause,
whan they man hae our help to pay their Debts: Dear Sir, whare wilt
come frae to pay a' this? And I trow, ye thats Lairds may look for ill
paid Rents, an ye get onny at a'; this'll be a Laed aboon a Burden, that
will gar monny a honest Man's back crack; in troth Sir, they may e'en as
well flea the skin aff our Faces, as gar us had up with thae payments; a
Year or twa wad herrie us: *a scad Man's head is soon broken,* wee reverence o' your Honour. But than another Wrack will fallow, whan we hae
it nae to pay, they'll send Dragoons to quarter on us, and tack awae a'
we hae, and that will raise great Murmurs and ill Blood, and wha kens
what this may drive poor Fock to: *Tramp on a Snail she'll shoot out her
Horns*: and a wiser nor ony o' ye a' said, *Oppression will mack a wise man
mad*: and after this, we'll get our Castles and strang Halds Garisond wee
Engles Sogers: its better hadden out nor putten out. But in the mean
time, I wonder what the Ministers is doen, theres no monny of them in
our Country browden for this Union, yet they say, theres some of the
Ministers in the East for it: But an I may speak wee reverence to their
Wisdoms, their Tribe has least cause of ony to be for't; I confess I hae
nae meckle skill, but I fear they wad nae be lang safe under the Tutory
of the *Engles* Bishops, that will hae mair of the Court and Parliament's
Ear and Hand too, nor our honest Ministers: and its well kent the Church
of *England* has ay been worken Wrack to our poor Kirk, and studed what
they could to pit down our Kirk Government, as being contrar to theirs,
and to get our Kirk made like theirs, I fear the ald Sprit is still to the
fore with them; And what will come of us an we get some new sort of
Aiths amang us that honest Fock will startle to take, and something or
other that will puzzle our learned Ministers themselves what to do about
it? I wiss my Een may nae see the ald Episcopal Wark of Hangen and
Headen and Persecuten come in fasson again, the *Engleses* will neer bear
mony things that our awn Fock thought fit to wink at: For the auld
of homologaten the supremacy, and homologaten Episcopacy, is not
our Country Focks head yet; yea this word's comen in Fasson
for now our Country Fock are callen the Union a homologaten the
the Solemn League and Covenant, a burien the Wark of Reforma-
or enen a Door for *Engles* Prelacy and Ceremonies: For a
Parlament may come to think it neither proper nor convenient,
not only different, but contrar Kirk Governments, baith settled
in one Kingdom. I fear I hae fashed your Honour wee
fickle and therefore I man leave aff: only I beseck you, (*For
a wise Man a Counsel at a time*) keep your Fingers free of

sic a foul Bargain, sae little to either the Honour or Profit o' the Nation,
and not only sae, but do what ye can, to keep us, as we hae been ay, a
Free and Independen Nation, an a cleanly Kirk: And to end Sir, whatever some Clatter of our bein Scarers of *Englands* Trade, whilk is the
takin Bait in this Business: there's mony wiser than I am, that says, we'll
nae ruise our seils meickle this gate; *Fair Heghts maks Fools fain*: for
the *Engleses* will surely gull us some gate or other do our best: Tack
things in time that ye prove nae your sels *Scotsmen. To be oner mickle wise
behint the hand*: but come o' Warld's Gear what will, I am sure, we hae
far better and surer Riches than they, that has the Gospel in purity, and
GOD's Worship without Man's Mixters, beyond ony other Kirk in
Christendom, the whilk GOD in his Mercy continue lang wee us; it will
be but a bach Bargain, an we quate wee Pearls for Pebles, we'll be *Penny
wise and Pound fools.* I wiss GOD may guide ye a', and gee ye the Grace
and Wit, to be baith True-hearted *Scotsmen,* and honest Presbyterians: it
will be a lasten Brand of Infamy on a Presbyterian Parliament, an a' the
Ruines that's like to come, be under their hand in bringen them on: My
Saul shrinks to think of the dismal Effects of this blind Block; I wiss
Slavrie, rank Poverty, Disgrace and Snares, be not the Bounteth of the
Bargain: I'm neither Prophet nor Prophet's Son, but I speak out what
mony Fock thinks, *A' is like to gae to the Pot together*: GOD forbid.

To His Grace Her Majesties High Commissioner and the Honourable Estates of Parliament.

The Heemble Petition of the peer Shank Workers and Fingren Spinners of Aberdeen, and Places thereabout.

Sheweth,

THAT we are right fain tee hear that your Grace and Lordships have in
your great Wisdom thought fit tee discharge the carrying away tee other
Quanties[1] tee Wool of this Kingdom. Our bread Benison light upon ye
all for this guid deed, & let it never gang by you, for this grit incouragement
to us peer things, who are fain to warble and wark late and air for a bit
of Bread tee our Mouths, and the Mouths af our peer Babies.

We are likewise right fain tee hear that we will all be made up by
this Eenion that's gane on between the twa Kingdoms, for the Cheeper
Lads that buy our Guids and Geer tell us, that we'le get a mikle better
off gate for our Shanks and Fingrens after the Eeuion than ever we had in
our Days. The reason they ga for it is, that they say all these sort of
Guids are mikle dearer in *England* than here, particularly they assure
us, that phan they ha taken in some pieces of our Fingrins wrapt about
their Packs of Linnen, they have Sold them for a third more than it coast
here, besides a guid piece of ourcome measure: They say the same thing
of our common Shanks, some of which they have Ventured to carry into
England tho there be Laws against the same, and these Lads tell us that
if they had withgate tee carry in Shanks Fingrins and other Guids we
make, into England, (as they say they may dee if ance the Eenion was
compleated) they could make very near double their Money by the return
of sick Guids as they could bring back.

[1] Quantries = countries.

Since we heard of the Eenion we ha ay been spearing at every body about it, & we ha learnt mikle annent it, that it will be a very Guide thing: among others pha ha tald us of the great vantages of it, we are informed by a gay aldfarane Carle, a Seaman who has beein in all the far aff Quintries, that he has been in places phar the *English* Trade tee, and that we may Trade tee after the Eenion, phat they will get mare than twenty pounds af Tobaco far an Ell of our Fingrins and 40 or 50 for a pair of Common Shanks that we sell for 14 or 16 shilling.

He sayt there is another far aff Quintry called the *African*, phar they get Goud Dust and Aliphan Teeth for Plaids and Killimeers slight Stuffs that may be there exchanged for great ventage, and that which incourages tee *English* to Teade thither, is that the Queen sends ov'r great Lords and Gentlemen ane errand to these Quintrys, to see that the peopl there do not wrong and Cheat her Subjects, and if they get not Justice deen them, they send hame word tee the Queen to stop all the Ships and Guids of the folk of these Quintrys that are in *England*, and if the ha nane there, Her Majesty will send o're mikle Ships with great Guns and destroy the Sea Coast Towns of these Quintries phere her Subjects have been abeased til sic sick time as full mends is made for the wrong done. He says in these far aff Quintries our folk dare not Trade for want of the like power to protect them, but if ance the Eenion were made up, the greatest King in the Warld will stand in aw to midle with a *Scots* man tee do him wrang.

But tee come hame again, we hear your Grace and the Lords of Parliament have sent for some of the Wool Merchants in *Edinburgh* to take Counsel about the Wool, and are about tee give some Inkiragement to the South Quintry Lairds for the loss they will suffer by discharging the Wool tee be carry'd away.

Ji a Curn peer things that ha na mickle Wot might advise Your Grace and Lordships, we wad say, midle nothing with the Wool Merchants of *Edinburgh*, for they'er a Curn Sivingeour Carles that care not phaes Bairn greet and theirs had its Toung, well ken we them, if they can get a six pence mare for a Stone of Wool in France than we wad give them, theyse carry it ov'r to Monsieer to Clead his Sodgers with, tho we and all our Babies should Starve at home, phan at the same time if it come tee our hands, we wald make it tee yield three times as mickle Silder in a foreign Mercat, if not mickle mare.

But we can tell your Grace and the Honourable Lords of Parliament, that the South Country Lairds need not be flyed for the Sale of their Wool if ance the Eenion ga on, for (short sighted and peer silly things es we are,) we can very well farsee that phan the ports of England and the other far aff places we ha spoke of are open tee Receive Our Fingrins, Shanks, Serges Plaids Pladings Stufts and Drogets &c, There will be a bra effaire for our Guides, and we'er na sick Feels but we ken how tee make our own vantage of sick a game, for if we find a few mae Chapmen at a Fair then ordinary we're as lordly with the Sale of our Guids as a Bony Lass that has half a Dozen of Wooers, and if we get a good off gate for our Guids, ilk ane o's will run faster tee the Wool Mercate than another and we na doubt but the Wool Masters and Merchants will ken how tee make their Vantage of that tee.

The Troubles and Abjections that some folk make that we'le be ne're able tee Card and Spain all the Wool of *Scotland* at hame, are so far from true, that if we had twice as mickle ther's na fear but we'le be able tee o're take it all, for litle ken they how far we are straitened to get our Living mony times for want of affgate for our Guids, and for that reson want Silder tee gate the wool Marcat are fain to Wirble kniting a pair of Shanks phan we could Card and Spin na litle Wool tee be Fingrens and other Cleath.

But not only so, are we oft Times Fain tee make mickle Work out of litle Wool, but mony of our Neighbours all the Kingdom o're, and most of our selves are fain to sit Idle mony times when we have deen with our Wool and cannot get our Guids sold tee ga tee the Marcat again, unless we sell it at a Wanworth, and our Merchants make their Vantage of our needeessity, phil in the mean time we sit with mony a Hungry Wame and mony a slight Mealtate.

We are told that some of the Wool Merchants that ha been before your Grace and Lordships; Compt that a hunder thousand Stone of Wool grows beyond Tay ilk year. We shall be ready to own all that and mickle mare, and wishes there were twice as mickle kening very well there is Hands enough in the Qountry to Card and Spin it all. Two Women will easily master half a Stone of clean Wool every Week at the mukle Wheel, that is 13 Stone in the year tee ilk Woman, thus 7 or 8 thousand Women will clear off a hunder thousand Stone of Wool in the year, and we are scere there is 4 or 5 times that number in the Quintry; They need not be flied, let us but ance see aff gate and Silder for our Wark, and we shall ply our Gardes and Fingers or the foul pair aff.

But as we said before, we are na at all flyeid but we will ha full aff gate and Silder for our Guids if the Eenion ga on, for not only will we ha *England* and all the other far aff places to carry the samen tee, but at hame phan we come to ha Bussiness and Silder, we'le e'ne take two Suits of new Cleass phan we cannot get ane now, so there na thing fleis us sa mickle as that we shanot get Wool enough, as we are very scere all tee Wool of this Kingdom will never be able tee Clead us all and be as mickle as a Bean in a *Barn* tee the other far aff Quintrys tee.

Ye need not trouble Your selves about your publick Malifactiries to get the Wool Carded and Spun, for if ance the Trade were opened by the Eenion, all the Women in the Quintray will flie upon the Wool like so mony Revens upon a dead Carion.

The Abjection some make that we cannot make Chaper Cleath here than in *England*, is not worth a Fig. for we ken fell well, according to the Proverb of the Chapmen that Trade with us, that *all the Winning lyes in the first buying* no Body can make it chaper than we, for Seer we are we can we leave as meanly and Work as sare as *any* shee that bears Fingers, and can scarce get our Bread of it, tho it is chaper with us then in *any* place of *England*, and we ken nane can Work for less, so let them do their best we shall afford our Guids cheaper than they can.

Neither *are* we fleid that all the *London* Cleath and Bra Claes that will be brought frea *England* will wrong our Trade *a* Pin. for that is only for your Gentles and Swagarers, and after all, the same may be said to be our own handy Work, for the Linnen Cleath, Tikings Dornick, and other things of Lint taken out here will bring *all* these things hame and mickle mare.

And tee tell your Lordships *a* tale of our Chapmen, phy there is less Silder due now by *England* to *Scotland* then no long sine, phan mickle *English* Guides was brought hither not only *London* Cleath, Silk Stifs Silder Shakers *and* all other sort of Bony Wallies, which are *all* now forbiden. They say just now there is mony of your great Folk phan in *England* buy these things with ready Money, which they eised tee dee by Trouk and that they could a brought mare of these bony Wallies hame with 70 pounds worth of Guids, nor your grit Folk can da with a hunder pound in Silder and for that Reason there is not so guid aff get for our Guids now as then.

We see mony other Vantages by the Eenion that we cou'd not tell all in a long Summer Day, such as the great aff gate that will be for our Linnen Cleath and all things made of Lint. That there will be a great Fishing set up, and Mony great Snips imployed in Trading with all manner of things tee and frea this Kingdom Great number of Hands imployed in biging of Ships and making all mannar of things for Sea Service, for our Snips are tee be made al here, which will be a great inkiragement to our own folk at hame, and keep mikle guid Silder in the Quintry.

For we hear the *English* are all for Inkiraging their work people and put on grit Customs upon sick sort of Guids as are brought hame fully made ready for eese, but little upon rough or unpared Guids that grows not in their ain Quintry. And on the other hand they say they inkirage all things tee ga out of the Kingdom, that is fully made ready. As for example they let na Wool ga aff guid Chap nor Dear, that in case any body take away Wool after it is Spun and made in Cleath *but not Lited and dressed they will ga them na encouragement, but suffar it to ga aff, but if it is Litted and Dressed, upon some sorts they give a dourough to take it away. We can na derny but this is a very canny auldfaren gate, and that it wald be mikle to our Vantage if it were sea here tee (as it will be by the Eenion) for then wald be in that case three Litsters and Wakers in our Town for ane.*

We wonder phat the Carles East and West the Quintry mean that make Addresses against the Eenion, and phat they waud be at against it, we're seer they man be very short sighted or mixed by na guid Spirit, we wish mony o' them be not Watermen, that is to look ae Gate and Row another.

We ha been deafened with Stories that the Customs,[1] *Excise and Cesses we will be put under by the Eenion will quite break and ruin us all, and after all we hear there is a little Book came out called Considerations on Trade Considered &c. Sold by Mr. Freebairn's in the Parliamet Cless, which makes it as plain as a niss on a mans Face, that the publick burdens will be less after the Eenion than just now, except phat is tee be laid upon Salt after 7 Years which wi'na be very mikle neither, for as we are tald, they sell it in England by weight as we do meal here, and that they allow 56 pound for a Bushel, which is 52 pound of our weight, and it pays 44 sh. of Custom.*

Since we heard this we have had the Kiriosity tee weight a peck of our Salt, and finds it tee be 9 pound and 2 ounces which according tee our Reckoning comes tee pay about 7 sh. and a plack Custom.

We ha likewise had the kiriosity tee spear at some auld farran House Keepers pha are uery nice in keeping Compt af every thing they ware upan ther Families and by their Account six pecks of our Salt is sufficient to serve a Family of 8 young and auld in a year, which comes tee 46 shilling Custom upon the 6 pecks, and being divided in 8 parts is just about

---

[1] ? Customs.

5sh. 6d. a head yearly, and we can very well farsee that we may then win two pence a piece a Day more than we can do now.

But af all the Carles that appose the Eenion, we wonder maste at the Phigs, and can na ken phat they wad be at, far seer we are if they stick na close like burs by the Phigs in *England*, and the Low Church men that brought in King *William* they need expect na mercy if there be a turn af affairs as phan King *Charles* came hame. However let them be doin they'l be the first that will rue it.

But having said mickle mair then we thought tee have said, we shalt conleid with gaing you our Benision out owr again, and prays ye may hastan forward the Eenion with all possible speed, for we lang as mickle tee see that happy day as we longed to be Wed phan we were Brides, or as those of us who are unmaried do so still, and wish that all the well meaning Carles pha are whidled into a beleif that the Eenion is an ill thing had our Speetkles, and that the Water men pha Row one Gate and look another would lay by their Oars, and put up Saill, that they may look and Steer one Gate.

To *Hir Grace Her Majesties high Commissioner, an te Honorable Estates of Parlment :*

Te Address far te Fishers on te Highland Coasts, an all uthers Inhapiting te Highlands, wha it ma concern,

Humbly Representing tat it will pe Exceedingly disadvantageous to Her nane sel, tat te Articles of te Union Concerning Salt, and Excise pe agreed to, without an Mendment in Case the Union is concluded.

Her nane sell having got notice tat tere is a Mariage or an Onion intended petween te twa Kingdoms, and farstanding tat tere are mony Tings of great Weight to pe well considerd pefore te same is Concluded, several People wad ha ingadged Her nane sell to ha joined with tem in making an Address against an Incorperat Onion wit *England*. Now to pe plain Her nane sell does not well Farstand tese Nice Points some Folk wha are not mikle Wiser tan Her sell pretend to Judge of, and terefore sall not midle wit any ting put fat Concerns Her nane sell, leaving tese kitle Points to pe Judged pe te Grit Lords and Duniwasles in Parliament, wha are able te give a petter Judgement of em tan Her nane sel, an has muele mare te loss tan Sae has if any loss to te Nation, sall tereby hapen, and wha she thinks will be as careful, for tere nane Concerns as other Foks are of teirs : on tese Considerations she sall Confin Her nane Speak to te Salt, an te Excise, whilk she far sees will touch Her nane sell Mickle, an na litle, in Case te Onion ga on.

Put pefore she pegin, ssie wad ha Your Grace, an te griet Lords of Parlment to Consider, tat Her nane sell was never pehind her Neighbours te Lalanders, in Loyalty te her nane Lord, to te King an to te Parlment, an terefore wad na pe farstood, as if she meant any ting against an Onion, put wit all she wad see it pe a Good Onion, far tat she likes wit all her Hart.

Put now to pegin she is informed tat seven Years after te Quion, te same Custom upon Salt is to pe Payed here as in *England*, which is Four and Twenty Mark upon te Pow, which together wit te price of te Salt its sell, will pe Therty Shilling a Peck, if not two Marks and a half, considering tat rer Few will Venture to pring it hame pecause of te grit Custom, for if tey should pring any quantity to ly upon ter hand owr year, it wad fash tem to get te Custom paid, so I tink te peak of Salt will pe cheap in tose dayes if it is not twa Marke and a half.

Now it is like Your Grit Duniwishes [1] may tink tis noting, pecause tey will gar 20 or 30 Mark mare a Year serve ter Families of Salt tan formerly, put tho her nane sell can *E*at her Meat wit as litle Salt as her Neighbours, yet she cannot make her hering, py which she wins her Preed, witout Salt, and tat a good qeantity too, which in such an event will be Salt upon Salt, and *I* tink Salt upon te top of tat Salt again.

Tat which will Certainly happen upon te Raising te price of Salt so very much, will pe, tat where formerly mony Folks who had put a Hunder Mark, two or tree, to Ware upon Harring, will not pe able to makemuch apove on half of tem, pecause te Salt will pe Dearer, or not muckle less tan all te other Charges; for in the present Case a Man tat has a hunder Mark to ware, many in a Year when a Good Take happens, make 30 Parrals of Harring wit Scots Salt, for he will get te Parrals for 18 or 20 Shilling a piece, Salt to each Parral for 14 shilling; Guting, Cowperage and Conveniency, where to make em for 4 shilling a pece, and the Harrings for 8 or 10 shilling a *P*arral, so tat tey will not pe muckle mare as 40 shiling a Parral put supose he give 20 or 30 shiling a parral for te Herrings, he will stil have 20 parrals for 100 Mark: put when the Salt is so dear he will not make 12 parrals under 30 pound or 50 Marks, for Salt only, and all te other *E*xpece as dear as formerly, Which in an ordinary way of reckoning he will not have apove half te Herring he can now get for his hunder Marks, and then if he lay on the Charge of his Attendence, and the *P*rofit of his Money upon the 12 parrals for which he can now he 24 parrals, te Harrings will pe very dear, Especialy when they are Cowped throw 3 or 4 Hands as they most pe from the place where they are made, to the place of Retail, and every one lay on the profit of their Money, as it is Resonable they should, from all which Salt Herring will not pe poor Folks Food, the only use tey will then pe for Greening Wives and for Dauntise to *P*eople that have Money to spare, in such a Case we may purn our Nets and Pirlins and go to te Plantations, or take on to pe Soildiers and leave our Wives and Pairns to Peg.

Your Traw-bakes will do us no Cood, for what ever encouragement may tereby arise to tose who carry tem aproad, it will be noting to hame Sale, and it is the hame Sale tat keeps up te price, for Folk are not obliged to sell to Marchants for Export Except they get a price, when tey know how to dispose of tem at hame, put in tat Case tere would be a Necessity to sell aproad, and I know not who will Ven*t*ar to bay Salt so dear and ly at the Discration of Merchants who will ever make teir own price, if they see the Herring plenty; and pesides, as Her nane sel said before, *M*erchants will be feard to pay mickle Salt, pecauiss of te great Custom, and in Case of a Cood Take, it may happen Salt is not to pe had for Money; so Fok what way she will, she can Tink of noting put of purning her Nets and Biriin, if te Onion go on, and tis Article pe not Mended.

Put farther te Traw-back is not Sufficent to pay the Extordinary price of Salt by muckle and no little 70 pounds woth of Salt will put make a last of *H*erring, and tho tese pe Push Herring, tere is put 18 pound

[1] Duniwishes.

allowed of Trawpack; so the Last of owr Herring will still be more tan 3 Marks a Parral dearer tan te Dutch, an a Marke saved at first Coast will enable te Merchant to sell twa Marks Chaper in te Marcat aproad, pesides te Tutch have te Voug in te Mercat already, an have teir Merchants pefore hand engadged oterways than owrs are like to get in hast.

Her nane sell farstands tat some Jody will say, jut we may make our Herring for home use wit Scots Salt, put allowing it to pe so, Scots Salt is likewise to pe raised py Taxations, which will make it half as dear as foreign Salt, so tat still her nane sels Trad will pe discouraged, so at she cannot make her lively hood of it.

Yea, even our Fresh Herring will pe spoild py te darth of Salt, far her nane sel wil pe sure te give em nane if possibly she can get em off her hand without it. Te Cowpers an Cadgers will pe sure te leave em without it, as lang as tey can want it, so in all propapility te Folk te whom tey are carried will get tem in a stinking condition.

Put it is na only Fishers tat are sa mickle discouraged pe te deer Salt, put it lys sad on te Peef too. An far tat Reason our Cows will na sell in te Lawlands as pefore, pecause te Country Folk tat were in use to buy em, about te Ladner time, will pe discouraged te buy em far te deer Salt, so tat not only wil tey buy nane of her nane sels Cows, put tey wil sel some of tere nane to England, so tat when her nane Cows go in to England te Mercats will pe stalled an te English when she sees bad Weather and a ful Marcaket, will een make te price her sel, so tat all te advantage of having no Custom to pay will not pe wit a Puttan albite it were tree times as muckle as it is.

Yea her nane sel hears tat te English have peen very pressing in te Article about Salt, an wonnot ha our Scots Skips pe Victuled with Peff or Fish Salted wit her nane Salt.

Tis she cannot farstand, nor can she see what te English wad pe at py it, unless it pe to hinder Scots Skips to Trade, for py tis means te English Skips can pe Victuled much Chaper tan te Scots.

Now I tink if te matter pe as it is represented, tat all te earnestness for an Onion upon te English side, proceeds from te Love an Affection tat tese who has now te Ruling of te Rost bear to us, then I am very sure when tis mattar is lade before tem, an te reasons given why we cannot consent to tis Article apout Salt, tey will pass from teirs seeking it, her nane Sels, Reason for it is tis.

If te English intend no mare py all tis Custom upon Salt jut to make a necessary Levy of Money for teir pressing Occasions, an tat tey look upon tis Branch of te Revenue to pe tat which may Raise most Money to te Crown, most in sensibly to te people as I tink all Government's ought to do, and tat te English desige no oter ting in it among tem sels; ten her nane sel is sure, is so far as it answereth not te scope or purpose in any part of te united Kingdom, it ought not to take place.

Put te proper way of Levying Taxes in all Countrys where tey consider teir own Interest, an te staning of te state, tey lay on most Customs upon such Goods as are Wasted an Consumed py People who ha Money to spare, or used py oters out of Vanity or some oter bad vice, which ought to pe discouraged, such as Pra Claes, danty Meats and Drinks &c. Now wat ever is laid upon tese comes out of Pockets where it is to spare, or from Fools tat ought to pe punished, put to put havy Taxations on poor Mens Laburs tat know not how to win a Mealath of Meat to temselves, is unacountable.

Put again if in *England* tis Custom is laid upon Salt only to Raise te Money Insensibly, an what is put litle to every Man, tho it doth Reach all Men, and tat very equaly, none makeing use of Salt to Excess, as many do Meat, Drink, and pta Claes, yet in *Sotcland* it shall Reach te People very unequaly, an most heavyly on tese who can worst bear it, because te poverty of te poor allows him not to go to Mercat frequently for fresh Meat, he most make use of Salt, which he puys at such seasons when he find it chapest, and it requires more ten five tims as much Salt to preserve te Meat as what is Sufficient to season it for te Eating, and where is te Euqety to make a poor Man who cannot buy Food for his Family in te proper Season, put must take it wen he may have it chapest, te pay 5 or 6 times as much for Salt to preserve it, as annother Rich Man makes use of who is in a Condition to buy dayly.

Another ting which maks it necessary for us to Salt Meat in *Scotland*, not only *Fish* which must be salted at te Place where tey are Catched, put also our *Flesh*, not only pecause many in the Country are *far form Marcat Towns and Scant of Silder, put more particularly pecause the Country his few or no Inclosures to keep Cattl in a good Condition, so tat most part of the Year none of tem are fit for Slaughter put such as are House fed or keept in some Cood Park or Inclosure which are not very rife.*

All tese tings and many mae Her might name, are reasons why Salt in *Scotland*, ought not to pe Charged at the same Rate as in *England*, and tis sall be a Touch stane to try whither the *English* seek an Onion wit *Scotland*, he[1] of kindness or for self ends, for if tey design noting put equal dealing, tey cannot refuse to alter tis Article upon Salt.

Put again, tat *Excise* is no less, yea a greater purden to many, for it will mak Usquebae dear, which her nane sell cannot well went, and Ale to Drunkards (which is no much matter) put it will make much less consumpt upon Corn, and tis shall touch your Laland Lairds wit a Witness, and in its turn come pack to us in the Highlands wit a Vengeance, for tey finding there will not pe use for so much Corn, must leave much of their Land Lie, and py tis means tey will pring up Cows to carry into *England*, and For-sta the Mercat upon her nane sell, tho the Laland Lairds will make but a sorry hand of it, tey will pe in doubt whither to leave their Ground Grass or make Corn of it, and tis dear Excise and Salt, will dry us up altogether, for Salt peing naturaly hot, and the dear Ale and little Money will not afford a Cooler.

LOST OR MISSING RECORDS RELATING TO SCOTLAND, FORMERLY IN THE ENGLISH TREASURY OF EXCHEQUER.

SIR FRANCIS PALGRAVE, in the volume entitled *Documents and Records illustrating the History of Scotland*, published under the direction of the Commissioners of the Public Records in 1837, referred to Bishop Stapleton's *Kalendar* which he had published in the previous year amongst *The Antient Kalendars and Inventories of the Treasury of His*

[1] ? he.

Majesty's Exchequer, under the heading 'Documents relating to Scotland antiently in the Treasury, but now lost,' in the following terms:— 'Several of the documents still existing in the Treasury are noticed in Bishop Stapleton's *Kalendar*, but this catalogue also points out many which are lost: the list, which is long, is well worthy the examination of the Scottish historian.' Little notice has been taken of this remark, perhaps because the volume *Antient Kalendars* is rare, and often strictly confined to the few Libraries in Scotland fortunate enough to possess copies. Mr. Hill Burton has referred indeed to one of the Documents in this List, the letter by Philip, king of France, giving Wallace a recommendation to his Lieges at the Court of Rome. This letter is printed in the *Wallace Papers*, published in 1842 by Mr. Joseph Stevenson, p. 163, from the original letter then in the Tower, so that it is not one of the documents lost, but other two letters mentioned in the *Kalendar*, No. 46, in favour of Wallace, one by Haco, king of Norway, and the other by John Baliol, king of Scotland, have not been found, and are probably irrecoverably lost along with 'the letters containing Ordinances and Bonds between certain Scotch Magnates and Wallace,' which were found on him when he was captured and 'delivered to Edward I. at Kingston by Sir John Seagrave.' All these Wallace papers are described as being in the Treasury of the Exchequer, when Stapleton made his Kalendar in the reign of Edward II., in a Hanaper made of twigs, of which Sir Francis Palgrave gives an interesting facsimile in the plates prefixed to the *Antient Kalenders*. It is impossible not to share the feeling of regret Sir Francis Palgrave expresses, that these documents relating to Scotland, which filled '*Certain forcers of leather bound with iron, four hanapers covered with black leather, nine wooden forcers, 18 hanapers of twigs, and 22 boxes,*' have now for the most part disappeared. It appears worth while to print the list in full for the benefit of future students of Scottish history, and with a faint hope that some of the missing documents may possibly still turn up, as a similar Hanaper belonging to the Treasury of the Exchequer was actually found in Berkshire and restored to its proper place of custody. With this object, the List, which is full of contractions, has been transcribed by Mr. W. K. Dickson, and is now printed in the *Scottish Antiquary*. Some remarks on its contents are reserved for a future occasion. It has not been printed in Mr. Bain's *Calendar of Documents relating to Scotland preserved in Her Majesty's Public Record Office, London*, although some of the documents contained in the List which are still extant will be found in that valuable publication.

.E. M.

Excerpt from Antient Kalendars and Inventories of the Treasury of the Exchequer, Vol. I. p. 127.

Kalendarium de Bullis Papalibus, etc., or Bishop Stapleton's Kalendar.
17 Ed. II.

XVII.

Scocia.

Obligaciones littere indenture quietaclamancie et alia memoranda diversarum personarum Scocie de diversis materiis ut patet in eisdem.

1. Obligacio *Willelmi* Regis *Scottorum* facta *Johanni* Regi *Angliae* de xv^{ml} marcis sterlingorum terminis infrascriptis solvendis, sine dato.

2. Littera communitatis Insule de *Man* facta *Edwardo* Regi *Angliae* per quam obligarunt se ad subjeccionem et dominationem ipsius Regis sub pena duarum milium librarum si aliquo tempore contra ipsum Regem insurgant contra hujus littere tenorem. Data etc. anno Domini mccxc.

3. Obligacio *Roberti de Brus* Comitis de *Carryk* facta *Edwardo* Regi Angliae de xl. libris per ipsum Regem eidem Comiti mutuatis.

4. Littera procuratoria Magnatum *Scocie* nomine tocius communitatis ejusdem Terre facta ad tractandum cum Domino Rege *Anglie* de statu terre ejusdem et ad faciendum et affirmandum omnia que eidem Domino Regi placuerit facienda pro statu *Terre* et Magnatum predictorum. Anno Domini mcccv. et regni Regis *Edwardi* tricesimo tercio.

5. Un endenture entre le Roi et ceux qi tyndrent le Chastel de *Bothcuill* de la rendue de meismes le Chastel lan . xxix.

6. La lettre *William* Counte de *Rosse* faite au Roi d*Engleterre* de son homage et destre foial et loial au dit Roi lan . xxxi.

7. Resignacio Domini *Johannis Comyn* Comitis de *Buchan* terrarum *Galweidie* facta *Johanni* Regi *Anglie* anno regni ipsius Regis secundo.

8. Endenture faite entre le Roi d *Engleterre* et la Countesse de *Rosse* et *Hugh* son fuitz eynez dautre dautre (*sic*) part sur la venue *William* Counte de *Rosse* a la foi le Roi et aussint de la demeore le dit *Hugh* en la compaignie le Roi lan . xxxi.

9. La lettre *Weyland de Stikelawe* tesmoignant sa venue a la pees le Roi d *Engleterre* et aussint que le Roi li baiila la garde du corps *Munes* (?) fuiz et heir le Counte de Cateneys, lan . xxxi.

10. Littera Regis *Francie* missa Regi *Anglie* apud *Liston Temple* xii. die Julii sub sigillis quorundam Scottorum, anno Domini mcclxxxviii. Data per capiam.

11. La lettre *Nicol de la Haye* tesmoignant la resceite de son heritage en *Essex* de la grace le Roi d *Engleterre* pur li et pur ses heir si *Gilbert* son fuiz veigne a la pees le Roi d *Engleterre* lan. xxxii.

12. Quietaclamancia *Johannis de Bar* per quam remisit et quiete-clamavit Domino *Edwardo* Regi et heredibus suis mille marcatas terre in *Scocia* quam ito ad hoc facultas se offeret pro mmm. marcis quas dictus Dominus Rex concessit predicto Johanni per manus Mercatorum Friscobaldorum etc. percipiendas. Data etc. anno Domini mcccvi.

13. Littera *Willelmi* Regis *Scocie* per quam concessit Johanni Regi *Anglie* ut maritet *Alexandrum* filium ejusdem *Willelmi* sicut hominem suum ligium infra sex annos et quod ipse et dictus filius suus fidelitatem servabunt dicto *Johanni* Regi et *Henrico* filio suo in omnibus et contra omnes tanquam ligio Domino suo. sine dato.

14. Littera . . . Archiepiscopi *Eboracensis* de inspeximus qualiter *Edgarus* Rex *Scocie* concessit quedam Maneria Regni sui *Sancto Cuthberto* et Ecclesie *Dunolmensi.* Datum inspectionis ejusdem littere etc. anno Domini mcclxxxvi.

15. Scriptum *Isabelle de Bello Monte* Domine de *Vescy* per quod reddit et reddit Domino *Edwardi* Regi *Anglie* et heredibus suis Manerium de *Caral* (Crail?) cum Portu *del Can* (?) in *Scocia.* Datum etc. regni predicti xxxiii.

16. Littera Domini *Johannis de Balliolo* quondam Regis *Scocie* sub

Magno Sigillo suo originali facta Domino *Edwardo* Regi *Anglie* filio Regis *Henrici* superiori Domino Regni *Scocie* super acquietacione cassacione et adnullacione tam de convencionibus promissis obligationibus et penis per dictum Regem *Anglie* dicto Regi *Scocie* et aliis de *Scocie* factis et concessis, antequam idem Rex *Scocie* seisinam ejusdem terre recepisset, quam de scriptis per dictum Regem *Anglie* apud *Northampton* xxviii. die Augusti anno regni sui xviii. quibusdam Magnatibus *Scocie* factis super prolocutione cujusdam maritagii faciendi inter filium ejusdem Regis *Anglie* et filiam Regis *Norwegie* Dominam et Reginam *Scocie*, in quibus scriptis contine-bantur diversi articuli concessiones promissiones affirmaciones et similia legum et jurium etc. dicti Regis Scocie et inhabitancium ejusdem Regni tangent. (?) Datum apud *Novum Castrum super Tynam* secundo die Januarii anno Incarnacionis Domini mcclxxxxii. et regni predicti Domini nostri *Edwardi* xxi et regni predicti Regis *Johannis* primo.

17. Item due littere de consimili materia sigillo dicti Regis Scocie et sigillis quorundam aliorum magnatum *Scocie* signate de datis predictis.

18. Littera Domini *Johannis de Balliolo* quondam Regis *Scocie* sub Magno Sigillo suo originale de homagio suo pro Regno *Scocie* Domino *Edwardo* Regi *Anglie* filio Regis *Henrici* Superiori Domino Regni *Scocie* in presencia quorundam Prelatorum et aliorum Magnatum *Scocie* facto apud *Novum Castrum super Tynam* in crastino Nativitatis Domini. anno Incarnacionis ejusdem mcclxxxxii. et regni Regis *Edwardi* pre-dicti xxi.

19. Item littera dicti Regis Scocie sub sigillo suo et sigillis quorundam Magnatum *Anglie* et *Scocie* testificans homagium predictum sub datis predictis.

20. Littera *Johannis* quondam Regis *Scocie* de Magno Sigillo suo testi-ficans fidelitatem quam fecit pro Regno *Scocie* Domino *Edwardo* quondam Regi *Anglie* Superiori Domino Regni *Scocie* in presencia quorundam Magnatum *Scocie*. Data apud *Novum Castrum super Tynam*, anno Gracie mcclxxxx. et regni dicti Regis *Anglie* xxi.

21. Littera centum et quatuor Magnatum de partibus *Anglie* et *Scocie* auditorum jurium et placitorum Petencium jus in Regno *Scocie* testimonialis quod satis ostensum fuit et prelatum atque dictum per *Robertum de Brus* ex una parte et *Johannem de Balliolo* ex altera, per quod Dominus Rex procedere potuit et facere judicium inter partes predictas, sub dato anno Domini mcclxxxxii., et regni predicti Regis *Edwardi*, filii Regis *Henrici*, xx.

22. Diversi rotuli sub sigillis quorundam Magnatum *Scocie* continentes placitum inter *Johannem de Balliolo* et *Robertum de Brus* super jure Regni Scocie. Dati anno regni Regis Edwardi filii regis Henrici xx.

23. Littera testimonialis sub sigillis Magnatum *Anglie* et *Scocie* de protestacione Regis *Edwardi* filii Regis *Henrici* quod littera quam ipse Rex fecit Magnatibus *Scocie* quod processus placitorum petencium jus in Regno *Scocie* determinari debet hac vice infra Regnum *Scocie*, non erit alias prejudicialis ipsi Regi, quin possit alias extra Regnum illud in *Anglia* vel alibi quo sibi placuerit in simili casu facere quod sibi placuerit vel debebit sicut Superior Dominus *Scocie*, sub dato anno dicti Regis *Edwardi* xx.

24. Scriptum per quod petentes jus in Regno *Scocie* obligant se ad petendum et recipiendum jus suum coram Rege *Anglie* Superiore Domino *Scocie*, et per quod concedent quod ipse Rex audiat et terminet jura sua

in dicto Regno *Scocie* sicut ei qui est Superior Dominus *Scocie* competit in hac parte, sub dato anno Domini mcclxxxxi.

25. Scriptum de submissione omnium Petencium jus in Regno *Scocie* quod pro rato habebunt quicquid eis consideratum fuerit pro jure suo in dicto Regno per Dominum *Edwardum* Regem *Anglie* Superiorem Dominum *Socie* et quod concedunt ei seisinam de Terris et Castris tocius *Scocie,* sub dato predicto.

26. Littere sub sigillis Domini *Edwardi* quondam Regis *Anglie* filii Regis *Henrici* et (aliorum Magnatum Regnum (*sic*) Scocie ut jus et hereditatem suam Petencium facere super reddicione Regni et Castrorum Regni *Scocie* in custodia diversorum Magnatum)[1] ejusdem Regni existencium per assensum dictorum Magnatum in manus dicti Domini Regis liberate sub dato predicto.

27. Quedam patens commissio Domini Regis Edwardi filii Regis *Henrici* sub sigillo ejusdem Regis pro regimine Regni Scocie deputato : Episcopo *Glasguensi* directa pro fidelitate de Magnatibus ejusdem Regni recipienda. Data anno predicto.

28. Indenture facte inter Reges *Anglie* et *Scocie* et quosdam ministros suos de diversis munimentis in Castro de *Edenburgh* inventis que per preceptu dicti Regis *Anglie* predicto Regi *Scocie* liberata fuerunt, sub predicto dato.

29. Littera *Dovenaldi de Insulis* et *Alexandri de Argathil* Domino Edwardo Regi *Anglie* filio Regis *Henrici* facta de bene et fideliter se habendo erga eundem Regem, anno regni Regis ejusdem xx.

30. Littera *Alexandri de Ergathil* et *Johannis* filii sui per quam promiserunt in presencia Domini Regis Anglie fideliter adjuvare Custodes Regni *Scocie* ad pacem ejusdem Regni servandam, data anno predicto.

31. Littera *Alexandri de Insulis Scocie* filii *Anegus* filii *Dovnaldi* facta Domino *Edwardo* Regi *Anglie* filio Regis *Henrici* quod pacem custodiet in partibus suis insularum usque ad parliamentum *Scocie* in xvᵃ Sancti Michaelis. Data anno predicto.

32. Consimilis littera *Alexandri de Ergathil de Insulis Scocie* eodem modo facta predicto Regi sub eodem dato.

33. Littera *Joannis* Regis *Scocie* per quam reddidit Domino *Edwardo* Regi *Anglie* filio Regis *Henrici* Regnum *Scocie.* Data sub sigillo predicti Regis *Scocie* anno regni sui iiii.

34. Rotulus continens leges et consuetudines Burgorum *Scocie.*

35. Item rotulus continens transcripta cartarum scriptorum et memorandorum apud *Edenburgh* inventorum in Thesauro Regis *Scocie,* anno Domini mcclxxxxi.

36. Item rotulus continens quedam transcripta bullarum et quarundam et quarum litterarum sub Magnis Sigillis Dominorum *Ricardi Henrici* et *Edwardi* quondam Regum *Anglie* cum transcriptis quorundam instrumentorum Regnum *Scocie* tangentium.

37. Item una cedula continens tractatum pacis et concordie habitum inter quondam Reges *Anglie* et *Scocie.*

38. Item rotulus continens appellaciones Septem Comitum Regni *Scocie* super jure ejusdem Regni ad eosdem Comites pertinente coram Custodibus dicti Regni per dictos Comites factas et perlatas.

39. Item due littere sigillis Comitum et Baronum Anglie sigillate que ordinate fuerunt Domino summo Pontifici transmittende super declara-

[1] Doubtful reading.

cione juris Regis *Anglie* de Regno Scocie, eidem summo Pontifici
intimanda, sub dato anno Domini MCCC.

40. Scripta tangentia tractatum de matrimonio contrahendo inter *In forcerio de
Edwardum* filium *Henrici* Regis *Anglie* et siiam Regis *Norwagie* cum *coreo ferro
ligato ad tale
signum. I.* quibusdam literis per Regem *Norwagie* quibusdam Magnatibus *Scocie*
directis.

41. Littere instrumenta et rotuli de articulis contra *Glasguensem* et *In forcerio de
coreo ferro
ligato ad tale
signum. II.* *Sancti Andree* Episcopos super adherencia ipsorum *Roberto de Bruys* in
principio rebellionis sue contra Regem *Anglie* et de inquisitionibus et
aliis in processu inde contra ipsos ex parte Regis exhibitis.

42. Instrumenta puplica super homagiis et fidelitate *Edwardo* Regi *In puchea de
canabo ad tale
signum. III.* *Anglie* factis per *Joannem de Balliolo* Regem *Scocie* et Prelatos et Nobiles
dicti Regni, et de submissione dicti Joannis facta dicto Regi *Anglie* et
libatione ipsius Johannis facta Episcopo *Vicentiani* secundum ordina-
cionem Domini Pape cum quibusdam rotulis et aliis memorandis de
eadem materia.

43. Rotuli et cedule de ordinacionibus per Regem *Anglie* factis *In parva puchea
de canabo ad
tale signum.
IIII.* super custodia Terre *Scocie* et Marchie ejusdem, et de municionibus
Castrorum et donacionibus terrarum Nobilibus *Anglis* per dictum Regem
factis.

44. Duo instrumenta puplica sub manu Magistri *Johannis de Cadamo* *In puchea de
canabo ad tale
signum. V.* et unum instrumentum puplicum sub manu Magistri *Andree de Tange* de
processibus contra Scotos.

45. Quatuor littere executorie *Eboracensis* Archiepiscopi et *Karliolensis* *In pixide lignea
ad tale signum.
VI.* Episcopi diversis Prelatis *Anglie* directe per mandatum *Clementis* Pape
quinti, ad denunciandum *Robertum de Brus* Comitem de *Carryk* excom-
municatum pro homicidio *Johannis de Comyn* in Ecclesia Fratrum
Minorum de *Dunfres* facto, et ad terras castra et villas predicti *Roberti*
et aliorum sibi adherencium in hac parte interdicto supponendas.

46. Quedam littere *Philippi* Regis *Francie, Johannis* Regis *Scocie* et *In hanaperio
de virgis ad
tale signum.
VII.* *Haquini* Regis *Norwagie* de conductu per eosdem Reges *Willelmo le Waleys*
concesso in regnis eorundem Regum eundo et redeundo, cum quibusdam
literis de ordinacionibus et confederacionibus per quosdam Magnates
Scocie prefato *Willelmo* facte, que littere invente fuerunt cum eodem
Willelmo, quando captus fuit, et Domino Regi apud *Kyngeston* apportate
per Dominum *Johannem de Segrave.*

47. Quedam littera *Alexandri* Regis *Scocie* patens cum litteris *In puchea de
canabo ad tale
signum. VIII.* diversorum Mercatorum de denariis ei libratis pro feodo quod percipiebat
de *Edwardo* Rege *Anglie* per manus *Gaufridi Newbaud* super custodis
Episcopatus *Dunolmensis.*

48. Item quedam instrumenta tangentia *Jacobum* Senescallum *Scocie,*
Episcopum *Sancti Andree* et Episcopum *Biblicnsem* cum quibusdam
litteris eorundem.

49. Item rotuli placitorum de parliamento Regis *Joannis Scocie* apud
Scone et *Strivelyn* anno regni suo primo.

50. Item quedam ordinaciones indenture et memoranda tangentia
ordinaciones de Terra *Scocie.*

51. Item duo rotuli continentes diversas ordinaciones[1] requisiciones
de diversis terris datis per Regem *Anglie.*

52. Item rotuli de nominibus Magnatum qui morabantur cum Domino
Rege *Edwardo* in guerra *Scocie,* anno regni sui xxxii.

[1] Word apparently wanting.

53. Item rotuli redditales de valore terre *Scocie* per annum.

54. Item quedam inquisiciones capte in diversis partibus *Scocie* per brevia de Magno et Privato Sigillis Domini Regis *Edwardi* filii Regis *Henrici* annis diversis de quibusdam personis qui venerunt ad pacem ipsius Domini Regis et eciam de quibusdam articulis temporalitatis Ecclesie Sancte.

55. Item rotulus de nominibus Magnatum et aliorum qui fecerunt homagium Domino *Edwardo* Regi *Anglie*.

56. Item quedam cedule transcripta literarum et memoranda tangentia Terram *Scocie*.

57. Item duo rotuli tangentes locucionem de pace *Johannis Comyn* et sibi adherencium.

58. Item rotulus responsium Religiosorum *Anglie* de cariagio accomodando Domino Regi pro guerra *Scocie*, anno regni Regis *Edwardi* filii Regis *Henrici* decimo.

59. Item littere quorundam Magnatum et aliorum de Terra *Scocie* de diversis materiis.

60. Item rotuli cedule et memoranda continentes informacionem juris Regis *Anglie* in Regno *Scocie* Curie *Romane* transmissam et responsiones *Scotorum* contra informacionem predictam et alia diversa dictam informacionem contingentia.

61. Item quoternus in quo continetur tractatus de vita et conversacione quorundam Nobilium *Anglie* et *David* Regis *Scocie*.

62. Item rotuli et memoranda de serviciis Regi *Anglie* prestitis contra inimicos suos *Scocie* per nobiles et ignobiles Regni sui et Terre *Hibernie*, et de providenciis faciendis in *Hibernia* pro guerra Scocie.

In puchea de canalo ad tale signum. IX.

63. Quedam memoranda de cronicis, ad mandatum Domini Regis *Edwardi* filii Regis *Henrici* ad informacionem pro jure suo in Regno *Scocie* habendam, per diversos de Clero *Anglie* tam religiosos quam seculares factis circa annum regni dicti Domini Regis xviii vel xix.

In forcerio ligneo in parte ferro ligato ad tale signum. X.

64. Littere sub sigillis Magnatum et Comitatum Villarum et aliorum diversorum hominum de Regno *Scocie* ad pacem Domini *Edwardi* filii Regis *Henrici* veniencium de bene et fideliter se habendo versus eundem Dominum Regem, et de homagio et fidelitate eidem Domino Regi per dictos *Scotos* factis, annis regni dicti Regis xxiiii. et xxv.

In hanaperio de virgis ad tale signum. XI.

65. Littere *Philippi* Regis *Francorum* et aliorum Magnatum tangentium (sic) treugas inter Dominum Regem *Anglie* et *Scotos*, ad instanciam dicti Regis *Francorum* per aliquod tempus initas, de diversis datis.

66. Item diverse alie littere quorundam Magnatum *Scocie* de carcere Domini Regis *Anglie* deliberatorum, de bene et fideliter se habendo, in auxilium eidem Domino Regi *Anglie* prestando, in guerra mota inter eundem Dominum Regem *Anglie* et Dominum Regem *Francorum*, de diversis datis.

In puchea de canalo ad tale signum. XII.

67. Bulle Papales diversorum Paparum plurimarum materiarum Regibus *Scocie* et aliis diversis ejusdem Terre directe pro statu dicte Terre, de diversis datis.

In coffro ferro ligato ad tale signum. XIII.

68. Coffrum plenum de diversis rotulis cedulis et alii memorandis, de tempore diversorum Regum *Scocie*, ac comitatum precium illarum ut de expensis Hospicii ipsorum Regum litteris ipsis Regibus directis, ac litteris ipsorum Regum aliis directis, ac eciam quampluribus aliis diversis de minimo valore.

69. Item sunt reposita in alio coffro de predictis memorandis usque

ad plenum billato, de materie predicta, per unam billam de verbo ad verbum.

In coffro ferro ligato ad tale signum. XIIII.

70. Octo pecie cuneorum Regni *Scocie* pro moneta facienda quasi dampnate, et sex pecie ponderum de plumbo, secundum consuetudine ejusdem Terre facte.

In una puchea de coreo ad tale signum. XV.

71. Munimenta Regum *Scocie* et aliorum diversorum ejusdem Regni ut de cartis Regiis per Reges ejusdem Terre, diversis factis, ac et cartis et scriptis diversorum Magnatum et aliorum dicte Terre, unam cum (*sic* Qy. unacum?) aliis variis memorandis, de quibus hic mentio expresse fieri non potuit pre (*sic*) confusione scripture et propter eorum minimum valorem, set sunt reposita, videlicet, in duobus forceriis de coreo, ferro ligatis, in quatuor hanaperiis, de coreo nigro cooptis, in ix. forceriis ligneis, in xviii. hanaperiis de virgis, et in xxxii. pixidibus, preter alia munimenta et memoranda ejusdem Terre antea isto libro per divisas perticulas et diversa signa, atque secundum ordinem numeri et secundum eorum facultates intrata et registrata.

In magna huchea ad tale signum. XVI.

AFTER FLODDEN.

SCOTLAND for years had been ringing with the armourer's hammer, and loud with the thud of the adze of the shipwright. In the fatal autumn of 1513, her preparations were ended: the hour for proof had arrived. Her fleet, headed by *The Great Michael*, with its wooden walls full ten feet thick, sailed away over the horizon and out of history, and her devoted army followed its quixotic and ungovernable king across the border to death and deathless fame. The general facts of the battle are agreed upon, and the death-roll of the feudal leaders is tolerably complete. The names of the valiant retainers who fell around them will never be known, but there is neither peer nor peasant to-day of Scottish descent who can say that no ancestor of his lies in Flodden Field. How the dread rumour of disaster reached Edinburgh, how the provisional government of city fathers, in the absence of their provost and magistrates with the army, ordered the weeping women out of the streets and into the churches to pray, and set themselves to put the town in a posture of defence; how the next Scots Parliament which met was a parliament of boys—are all matters of familiar history. But the strength of the self-possession and resolution of the country in its distress and danger is not to be ascertained without reading the Register of the Acts of the Lords of the Council, who carried on the affairs of the state, both legislative and executive, through that period. These *Acta Dominorum Concilii* are still in manuscript, and almost or altogether unknown to our historians, and yet they contain the only official record of the government of that date. They exhibit the Lords sitting from day to day and attending to their duties, both routine and exceptional, with the equanimity which belongs to times of profound peace and security. Among the records of their ordinary decisions, regarding civil disputes between individual citizens, are the entries of their public acts, and of a considerable number of private proceedings arising out of the battle of Flodden. They arrange for the immediate coronation of the young king; for the issue of brieves of inquest of heirs of those who had been slain, with special provision for those cases where the sheriff of the county to whom the brieves should have been addressed had also been slain. They order the munitions of war, which were in Dumbarton Castle, to be taken to Glasgow, and thence to Stirling. They record the complaint of the Governor of the Castle of Edinburgh that that castle is not in a proper condition for defence, etc.; they send an embassy to Denmark to ask help for the country; they provide for a council of four to be constantly in waiting on the queen; they ordain the holding of weaponshaws, and give a licence to the possessors of spoil taken on the battlefield to sell it in any Scottish burgh they like, but they make it treason to sell it in England; they sit on the questions of ransom, etc., etc.

The Rev. Walter Macleod has selected, and contributes the following extracts from this Register. ED.

EXTRACTS CONCERNING FLODDEN FROM THE *Acta Dominorum Concilii*, 1513-14.

Acta Dominorum Concilii, vol. xxvi. fol. 2.—[At T]wesilhauch in Northumberland the xxiiij day of August the yer of [God] j^m v^c and xiij yer. It is statut and ordanit be the kings hienes witht avis of al his lords being thar for the tyme in his ost in this forme as efter follois, that is to say gif ony man beis slane or hurt to deid in the kingis army and ost be Inglismen, or deis in his army, enduring the tyme of his ost, his airis sall have his ward relief and mariage of the king free, dispensand with his aige quhat eild that ever he be of and ordanis the kingis lettres to be direct herupon to the effect forsaid necessar as efferis: Extractum.

Ibid. fol. 3. Apud Striveling xix° Sep[tember anno] domini millesimo quingentesimo decimo [tertio].

Sederunt Jacobus archiepiscopus Glasguensis Williclmus episcopus Abirdonensis D[avid] episcopus Candide Case Jacobus episcopus Dunblanensis Andreas Cathinensis David Lismorensis Eduardus Orkadensis Archibaldus comes Augusie Alexander comes de Huntlie Joannes Colinus Johannes Hugo Willelmus et Johannes comites de Mortoun, Ergyle, Levinax, Eglintoun, Glencarn et Athole Johannes prior Sancte Andree Georgius abbas Sancte Crucis Robertus de Pasleto, Robertus de Melros Patricius de Cambuskenneth Alexander dominus Hume Willielmus Ruthvane Laurencius dominus Oliphant.

The Lordis forsaid thinks expedient and it pleis the quenis grace that the king our souerane lord be crounit on Wednisday nixtocum the xxj day of this instant moneth of September in the kirk of the Castell of Striveling and that my lord of Glesgw be executor officii and provyde therfor and that all uther necessar provisioun be maid for the said coronatioun againe the said day.

Sederunt.

Thir ar the Lordis ordanit be the generale counsell to sitt uponn the daily counsell for all materis occurrand in the realme or ane sufficient part of thame and euer thre spirituale and thre temporale of thir as it lykis the queyn to command.

The Secretar
The Clerk of Register

The Archibischop of Glesgw
The Bischop of Abirdene
The Bischop of Galloway
The Bischop of Dunblane
The Bischop of Caithnes
The Bischop of Ergyle
The Bischop of Orknay
The Prior of Sanctandrois
The Abbot of Halyruidhous
The Abbot of Paslay
The Provest of Sanct Gelis kirk
The Dene of Dunkeld
The Dene of Glesgw
The Provest of Crechtoun
Master David Setoun
The official of Lothiane

The Erle of Angus
The Erle of Huntlie
The Erle of Mortoun
The Erle of Ergyle
The Erle of Craufurd
The Erle of Levinax
The Erle of Eglintoun
The Erle of Glencarn
The Lord Chaumerlane
The Erle of Athole
The Lord Ruthvane
The Lord Drummond
The Lord Forbes
[The names of two noblemen and two lairds have been obliterated.]

Ibid. fol. 4.   Apud Striveling xxij Septembris, anno.

Memorandum—That the Lordis of Counsell ordains that brevis be gevin of inqueist till every persone that had thair faderis or freyndis slane in this last feild in Northumbirland in this forme that is to say gif the Shireffis of the schyris quhar the landis lyis war slane in the said feild that brevis be directit till shireffis be speceale commissioun of the Chancelary in dew forme as efferis with all clawsis necessar and gif the shireffis of the schyris quhar the saidis landis lyis be on live that the saidis brevis be directit to thai said shireffis and thair deputis without ony uther speciale deliverance or ony commissiounis for the serving of the saidis brevis quhat aige that ever thai be of efter the forme of the act and statut maid be the kingis graice at Twesill in Northumbirland with avis of all his lordis being thar for the tyme and ordains the samyn to have the strentht of act gevin in jugement.

Ibid. fol. 4.   Apud Edinburgh xxvj[th] Septembris.

Memorandum, that lettres be written at the quenis instance and lordis for the Lord Maxwell to comper befor the lordis in continent to avis apon certane materis concerning the gud and wele of the Realme.

The quhilk day the saidis lordis ordanis as tuicking certane castellis and housis takin be certane That is to say the hous of Uchiltre Cumnok, Duchell and Langnewtoun That lettres be written of the kingis tuiching the hous of Uchiltre to David Coluile and James Coluile, and for the hows of Cumnok tyll Johnne[1] Cuthbert Dunbar of Interkin and Patrik his bruther And for the hous of Duchell to George Liell And for the hous of Langnewtoun to Adam Ruthirfurd and to the remanent of the personis being in the saids housis for the tyme or that happinis to be in the sam-mynis ay and quhill the deliverance of the saidis howsis chargeing thaim at the saids howsis or be opin proclamatioun at the mercat corsis of the principall burrowis of the schyris quhare the saidis howsis ar situat becaus

_____
[1] 'Johnne' is written above 'Cuthbert.'

thai have attemptit and takin thir howsis in contrar of our soverane Lordis proclamatioun of gud mynd laitly maid quhilk was under the pane of tresone that nane of his liegis suld mak ony slauchtir reiff spoliatioun revising of wemen nor uthir public innormyteis agains utheris now in the tyme of his host, cumand therto nor returnand therfra, and becaus the said host was not perfitlie completit nor his liegis gane hame therfra thir atemptatis ar committit, that therfor thai deliver and caus be deliverit the saidis howsis to the awnaris therof ther aieris tutoris procuratoris factoris or beraris and presentaris of thir lettres in continent efter thai be chargeit undir the said pane of treasone and that nane fortefy supple nor vittale ony of the saidis howsis nor personis being therintill under the said pane and als at the personis takaris and intromettaris with the said howses be summond to comper befor the king and his Lordis of Counsell to ane certane day lymmitt to thaim till ansuer in it at salbe said to thaim for the taking of the saidis howsis and in all uther thingis on that behalve and ordanis our soverane lordis lettres be direct herapon.

Ibid. fol. 6.—Memorandum In primis as tuiching the gunnis puldir bullettis pikkis mattokis and other munitiouns send be the king of France to the Kings grace it is ordanit be the Lordis of Counsell that the comptrollar sall bring all the saidis munitionis be watir furth of Dumbritane to Glesgw and that my Lordis of Glesgw, Paslay, and Newbottill and utheris that has thair landis nixt adjacent cary the said munitionis furth of Glesgw to Striveling and thair to remane quhill the quenis grace and the Lordis avis quhat sall remane thair and quhar the laif salbe cariit to.

Ibid. fol. 9 —The quhilk day the Lordis has divisit and ordanit that ane man be send to the King of Denmark that is to say —— till expone to him how this cais is hapnit and to undirstand quhat help we may lippin to him for the help and defence of this realme now as the cais standis.

Ibid. fol. 9.—Item it is thocht expedient be the said lordis that this Franche knycht and the remanent of thame now being in Edinburgh remane still quhill word cum fra the King of France and in the menetyme that thair expensis be furnist be the thesaurar.

Ibid. fol. 10.—Thir ar the Lordis ordanit to remane daily with the queny's grace to gif hir counsell in all materis concerning the wele of the realme and four or thre.

The spirituale lordis	The temporale lordis
In primis My Lord of Glesgw chancelar	The Erle of Angus
	The Erle of Huntlie
My Lord of Dunkeldin	The Erle of Craufurd
My Lord of Abirdene	The Erle of Ergyle
My Lord of Dunblane	The Erle of Glencarn
My Lord of Galloway	The Lord Hume
My Lord of Caithnes	The Lord Borthuic
My Lord bischop of Ergyle	The Lord Drummond
My Lord of Orknay	The Lord Ruthven
My Lord prior of Sanct Androis	The Lord Erskin
The Provest of Sanct Gelis kirk	The Lord Lindesay of Byris.
The Dene of Dunkeld	
The Dene of Glasgw	
The Provest of Creichtoun	Witht the officiaris of the Court

And four or thre at the leist of Ilk stait of thir to remane contineualy apoun the queyn for gud rwle to be kepit within the realm and thai personis to be nemmit and sall begyn now and to continew ay and quhill utheris be nemmyt and the nominatioun of the said persouns of the first diet to be at the quenys plesour and to remane the space of xl dais and efter the ryning of the xl dais uther iiij or iij of ilk stait to be nemmit and remane elykwys and sa furtht quhill all the personis nemmyt heir have remanyt xl dais and than to begyn agane.

Ibid. fol. 12.   Apud Pertht xxix Octobris.

Item as tuiching of the article maid for the defence of the bordouris and resisting of the Inglismen, it is statut and ordanit be the Lordis of Counseli that wappynschawnis be maid in every schire of the realm, and that letres be direct to the shireflis therapon, and at thai caus all the kingis liegis within thar bowndis to reforme thair harnes and abilzementis for weir and mak thame fensable wapinnis sic as speris, leitht axis, and Jedwart stavis, halbertis, and gud twa handit swerdis, and all uther neidfull wapinnis for resisting of the Innymyis of Ingland and defens of the realme and bordouris, and to be reddy at all howris quhen thai ar warnit for defens of the samyn as neid beis, and that balis be maid upon all partis of the bordouris, in Lothiane, and all uther partis adjacent therto as the auld use and consuetud has bene in tymes bygane for the warnyng of Scottis men in the resisting of thair inimyis.

Ibid. fol. 12.   Apud Pertht xxix Octobris.

We do yow to wit that forsamekle as now at the last feild of Northhumbirland thair was divers gudis and geir recouerit be our liegis, sic as palzounis, harnes, jakkis, crelis, rubouris, and uther necessaris for osting, quhilk as we understand was leifful to thaim to do and necessar to this our realme in plane feild, quhar the personis that aucht the said geir, part war slane, part takin, and part removit therfra, throw the quhilk thai mycht not cum to thair awin ger forsaid, and without our saidis liegis had recoverit the said gudis and geir our inymyis of Ingland had takin the samin with thame, certifying onto our liegis forsaid that it salbe leiffull to thame to cum and sell and mak lefull merchandice of the said geir recouerit as said is in ony burgh of our realme or in ony uther placis as thai think expedient within the samin without ony accusattioun of ony juge, spirituale or temporale, therfor, praying thaim and als chargeing that thai bring the said gudis and stuff recouerit in the said feild till all burrowis and merkatis quhar thai lyke best within our said realme, sa that our liegis may by therof and be furnist to thair ois and utilite, and that nane sell sic thingis in Ingland or to Inglismen under the pane of tresoun, and that lettres be writtin to my Lord Chamerlane chargeing him that he be opin proclamatioun in all placis neidfull within the boundis of his office command and charg that nane of our souerane lordis liegis tak apon hand to mak ony merchandice with Inglismen or sell thame ony maner of stuff on the Calfhill or in ony uther place within this realme or utouth under the said pane of tresoun, and this ye do and ever ilk ane of yow as ye will report speciall thank therfor.

Ibid. fol. 13.—Patrick M'Lellane of Gelstoun was slain at Flodden. (In petition of Isabel Dunbar, his widow.)

Ibid. fol. 16.—14 *November* 1513. Anent the term assigned to Walter Cellar and William Bow to have heard and seen them decerned to pay to David Bonar the sum of 14 angell nobillis for their ransomes, that is 7 angellis nobillis, because the said David became surety for them to their captors, which should have been paid at a certain day in England and lyes in hostage thereof, and failed of payment at the said day, together with an English grote for the said David's expenses each day: The said David compeired by his procurator, and the saids Walter and William being lawfully summoned, oftymes called, and not compeared; the Lords assign the last day of November instant to compeir and prove the payment of the said ransoms.

Ibid. fol. 31.—10 *January* 1513-14. Memorandum to consider how the strenthis and castellis of Fast-castell and Dunbar salbe provydit in men, artalzery, and vittale, and to mak the said castellis to be providit with sic maner of provision in all possible hast, and the captanis and keparis of the said castellis be send for in all hast that it may be understandin be thame quhat the Quenis grace and lordis may lippen to.

Ibid. fol. 33.—10 *January* 1513-14. Memorandum anent the furnising of the castell and fortalice of Fasteastell. The Lordis being avisit with the captane therof ordanis ane pece of gret artalze be send to the said castell that will brek bulwerkis, togiddir with certane gun powdir for the defence and kepin of the samin.

Ibid. fol. 7.—27 *January* 1513-14. George E. of Rothes became surety for the relict of David Allerdes of Scatoquhy who died in the King's Army.

Ibid. fol. 11.—31 *January* 1513-14. Robert Gordon of the Glen became surety for the relict of Gilbert Ferguson who died in King's Army.

Ibid. fol. 33.—Madame, unto your gude grace and to the reverend and nobill lordis of Counsale, humelie schewis, I, your servitour, Patrik Crechtoun of Cranstoun Reddall, knycht, Capitane of the Castell of Edinburgh, That quhare as your grace and Lordschipis knawis the said castell, quhilk is ane of the principale strenthis of the realme, is now desolat of artalzery and uther thingis necessar for defens and keping therof, and now lately Monsieur de Lebawty and Robert Borthuik hes of your causing visit the said castell and hes devisit bulwerkis and trinchis to be made before the place and siclike within the castell to be stuffit with men and artalzery for defens therof in tyme of assalt, gif ony beis maid be our Inymis, The quhilk devise without it be put to executioun and fulfillit in deid is in vane, heirfore it will ples your gude grace and Lordschipis, for honour and proffet of the Kingis hienes and his realme, to caus werkmen be put incontinent to fulfill the said devise as salbe schewin to thame be Robert Borthuik and uther wismen sic as ye ples to assigne therto, and that without delay, sen thar is gret werk to be maid baith within the castell and utouth, and the tyme is schort, for the symmer sesoun approchis fast, and als that ye will provide in tyme for furnissing of the said castell with men, vittalis, artalzery, fewell, and sic uther thingis as is necessar for keping therof in tyme of were, and als that ye will caus me to have pament of my pensioun assignit for keping of the said castell, for the forest stedis that war assignit to the payment therof ar layt waste and my gudis that war theron reft and stollin, and I man now in tyme of trubill and of the kingis less age mak for largear coft upone the keping of the said hous in wachmen, garatouris, portaris, and utheris servandis, than wes maid theron of before, and that ye will avise heiron in tyme and do that accordis to be done without delay, ffor I am and salbe reddy with my kyn and freindis to do heirin all that accordis me to do eftir my power, sa that God willing thar sall na falt be fund in me And your ansuere heirupone.

Ibid. fol. 50.—13 *March* 1513-14. Anent the complant maid be William Tait apon William Turnbule, that quhar the said William Tait was in the feild with our souerane lord, quhem God assolze, and deliverit his hors quhilk was wortht x merkis in keping to David Strachachin, servand to his maister for the tyme, Maister Thomas Diksone, and in the tyme of the feild the said Wylliam Turnbill come and reft the said hors fra the said David masterfully at his awin hand, howbeit he knew that the said hors pertenit to the said William Tait, lyk as at mair lentht is contenit in the said complant. Baith the saidis partiis being personally present, the said Williame Turnbule grantit that he tuk the said hors and efter at he was cumand fra the said feild he was strykin fra the said hors and the samyn tayne fra him, Tharfor the lordis assignis to the said William Tait the xiiij day of Merche instant to preif at the said hors was reft fra the said David Strachachyn be the said William, and the avale and price of the said hors, and the partys ar warnit heirof apud acta, and to heir the witnesses sworn.

Ibid. fol. 52.—Anent the terme assignit be the lordis of Counsale to William Tait to preif the availe of ane gray hors pertening to him, and takin be William Trumbule, seruand to umquhile ane maist reverend fader in God, Alexander, archbischop of Sanctandrois, for the tyme, fra David Strathachin, seruand to umquhill Maister Thomas Dikson, Dene of Lestalrig, in the last feild in Norththumbirland quhilk had the said hors in keping, and withhaldyne be the said William Trumbule fra the said William Tait lyk as at mair lenth is contenit in the act gevin therapon of befor. The said William Tait being personali present, and the said William Trumbule being lauchfully summond to this actioun oftimes callit and nocht comperit, the partiis present richtis resounis allegatiouns and productioun of witness being hard sene and understand, and therwith being riplie avisit, the Lordis of counsell directis and deliveris that the said William Trumbule sall deliver and restoir again to the said William Tait the said gray hors als gud as he was the tyme at he was takin in the said feild, and failzeing therof sall content and pay to the said William Tait aucht merkis usuale money of Scotland for the said hors lyk as was sufficiently previt befor the saidis lordis, and that lettres be direct to compell and distrenze the said William Trumbule his landis and gudis therfor as efferis.

Ibid. fol. 90.—' At Striveling. the secund day of June the yeir of God, jᵐ vᶜ and xiiij yeiris, in presence of the queinis grace, and the Lordis of Counsale ' therein mentioned ' has decretit and ordanit in the generale counsale haldin at Striveling day and yeir forsaid, quhar ony personis havand takkis or malingis of the kingis grace, or of ony utheris thair lordis and masteris spirituale or temporale duelland apon the ground and takkis, and cumand with thair masteris to the feild that thai have the takkis off. or with their balzeis or deputis in thair name, war slane with the said kingis grace or ther masteris under the kingis baner at the last feild in Northumbreland, or happinis to be slane under our said souerane lordis baner in tymis cuming in ony place in the defence of the realme, his wiff and eldest son sall have his takkis and stedingis quhilkis he had of the kingis grace, or of his lord and master for the termis of thre yeiris nixt efter the terme of Witsonday immediat following the slaughter of the said man or persoun that happinis to be slane under the kingis baner, and falzeing of his wif and eldest son, his second son, and failzeand of his secund sonn, his thrid sonn, and sa furth for als mony sonnis as the man has, and falzeand of his wyf and sonys as said is his nearest kynsman that is able to do the kingis grace service, and his master to have the said tak for the space forsaid, providand alwayis that quha evir happynnis to succeid to the said takkis be deces of this man be the space of thre yeris as said is sall find ane sufficient persoune to do the king and his maister service in the kingis weris quhen thai are requirit therto thai payand therfor thair dewiteis mailis and gressomes aucht and wont as efferis.' Extractum, etc.

Ibid. fol. 96.—15 *July* 1514. Anent the summonds raisit at the instance of David Bonar against Walter Sellar that quhar the said David was hurt and takin prisoner in the last feild in Northumbirland be Johne Smyth, Robert Mortoun and thair complices Inglismen, And als the said Walter and ane callit Bulle was takin with the sammyn and maid thair ransomis for xvj angell noblis and xij grottis, and the said Walter causit the said David to be sourtie for payment thairof or ellis to entir himself again within xv dais and oblist him to keip the said David scaithles therof and to refound his expenses sa lang as he remanit presonere for him, and as yit the said Waltir has nothir payt his ransome nor enterit again to freiht the said David as he was oblist quharthrow the said David was haldin in presone for the said Walter fra the tyme of the feild quhill Monnday in Pasche olk last by past extending to vij monethis with the mair lyk as at mair lentht is contenit in the said summondis. The said David being personaly present and the said Walter being lauchfully summond to this action oft times callit and nocht comperit, The Lordis of Counsell decretis and deliveris that the said Walter Sellar sall content and pay to the said David Boner, Sextene angell noblis and ten grotis Inglis, becaus the said Walter causit the said David to cum sourtie for the sammyn, and als sall content and pay to the said David ten angell noblis for his expensis maid the tyme that he lay in presone as sourtie for the said Walter be the space of vij monethis with the mair, according to the said Walteris promit and oblissing maid to the said David theruppon the tyme he fred him furtht of presone as was clerly previt befor the saidis lordis, and ordainis our Souerane lordis lettres to be direct to compell and distrenze the said Walter his land and gudis therefor as effeiris.

WILLIAM ERSKINE, ARCHBISHOP OF GLASGOW.
(*Vol.* xii. *p.* 62.)

I SUGGESTED in reference to this man that he was a son of James Erskine of Little Sauchie and Balgownie. J. Maitland Thomson, Esq., Curator Hist. and Antiq. Dept., General Register House, Edinburgh, has most kindly furnished me with proof of the correctness of my view, taken from the MS. Calendar of the Register of Deeds: 'Archibald Prestoun of the Valafeild and James Prestoun his son and apparent heir, on one part; and James Erskyne of Lytill Sauchy and Gene Erskyne his daughter (and Robert Erskyne, son and apparend heir to the said James, and William Erskyne, second son to the said James and persone of Campsie, cautioners), on the other.' Contract of marriage (between James Prestoune and Gene Erskyne), 2nd April 1567 [vol. ix. fol. 103]. It should be possible to discover the names of his wife and children.

A. W. CORNELIUS HALLEN.

OLD SCOTS BANK NOTES.
(*Continued from p.* 73.)
Douglas, Heron and Co., Bankers in Air.

AFTER the lapse of more than a century the recollection of the hopes wrapped up with the Ayr Bank-note when it first appeared is dead and gone, but the memory of the sorrows which it brought in its train is still alive in the families of the south-west of Scotland which were so unfortunate as to be principally connected with it.

In the year 1769—a time of some financial uncertainty, when the private banks in Scotland were unable to indulge in large commercial ventures, and the public banks were declining to do so—there appeared the firm of 'Douglas, Heron and Company, Bankers in Air,' known for short as 'The Air Bank.' The partners of this concern 'considering that the business of Banking, when carried on on proper principles, is of great public utility, particularly to the commerce, manufactures, and agriculture of a country, at the same time that it may yield a reasonable profit to the Bankers concerned in it; and likewise considering the necessity there is, in the present situation of the country, that a Banking Company should be erected on proper principles at this juncture, have therefore resolved to establish a Banking Company upon a solid, creditable, and respectable footing.' So began the preamble of the Contract of Copartnery of the Ayr Bank. The Duke of Queensberry and Dover headed the list of subscribing partners, which contained the names of peers, landowners, and men of every profession save one, and that exception, says an expert in banking (Graham, —*The £1 Note*) was the profession of banker. The Bank opened its doors on 6th November 1769, and there has never been a doubt that the great body of its original shareholders were actuated by the laudable desire of, it may be increasing their private incomes, but of doing so by engaging in a business of public utility. With the prestige of such distinguished names on its share list, and a subscribed capital of upwards of £160,000, a career of both public and private advantage lay open before the Company. But in less than three years the Ayr Bank came to grief in a manner which was disgraceful to its managers and disastrous to its shareholders. 'That a Company established on so solid a bottom,' exclaims the Shareholders' Committee of Inquiry appointed after the fall (*The Precipitation and Fall of Douglas, Heron and Co.*, 4to, Edin. 1778, p. 2) . . . 'and embarking on a business which, when conducted with any tolerable degree of prudence, cannot from its nature be attended with great risk, should, by the transactions of a very few years, have incurred so enormous a loss as not only to exhaust the whole of so large a capital, but to require the additional aid of a very large sum, the amount yet unknown, is an instance which it was hardly to be imagined could have sprung from the enterprise of so narrow a country, and of which perhaps there are few examples in any country.'

It may easily be true that the shareholders whose contributions to the stock of the Company made its operations possible, were actuated by honourable and sensible motives, but it appears to be equally true that from the beginning they were in the hands of a gang of at first designing, afterwards of reckless, speculators.

The Committee of Inquiry are naturally loth to admit that the shareholders were duped from the beginning. 'The general error in the conduct of the affairs of this Banking Company seems,' they say, 'to have been that of over-trading and endeavouring to force a circulation of the Company's paper beyond the natural limits. . . . Hence may be derived the source of our calamities.' But when the Committee proceeds to details, it formulates a series of charges against the management of the Company of such a nature that, if justified, leave little doubt that whatever the first false step may have been, the ruin of the Bank did not wait on errors of judgment in over-trading or over-issue of paper, but was immediately due to actions of the managers which cannot be called banking operations, however misguided.

The business of the Bank was conducted at three centres, of which Ayr was the principal. Edinburgh and Dumfries were the other two. At the very start of the Bank large credits were granted, without security, to a limited and favoured circle of traders by the Ayr branch. The other branches protested at first, but ultimately followed suit, and all three practised 'an open disregard, not only of the principles of the co-partnery, but of the express and positive rules and regulations laid down for the managers.' In each of the departments of banking—cash accounts, accounts current, discount of bills, bills of exchange, and circulation of paper—the Committee bring specific charges against the management. As to the last they say: 'It seems to have been a favourite topic at all the offices to endeavour not only to force a circulation of the Company's paper beyond the natural limits which must always regulate and confine such operations, but also to supplant the circulation of other banking companies. In this view it appears to have been a common practice to give out to particular persons, without receiving any proper security, large sums in the Company's notes to be circulated by them in different parts of the country, and the value to be returned within a limited time in bills of exchange, specie, or the notes of other banking companies.

'This dangerous and unconstitutional practice was carried to great excess; and the consequence of so idle an expedient was such as might have been expected. The Company's paper, forced into the circle in this manner, was immediately picked up by the agents of other banking companies, and generally came back upon the Company to be exchanged for other value, long before the returns were made by the circulators; and by this means the Company, instead of reaping any advantage or relief from this sort of traffic, was actually a real sufferer by it, independent of the danger and risk attending such loose dealings. It was beneath the dignity, as well as adverse to the interest, of a banking company acting upon fair principles to resort to so mean an expedient; but we find that it was likewise very soon shamefully abused, and converted into an additional mode of private accommodation . . . except in a very few instances it was issued without any visible authority at all, not to mention the authority of a legal quorum . . .'

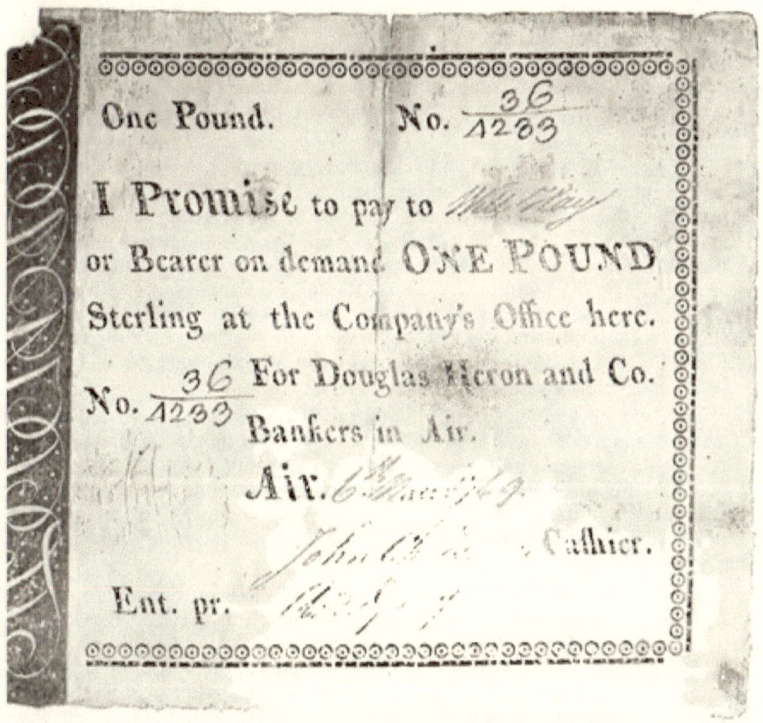

When it was seen that the Ayr Bank was to follow the fate of several of the weaker or worse managed concerns, the Edinburgh banks, anxious to minimise the panic which would ensue, advertised that they would cash its notes. But this measure, though beneficent, did not materially soften the lot of the unfortunate shareholders. It has been calculated that half of the lands of Ayrshire changed hands in consequence of the calls which were made to pay the bank's creditors.

The note which is reproduced above is a specimen of the first issue of the Bank, dated 6th November 1769. The full length of the note is about 5¼ inches. The water-mark consists of a winged heart and the capital letters D. H. & Co.

A HIGHLAND TOUR IN 1814.

THE following Directions were found among the papers of Robert Cadell of Ratho (Sir Walter Scott's publisher, *b.* 1788, *d.* 1849), and are docqueted in Mr. Cadell's handwriting, '1814, A. Pact's Directions for a Highland Journey.'   J. H. S.

DIRECTIONS TO MR. CADELL FOR A *FIVE DAYS'* TOUR THROUGH THE HIGHLANDS OF SCOTLAND.

1st day.—Breakfast at N. Queensferry—dine at Perth, and if convenient walk to the top of the rock of Kinnoul, from whence you have a full view of the Carse of Gowry and all the view in the vicinity of the city—drive to Dunkeld, afternoon, and if possible walk to the top of Kingsbarns, the evening view will well repay you—you must by all means see Ossian's Hall.

2nd day.—Engage a chaise to Kenmore, there is none at the half-way house—get out early and take the road by Inver to Balnaguard, where breakfast—the whole of the ride beautiful and interesting, in particular the house and Rock of Kinaird. If you have time, there is a most romantic fall, very little known, about half a mile up the burn from Balnaguard. Alight at Aberfeldie and view the falls of Moness. The whole of your ride to Kenmore is beautiful and picturesque. Dine at Kenmore, and drive to Killin that night, though late. Cause the postilion to take the south side of the loch, and alight by the way and walk to the Earl's Hermitage—it is worth your while.

3rd day.—I find you must abandon the idea of going from Killin by Loch Lomond. There is a part of the road at present so bad that even the Highlanders can only pass with their carts half laden; besides, you have nothing in the world to see, and you miss the fine scenery of Loch Earn and Loch Ludnich, which will never do. From Killin then breakfast at Loch-Earn-head and dine at Callander—visit the bridge of Braklin, afternoon.

4th day.—Rise early—post it to the Trossachs and breakfast at Stewart's house there—view the scene and sail to the lonely isle. Return with the chaise to the bridge of Turk—dismiss it and walk across the hill to Aberfoyle to dinner. You have a tolerable good path, and will get a fine view of the whole scenery about Loch Lomond, Loch Ard, Loch Katherine, etc., etc. You may lodge at Aberfoyle, or walk a short stage in the evening by the loch of Monteith toward Stirling. This is all that you can possibly accomplish, if not more.

5th day.—Return to Edin.

THE MEMBERS OF THE EDINBURGH MERCHANTS COMPANY—1687.

The MS. of the following early list is in the Privy Council Papers. The meaning of the asterisks does not appear.—M.

ANE EXACT LIST OF ALL THOSE WHO ARE MATRICULAT IN THE COMPANIE OF MERCHANDS OF EDENBURGH PRECEIDING THE TWENTIE FYFTH DAY OF JUNE J^M VJ^C EIGHTIE SEVEN YEARS.

A

Harie Anderson.
James Alstowne.
James Arbuckles.
James Aitkine.
John Armstrange.
Mr Wm Allan.
John Auld.
Andrew Aitkine.

B

Mr Rot. Blackwood.
William Blackwood.
Robert Blackwood.
James Broadfoott.
Bailzie Brand.
Hugh Blair.
Robert Browne.
James Bawden.
Sr Rot Baird.
Stephen Bruntsfeild.
William Beck.
George Bell.
John Browne.
Hugh Blaikie.
George Begg.
Andrew Browne.
Robert Bogle.
Geo: Browne.
James Browne.

C

Bailzie Chemcellar.
William Cleiland.
Ab. James Cleiland, elder.
John Chatto.
Charles Charters.
Alex^r Crwickshankis.
Georg Clerk, elder.
George Craighead.
Tho: Crichton.
Alex^r Clerk.
Hugh Cuninghame.
Hugh Campbell.
Alex^r Campbell.
James Clerk.

John Corsbie.
Wm Corsar.
Robert Campbell.
John Clerk.
Alex^r Chamcellar.
John Colquhowne.
*William Cockburne.
James Corsbie.
*Robert Cuninghame.
*Patrick Crawford.
Mr Hugh Craig.
Robert Coventrie.
Walter Cheislie.

D

Sr Geo: Drumond.
Mr John Duncan.
George Drumond.
John Drumond——
Laurence Donaldsone.
Arch: Duncan.
Robert Drysdaill.
James Dowglas.

E

Hendry Elphingstone.
David Eistone.
James Edmingstoun.
Charles Erskine.

F

Sr James Fleiming.
Thomas Fisher.
David Falconer.
James Fergus.
James Fleiming.
Alex^r Fergusone.
Robert Finning.
Robert Fleming.
David Forrest.

G

Bailzie Grahame.
Ab. William Gordone, ex.
Robert Gibsone.

James Gibb.
John Gray.
Lawrence Gellatlay.
John Gawdie.
*Charles Gray.
William Gladstons.
John Glendinning.
Robert Griersone.
Tho: Goodshir.

H

John Hay.
John Handysyde.
George Home.
Arch: Hamiltone, elder.
John Huntar.
John Hendersone.
Alexr Heriott.
John Hepburne.
Arch: Hamilton, younger.
*James Heart.
William Hopkirk.
*William Huttone.

I

Pat: Johnstone, elder.
Josias Johnstone.
Archd Johnstone.
John Jolly.
Pat: Johnston, younger.
Andrew Irvine.
Mr Geo: Jolly.

K

Sr Tho: Kennedy.
John Ker.

L

Tho: Laurie.
John Litle.
Mr Charles Lumsden.
George Lawsone.
Alexr Lawrie.
John Lindsay, elder.
James Loch.
Colline Lawder.
George Liddell.
John Lamb.

James Lithgow.
[A name here rendered
illegible by the fold of the
paper.]
Walter Learmont.

M

Duncan McIntoshe.
William Menzies.
Samwell McCleland.
Robert Miller.
William Montgomrie.
David Montier [or vir].
*George Mosman.
John Marjorbanks.
John Moore.
Edward Marjorbanks.
John Miller.
John Marshall.
George McKenzie.
Thomas Montgomerie.
John Murray.
John McIlwrath.
Henrie Mein.
*William McHendry.
Robert Murray.
*William Mosman.

N

Bailzie Nicolsone.
Alexr Neilsone, elder.
Andrew Neill.
Alexr Neilson, younger.
David Neish.
John Neill.
James Newall.
John Naismith.
George Nicoll.

P

Dean of Gild Prince.
William Pattowne.
John Pattersone.

R

James Rowe.
James Reid.
William Reid.

John Ritchie.
William Ramsay.
*Thomas Row.
James Ritchie.

S

David Spense.
George Smellum.
Walter Stewart, elder.
William Stevinsone.
James Simpsone.
James Smeittone.
Gilbert Stewart.
*Robert Smith, merch'.
Robert Smith, wryter.
George Saudry.
Thomas Scott.
John Simpsone.
James Spense.
William Smeittone.

T

John Thomson, elder.
John Thomson, younger.

James Tait.
John Tait.
John Tailzeir.
Jo: Trotter.

W

Thomas Wyllie.
George Warrander.
George Wedderburne.
Robert Walwood.
Arch: Walker.
John Wallace.
Alex' Wright.
Henry Wyllie.
Alex' Watsone.
*John Wright.

V

Thesawer Young.
Joseph Young.
William Yowng.
Thomas Yowng.

Dan'll Mackpherson.

LETTER TO THE EDITOR.

JOHN GRAHAM OF KILBRIDE,

OR BROTHERS WITH SAME CHRISTIAN NAME.

(*See vol.* xi, *p.* 108, *and vol.* xii, *pp.* 33 *and* 36.)

'B.' is inclined to take too much for granted; and, despite his five quotations, there are people who do not believe that there are 'numerous instances' in old Scottish families of two brothers with the same Christian name being alive at the same time—*legitimate* brothers, that is. Of the five instances he gives, there is but one with any show of reason—Seton, the others are unsupported by the slightest evidence; and the opinion of Mr. Riddell, who was the greatest legal antiquary in Europe, that such duplicate names denote illegitimacy in one or the other, is of more weight than 'B.'s' to the contrary, unless he has a great deal better evidence to adduce, which does not appear to be the case. Even the Seton instance is more than suspicious. The second Lord Gordon (Alexander de Seton, first Earl of Huntly), was thrice married according to old genealogists, but the present Lord Huntly in *The Records of Aboyne* calls the first marriage in question on tolerably good grounds. It is with the two other marriages we are concerned. It is quite clear that there was an Alexander by both—Alexander, the only son of the first, and Alexander, the second of the other, whose elder brother-german was George. But it was George, the first-born of the last marriage, and not his elder half-brother Alexander, who succeeded to the peerage. This fact at once fixes attention, and at the first blush

I

suggests the illegitimacy of Alexander, a suspicion by no means dispelled
on closer examination. The elder Alexander was son to the first Earl of
Huntly by Egidia Hay. heiress of Tullybody, Touch, etc., and the charter
by King James I. in 1426 settled these lands on the Earl and the said
Egidia and the longer liver of them, with remainder to *the legitimate heirs
of Egidia*. If Alexander was beyond doubt born in wedlock he was
clearly entitled to such lands, and no question of heirship to them could
have arisen. But a question did arise, and Douglas in the *Baronage*
(p. 167), tells us that there were 'several contests' between Alexander and
George (son of Elizabeth Crichton), about the succession to those lands.
Why was this if the legitimacy of Alexander was not called in question?
It could be the only ground. And the Earldom of Huntly was put past
Alexander. What also favours the suggestion is, that although the title
Earl of Huntly, by a new grant in 1449 descended to George, that of
Lord Gordon did not, the undoubted heir to which, were he legitimate,
being Alexander : but the Barony of Gordon became dormant *or extinct* at
his father's death in 1470. Neither Alexander, his son, nor their
descendants made any pretence to it. Mr. George Seton, in his
sumptuous work *The Family of Seton*, bears testimony to there being
irregularity. On page 381, he says the Earl of Huntly was married, *before*
8th January 1426, to Egidia Hay, somehow overlooking what on page
378 he had previously stated, that in 1427 a charter was granted by
James I. to him (the Earl), and Egidia or Giles de Haya, daughter and
heiress of the deceased John de Haya de Tullibothe, 'whom, by God's
grace, he shall marry.' There is here not alone a serious discrepancy,
but very unusual wording. The 1427 charter is not in the *Registrum
Magni Sigilli*, but that of 1426 is, and (without the testimony of the 1427
charter) it is most significant that Egidia in it is not referred to as spouse,
or as one betrothed, after the custom of the Register. It might satisfy
Lord Huntly's objection (p. 393, *Records of Aboyne*), to their having been
an earlier marriage (with Jean Keith) if we recognise—as indeed it
does not seem we can avoid doing—that singly, or in conjunction, the
references of 1426 and 1427 to Egidia point to her as having been, prior
to 1428, and probably in the lifetime of Jean, the mistress of the first Earle
of Huntly. He divorced her before 26th November 1438 ; and the
sequel is, to say the least, most curious if their son was born after their
marriage, for as per the 1426 charter he would have succeeded as ultimate
heir of his mother's estate. Yet the lands were gifted by the father, after
the mother had granted them to him *in liferent only*, to the son begotten
between them. There is another reference to Egidia which emphasises her
character for skittishness. On 7th August 1440, Egidia, Lady of Tullibody,
in her pure widowhead (she was not Huntly's widow, as he lived till 1470), for
the many faithful services rendered to her by Sir William Forbes, Knight,
grants him a charter of the lands of Achonwery with the pertinents (p. 394,
Records of Aboyne)- an unusual proceeding for a young widow who
protests her virtue. The weight of evidence favours the illegitimacy of
Alexander, which the writer does not doubt. If he were legitimate, the
succession to the Barony of Gordon is open to the Seton baronets of
Abercorn. That Alexander should keep his patrimonial name of Seton,
and not, like his undoubtedly legitimate-born brothers, take Gordon for
surname, may be taken as another piece of evidence against his legitimacy,
and of his abandonment of all right to the Barony of Gordon. Of 'B.'s'

other instances of two legitimate brothers of the same name little need be
said. Riddell disposes of the two Maurices, and the like objection holds
good in all cases where there is not direct evidence to the contrary. No
proved case presents itself in official records or family histories. Mr.
Alexander Mackenzie's great weakness is that he rarely gives any authority
for his statements, and without authorities mere modern statements on
questions genealogical are not evidence. Mr. Mackenzie gives no
authority whatever for stating (p. 76, not 108) that Kenneth was son
of the second marriage of Sir Kenneth Mackenzie of Kintail, who
died in 1491. Likewise in the Fraser case, Mr. Mackenzie says,
'Hugh, sometimes called Simon, Master of Lovat.' It is important to
have the evidence for this. It is more likely that his name in reality
was Simon, and that he on some occasion got miscalled for his
father. The same author puts a younger Hugh as fifth son, who
is not mentioned by Douglas. Where was he found? Unless Mr.
Mackenzie has old documentary proof that he was a son of the second
marriage the chances are, in event of his elder brother being Hugh and
not Simon—he could not be both—that he was a bastard if son at all of
Lord Lovat. If he was genuine, it goes to prove that his elder brother was
Simon and not Hugh. 'B.'s' last instance is Stewart of Glenbucky: but
he is without warrant for assuming that because there are two Johns
mentioned—the one as John, the other as John Beg—that the distinguishing
addition 'little' shows that both must have been alive at the same time.
'Beg' denoting a *man* of extraordinary low stature and not a little or
lesser child. Did 'B.' ever read of, say, John, father and son, being
distinguished—the first as 'more,' the second as 'beg'? Surely not,
although it would be more applicable. But, again, were two Johns proved
to be alive at the same time, Riddell's objection is to be upheld. The fatal
point is that the first Earl of Menteith would not have had a legitimate
son called John, if John Graham of Kilbride had been alive in 1478. We
find Robert II., with two sons called Robert. But one, the elder (who was
christened *John*), for State reasons *adopted* his father's name when he succeeded to the throne, abjuring that of the despicable Baliol. The reason here
is plain, and, so far from helping 'B.' in his pleading, discredits his case:
Robert, the elder, being in reality John. This is the only authentic instance
so far as made known. There may be instances, but they could have no
bearing on John of Kilbride.

A person who deliberately writes that there are few records which are
absolutely correct, and that he had never seen one, may be pitied but
cannot be helped.

'B.' has not shaken the testimony of the *Acta Dom. Concil.*, that John of
Kilbride was son *and heir* of Earl Malise in 1469, and it is a legal formula
that where words spoken or written were used they must have their
ordinary signification, unless there was something which obliged giving
them a meaning other than their ordinary meaning.

The 'crucial point' of the service of John's widow's brief of terce (in
1492) is no point at all, for had it not been for the dispute which then fell
out among several parties interested in Kilbride, she being one, it would
never have been heard of. John of Kilbride was beneath the sod, drowned
or 'witched away,' like the Rev. Mr. Kirke of Aberfoyle, before 19th April
1471, when his brother Patrick of Gartrenich (father of the second Earl
of Menteith) was son *and heir* of his father.

WALTER M. GRAHAM EASTON.

THE COMMISSARIOT REGISTER OF SHETLAND.

(*Continued from vol.* xii. *p.* 40.)

690. Laurence Stove in Garth.

691. Gilbert Sinclair in Norst, died 10th September 1641, given up by William Burgie, now spouse to Grissel Forester his relict, on behalf of Martha his daughter.

692. Janet Alexander, spouse to John Bannatyne in Hillwall, died September 1645.

693. David Sinclair in Quharne, died September 1648. William, Mary, Janet, and Barbara his children.

694. Euphane Cranstoun, spouse to Nicoll Whyte, minister of Dunrossness, died 6th June 1640. Katherine, William, Barbara, and Robert her children.

695. James Sinclair in Quendale, died 21st September 1647. Barbara Stewart his relict, Harie and Robert his children.

696. William Smyth in Lie, died March 1648.

6th July 1648.

697. Andrew Mitchell in Meilles, died April 1648.

698. William Sinclair in Swinbuster, died April 1620? . . . . Bannatyne his spouse, Barbara his daughter.

699. Malcolm Christie in Bluidbuster, died February 1644. James, Gilbert, Arthur, and Magnus his children.

700. Arthur Magnussone in Bandone, died April 1643.

11th July 1648.

701. Peter Olasone in Twatt.

702. Agnes Cheyne, spouse of Ola Petersone in Aith.

13th July 1648.

703. Nicol Wishart in Brinzesetter.

704. Harry Cheyne of Stapness, died December 1643. Janet Bell his relict, Margaret his daughter.

705. Walter Christophersone in Middale.

706. Anna Gilbertsdochter, spouse to John Anderson in Netherlaill.

707. Marie Magnusdochter in Hislagar.

708. Robert Coutts of Futabrough, died February 1648. Janet Henriesdochter his relict, Henry, Christian, Clara, Agnes, and Margaret his children.

14th July 1648.

709. Nicol Mansone in Papa Stour, died February 1643.

710. John Erasonsone in Papa Stour.

711. John Strachan in Papa Stour.

712. Robert Cheyne of Northhouse, died 14th June 1641. Margaret Androisdochter his relict, Patrick and Agnes his children.

713. Henry Lasone in Brabister.

18th July 1648.

714. Andrew Smyth in Nethersetter, Northmaven.

19th July 1648.

715. Thomas Scott in Elvesta, Walls, died August 1647. Janet Hendrie his relict, William his brother, Katherine and Margaret his sisters.

716. William Hay, archdeacon of Zetland, died July 1647.

5th August 1648.

717. John Smyth in Keldebister, in Brassey.

14th August 1648.

718. Margaret Sinclair, spouse to James Mount of Ollaberry, and March 1645. Gilbert, James, Barbara, Margaret, and Janet her children.

719. Gilbert Williamson in Arnisvale.

720. Donald Nicolson in Clothasetter.

721. Henry Pitcairn in Gravaland, died March 1648.

722. Janet Magnusdochter, spouse to Harie Anderson in Hammer.

723. Christian Bruce, spouse of Barthelmo Symonsone, died November 1645. She is called a bastard.

16th August 1648.

724. Orne Johnson in Nibaboch, Yell.

725. Garthrow Erasmusdochter, spouse of Garth Salmonson in Yell.

726. Sulomone Erasmusson in Coppisetter, Yell.

727. Barbara Bie, spouse of Bothwell Erasmusson in Hamnavoe, died February 1648. Laurence, Edward, and Andro her sons.

728. Isabel Ornesdochter, spouse of David Manson, died February 1645.

729. Ingagarth Georgesdochter, spouse of Mathew Hawick in Southladie, Yell, died February 1645. Daniel, Matches, James, Thomas, and Christian her children.

18th August 1648.

730. Gilbert Scott in Kirkabister, died February 1642. Ingagarth Olasdochter his relict, Matches, Peter, and Sinnevo his children.

19th August 1648.

731. John Folleslaill, Lumbuster, died June 1645. Margaret Magnusdochter his relict, David, Ola, Janet, Breta, and Barbara his children.
732. Ola Petersone in Basta.
733. Magnus Swynson in Bousta.
734. Christian Foaller, spouse to Francis Nicolson in Hamagairth, Unst.
735. Margaret Dunt, spouse to Magnus Erasmusson in Enawbuster.

23rd August 1648.

736. Laurence Olasone in Utterska, Unst.
737. Christian Smyth, spouse of Steven Manson, Unst.

25th August 1648.

738. James Sinclair in Baltasound, died August 1645. Helen Wood his relict, William, James, and Thomas his children.
739. Christian Nicolsdochter, spouse of Thomas Nicolson in Deall.
740. Anthonie Manson in Hammer.

26th August 1648.

741. James Williamson in Vigga.
742. Magnus Bernardsone in Vigga.
743. Margaret Anthonisdochter, spouse to Andrew Still in Huggaland, Unst.
744. Andrew Bruce, elder of Mowness, died 12th February 1625. Andrew his only son.

27th August 1648.

745. Harie Isaksone in Hine.
746. John Johnstone in Langhouse.
747. James Laurenceson in Howle.
748. Anthone Laurenceson in Howle.
749. Agnes Henriesdochter, spouse to John McRitchie in Howsder.
750. John Nicolson in Mervis in Ballista.
751. Katherine Thomasdochter, spouse of Thomas Couttis in Balbiesta.
752. Andrew Manson in Toft of Burrafirth.

31st August 1648.

753. Magdalen Scott, spouse to Nicol Polsone in Mungarsdaill, Fetlar.

31st August 1648.

754. Jean Archer, first spouse to Daniel Polsone in Clothen.
755. Andrew Nicolson in Urie.
756. Marion Nicolsdochter, spouse to Hermane Stevensone in Urie.
757. Magnus Mansone in Clivak r, Unst.
758. Breta Allansdochter, relict of Erasmus Dicksone in Aith.
759. James Sutherland of Meicklegarth, died Dec. 1647. John his only surviving son.

760. Agnes Davidsdochter, spouse to John Robertson in Cullenstoft.
761. David Williamson in Howle, in Fetlar.
762. Elizabeth Jonsdochter, spouse to Magnus Culstone in Cullenstoft.
763. Donald Gilbertson in Brigh.

5th September 1648.

764. John Walkerson in Otterswick, Yell.
765. Sinnavo in Gosalaith, spouse to Walter Jameson in Snasetter.
766. Anna Henriesdochter, spouse to Laurence Anderson in Otterswick, Yell.

8th September 1648.

767. Jean Chrichtone, spouse to Arthur Javens in Laxo.

9th September 1648.

768. Arthur Polsone in Ska.

10th September 1648.

769. Robert Hawick in Firth, died December 1645. Margaret Arnot his relict, John, Thomas, and Christian his children.
770. Oliver Simsone in Sandwick, Whalsay.
771. Elspeth Hawick, spouse to Andrew Stewart in Sandwick, died September 1648. Bartholomew, Sara, and others, children.
772. Edward Sinclair in Ska, Whalsay, died May 1646. Susana Antonsdochter his relict, Sheward, Andrew, Marian, and Christian, children.
773. Agnes Thomasdochter, spouse to James Arthurson in Skail, Whalsay.
774. Sewart Williamson in Luning.

12th September 1648.

775. Gullis Weymes, spouse to Thomas Linklater Smith in Laxfirth.

15th September 1648.

776. Alexander Bruce of Shelbeis, in Lunesting, died July 1648. Katherine Giffart his relict, Andrew, Jean, Lilias, Margaret, and Agnes his children.

20th September 1648.

777. Euphane Strang, spouse of Alexander Williamson in Eswick, died April 1648. Laurence only child.

23rd September 1648.

778. Erasmus Smith in Urasetter, Dunrossness.
779. Malcolm Tulloch in Cumlewick, Dunrossness.

780. Marjorie Bruce, spouse to John Cheyne of Tangwick, died 4th April 1645. George, Andrew, and Patrick her sons.

781. Christine Philip, spouse of Arthur Clerk in Breck, Walls, died July 1648. Nicol, Peter, Thomas, James, Henry, and Robert Edwardsons, her bairns by Edward Nicolson her first spouse.

782. William Dempster in Skellester, died 30th June 1647.

27th September 1648.

783. Agnes Wright, spouse to William Forsyth in Scalloway, died 31st May 1648. Arthur Forsyth only child.

784. Margaret Umphray, spouse to Henry Sinclair, brother to Laurence Sinclair of Burgh, died 4th March 1645. Hew, Patrick, Helen, and Jean her children.

785. Jean Bruce, relict of Hew Sinclair of Burgh, died 8th March 1644. Laurence, Henry, and Alexander her children.

786. Margaret Sinclair, spouse to Laurence Sinclair of Burgh, died 28th April 1646. Hew her only son.

787. Patrick Cheyne of Vaila, died 23rd December 1643, given up by James Cheyne of Raewick, uncle to Patrick. Agnes, Katherine, Christian, and Marjorie his children.

30th September 1648.

788. Andro Georgeson in Middale, died 20th Feb. 1648, given up by Andrew of Melby in absence of Janet Gibson relict, in name of Marbrun and Agnes Georgesdochter his sisters.

789. Ursella Edmeston, spouse of Ninian Nevin of Windhouse, died 8th December 1646. Gilbert, James, Rodger, Andrew, Barbara, and Bessie his children.

18th September 1648.

790. Turvell Nicolson in Hamysragarth, Weisdale.

791. Erasmus Jameson in Hamragie, Weisdale.

792. John Brown in Bardister, Walls.

28th August 1649.

793. Christian Johnson, relict of Magnus Williamson in Neip, Nesting.

794. Anna Magnusdochter, spouse of Olaus Reid in Barddall, Sandness.

795. Elspeth Magnusdochter in Sandwick.

796. Magnus Olasone in Levenwick, Dunrossness.

797. Erasmus Irvingson in Deall.

798. Magnus Nicolson in Elister.

799. David Simonsone in Giuss, Northmaven.

800. Harie Robertsone in Bardister, Walls.

801. Bessie Redland, spouse to Gilbert Christopherson in Elvister, Walls.

802. William Hay, minister at Walls, died 20th October 1647. Barbara Hay his relict.

803. Laurence Cheyne of Gutabrid, died July 1648. Eliza Sinclair his relict, Anna his daughter.

804. Vincens Gregorsone, merchant, Brassey.

805. Elizabeth Nicolsdochter, relict of William Olasone in Nibon, Northmaven.

806. Marion Turvelsdochter, spouse of Olaus Jamiesone in Weisdale.

807. James Magnusson in Bragh, Burra.

808. Janet Tulloch, spouse to Mathew Sinclair in Bragh, Burra, died April 1646. Laurence, Elspeth, and Margaret her children.

809. Malcolm Sinclair in Westager, Dunrossness, died June 1646. Adam, Laurence, and James his children.

810. Bartholimo Tulcoche in Kirkabister, Lunnasting, died September 1649. Walter his son.

END OF REGISTER.

Uycasound, 11th December 1650.

811. Christian Edmondston, spouse to William Spence of Houlland, Yell, died April 1650. Osca, John, Sinnevo, and Christian her children. John Neven, Commissary Substitute.

July 1686.

812. Mr. William Campbell, minister of Fetlar, died March 1686. Bess Ross his relict and sole legatee, under will dated 11th March 1686. Francis Murray, commissary, James Scott, younger of Voesgarth, cautioner.

COMMISSARIOT OF EDINBURGH.

14th September 1608.

813. Margaret Stewart, spouse of William Bruce of Symbister.

27th August 1669.

814. Gilbert Mowat of Ure.

2nd February 1706.

815. James Smellam, portioner of Preston.

27th May 1708.

816. George Scott of Gibblaston.

11th December 1718.

817. Andrew Bruce of Mowaness and John Bruce his brother.

10th February 1719.

818. Charles Sinclair of Scalloway.

13th June 1722.

819. Mr. James Milne, minister of Lerwick.

15th July 1725.

820. Arthur Nicolson of Lochend.

27th April 1727.

821. James Kelday, jr., merchant, Lerwick.

20th February 1730.

822. Charles Mitchell of Uresland.

19th November 1735.

823. Alexander Scott, eldest son of deceased James Scott, who was son of Alexander Scott, goldsmith, Edinburgh, and Agnes Wachnope, Dowager Countess of Linlithgow.

17th May 1763.

824. Andrew Scott of Greenwall, given up by John Scott, his only son.

QUERIES.

TUSTIMAS IN CAITHNESS.—After mentioning the fairs in Wick parish, the writer of the article on that parish in the *New Statistical Account of Scotland* (Caithness. p. 176 note), says: 'Besides Margaretmas and Fergusmas, mentioned above, there are in the county Colmsmas, the term on the twentieth of June; Petermas, twenty-ninth of June, O.S.; Georgemas, fifteenth of July, O.S.; Marymas, fifteenth of August, O.S.; Lukesmas, first Tuesday of October, O.S.; Mansmas, or Magnusmas, first Tuesday of December, O.S.; Tustimas, fourth Tuesday of November, O.S.; and a number more masses.' What saint has his name embodied in Tustimas? W. G. G.

ST. ALEXANDER.—*Sub voce* Alexander, August Sixth, Bishop Forbes in his *Kalendars of Scottish Saints*, remarks: 'Camerarius gives a doubtful saint of the name, who, being the son of a king of Scotland, joined the Cistercian order in France. He was brother of a Saint Mathildis. There is a fair of St. Alexander at Keith.' On March 31st, 1582, as we learn from the Retours (Stirling), Alexander Levingstoun was returned as heir of his father, John Levingstoun, 'in terris capellae Sancti Alexandri vulgariter nuncupatis Kirklands et parva silva vocata Sanct Alexanders Cuthill cum Cuthilbrae in baronia de Herbertschyr.' In another retour of date April 15th, 1685, we find a reference to 'terras Sancti Alexandri capellae, infra parochiam de Dunnipace. unitas in baroniam de Dunnipace.' Perhaps some reader of the *Scottish Antiquary* can supply information regarding the saint Are there any other traces of his cultus north of the Tweed? J. M. MACKINLAY, F.S.A., Glasgow.

SMITH OF FORRET, COUNTY OF FIFE.—Is anything known concerning the ancestry of Robert Smith of Forret, County of Fife, a doctor in Montrose, where he died August 1752? He married Elizabeth, eldest daughter and one of the co-heirs of John Moodie of Arbekie, County of Forfar, and had at least three sons—William, James, afterwards tenant of Balgonie, born 1730, and John, baptized in Montrose, 16th August 1738—and probably a daughter, who married —— Bonthron.

Neither the Logie nor Montrose registers help in this matter.

Any information will greatly oblige RUVIGNY

(MARQUIS DE RUVIGNY AND RAINEVAL.)

563 ROMFORD ROAD, ESSEX.

Ross, Abbot of Ferne.—Thomas Ross, Abbot of Ferne, died in 1505, leaving two sons—Walter, from whom the family of Ross of Morangy, and William. Can any of your readers give me any information concerning the descendants of this William Ross, whose son, Alexander Ross, was alive about 1660? J. C. R.

Robert Campbell of Rachane.—According to Irvine's *Book of Dumbartonshire* (vol. ii. p. 280), Robert Campbell, a younger son of John Campbell of Ardkinglass, acquired the lands of Rachane. What proof is there of his parentage, and when and from whom did he acquire the lands? Was it from John Campbell who was 'of Rahevin' in 1622 (*Reg. P. C. Scot.*, vol. xiii. p. 30)?

The titles of Rachane as given in *Rosneath, Past and Present* (pp. 238, 230), show that Donald Campbell acquired the lands from Walter Leckie of that Ilk in 1580. and that he transferred them in 1598 to his son John. From the same it appears that an Archibald Campbell was of Rachane in 1669. Was he son of Robert? A. W. G. B.

John Graham of Killearn, 1716.—Can any reader of the *Scottish Antiquary* give me the dates of his birth, marriage, and death, and the names of his wife and children; also the names of his father (John?) and his mother, and the dates of his father's birth and death?

A. W. G. B.

Elizabeth Stirling. — Robert Buchanan of Leny, who died in January 1615, aged about 38, married Elizabeth Stirling, said by Buchanan of Auchmar to have been a daughter of Stirling of Ardoch. Sir William Fraser in *The Stirlings of Keir* makes her a daughter of William Stirling, first of the Ardoch family. The dates, however, make it seem more probable that she was daughter of Henry Stirling of Ardoch and grand-daughter of William. I will be glad of any information which will clear up this point. A. W. G. B.

MacGregor of Glengyle.—I shall be glad if any one can supply me with the pedigree of the original MacGregors of Glengyle, sometimes termed of that Ilk, from Gregor MacGregor, who died in 1626, downwards. An account of the family appears in Burke's *Landed Gentry* for 1872, but it leaves out several generations. These I would like supplied. Gregor married Janet, daughter of Thomas Buchanan, third of Carbeth, and not a daughter of Buchanan of that Ilk as stated, and which Janet was sister of Thomas, fourth of Carbeth, whose wife was Issobell Leckie. At the time of the 1715 rebellion there was a firm bond between the Leckies and MacGregors of Glengyle, under Rob Roy, which resulted in the flight (to Ireland) and forfeiture of the Leckies. Tradition has it that a sister of Rob Roy's was the wife of John Leckie of Croy-leckie, who with his sons fled the country. Thereafter the head of the family seems to have been the Rev. Thomas Leckie of Kilmaronock. This tradition was believed in by my relative, the late Mr. William Leckie Edmonstone of Armgomery, heir of line of the Rev. Thomas.

W. M. Graham Easton.

Croy Hall, Larbert, Stirlingshire.

JOHNSTONS OF WAMPHRAY.—I shall be much obliged if any of your readers can supply me with the following information, viz.:

The dates of births and deaths of the children of Robert Johnston of Wamphray, who died in 1733, and of Isobel Rollo his wife. The children were, according to Douglas: (1) Robert, died young; (2) William, died unmarried; (3) James, a captain in the army, died unmarried; (4) Andrew, died young; (5) Robert, who succeeded his father.

In the London *Notes and Queries* it has been hinted that the above Captain James Johnston did not die unmarried. I should like especially some information regarding this individual. Sir William Fraser in his book of the Johnstones refers to a John Johnstone of Wamphray, who joined the rebellion of 1745, and was warded in the Castle of Wamphray, from which he escaped, thanks to Johnstone of Kirkhill, who took his place. There was no John Johnstone of Wamphray at that time, so the John referred to was evidently the James whose fate I wish to know. Will some of your readers kindly assist me?   ENQUIRER.

JOHN JOHNSTON, VICAR OF ——?—'Hic jacet Maria Johnston Johannis Johnston hujus loci Vicarii Dilectissima Conjunx ë veteris Bruceorum Familia oriunda Pietate Virtute morum Pulchritudine Eruditione Facundia et Ingenii acumine Sexui ornamento et Decori. Liberos habebat Jacobum Thomam et Jeanam Superstites et Eheu Pregnans obiit 25 Die Octobris Anno Dom 1714 aetatis Suae 38.'

Information desired with regard to the above inscription—of what parish John Johnston was vicar, and any particulars about him and his children. There are grounds for thinking he was connected with James Johnston, minister of Crimond (but was not vicar there), who died in 1796, without issue, aged 83, and left a bequest to King's College, Aberdeen, for bursaries.   R. P. W.

JAMES GIFFORD.—About 1660 he lived in the village of West Linton, Peeblesshire, and left some carved stones which decorated his houses. His wife's name was Euphemia Veitch, and he set up a statue of her in the village. One of the carved stones referred to has four panels, each inclosing two figures in low relief, and inscribed thus:—'Ye first man is J. G. brother of Shirefhal (1440).' also 'Six progenitors of James Gifford. wᵗ his awne portracte, and eldest sone,' and 'Wrought by me J. G. architector, ye 7ᵗʰ May 1666.' This James Gifford espoused the Covenanting cause, and was at Rullion Green. Any information relative to his ancestors and descendants, also his death, etc., will oblige,
A LINTON LAD.

REPLIES.

PELDER.—Dun-pelder [or Dunpender], the ancient name of Traprain Law, is derived from 'two Gaelic words signifying "steep hill."'— (*Historians of Scotland*, vol. v. p. 322.)   A. W. G. B.

PELDER (see vol. xii. p. 94).—In a fragment of an early life of St. Kentigern, printed in the fifth volume of the *Historians of Scotland*, it is stated that his mother was taken to the top of a hill called Kepduf, a few miles from Aberlady, and precipitated from it. In Bishop Jocelyn's Life of the same Saint the hill is named Dunpelder. It has also been called Dunpender, and is now known as Traprain Law, from a place beside it. (See Skene's *Celtic Scotland*, vol. ii. pp. 180 and 185.) In the *Ordnance Gazetteer* (Jack, Edinburgh, 1886), the ancient name of Traprain Law is said to have been Dunpender, 'from two Gaelic words signifying a steep hill.' Dun, of course, is a fort or a fortified height, but there seems to be no Gaelic word like Pender. It may be, however, that Pender was originally Beinn doirbh, the difficult hill—the whole then meaning 'the fort on the difficult hill,' and applied generally to the hill itself. But the etymology of it is, I fear, not less difficult than the hill itself.

J. L. A.

EDINBURGH.

If the shape of the hill may have originated the name it might mean *Spelder*—spread out, in opposition to the cone shape of North Berwick Law. It might again be said to have the shape of a pedler's basket turned upside down. The Scottish word for a pedler *pedder*, or his basket *peddle*, might afford a clue.

J. J. D.

ST. MARTIN OF BULLION'S DAY (see vol. xii. p. 92).—St. Martin's day was known on Donside as 'Martin Bulg's Day'; in the Buchan district of Aberdeenshire it is called 'Marcabillin's Day.'

G. W.

OGILVIE OF AUCHIRIES.—Patrick Ogilvie of Auchiries died February 1710, and was succeeded by his son James.

James Ogilvie of Auchiries was father of Alexander, William, and John, who were out in the '45 (*List of Persons concerned in the Rebellion, 1745-46*, pp. 94 and 96). He had also a daughter Rebecca, who married, 2nd August 1750, John, Master of Pitsligo, and died without issue at Aberdeen, 29th January 1804, aged 85 (Wood's *Douglas's Peerage*, vol. ii. p. 370). James Ogilvie died in 1741, and was succeeded by his eldest son Alexander.

Alexander Ogilvie of Auchiries had a daughter Margaret, who was second wife of William Urquhart of Craigston (Burke's *Commoners*, vol. ii. p. 300).

George Ogilvie of Auchiries died before 10th January 1807, when his son Alexander was served heir general.

The *Indexes to the Services of Heirs in Scotland* are the authorities for the above, except when stated otherwise.

A. W. G. B.

DALGLEISH OF TINNYGASK.—1582, April 17th. Confirmation of Charter by Robert, Commendator of Dunfermline, in favour of James Murray of Perdewis, and Agnes Lindsay his spouse, of 'terras de Tunygask, per Robertum Dalgleis occupatas' (*Registrum Magni Sigilli*, 1580-1593, No. 392).

1590, July 18th. 'Robert Dalgleische of Dunnygask' (*Register of the Privy Council of Scotland*, vol iv. p. 511).

1654, June 6th. 'Katherin Wardlaw spous to James Dalgleische of Tynygask, heir of Hendrie Wardlaw of Foulford, *her brother germane*, in the lands of Dewarsbaith *alias* Foulford, within the pareochin and regalitie of Dunfermling.—*E.* 86 *l.* 8 *d.*' (*Inquisitiones Speciales, Fife*, 831).

Dalgleish, Robert, of Tunny-Gask, to his father, Robert Dalgleish of Tunny-Gask, who died 23rd September 1830, heir special in the lands of Tunny-Gask, Fifeshire, dated 10th June 1831 (*Decennial Indexes to the Services of Heirs in Scotland*, 1830-1839). A. W. G. B.

ALEC BURNETT.—1787, April 19. ' At Caskiebain, Alexander Burnet, Esq. of Caskiebain' (Deaths, *Scots Magazine*, vol. xlix, p. 207).

Robert Irvine, merchant in London, and William Young, merchant in Aberdeen, were served co-heirs of provision general to Alexander Burnett of Caskieben, 18th May 1791 (*Indexes to Services of Heirs*, 1790-1799).

Alexander Burnett may have been of the Elrick family. According to Burke's *Peerage*, Andrew Burnett of Elrick married Marjory, elder daughter and co-heiress of Sir John Johnston, Bart., of Caskieben (formerly Cordyce), parish of Dyce, Aberdeenshire. Cordyce (now Caskieben) was a purchase of Sir John Johnston himself, and may, perhaps, have passed on his death in 1724 to his daughter Mrs. Burnett

A. W. G. B.

NOTICES OF BOOKS.

The Arms of the Royal and Parliamentary Burghs of Scotland, by John, Marquess of Bute, K.T., J. R. N. Macphail, and H. W. Lonsdale. (Edinburgh. William Blackwood and Sons.) 1897. 4to, pp. 392 ; price £2, 2s.

By the irony of fate, the first historical enquiry into any class of Scottish Arms, which has appeared since the office of Lyon has been placed in the hands of commoners, has been made by a peer (albeit he is descended of Sir George Mackenzie of Rosehaugh), and the arms which have engaged his pen are those of the ancient rivals of feudalism. It has been denied that burghs should have 'arms' at all, but the denial is based on the confusion of simple armorial ensigns with genealogical achievements, which armorial ensigns only sometime are, and never were originally. The hereditary coat worn undifferenced by the representative of many an ancient house might have been worn as it was by any of many of his predecessors. Heraldically, it does not tell whether he is the founder of his family or the 'twentieth accident of an accident' in unbroken noble descent. Alongside of these ancient hereditary houses have lived the undying corporations, the Royal Burghs. As early as 1295 the seals of the burghs of Aberdeen, Perth, Stirling, Edinburgh, Roxburgh (afterwards deposed for incurable treason), and Berwick were appended to John Balliol's treaty of alliance with France. The seals of the *majores communitates* were affixed to the settlement of the Crown on Edward Bruce in 1326, those of Aberdeen, Dundee, Perth, and Edinburgh to a Commission in 1356 to the Ambassadors to England to treat for the liberation of David II., and so on. And it is certainly a matter of antiquarian and historical interest to know, and perhaps to see still in use, the armorial ensigns which constituted the ancient signature of the burgh to its deeds in time of peace, and which also set a common seal on the stout burgesses who accompanied the king's host to the border in time of war. For it is an error to suppose that 'watching and warding' within the walls, and the curbing of their own turbulent apprentices, constituted the whole military duty of the Royal Burgh ; it was liable to furnish its contingent for national

defence and attack, and its magistrates were bound to accompany the
king when he took the field. There is an unbroken historical succession
from the civic trained bands and town guard down to the modern burgh
police force, and though 'the force' carries no banners and wears neither
red coats nor cross belts, it still carries the arms of the burgh—in some
burghs at least—on its helmet.

A large majority of the burgh shields are absent from the Lyon
Register, and though many of them have been collected and described by
various authors, and chapters and monographs have been written on
individual seals, the majority is to be found in no official register nor, till
now, in any authoritative work.

The scheme of the book is that of a series of eighty-seven chapters or
thereby, some long and some short, a chapter being devoted to each burgh.
Each chapter, save one, is headed with the arms of the burgh in question,
in a shield of the quaint pattern rendered classical in Scotland by its having
been adopted by Sir David Lindsay in his well known Heraldic MS. These
shields are also crowned with mural crowns. They are not, however, the
only illustrations in the book. All distinct versions of the burgh arms,
other than those registered or presently in use, are inserted in the text,
and here and there are 'process' reproductions of remarkable seals. Another feature of the book is that when it has seemed good to the authors
to suggest a new shield as manifestly more correct for a burgh to use than
its adopted coat, they do not hesitate to illustrate their suggestion with a
woodcut. In the case alluded to above, where the burgh has no coat of
arms, the authors of the *Royal Burgh Arms* have taken upon them the
charitable work of making a coat for it. The shield which they suggest
bears an iron furnace in full blast on a sable field, a most effective, if
rather terror striking, achievement.

Of the Royal Burghs more than thirty have emblems of religion on
one or other of their seals, figures of the Crucifixion, of Virgin and Child,
of Patron Saints, etc., and here specially as well as elsewhere through
the book it is clear that Lord Bute is the predominant partner in the
collaboration. Hagiology has not been a strong point at either Lyon
Office or the College of Arms. Heralds must now be more careful. But
it is not in this department only that the work before us excels. Its careful
inquiry into the history of every burgh achievement of every sort, places
it on a totally different basis from the usual works which found on *ex parte*
statements, and then blazon shields true or false without explaining or
accounting for them. It is the standard work on its subject, and without
consulting it no historical book dealing with a Scottish Royal Burgh
can now safely be written. And apart from considerations of historical
value, it is a work which will dignify municipal institutions if literature
and art can do so. Mr. Lonsdale's gothic and idealistic drawings of the
shields of arms are exceedingly beautiful. In historical investigation,
literature, and art there is no heraldic equal to the book which Lord
Bute and the two friends whose names he places along with his own on
the title-page have presented to the public.

It is impossible within the limits of the space at our disposal to follow
this time the authors in their progress through all the burghs. They begin
with Aberdeen, the first burgh on their alphabet, and trace the present
Arms of Saint Michael and the children in boiling chauldron back to an
early Saint Nicolas and the children in the salting-tub! Airdrie

comes next with the Aitchieson eagle, etc., on its shield, and the circumstances which lead that burgh to bear these arms are narrated. The
chapter on Annan succeeds. It contains a historical disquisition to
account if possible for the coat which that burgh carries. And so on they
go through the whole catalogue—here meting out praise to an old-time
local herald painter, and there dealing a buffet at Lyon Office, and every
now and then startling the sober reader with sallies of wit and humour
which are unexpected in such works, and are to be sternly reprobated by
people who find that it hurts them to laugh suddenly. The book is very
handsomely produced with ample margins, and on a superior kind of
paper which leaves it open to the possessor of a copy to colour the outline
illustrations. It is bound in white buckram. As the issue for sale
consists only 200 copies, the book on that account alone is a prize to the
book collector.

*Aisle and Monastery: St. Mary of Geddes Aisle in the Parish Church of
Peebles: and the Church and Monastery of the Holy Cross of Peebles,*
by Robert Renwick. (Glasgow, Carson and Nicol). 1897. 8vo, pp.
viii + 83.

IN this short monograph Mr. Renwick continues his admirable work
among the antiquities of Peebleshire. After a brief survey of the introduction of Christianity into Scotland, in which he follows Dr. W. F.
Skene, the author traces the history of the two ancient churches of
Peebles from their foundation in the 12th and 13th centuries. With
the earlier of the two, the Church of St. Andrew, Mr. Renwick is concerned chiefly on account of its Geddes Aisle, the endowment and history
of which he relates in full. A facsimile of the Charter endowing the
chaplainry attached to this Aisle is given in the Appendix, dated 4th
December 1427. The Church of the Holy Cross, founded some 70 years
later than the Church of St. Andrew, survived as a place of worship till
the close of last century. Its history and that of the monastery attached
to it, belonging to the order of the Trinity Friars, are well told. Mr.
Renwick unearths many interesting facts concerning the various gifts by
which the Church and Monastery were enriched from time to time, and
their ultimate absorption by the king and his nobles. Besides the facsimile already referred to, a number of interesting documents—Charters
and Instruments—relating to the revenues, inductions, feasts, etc., of the
two churches are given in the Appendix. The book is well illustrated
with drawings of the ground plans of the Churches (executed by Mr. A.
A. Thomson), and also with photographs of the buildings as they were in
1790 (in an Grose's *Antiquities of Scotland*), and as they are now.

The Art Student. An Illustrated Quarterly by the Students of the Edinburgh
Schools of Art. Vol. I., No. I. Large 4to, price 1s. Publishing
Office, 70 Princes Street, Edinburgh.

THIS new Art magazine deserves our attention and support on its own
merits, as well as for the excellent objects for which it has been started,
namely, of bringing together the Art Students living in Edinburgh, and
encouraging their artistic development by soliciting and publishing contributions on Art in all its branches. This, the first number, is presented
to us in so artistic and attractive a form that its success must be assured.

The supplement, a photogravure of Raeburn's portrait of Sir John Wauchope, is in itself a delightful possession, and, we hope, the forerunner of many others equally good.

Quarterly Statement of the Palestine Exploration Fund. Office, 24 Hanover Square, London, W.

This Statement is, as usual, full of interest. Among the most important are the representations of the Cufic inscription lately discovered near the Church of the Holy Sepulchre, and the seal found on Ophel. There is also an interesting and fully illustrated article on the Great Mosque of Damascus, and many other papers of excellence.

County Histories of Scotland Series. A History of the County of Inverness (Mainland), by J. Cameron Lees, LL.D., F.S.A. Scot. (William Blackwood and Sons, Edinburgh and London.) 8vo, pp. xx+376, 2 maps, price 7s. 6d.

In his preface, Dr. Cameron Lees tell us his object has been 'to view the history of Inverness-shire from the standpoint of the general history of Scotland.' There can be no doubt that he was right in doing so. Possibly it results in the omission of many details with which the antiquary is especially concerned, but it adds greatly not only to the general interest of the work but to its historical perspective. Dr. Lees has carried out his purpose most admirably. He has given a remarkably clear picture of the various phases through which the great Highland county passed from its incorporation in the kingdom of Scotland, under Malcolm Canmore, to its practical annexation to-day by the Sassenach sportsman. During the whole period, Inverness-shire played no unimportant part in the history of our country. As Dr. Lees points out, its history readily divides itself into four epochs: the first, marked by the rise of the clans, and their consequent feuds, varied by conflicts with the Crown; the second, by their union in defence of the Stewarts; the third, and most mournful, inaugurated by the almost incredible butcheries of the Duke of Cumberland and his Hanoverian soldiers after Culloden, and ending in the breaking-up of the Clan-system and the great wave of voluntary emigration that lasted to the beginning of this century; the fourth, or modern epoch, which may be said to date from the middle of the century, when the southerner began to realise the unequalled facilities for sport which the county provides, when, sheep began to take the place of men throughout its glens, and deer forests to spread over its mountains. Dr. Lees does not enter largely into the social and economic questions raised by these sweeping changes, although he shows he has no sympathy with the terrible evictions of the middle of the century. He states, however, some remarkable facts regarding the influence of the sportsman proprietors of the county on its material prosperity. He takes adequate notice of the condition of its agriculture past and present, its educational facilities, its famous men in war and peace, and, not least, of its bards. The author has produced a very interesting and most readable book. The style, if sometimes graphic, is always clear and never dull. Although written with abundant sympathy with the Highlands, the book is remarkably free from all exaggeration or partisanship, and no one could wish for a fairer or more intelligible account of the part which Inverness-shire has played in the general history of Scotland.

Mary Queen of Scots: From her Birth to her Flight into England: A Brief Biography, with Critical Notes, a few Documents hitherto unpublished, and an Itinerary, by David Hay Fleming. (London, Hodder and Stoughton.) 1897. 8vo, pp. xii + 543; price 7s. 6d.

MR. HAY FLEMING tells us that this short life of Mary Stuart contains the fruit of three years' almost continuous labour. One cannot help thinking that if all historians had been as painstaking, as conscientious, as lavish of time and labour as he has been, we should now be in possession of *less controversy, fewer histories, and more history*. He has gone direct to the fountainhead for his information. The smallest detail of fact has been verified, every tradition investigated, every myth sifted. One-third only of the volume is narrative, and two-thirds is devoted to original documents hitherto unpublished, notes and references, and an itinerary, which show the original sources of his information.

It cannot be said that the memory of our most unhappy Queen is greatly exalted by this searching inquiry into her life and times. We are filled with pity for her, and for the evil times on which she fell. The daughter of a Guise, the pupil of a Guise and of a Lorraine, the chosen friend of a Poictiers, and the beauty of a French Court, she was no more than the deplorable outcome of deplorable circumstances. The student of history need not brand Mary Stuart as the most abandoned of her sex and nation, because she did not, in spite of heredity, environment, religion, and education, rise superior to the most trying circumstances in which frail woman ever found herself. But, on the other hand, it is not necessary to prove a miracle on her behalf, and believe that she was as pure and good as she was cultured and beautiful.

No greater proof has been seen of the power of beauty and misfortune than the never-ending controversies which have raged round the name of this most beautiful and most ill-starred Queen. One hopes that now that Mr. Hay Fleming has put us in possession of the recorded facts, we may form our opinions for ourselves, and cease to range ourselves behind the partisans of either side of the question. Then perhaps the war may cease, and Mary Stuart be allowed to rest in peace. Mr. Fleming in no way spares Queen Mary's apologists. His text has been almost entirely drawn from the State Papers, official records, and letters of the period, and from contemporary histories and chronicles. Controverted points are freely dealt with in the notes and references, and it must be confessed that two at least of Queen Mary's biographers cut but sorry figures. He says of Father Stevenson that 'he has dimmed his great reputation as an historical student by prejudice, partiality, and perversion'; and that Skelton 'not only rivals him in these faults, but is so reckless in matters of fact and so careless in quotation, that no reliance can be placed on his statements, no weight on his opinions.' And certainly if any reliance is to be placed on contemporary chroniclers, very little is left for either of these distinguished biographers.

Mr. Fleming proposes to deal in a future volume with Mary's life in England, and to discuss, in connection with the conferences at York and Westminster, the Casket Letters. He has given us so many fresh facts, and exploded so many pet theories in his present volume, that his next will be waited and watched for with keen interest and impatience by all students of Scotch history, and with some anxiety by those champions of the House of Stuart, to whom Mary is only the most maligned as well as the most sorrowful figure in modern history.

Abstracts of Protocols of the Town Clerks of Glasgow. Edited by Robert Renwick, Depute Town Clerk. Vol. iv—William Hegait's Protocols, 1568-76, with Appendix (including Michael Fleming's Protocols) 1530-67. Glasgow, 1897. 4to, pp. viii+157.

It is difficult to exaggerate the satisfaction with which one finds himself in possession of another volume of these early protocols, which furnishes him with not only a legible and convenient abstract—sometimes a full transcript of the protocols themselves, but with indices of persons and places, and a glossary to Fleming's vernacular. This volume contains also certain additional documents, including an excerpt from a letter from Queen Mary to the Archbishop of Glasgow, dated 20th January 1566-67, written for the purpose of inducing him to dismiss Hegait, the Town Clerk, for circulating rumours regarding variances between her and her husband Darnley.

A translated abstract of Heygate's Protocols occupies the first twenty-six pages of the book, while the next ninety pages are filled with the earlier and vernacular protocols of Michael Fleming. There occurs among these latter protocols an interesting case of a claim for *maritagium* from an heir. It is recorded that on ' 11 February 1536-7, at 4 p.m., Mr. John Walker, procurator for Elizabeth Steward, daughter of quondam Robert Steward of Myntto, went to the presence of Robert Maxwell of Calderwood, and there read and intimated to him the letter of the King, under his privy seal, granted to the said Robert Steward, upon the gift of the marriage of the said Robert Maxwell; also an instrument of assignation, granted by the said Robert Steward to the said Elizabeth, of the said marriage, and a procuratory of hers, in virtue of which the said Mr. John warned the said Robert Maxwell to compear in the parish church of Cowper, situated within the burgh thereof, on the 24 day of April next to come, at the tenth hour before noon, to marry and take as his spouse, Elizabeth Barclay, daughter of the late David Barclay, of Cwllarnye, knight, and that in virtue of the said royal letters and assignation of the said Robert Steward, expressly intimating to the said Robert Maxwell, that if he should marry any other woman than the said Elizabeth Barclay, he should pay to the said Elizabeth Steward the double of the said marriage ; and solemnly protesting that in case he failed in the premises, and did not complete and solemnise marriage with the said Elizabeth Barclay, the said Robert Maxwell should pay the said double of the marriage to the said Elizabeth Steward, according to the tenor of the said royal letters, and the usage and custom of the kingdom of Scotland. Done at the manor called the Mowchlynhowll, near the town (*oppidum*) of Calderwood. Witnesses—Alexander Maxwell, Jasper Petigrew, Robert Hammylton, and John Hammylton.' The Editor adds, in the course of a footnote on the double and single avails, that what the result of this summons was has not been ascertained. The abstracts, as the Editor announces in his preface, have been made by the Rev. Walter Macleod, who is so well known as an authority on Records.

The old Ludgings of Stirling: Being the Ancient Residences of the Nobility, Clergy, and Civic Dignitaries, not hitherto delineated and described, by J. S. Fleming, F.S.A. Scot. (Eneas Mackay, Stirling), 1897, pp. xvi + 139. Foolscap 4to, 7s. 6d. net. Illustrated by forty-one pen-and-ink sketches by the Author.

Forester of Logie's Ludging

THIS is a most important addition to the interesting literature already existing on Stirling and its ancient buildings. It follows quickly on Mr. Small's *Old Stirling, measured and drawn for the Stone,* a notice of which was given in the last number of the *Antiquary.* In the old days, when

Stirling Castle was a royal residence, and the old town was the residence of the Regents—Lennox, Mar, Morton, Moray—the nobles, high dignitaries of the Church, and lairds of the surrounding country all had their 'ludgings' in Stirling. It is the memory of these historic and picturesque buildings that Mr. Fleming is resolved to perpetuate, many of which would otherwise have no permanent record, and must, in the ordinary course of events, disappear. Amongst the most interesting architecturally, as well as historically, are 'The Town Clerk Norie's Ludging,' 'Forester of Logie's Ludging,' 'Jonet Kilbowie's Tavern (Darnley's House),' 'J. Bowie's Ludging and Court ("Serjeant of His Majesty's Wine Cellars"),' and 'Bothwell or "Bogle Ha'" (Sir Robert the Brous) Ludging.' All are charmingly illustrated by pen-and-ink sketches by the author. The two Ludgings of Forester of Logie, the illustration of one of which we insert by kind permission of the publisher, are perhaps the most important in point of size and architecture. Besides the Old Ludgings, Mr. Fleming gives us some curious extracts enumerating the legal symbols used in taking sasine, selected from ancient documents in Sir M. Connal's Burgh Records, which may come within the special province of the antiquarian and the lawyer, but which will be read with the liveliest interest by the layman as well. Such old rites and customs as 'taking sasine' of property by receiving from the hands of the seller a handful of earth, stones, and a cup of water. 'Breaking sasine' (by breaking dishes and throwing them forth with earth and stones from the ground), an old formality of protest that a sasine has been improperly obtained, was found recently, by Mr. Renwick, to have been in use in Glasgow (see Glasgow Protocols, No. 801). Mr. Fleming finds that the custom was in use in Stirling also. The book ends with a notice of the marriage of an Argyle with a Montgomery, which was celebrated with an admirable simplicity, at the *door* of the parish church of Dollar, April 21, 1478. It seems to have been the custom in those days to solemnise the marriage at the *door* of the church, not inside, but the event is described as 'Done *in* the Church of Dollar, the tenth hour before noon or thereby.'

Reviews of several books unavoidably held over.

The Scottish Antiquary

Northern Notes and Queries

VOL. XII. APRIL 1898. No. 48.

RAISING DRAGON.

WHEN Bruce killed Comyn in February 1306, there speedily followed the mission to Aymer de Valence, Earl of Pembroke, to suppress the Scottish insurrection. Barbour (bk. ii. line 205) states that Edward's instructions to him were to ' byrn and slay and raiss dragoun.' The last phrase has occasioned difficulty. Barbour has been fortunate in his editors ; could he have guessed that his great work would be sponsored to the nineteenth century by Jamieson and Skeat, it might have helped him to die happy. Yet not even in their monumental editions are we furnished with a full and final explanation of the unique locution to 'raise dragon' which has been glossed variously as meaning (1) military execution ; (2) to harry ; (3) to act tyrannously, and (4) to play the devil. For this last rendering a passage in the *Song of Roland* (line 1641) is invoked with the purpose of showing that there the dragon was the devil's standard raised by a pagan host. This contention, however, is not tenable, as 'dragun' in the line in question, as elsewhere throughout the great French romance (lines 3266, 3330, 3550), means no more than the standard of King Marsile and his Mohammedan army. M. Léon Gautier, in his glossary to the *Chanson*, says simply that it was the standard of the pagans ; and this quite accords with Ducange's proofs that the word in that general sense of standard or ensign was familiar to Europe at large. A very explicit drawing of such a dragon, an image, not a flag, carried by a horseman, has been found in an eighth-century MS. (Woodward's *Heraldry*, 1896, vol. i. plate ii.) The dragon borne in ecclesiastical processions to denote the devil or symbolise heresy obviously was a very different thing from the military ensign, and the two must not be confounded. It is, of course, not in the least likely that so many sections of Christendom would march to battle following an image of the devil. It may be asserted, therefore, that the true sense of the phrase in Barbour is still in some respects to seek. It will have to be sought in English history, for the dragon banner was once well known there.

The dragon, as a military sign like the more familiar eagle, is supposed to have been introduced into the Roman army after contact with the Dacians and Scythians who employed it. Amongst the Saxons also we have the warrant of Widukind (i. ch. 11) for believing that the dragon figure was a sacred ensign. According to Vegetius (bk. ii. ch. 13), the Roman legion as a whole had its eagle while the component cohorts had their dragons. St. Chrysostom, in the beginning of the fifth century, describes the golden dragon as an imperial emblem embroidered on the robes of Arcadius (Gibbon, ch. xxxii.). The golden dragon makes its debut in mythical English history early, like that long-lived and powerful allegory of Merlin and the battle between the red dragon and the white—between the Celt and the Saxon. Utherpendragon is declared by Geoffrey of Monmouth (viii. ch. 17) to have taken his name from the golden image of a dragon which he bore as his war ensign. Hence no doubt romance, wearing the mask of history (*R. of Brunne*, R. S., line 13345), described King Arthur's banner in kindred terms—

> 'the dragon
> That Arthur bar for gonfanoun.'

There is less doubt about the verity of Henry of Huntingdon's allegations in his history, (1) under the year 752, that the standard of the kings of Wessex was a golden dragon, and (2) under the year 1016, that the king's station in battle was between the standard and the dragon (*Monumenta Hist. Brit.* i. 728, 756).

Emblems of royalty have many indications of their origin in a worship of brute force to which the ethical concept subsequently applied was really foreign, and not always a very appropriate afterthought. The eagle and the lion, the most famous of all these symbols, are fundamentally types of ruthless strength. The dragon, a very exorbitant reptile indeed in the sense of heraldry, was of the same category, and even apart from his imperial associations, was quite worthy to rank with them. The middle ages, exploiting and expanding Pliny, Solinus, and Isidore, assigned him many strange attributes (*Bartholomaeus Anglicus*, ed. 1488, xviii., ch. 37 ; Jaques de Vitry, *Historia Orientalis*, ch. 89, Neckam, etc.). A gliding serpent without feet (unlike the griffin), he was by some authorities reckoned the largest of all animated things ; great and terrible was the fighting virtue of his tongue and of his tail ; his raging and unslakable heat and thirst were not quenched by the blood of a whole elephant. He therefore had a fit enough place as a cognisance for mediæval royalty, less given to rule by love than fear.

The chronicles are practically unanimous that at the battle of Hastings there was only one English standard, although there is mention of minor banners. William of Malmesbury says King Harold's vexillum was a figure of a fighting-man. The Bayeux tapestry, on the other hand, represents a dragon figure. Mr. Freeman (perhaps to some extent influenced by the already cited statement of Henry of Huntingdon) combined the two accounts, and accepted both, inferring that the fighting-man was a personal ensign, and the dragon national. It may well be doubted, however, whether Harold had more than one. The day of heraldry was not yet ; and the distinction between the standard of a king and of his kingdom— the personal and the national—is scarcely likely to have been fully developed by that time. In any case the outstanding fact is that the tapestry shows Harold fighting and falling beneath the dragon, carried

closely in front of him by his vexillifer. Thus, although hereditary royal
and national, it was none the less in the strictest sense a personal ensign
too.

One gleam of light on the subject which Scotland has to offer is from
the battle of the Standard. There it will be remembered the king of
England was not present, but the king of Scotland was. The English
standard, which we know was not a dragon, is styled the royal standard
by Ailred. King David's royal vexillum, on the other hand, was 'a
figured image of a dragon.' Ailred (*Decem Scriptores,* 339, 346) tells how
the repulsed and fugitive Scots knew when they saw it that their king had
not fallen but was retreating. That this dragon therefore was quite as

HAROLD'S DRAGON ENSIGN AT HASTINGS (BAYEUX TAPESTRY).

much a personal as a royal and national standard is to be deduced from
the single authority known for its existence.

In the Crusades, whilst heraldry was still embryonic, we are told
(*Itinerarium Ricardi,* v. ch. 48) of pennoncels with golden flying dragons
upon them. Hoveden (ed. R. S., iii. 129) distinguishes between the royal
standard (signum) of King Richard and his dragon, the hereditary honour
and office of bearing which were in 1191 the subject of dispute. Ducange
suggests that the dragon of Richard was his standard as Duke of Nor-
mandy, and cites from an old French register a tenure of barony by the
service of carrying 'le Dragon du Duc.' He also cites (*voce Draco*) an
interesting passage from Gervase of Tilbury, who records that he had
himself seen Richard's dragon displayed, and that it had a golden head.

So far, however, there is no indication that the hoisting of the dragon involved any particular threat of uncompromising severity. At least twice in Merlin's prophecies, as reported by Geoffrey of Monmouth, the dragon— the monster itself, that is, not the mere image of it—connotes extermination (bk. vii. chaps. 3 and 4, ed. Caxton Soc., pp. 120, 127). This signification passed to the banner. In the thirteenth century that sense obtained for a time, and the chroniclers tell of the dragon as a menace of death, a denial of pardon to a rebellious enemy. Their agreement demonstrates a contemporary understanding that it was a gage of hostility too deep and bitter to admit of quarter or reconciliation, that in short the dragon must have blood.

To the dragon of Henry III. history has allotted a most important, though not particularly tragic rôle. In 1244 Henry directed a dragon to be made of red silk embroidered with gold, his tongue to look like fire and as if in constant motion, and his eyes to be of jewels appropriate (Bentley's *Excerpta Historica*, p. 404, Woodward and Burnett, 1st ed. 291). The Welsh, who had given serious trouble in 1229, had risen again, and the dragon was for their benefit. The king marched into Wales in 1245 with a great army, believing that he would very soon subjugate the Principality. 'He was so greatly moved with wrath,' says Hemingburgh (i. 301). 'that he hoisted the dragon standard and commanded his forces to march for the death of the Welshmen.' But neither he nor his dragon quite effected the purpose in view. Again Matthew of Paris (*Chronica Majora*, R.S. v. 648), adopting an allusive phrase to moralise two meanings in one word, states that King Henry, in 1257, after marching to Chester, 'unfurled his royal banner like a dragon (*quasi draconem*) which knew not how to spare, and threatened Wales with general extermination.' During the barons' war (see Blaauw, ed. 1871, pp. 190, 191), the dragon was turned against Englishmen, fulfilling, albeit by anticipation, the poetical prediction that one day they would be 'seized in the dragon's mouth' (Bower's *Scotichronicon*, ii. 309). It was displayed by the king on the march to Northampton in 1264 (*Annales Monastici*, R.S. iii. 229). In the subsequent advance towards Lewes, and at Lewes, it was still flying. Langtoft (ed. R.S. ii. 142), has the simple phrase unglossed *Le dragon est levé*, while his translator (R. of Brunne in Hearne's *Langtoft*, i. 217), says—

'The kyng schewed forth his scheld, his dragon fulle austere.'

According to the *Flores Historiarum*, and two slightly divergent chronicles by Rishanger (*Flores*, R.S., year 1264, ii. 495. Rishanger, R.S. 26. Rishanger, *Camden Soc.* 32, Rishanger in Wats's *M. Paris*, 995), in the differences of which a cause of confusion has been the impossibility of distinguishing in the manuscripts between the words *indicium* and *judicium*, the dragon was either a symbol, or a sentence, of death. Probably the best reading and most authoritative text is that of the last edition of the *Flores*, to the effect that the king's army was 'ensigned with the royal standard, which they call the dragon—holding out an inexorable sentence of death.' The Rishanger variants omit the inexorable, and leave it an open question whether we are not to read instead of a sentence, a symbol or message of death, but add that the dragon was carried in front of the king. John of Oxenede (R.S. 223, also in Rishanger, *Camden Soc.* 131) similarly says: 'The king's banners advance following the dragon, which,

when it is seen in the army is the signal of slaughter to the uttermost.'
As matters turned out, the defeat of Lewes deprived the signal of its
terror. 'O dolor draconis!' was the unsympathetic apostrophe of
Oxenede, who was not on the side of the dragon. Neither was Langtoft,
who metonymically puts the fact rather neatly in saying that Simon de
Montfort cast down the dragon—*le dragoun avalait.*

It was certainly an unlucky emblem for Henry III., this 'dragon full
austere,' and after his time it is seldom mentioned as in use. The *Flores*
repeats Matthew of Paris's observation (*Chron. Maj.* i. 228), that it was
still the custom of the kings of England in their warlike expeditions to
have the dragon carried in front of them for a vexillum. Historically it
seldom had the chance of proving itself as cruel as the chroniclers painted
it. Indeed the present writer is unaware of its being associated with any
great victory except that of Crecy in 1346. A very interesting chronicle
of distinctly military spirit (*Galfridus le Baker de Swinbroke*, Caxton Soc.
164, 165), describes the standard of Edward III. as a 'banner in which a
dragon was depicted clad in his (*i.e.* Edward's) arms, and which therefore
was styled the dragon, signifying that the pride of the lion and the
gentleness of the lilies had been laid aside and had been transformed into
the cruelty of the dragon.' This explanation of a curious example of the
heraldic 'single supporter,' is given as contrast and sequel to a note on
the Oriflamme, purporting that when that renowned gonfanon of France
was displayed no man might under pain of death take a prisoner under
assurance of quarter.[1]

The possible inaccuracy of these ancient and weighty comments on the
dragon and his significance is, for present objects, of quite secondary
moment. The material point is, that in the middle of the fourteenth
century, and later, there was still prevalent the conception (vouched as
existing, by contemporary proofs, nearly a hundred years before) that the
dragon banner was a token of hostility more deadly than the ordinary
conditions of feudal and chivalric warfare countenanced. Its display in
every example adduced was against subjects in revolt, however sup-
posititious, as at Crecy, the claim of sovereignty might be. The explanation
common to so many chroniclers of the period manifestly offers to
Barbour's words a gloss capable of historical test. What then were
Aymer de Valence's instructions about the Scottish enemy, and what was
actually done? The instructions were tolerably distinct and firm. In
June 1306, King Edward wrote to Valence to put to death all enemies
and rebels, and to reserve only prisoners of consequence till Edward
himself could decide their fate (Bain's *Calendar*, ii. 1790, compare 1782,

---

[1] Most probably this statement of Geoffrey Baker about the historic French banner
is to be reckoned as more popular than critical; still it does appear fairly clear that just as
from the end of the eleventh century the Oriflamme was never (except once—at Agincourt)
raised in battle in the absence of the French King as banner-bearer of St. Denys; so the
royal dragon of the kings of England would seem never to be recorded as displayed in
any battle where the monarch was not himself in the field. At least the present writer
has found no instance. Note the chronicler's remark that the dragon was carried in
front of the king—just as it is shown in the tapestry picture of Harold's death. The
author of the *Song of Roland* supposed the Oriflamme to have been the banner of
ecclesiastical Rome. 'St. Peter's it was, so then it had the Roman name' (*Seint Piere
fut, si aveit nom Romaine*, line 3094). St. Peter may have been somehow associated
with the English dragon too; at all events, that of Henry III. was originally placed in
the church of St. Peter at Westminster (*Excerpta Historica*, 404).

1786, 1787). Barbour tells (ii. 455) that when news of prisoners came, Edward was blithe,

> 'And for dispyte bad draw and hing.'

Hemingburgh, too (ii. 250), speaks of the king's special order (compare Bain's *Calendar*, ii. 1811) under which, in that fierce autumn of 1306, so many Scotsmen, gentle and simple, died cruelly by traitors' deaths on the scaffold. The commission to the judges was to pass sentence of death, not to try the prisoners, who were not to be allowed to answer. 'Sum thai hangyt,' says Barbour (ii. 467), 'sum thai drew.' Although Valence did not in fact raise the dragon, his entire work answered closely to the hypothetical consequences of the display of that austere and inexorable symbol as illustrated by old opinions dealt with in this essayette.

BARON MUNCHAUSEN'S MINERALOGICAL DISCOVERIES IN SCOTLAND.

RUDOLPHE ERIC RASPE was born at Hanover in 1737. Librarian at first of the library of his native town, he was afterwards appointed Professor of Archæology in the Caroline College and Curator of the Cabinet of Antiquities of Coins and Medals at Hesse-Cassel. For these positions of distinction he seems to have been peculiarly suited. He could write and speak well in Latin, French, and English, as well as his native German, and wrote several learned works on mineralogy and geology in these languages. He reviewed Ossian's *Poems* and Percy's *Reliques*, translating portions of these works; and was author of a poem having chivalry for its theme and entitled *Herman und Gunilde*. A communication of his in Latin on Fossil Teeth, read before the Royal Society of London in 1769, procured his election as an honorary member of that learned society. Having, it is alleged, appropriated to his own use money realised on the fraudulent sale of the coins belonging to the Museum, he left Germany. He next appears in London about 1775, where we find him a year later publishing a book on extinct German volcanoes. In 1781 he published a transcript of a MS. by a German monk of the eleventh century in which it appeared that the use of oil colours had been known long before Van Eyck, to whom Vasari had incorrectly attributed the invention. Raspe's discovery was much appreciated by Horace Walpole, at whose expense the book was published, and about this time he received employment as overseer at Dalcoath Mines in Cornwall where he probably spent some six or seven years. It was while in Cornwall that Raspe wrote and published the trivial work that has rendered him more famous than all his learned treatises. This was *Baron Munchausen's Narrative of His Marvellous Travels and Campaigns.* It was first published in 1785, and at once attained immense popularity. It was translated into German two years later by Bürger, to whom its authorship has often been attributed. Raspe was first definitely stated to be the author in 1824, by Karl von Reinhard, the friend of Bürger and editor of his works.

We have said that Raspe probably remained in Cornwall till about 1788. We know for certain that during the summer and autumn of the following year, if not for a longer period, he honoured Scotland with a

visit on mineralogical discoveries bent. Most of the time during which
he was resident in Scotland appears to have been spent either in Edinburgh or with Sir John Sinclair at Ulbster. In the *Scots Magazine* of
October 1789 there appeared the following grandiloquent account of some
of these discoveries:—

'AFFAIRS IN SCOTLAND.

'Mr. Raspe, the German mineralogist, after having examined the greater
part of the Western Highlands and Islands, has at last begun his survey
of Caithness. He has been successful in discovering mines of copper,
lead, iron, cobalt, manganese, etc., and he will probably publish an
account of these discoveries. It must give the greatest satisfaction to
every friend to the prosperity of the Highlands, to understand that the
marble of Tirie, belonging to the Duke of Argyll, the lead in the property
of Lord Breadalbine, and the iron on the estate of Glengarry, are likely
to turn out of great value and importance. From Sutherland he has
brought specimens of the finest clay, and there is reason to hope that this
country [county] will yet make a figure as a mining district, there being
every symptom of coal, and a very promising vein of heavy spar mixed
with lead having been discovered. On the whole, it is believed that the
tour of this ingenious traveller will turn out of great public, as well as
private utility, and will do credit to those who have promoted it.'

Who contributed this paragraph to the *Scots Magazine*? It can
readily be understood that at the close of the eighteenth century the
periodicals of Scotland did not enjoy the advantages of the modern
system of newspaper reporting or correspondence. The monthly maga-
zines of that period partly fulfilled the functions of the newspaper and
relied for the news they contained on any voluntary correspondent whom
circumstances had placed in possession of some curious or interesting
item of news. Stirred by different motives, some correspondents would
send their communications to their favourite periodical with the laudable
desire of imparting to others what they had themselves learned; others
possibly might feel impelled to write while suffering from an innocent
attack of *cacoethes scribendi*. [*See articles by the present writer in* Scots
Magazine, *February and December* 1896.]

It is evident the writer of the paragraph under review was no mere
local scribbler, but one not only cognisant of Raspe's visit to the Highlands, but also acquainted with his visit further north. While composed
with terseness, it is so complete and comprehensive a report of the famous
geological excursion, that we are possibly justified in concluding that
Raspe wrote it himself. Sir John Sinclair could have done so, as he
would have been in possession of the facts from his visitor, but as the
concluding sentence implies praise to Sir John, at whose expense it would
almost appear the western tour was undertaken, the report must have
been written by another, and who more likely than his guest, the ingenious
and imaginative author of *Baron Munchausen*. It may also, if necessary,
be borne in mind that at this time Sir John Sinclair was engaged in
writing on the Geology of Caithness for the *Statistical Account of Scotland*, so there was no necessity for him to write to the *Scots Magazine* on
the same subject.

If we are right in our surmise regarding the parentage of the paragraph we have quoted, the author was actuated by neither of the motives

which we have attributed to ordinary correspondents. The somewhat lofty style of the writer is not unlike that of the general tone of *Munchausen.* It is amusing to observe the easy grace with which the mineral wealth is distributed with a generous hand amongst the great landowners of the west and north of Scotland. The Duke of Argyll, the Earl of Breadalbane, the Duke of Sutherland, the laird of Glengarry, and the philanthropic agriculturalist of Ulbster has each a tempting bait dangled before his eyes. The latter, Sir John Sinclair, had probably been already hooked and landed. What these landowners were expected to do, was to employ the enterprising German mineralogist to work the minerals for all they were worth. Raspe lived a hundred years before his time. In 1898 his talents would be employed to full advantage in the interests of some mighty gold syndicate as prospecting mineralogist in South Africa, Westralia, or Klondyke. However modestly Raspe may have issued *Munchausen* from the press, it must be confessed that we have in the *Scots Magazine* episode as excellent an example of the art of blowing one's own trumpet as any ever practised by a modern novelist. This different line of conduct in Raspe does not militate against our theory. Raspe's avowed profession was that of a dealer in facts, not fancies. It would not have enhanced his professional reputation that he should have been identified with the author of *Munchausen.* He might reasonably have thought, in the words of his own Baron, 'the little regard which this impudent knave has to veracity, makes me sometimes apprehensive that my real facts may fall under suspicion by being found in company with his confounded inventions.' To show the position which this versatile man occupied in contemporary estimation in respect of his acknowledged writings, it may be mentioned that his name appears in the catalogue of five hundred celebrated authors of Great Britain, which was published in London in 1788.

We obtain some additional information relating to Raspe's mineralogical discoveries in Scotland from the work entitled *An Economical History of the Hebrides and Highlands of Scotland,* written by Dr. John Walker, Professor of Natural History in the University of Edinburgh, and published at Edinburgh in 1808. In the second volume he writes: 'In the Island of Icolumb-kill there is a white saline marble, sometimes veined with black, and sometimes containing veins of a greenish mica. A large altar table which formerly existed in the ancient abbey, upon the island, was formed of this marble. A quarry upon it [the island, not the altar] was opened some years ago by Mr. Raspe, a German miner, and some pieces of it brought to Edinburgh, which were much esteemed.' Walker has also something to say of the marble of Tiree, which he claims to have discovered, and states to be of very uncommon variety, of a 'carnation colour, and the concretions are of a green chrystalised schorl.' A block of it was taken to Edinburgh, from which a table was formed for the Duke of Argyll, and placed in Holyrood Palace. From this account it would appear that Raspe did not deal entirely in fiction, but he exaggerated the truth until it became in effect as prejudicial as an untruth. A poor vein of a mineral is for practical mining purposes equivalent to no vein at all.

Raspe exaggerated the finds he himself made, or others had reported. Thus, as we shall afterwards see, where Sir John Sinclair's miners found a vein of ore three inches thick, Raspe had found one of three feet !

In 1787, Sir John Sinclair of Ulbster had discovered indications of the presence of some mineral deposits on his estate at the Hill of Skinnet, four miles from Thurso. In tracing the course of a burn, there was found a small vein of yellow mundick about three inches in breadth, and at a greater depth some white mundick was discovered. Sir John referred these discoveries to some Cornish miners, who told him the mundick itself was of little value, but was a good indicator of the near presence of other minerals of greater value. 'White mundick,' according to their proverbial philosophy, 'was a good horseman and always rode on a good load.' In 1790, Sir John wrote to a lead company in London, but failed to get it interested in the problematical discoveries of Caithness. The reference to the Cornish miners rouses our curiosity to know what connection, if any, the quondam overseer of Dalcoath mines may have had with them.[1]

In the *Statistical Account of Scotland,* we find the following allusion to the subject of the discoveries: 'Mr. Raspe, a German mineralogist, having come into the country of Caithness last autumn [this was written in 1790], was employed by Sir John Sinclair to make trials in the same place ; and not far from the mundick, he discovered a regular vein of heavy spar, mixed with lead and crystals, three feet in breadth, and very near the spot where the mundick was found. No further progress was made than merely to ascertain the size of the vein, and the nature of the metal which it contained.'

No mention is made of these supposed discoveries in the *Memoirs* of Sir John Sinclair, written by his son. Miss Catherine Sinclair, however, states that she had often heard her father relate the story of the imposition, but never with the slightest tinge of bitterness. Although the acute mineralogist wheedled Sir John out of a considerable sum for the discovery of minerals which it was suspected had been previously procured from Cornwall and placed where afterwards found, it was considered by the Sinclair family that they had been amply compensated by the amusement which their intelligent and facetious guest had given them. From this we may assume that one phase of Raspe's character may possibly have been indicated in the Preface to his romance when he describes Munchausen as one who, when the conversation threatened to become argumentative, directed the talk into the more peaceable channel of humorous story-telling. 'The Baron was,' he says, 'a man of great original humour : and having found that prejudiced minds cannot be reasoned into common sense, and that bold assertors are very apt to bully and speak their audience out of it, he never argues with either of them, but adroitly turns the conversation upon indifferent topics, and then tells a story of his travels, campaigns, and sporting adventures in a manner peculiar to himself, and well calculated to awaken and shame the common sense of those who have lost sight of it by prejudice or habit.'

---

[1] Raspe may have been introduced to Sir John Sinclair by Dr. Watson, Bishop of Llandaff, and Professor of Chemistry at Cambridge. In an 'Essay on the Rise and Progress of Chemistry,' Watson quotes a statement made by Raspe in the preface to his translation of Born's *Travels in Hungary,* etc., regarding the cobalt ores of Hesse. Watson was an intimate friend of Sinclair, and it is not unlikely he was also acquainted with Raspe. Baron Born, several of whose works Raspe translated, was the most distinguished mineralogist then living, and, curiously enough, was not unlike his English translator in being celebrated as a humorist, his *Natural History of Monks,* and other humorous works, enjoying a wide popularity throughout Europe.

This seems to have been the manner in which Raspe comported himself while amusing his hosts at Thurso Castle.

In *The Antiquary*, Sir Walter Scott makes Sir Arthur Wardour stand for Sir John Sinclair, and Herman Dousterswivel for Raspe. In the novel too many of Reginald Scott's beliefs in astrology and witchcraft are attributed to the Dutchman for it to be anything like a true portrait of Raspe; the latter, besides, spoke good English, and not the broken jargon put into the mouth of Dousterswivel; but nearly thirty years had intervened between the explorations at Caithness and the writing of *The Antiquary.*

Either before or after his visit to Thurso, Raspe was employed by James Tassie of Edinburgh, in cataloguing his unique collection of casts and impressions from ancient and modern gems. A preliminary conspectus of the arrangement and classification of the collection was first issued, and was followed in 1791 (but dated from Edinburgh 16th April 1790), by a 'Descriptive Catalogue,' in which over fifteen thousand casts of ancient and modern engraved gems, etc., were described in French and English. Mr. Seccombe, one of Munchausen's editors, says Raspe went north in 1791 after his work for Tassie was finished, but we have seen from the contemporary accounts in the *Scots Magazine* and the *Statistical Account*, that he was at Thurso Castle in 1789.

The last we hear of Raspe is that he received an appointment as manager of mines at Muckross in Ireland, and died there from an attack of scarlet fever in 1794.   G. W. NIVEN.

THE MOVING WOOD: A POSTSCRIPT.

By far the most stirring parallel to the Macbeth incident is older than any yet cited (*supra*, pp. 49-56). Appearing in the chronicle of Aimoin, a monk of Fleury-sur-Loire, who is believed to have died in 1008, it relates to an event still earlier by nearly half a millennium—the battle of Droissy, near Soissons, in 593 (Bouquet's *Recueil*, iii. 107; *L'Art de vérifier les dates*, 8vo, ed. 1818, v. 394). On the death of Gontran, Childebert II. attempted to wrest the sceptre from his child-cousin Clotaire II., king of Soissons, and son of Frédégunde. Childebert's army was under the command of two generals, Wintrio, Duke of Champagne, and Gundoald. Landeric was the commander for the dauntless Frédégunde, who, carrying her boy in her arms, rode at the head of her troops until contact with the enemy was imminent.

Meanwhile Wintrio and Gundoald lay encamped. One morning at early dawn a sentinel in their host detected something unusual just outside the lines, and drew a comrade's attention to the fact. 'What is that wood,' he said, 'which I see now? Last night there was none, scarce even the smallest scrub.' His comrade was incredulous, and rallied him on his powers of imagination; surely the wine of the night before was in his head still, or he would have remembered that the horses of the army were at pasture in the wood. 'Why!' said he, 'do you not hear the tinkling of the bells hanging from their necks?' Aimoin reminds us that the use of such bells was an old custom to facilitate the recovery of the animals if they strayed.

The first sentinel, however, had the truer instinct. The wood had not been there the night before, neither had the bells. Landeric had determined to effect a surprise. He had lopped off a branch from a tree in the wood through which his line of march lay ; next he had fastened a bell to his horse's neck. The whole army, obeying his order, had done the like, and now, as the first streak of morning light rose on the horizon, they stood with their boughs for ambush, in readiness to storm the slumbering camp of Wintrio.

Whilst the two sentinels were yet discussing, the branches were thrown down ; what had seemed a dense wood was in a moment revealed as an arrayed battalion flashing with the sheen of arms. The attack was instant and overpowering. Wintrio himself barely managed to escape by the swiftness of his steed. Frédégunde took full advantage of her victory, and the aggressive Childebert never recovered from the effects of the disaster.

A friend of mine, whose learning and penetration are only slowly getting to be known, as they deserve, in this country—Dr. Alexander Tille—has directed my attention to the late Professor's Karl Simrock's *Handbuch der Deutschen Mythologie* for certain minor German analogues. Professor Simrock says (p. 584) that in the old folk-tale, when the May king returned from the wood, he and his whole company were clad in green, and so hidden under green branches that it seemed as though the whole wood came walking. And in the legend of König Grunewald (King Greenwood), his daughter, terrified by the approach of the enemy under cover of green boughs, cried to him to yield for the green wood was come walking :—

> Vater, gebt euch gefangen ;
> Der grüne Wald kommt gegangen.

(See Grimm's *Deutsche Sagen*, i. 148; also Wolfgang Menzel's *Geschichte der deutschen Dichtung*, i. 164.)

King Grunewald, Professor Simrock assures us, was a winter giant whose reign came to an end when the May festival began, ushered in by the walking greenwood. Dr. Tille points out in the Droissy narrative the singular conjunction of the names Gundoald and Wintrio with the greenwood stratagem. To him it suggests, by the affinity of names and parity of circumstances, a possible relationship with the nature-myth—if it indeed be a nature-myth—of the winter-king Grunewald vanquished by the actual 'grüne Wald' of summer. The problem may be left to the folklorists, but for their assistance it is worth mentioning that in England of the fourteenth century both 'summer king' and 'greenwood king' were known terms, if not specific personalities of romance. English writers said in scorn that Robert the Bruce's queen had told him he was but a 'kyng of somere' (*Political Songs*, Camden Soc.. pp. 215, 380), a *rex aestivalis* who would probably never be (*hyemalis*) a winter one (*Flores Historiarum*, year 1306) ; monarch only with his queen like boy and girl in their game of summer-time (Hemingburgh. ii. 250). Again, in 1308, Edward II. in an unpopular tourneying match took the name of Greenwood King—*Rex de viridi bosco* (*Chron. Edward I. and II.*, R.S., *Annales Paulini*, p. 264)—a title which supplied a caustic annalist with a fine chance to point a sentence with a sarcasm about the green tree being quickly turned into dead wood.

Although the French legend of Droissy was not at first common property amongst the chroniclers of France, it was yet known in more forms than one before the end of the 13th century (*Bouquet*, iii. 256), and likely enough might have some currency in Scotland through the French alliances resulting from the wars with the three Edwards. It would not be surprising, therefore, if its influence could be shown to have contributed something to our tale of Birnam Wood.　　　　　　　　　　G. N.

THE INSIGNIA OF THE BARONETS.

THE cognisance of a member of any of the orders of the baronetage, save the Scottish order, consists merely of an honourable augmentation surmounting his coat of arms. This augmentation is a canton of the Royal Arms of Ulster, viz. :—*Argent*, a hand *gules*. The hand is generally, but not unanimously, said to be a sinister hand. In practice the 'canton,' which contains the Ulster coat, is not always the sub-ordinary of that name. Thus in Burke's *Peerage and Baronetage*, it is always smaller than the sub-ordinary, and is generally in the form of an escutcheon. It is also treated to some extent as a charge, or a mark of difference, and is placed in different parts of the shield, according to circumstances. Sir William Abdy, who somehow is always out of his alphabetical place in Burke's annual, has his Ulster escutcheon there in the middle chief. The Rev. Sir David Hunter Blair carries his in the dexter chief, Sir Hervey Bathurst bears his in the sinister chief, and in Sir George Baker's case, it is on the field of his coat of arms, immediately under the centre of his chief. In all these cases the 'canton' is bounded on at least one of its edges by one of the bounding lines of the coat which it surmounts, or, as in Sir George Baker's case, by the bounding line of an honourable ordinary. In this respect it resembles the canton in its treatment, but where, as in Sir Hugh Beavor's shield, it is placed in the fess point, as if it were an escutcheon of pretence on a small scale, it is an inescutcheon, surrounded by the shield on all sides, and in no respect a canton.

On the institution of the Scottish or Nova Scotia Order of baronets, the arms of Nova Scotia were assigned as the badge of membership of the Order. In the Charter under the Great Seal of Scotland, 25th May 1625, to Sir Robert Gordon, the premier baronet of the Order, King Charles grants him, firstly, a part of the region of Nova Scotia, and proceeds that he has created an order of baronets of which he makes Sir Robert the first, and that 'dicti baronetti gererent vel in paludamentis vulgo lie cantoun in thair coatt of airmis, vel in scutis, thair scutcheonis pro suo arbitrio, arma Nove Scotie.' These provisions are repeated in all the earliest creations of baronets, and afterwards, when omitted, they are referred to.

The language of the charter is unintelligible. The terms of the Royal signature on which it proceeded are, however, clear. 'The said Sir Robert and his saids aires male sall and may have and beare for ever heirafter … r in ane canton in their coat of armes or in ane inskutcheon at their …on the arms of the said countrie of New England which ar—' (*Regr … otars*, vol. 46). All the early Signatures and charters have a blank … arms of Nova Scotia had apparently not been decided on. What … remarkable in the terms of the Great Seal charter is not that in a matter of heraldry the clerk should talk nonsense, but that its language

—the Latin of it being taken alone—should import a clearly defined grant, but one totally different in kind from that contemplated in the Signature. That the baronets 'gererent arma Nove Scotie vel in paludamentis vel in scutis,' means that in their option they may place the badge of their knighthood on their mantle or on their shield. It is spoken like a herald, and is a much more sensible grant than that in the Signature. The suggestion is, perhaps, admissible that when the Latin charter was in draft, the terms of this clause were altered for heraldic reasons, but that the alteration was stultified by the addition of the gloss in the vernacular taken from the original Signature.

Nisbet, and an entry in the Lyon Register, made probably about 1678, supply the blazon of the Nova Scotia arms omitted in the Great Seal Register, which in Nisbet's words is—'Argent, a cross of St. Andrew azure (the badge of Scotland counterchanged), charged with an escutcheon of the royal arms supported on the dexter by the royal unicorn, and on the sinister by a savage or wild man, proper, and for the crest a bunch of laurel, and a thistle issuing from two hands conjoined, the one being armed, the other naked, with this motto—'Munit haec altera vincit.'

'The badge so trimmed with supporters, crest and motto,' adds Nisbet, 'I have never met with on any paintings; neither can I conceive how it could be carried in a baronet's shield of arms with these exterior ornaments, either by way of inescutcheon or canton. However, these exterior ornaments were soon taken away, for in the year 1629, after Nova Scotia was sold to the French, his Majesty was pleased to authorise and allow the baronets, and their heirs-male, to wear and carry about their necks in all time coming an orange tannie silk ribbon, whereat hung a scutcheon argent, a saltier azur, and thereon an inescutcheon of Scotland, with an imperial crown above the escutcheon, and encircled with the motto "FAX MENTIS HONESTAE GLORIA." The wearing of which badge about the neck was never much used, but carried by way of canton or escutcheon in their armorial bearings without the motto, of which I have given some examples in plate 8, Fig. 20, etc., by way of canton, dexter, and sinister; also by way of an inescutcheon. There's this difference to be observed, when the badge of Nova Scotia is placed in a canton, and when on an inescutcheon; in the first, the inescutcheon of Scotland is ensigned with the imperial crown, whereas the canton cannot be ensigned by reason of its position; in the last, the escutcheon which contains is ensigned with the imperial crown, and not the inescutcheon contained' (Nisbet, i. 101).

The terms of the royal letter were: 'We authorise and allow the said Lewetennent [Sir William Alexander] and Baronettis and every one of them and their heirs male to wear and carry about their necks in all time coming, ane orange tauney silk ribbane, whairon shall hing pendant in a scutchion argent, a saltoire azuer, thairon ane inescutcheoine of the arms of Scotland, with an imperiall croune above the scutchone, and incircled with this motto: FAX MENTIS HONESTAE GLORIA, which cognoissance oure said present Lieutennent shall deliver now to them from us, . . . and we ordain that from tyme to tyme as occasione of granting and renewing their patents or their heirs succeiding to the said dignitie shall offer, that the said powars to them to carie the said ribbone and cognoissance shalbe tharein particulariie granted and inserted.—17 November 1629. This letter was forthwith embodied in an Act of the Privy Council, which appears to subsist still as an enactment conferring on each possessor of the dignity of a Scots baronetcy the right to the distinction of wearing that badge as a personal decoration.

The accompanying plate bears full-size representations of two of these badges belonging to Sir William Liston Foulis, Baronet, who has kindly allowed them to be photographed for the illustration of the present article. They are of gold richly enamelled in the proper heraldic colours; the oval on which stands the motto is enamelled blue : the letters are of gold. The ribbons are of watered silk, the older ribbon—on the smaller badge—is now at least more tawny than orange. Neither Nisbet nor the original letter of 1629 gives the tincture of the oval on which the motto is placed. In Watson Gordon's portrait in the Parliament House, Edinburgh, of Sir James Wellwood Moncreiff (Lord Moncreiff), the oval is gold. It is gold in the last two instances in which it appears in the Lyon Register, viz. in the arms of Sir John Sinclair of Dunbeath, 1886, and Sir Walter Hamilton Dalrymple, 1889, but the general practice in the Lyon Office has been to make it blue. Etherington Martyn, in his Heraldic MS. (Adv. Lib.), anno 1794, makes the oval of Carr of Etal's badge green. It is probably owing to a freak of the enameller that the ornamental curls at each upper corner of the silver, or rather white, shield in the smaller Foulis badge are green.

There is a long discussion of the same subject of the distinctive marks for baronet's shields in the so-called second volume of Nisbet which appeared in 1742. He is made (p. 124) to denounce the heralds for placing on baronets' coats of arms badges which fell short of the full arms of Nova Scotia, thereby depriving the bearers of part of their rightful honours. He is further made to argue that the badge on the shield was intended in 1629 to be superseded by the ribbon and pendant badge which were then conferred on the members of the Order as a personal decoration, and which, like the collars of the knightly Orders, should be hung round the bearer's shield of arms. He puts the crown on the gold, and not the silver, shield of the badge. The passage is certainly none of Nisbet's. But it has its importance because at the time of its publication, and for that part of it for a hundred and fifty years afterwards, it was accepted as Nisbet's.[1] There is no indication either in the King's letter of 1629 (November 17), or in the Act of the Scots Privy Council which followed on it, nor any suggestion in Nisbet's first volume, nor in his MS. on Exterior Ornaments (preserved in the Lyon Office), which is the foundation of the chapter alluded to in the volume of 1742, that the personal decoration was intended to be added to the baronet's armorial ensigns, or to supersede a badge on his shield. It was after the baronets received the right to the decoration that Sir William Alexander, the Hereditary Lieutenant of Nova Scotia, and now Viscount Stirling, was granted the right to place the badge in an inescutcheon on his shield (15th March 1632). When nearly three years later (28th January 1635), the king granted him, by this time an Earl, the right to bear the Nova Scotia arms on a quarter instead of in an inescutcheon, the express purpose of the grant was to distinguish the Lieutenant from the rank and file of the Order. ('The letters containing

---

[1] For the exposure of the fraud of this second volume, see the Introduction by Mr. A. R. Ross, to Nisbet's *Heraldic Plates*, edited by Ross and Grant. 4to (Edinburgh, 1892. The passage in the print, which is cited above, does not appear in Nisbet's MS. which is preserved in the Lyon Office.

BARONET'S RIBBONS AND BADGES, BELONGING TO SIR WILLIAM LISTON FOULIS, BARONET

these grants may be seen in the Nova Scotia volume edited by David
Laing for the Bannatyne Club, 1867.) Still volume ii. of the *System of
Heraldry* was supposed to be Nisbet's, and its influence may be detected
among the variations in the practice of the heralds in the distinguishing of
the arms of the baronets, as in other heraldic matters.

It is difficult to defend the practice of placing the crown on one shield
when the inescutcheon was used, and on the other when the arms were
placed in a canton. In the painting of Viscount Stirling's arms, formerly
in volume S. 9. A. in Lyon Office, now in the folio volume there, *Arms of
Scottish Peers*, the inescutcheon is adopted, according to the grant of
1632, but in it the crown is on the gold shield of Scotland. In MS. 21 the
inescutcheon is represented on a larger scale—properly so, and with no
crown at all. In both these cases the MSS. date from about 1638, the
arms are attributed to the Earl of Stirling, and are ensigned with an
Earl's coronet. The inescutcheon appears also on the Alexander arms,
still over the porch of the main door in Argyle's Lodgings in Stirling. I
have not seen an exemplification of the Earl's coat, with the quarter,
granted him in 1635.

In the earliest volume of the Lyon Register, the verbal blazon of the
arms of Sir Alexander Abercrombie of Birkenbog, who matriculated in
1678, runs, '*Argent*, a chevron *gules*, betwixt three boars' heads erased
azure, with the badge of Nova Scotia as being Baronet.' In the painting
of these arms on the margin of the page, the 'badge' is in the form of an
inescutcheon placed on the fess point of the shield, and is crowned with the
crown imperial. The inescutcheon bears *argent* a saltire *azure*, and in its
turn is surmounted by an inescutcheon of the Royal Arms of Scotland, viz. :
on a lion rampant *gules*, armed and langued *azure*, within a double tressure
flory counter-flory of the second. The badge on Sir Alexander's shield is
thus heraldically the same as Sir William Foulis's jewels, figured above,
save that it has no motto round it. This volume of the Lyon Register
consists of a collection of verbal blazons of arms arranged according to
their bearers' surnames—roughly alphabetically, and the first entry under
each letter is accompanied by a painting of the arms, executed apparently
of the same date, on the margin. It thus happens that we have a
painting of the Abercrombie Arms, and in the same way we have a
painting—by the same hand, of the arms of Sir Henry Wardlaw of
Pitreavie. In this case the badge is the same. In these official paintings
the crown ensigns the silver and not the golden shield. The date of these
paintings may be said to be 1678, but the volume in which they occur was
still in use in Nisbet's time, and still so when the volumes of his system
successively appeared—1722, 1742. In the entry, well down under the
letter G., of the arms of the Hon. Sir James Gordon of Invergordon,
Baronet, whose matriculation is dated in 1756, there is, in a style apparently of the period, one of the few paintings in this volume of the
Register, which are not among those already alluded to. 'Nisbet's'
second volume version of the badge is adopted in this case, so far that
crown on the badge ensigns the gold and not the silver shield,
the supporters and crest which it mentions, and which it says it is
improper to omit, are still omitted. After this date, however, the
practice of the Lyon Office alters further, and the 1742 contention is given
effect to, viz. that the inescutcheon should be altogether omitted and the
ribbon and badge, the personal decoration, hung round the shield. This

is done in the following representative cases: in 1808, in the case of Ramsay of Balmain; in 1842, for Forbes of Craigievar; and in 1850, for Dick-Cunningham. In these cases the heraldry of the badges has reverted to that exemplified in our illustrations, but in 1865, in the case of Forbes of Pitsligo, and in 1880, in Fergusson of Kilkerran's, the crown is again transferred to the inner inescutcheon.

Nisbet, in his first volume, plate No. 8, gives examples of baronets' coats of arms, in which so far as the engraver has permitted him, he observes the rules of the blazon which he gives in the text of his book, and with them agree the plates recently discovered in the Lockhart repositories, and published for the first time by Messrs. Ross and Grant. In both books the coat of Ogilvie of Barras appears with Nova Scotia arms in a canton in the sinister chief with the golden inescutcheon crowned. In the arms of Seton of Pitmeddan, given in the *Heraldic Plates*, the Nova Scotia ensign is in an inescutcheon with the crown on the silver shield. In both books, Fleming of Ferme's coat carries an inescutcheon in which the engraver has succeeded, if possible, in making the crown ensign both shields. Etherington Martyn's Heraldic MS. (Adv. Lib.), anno 1794, places an inescutcheon with the crown on the silver shield, in the dexter chief, in Dick of Braid's arms, and omits the badge from the shield and substitutes a ribbon and jewel pendant below the shield in the case of Carr of Etal.

After so long a disquisition, it is scarcely necessary to advert to recent works on Heraldry save to remark that Edmonstone accepts both Nisbet's first volume, and his so-called second which is inconsistent with the first; Seton accepts both the Nisbets, and Edmonstone also; Cussans, blundering Nisbet's descriptions of two different things, adds supporters, crest, and a wrong motto to the pendant badge or jewel, which he says 'was suspended to the necks of the Baronets of the Province by an orange ribbon.' Clark changes the silver shield of the pendant jewel to gold, and crowns the inescutcheon of Scotland. Burke (*Peerage and Baronetage*) acquiesces in the statement of the Nisbet of 1742 that the inescutcheon and canton were superseded in 1629, and in practice omits them, but does not substitute the ribbon and jewel. Boutell (Aveling's ed.) says that all baronets carry the badge of Ulster, 'and generally upon a small shield of pretence.'

According to practice, the shields and crown have been borrowed from the pendant badge, and placed as an inescutcheon on the shield, or, with the crown transformed from the silver to the gold shield, been used as the bearings of a canton. This practice was not contemplated at first, and it is open to question whether it is defensible. When the original grant of a badge was made the arms of Nova Scotia were evidently not yet fixed, but the arms contemplated, in the Royal Signature, at any rate, were such as might be placed, like the Ulster badge already familiar to every one, on either an inescutcheon or a canton. Had the inclusion of exterior ornaments been contemplated, a tincture or metal for the field of the canton or the inescutcheon which were to contain the achievement must have been granted. The crown, which was afterwards included in the grant of the pendant badge, was, according to the Lyon Register, and Nisbet, no part of the original Nova Scotia arms. This is borne out by the arms prescribed by the king in 1628 to be used on the seal of the office of the Admiralty of that country—'The said seale having a shippe with

ail her ornaments and apparelling, the mayne sail onlie displayed with
the arms of New Scotland bearing a saltoire with ane scutcheon of the
ancient armes of Scotland, and upon the head of the said shippe careing
ane unicorne sittand, and ane savage man standing upon the sterne both
bearing St. Andrew Croce' (Nova Scotia volume, *ut sup.* p. 42). This
being a blazon for a seal, the tinctures are not given for the sail and saltire.
The first-mentioned painting of Viscount Stirling's arms with the badge in
an inescutcheon, in the large folio MS. in Lyon Office, would be interesting
were it official and contemporary, which it probably is not. Still it
proves nothing, as it was painted after the invention of the pendant, and
its adoption as the badge to be placed on the shield. Beside it also
stands MS. No. 21, also mentioned above, which has no crown on or in the
badge. This MS. 21 may stand alone in thus adding no crown to the
inescutcheon, but if an instance can yet be found of a Nova Scotia
canton or inescutcheon of a date prior to 17th November 1629, it may
reasonably be expected to be simply—*argent* a saltire *azure*, on an inescutcheon the royal arms of Scotland, viz. *or*, a lion rampant *gules*, langued
and armed *azure*, within a bordure of the second. ED.

A MUNICIPAL RELIC OF OLD STIRLING.

AT the January meeting of the Stirling Natural History and Archæological Society Mr. W. B. Cook exhibited a bell-shaped weight of the
sixteenth century, with an inscription relating to a Provost of Stirling.
It formed part of a small collection of curios which had belonged to a
Renfrewshire gentleman, and was sold by auction in Glasgow in 1889,
but beyond this nothing is known of its history. It is now preserved in
the Kelvingrove Museum. It is made of bronze, is 6½ in. high, 3¼ in.
in diameter, and 16 in. in circumference at its widest part. The iron
ring attached to it is made of ⁷⁄₁₆ in. metal, and is 3⅝ in. in diameter.
The inscription, which is in raised Gothic letters, runs round the weight
in three rings, divided by a projecting line, a simple ornament in the first
ring, and a *fleur-de-lis* in the other two rings marking where the inscription begins and ends. There is also a *fleur-de-lis* between the last two
words of the inscription, which reads as follows:—

> John cragingelt of gat itk me cõbing
> maid qubē he bco proucot of ßtribiling
> anno dñi m d l iii : in : habcs | coqbrcn.

This is all simple enough as far as the date—the last word of the first
line is supposed to stand for 'commanding'—but the last three words form
a puzzle of which no satisfactory solution has yet been suggested. The
last word seems to read coqbrcn, and may be an old spelling of Cochran,
the name of the founder who cast the weight. Mr. Cook has failed to
find any such name among the sixteenth-century bellfounders of the Low
Countries. Then it is suggested that the colon after in implies a contrac-
tion, and that we should read jn., meaning 'John,' and habcs, or 'Hawes,'
as John's surname, this John Hawes being the maker of the weight, and
the mysterious final word the name of the town in which he lived. There
is not, however, any place resembling 'Coqhren' in the map of the
Netherlands.

The weight itself furnishes another problem. What was it, and what was it used for? It weighs exactly 20 lbs. 3½ oz. avoirdupois. The label attached to it in the Kelvingrove Museum describes it as the Stirling tron stone, but what was the weight of the Stirling tron stone? There is nothing to guide us in this matter, because notwithstanding the laws dealing with weights and measures, every burgh in Scotland seems to have

THE CRAGINGELT WEIGHT.

been a law unto itself, and no two tron stones were alike. In Provost Cragingelt's time, hay and tallow were two articles that were sold in Stirling by the stone, but was it the tron stone or the Lanark stone? The Records of the Convention of Royal Burghs show that in 1552 the Commissioners resolved that the whole burghs of the kingdom should receive their measures from the standards following, viz. the stone weight of Lanark, the pint of Stirling, the firlot of Linlithgow, and the ell of Edinburgh, and the Commissioners for these towns were ordered to attend a meeting to be held a few months later and produce the standard measures.

The Commissioner for Stirling was Provost Cragingelt, who was present at this meeting, and he attended the following meeting and produced the Stirling 'stope.' The Commissioner for Edinburgh produced the elnwand, but neither the Lanark stone nor the Linlithgow firlot were forthcoming. It is possible that Provost Cragingelt at this time ordered a duplicate of the Lanark stone to be cast for Stirling—unfortunately, the Council Records for 1553 are lost, and there is no extant notice of the matter—but the difficulty is that the weight in question cannot be assimilated to the Lanark stone, if it be the case that the latter weighed 16 lbs. of 7620 imperial grains. And if it be the Lanark stone, then it cannot be the tron stone, for they are quite different in weight.

NOTE ON A LETTER OF THE EARL OF MAR, 1715.

THE following letter from the Earl of Mar to Lord Kilsyth is in the possession of Alexander Thomson, Esq., Trinity Grove, Edinburgh, by whose kind permission it is now printed, for, it is believed, the first time. It is an interesting addition to the documents of the '15.

The letter is dated from the camp at Perth, October 13th, 1715. By that time Mar had been nearly a month at Perth, and was building up his 'unenviable renown for inactivity'—to use Mr. Hill Burton's phrase. His army was ill-paid and was getting out of hand, and there was no appearance of the expected succours from France. The Master of Sinclair, in his ill-natured *Memoirs*, tells us how the time passed. 'Mar,' he says, 'after coming into Perth, did nothing all this while but write; and as if all had depended on his writing, nobodie moved in any one thing; there was not a word spoke of fortifieing the town, nor the least care taken for sending of powder to any place; we did not want gunsmiths, and yet none of them was imployed in mending our old armes. Whoever spoke of those things, which I did often, was giving himself airs; for we lived very well, and as long as meat, drink, and monie was not wanting, what was the need of anie more; most of us were goeing home everie day for our diversion, and to get a fresh supplie of the readie. In that we followed strictlie the rule of the gospell, for we never thought of to-morrow.'

Mar certainly was a bad general, and certainly stayed far too long at Perth. Still, apart from any question of waiting for French aid, it was necessary that he should stay there for some time to gather his forces. The letter now printed expresses his own view as to this. When it was written his force amounted to some 12,000 men. His counsel to Lord Kilsyth with reference to the latter's tenants reminds one of his own famous letter to 'Black Jock,' John Forbes of Invererman, Baron Bailie of Kildrummie. 'Let my own tenants in Kildrummy know,' he wrote, 'that if they come not forth with their best arms, that I will send a party immediately to burn what they shall miss taking from them. And they may believe this not only a threat, but by all that's sacred, I'll put it in execution, let my loss be what it will, that it may be an example to others.'

Lord Kilsyth, to whom the letter is addressed, was the third Viscount, who married Claverhouse's widow. He was attainted for his share in the '15, and died in Rome in 1733. Lord Strathallan, William Drummond of Machany, who succeeded his cousin in the peerage, was taken prisoner at Sheriffmuir, but no proceedings were taken against him. He was one of the well-known leaders of the rising of 1745, and was killed at Culloden. W. K. D.

LETTER, THE EARL OF MAR TO VISCOUNT KILSYTH.

MY LORD,—By advices just received from Lord Strathallan I have got news that will make all right from Bampff, and we can now proceed with more diligence than has been done formerly. But befor doing anything you will know that we have not got so many together as we would have liked, and befor His Majesty comes I would like to have double the quantity of Men under Arms, as he will bring with him a good many Implements and we must have men for them. I do ask you to make all your tenants rise to a man as I have done and give them no mercy should they refuse, and you will soon have a goodly number because the idle fellows know not what is either due to their King or their Chief, and some examples will be made to hasten the rest. My humble services I place at your command and those gentlemen with you who deserve the highest praise. I long exceedingly to hear from you, and hope you will find a way of sending safe, but I have no fear as the country is quite open to all our men. I wait in the meantime for General Gordon who has been kept back by some things, but I doubt not you will see him and put him in Mind of my Anxiety to have as many as he can get with him. Wishing, My Lord, all success, I am with all esteem, Your most obedient humble Servant, MAR.

From the Camp at Perth, October 13, 1715.
Addressed—To my Lord Viscount Kilsyth.
With all speed.

A BOOK-PLATE (*EX LIBRIS*) STAMPED ON A TITLE-PAGE.

THE following description of a book-plate (*ex libris*) may be interesting. It is found in a folio volume entitled "The whole Proceeding upon the Arraignment, Tryal, Conviction, and Attainder of Christopher Layer, Esq. for High Treason, 1722." The book is a large-paper copy, and is in a handsome contemporary binding of red morocco, prettily gold-tooled with a border formed of *fleurs-de-lis* and scroll-work, and a large diamond openwork design in the centre.

It is peculiar in one respect. Instead of being printed on a separate sheet and pasted inside the cover, or, as is sometimes the case, on the back of the title, it has been impressed direct from the copper upon the back of the title-page, and this must of course have been done before the book was bound. The plate-mark is 5 × 2¾ inches. The plate, which is heraldic, consists of a shield with supporters, helmet, and crest. The shield bears *argent* two chevronels *sable*, a label of three points *azure*. Above an esquire's helmet is the crest—a lion's head issuing out of a ducal coronet, the supporters are two lions rampant regardant, addorsed, or, in other words, in the rather stultifying attitude of leaving the shield to support itself. The compartment on which they stand is a sort of pedestal, resting on scroll-work. Immediately underneath the shield is a ribbon bearing a motto in something like Russian characters. Underneath is a draped sheet suspended from the tracery bearing the legend: 'Abel Ketelby of the Middle Temple, Esqr, F.R.S., MDCCXXI.' Burke's *General Armorial* gives Ketelby the arms and crest but omits the supporters and all mention of a motto. G. P. J.

BROTHERS WITH THE SAME CHRISTIAN NAME.

THE parental selection at the present day of the 'Christian' name which is to be bestowed on a child at baptism is influenced in different cases by different considerations, but distinctiveness is always one of them. In mediæval times, however, and, indeed well on in the seventeenth century, there are frequent cases of brothers alive at the same time and bearing the same Christian name, and, after the introduction of hereditary surnames, the same Christian and surnames. Whether these cases indicate the name of the patron saint of the family, or the saint at whose festival the child was born, might be made the subject of a not altogether useless inquiry. That the bearers of the identical names must have been distinguished by personal soubriquets afterwards conferred on them is obvious. These surnames were of course common wherever a distinguishing mark was needed—thus, for an example of the commonest form in which this has occurred among ourselves in the seventeenth century, we find Hugh Fraser in Leadclune, ancestor of the present baronet, has a son of the same name. The father is called Huchon More and the son Huchon Oig.

In a Diploma de Petri d'Elphinstone, Anno 1610 (a copy of it is in the Register House, and a transcript in the Adv. Lib.: MSS. 34, 6, 3), we find it stated as if it were a fact of ordinary occurrence that, about 1450, John de Elphinstone, son of John de Elphinstone, and his wife, a niece of the Earl of Eglinton, had a younger brother John 'ittem cognomine,' and that this second brother had three sons, John, William, and John. 'quem nostri vulgari appellationem ad majoris natu distinctionem, Jockum nuncuparunt.' A correspondent[1] affirms in the *Scottish Antiquary* of January last, that such an occurrence of two brothers of the same Christian name shows the illegitimacy of either of them; and he cites Riddell the great Antiquary and lawyer in support of this opinion. But the opinion is untenable. We do not at present recollect any passage in Riddell's works which convicts him of ever having held the opinion, but an easy test may be applied to that authority by referring to the words he uses in discussing the case of the Earldom of Caithness, where both parties admitted that there were two half-brothers called William, sons of the Chancellor Earl. Here Riddell says (*Peerage Law*, p. 608) the 'Comitatus of Caithness was constituted [by Royal Charter dated December 7th 1476] in the person of William Sinclair, youngest son of William, Earl of Orkney and Caithness,—the first Earl Caithness of his line, in exclusion of his two elder brothers,' and he adds in a footnote, 'these were William senior who was mainly disinherited, . . . and Sir Oliver.' Thus Riddell here accepts the fact of the two legitimate half-brothers of the same name, co-existing with each other, and as he

[1] The correspondent alluded to, in an argument to show that the first Earl of H...... two sons named Alexander were not both legitimate, adduces as a fact that the ... did not succeed to the title of Lord Gordon. If the fact is conclusive of ... it may be worth while to consult the Hist. Com. Report. xii. App. Part viii.

accepts it without observation, he does not appear to have thought it anomalous.

Sir David Lindsay of Rathillet, who was Lyon King at Arms from 1568 till 1591, was a younger brother, on the father's side at least, if not brother-german, of the greater Sir David Lindsay of the Mount (Laing's Memoir prefaced to his edition of Lindsay of the Mount's *Poetical Works*, p. ix.; Seton's *Heraldry*, p. 482). George Elphinstone, grandson of the already mentioned John, the elder brother of Jock, had two sons, both named George. The second of these is described in the *Register of Acts and Decreets*, 8th June 1586 (vol. 105, f. 62), as 'umquhill George Elphinston of Blythiswode, heritor of the few maill efter specifiet, quha was brother and air of umquhill George Elphinstone of Blythiswode.' The younger brother is a witness to a discharge to the elder on 30th May 1563, where they are merely described as 'George Elphinstone, elder,' and 'George Elphinstone, younger.' On the same day the younger brother is witness to a bond by his elder brother, who here styles him in the testing clause 'George Elphinstone my brother' (*Register of Deeds*, vol. vi., 30th May 1563). In the *Acts and Decreets* (vol. 91), 11th January 1582, we find an action brought against Walter Lawson, burgess of Aberdeen, for payment of the thirds of the goods which pertained to 'umquhile David M'Kellan, indweller in Glasgow, brother and heir of umquhile David M'Kellan quha deceist in Deuchland.' In the *Register of Deeds* (vol. xxiii. f. 396), 18th August 1585, we learn that 'David Donald, burgess of Glasgow, Johne Donald, and Johne Donald his brother germene,' purchase 'all and haill the equall halff of ane bark callit the Williame, with ankeris, saillis, maistis, towis, cordage,' etc. John Hamilton of Muirhouse, Apothecary in Edinburgh, had two sons, half-brothers, both called John. John the father had married, first : Christian Wright, and in 1645 their son John inherited Muirhouse under an entail by which, failing himself, the estate passed in succession to his brothers James, Thomas, Alexander, Henry, and John. This second John was a son of his father's second marriage—with Catherine Brown. (*Edinburgh Register of Sasine (Part)*, vol. xxxiii., 18th March 1645.) Were it necessary we might cite parallel cases on the Continent : how, for example, John, Duke of Brittany, who died in 1341, was brother of John, Count of Montfort (Guigot's *History of France*, ch. xx. vol. ii. p. 79), and many other instances could be obtained, with comparatively little trouble, from our own Records.

ED.

BLAW OR BLOW FAMILY

(*Vol.* viii. *p.* 64).

AMONG a number of manuscripts purchased at a sale by auction in London a year or two ago were the following :—

1574 (18th Nov.). Sasine of Andrew Gibson, burgess of Culross, and Isobelle Suderland, his spouse, in annual rent of 10 merks from the lands of Castlehill on precept granted by James Blaw of Castlehill. Present— John Blaw of Westkirk, jun. ; Alexander Suderland, son of Patrick Suderland, and Cuthbert Lindsay, servitor to the said Patrick.

1582 (21st April). Sasine of James Blaw of Castlehill, jun., and Cristine Schorthouse (daughter of James Schorthouse, burgess of Dunfermline), his spouse, in half the lands of Castlehill, on resignation to

Alexander, commendator of Culross, superior, by James Blaw of Castle-hill, sen., in implement of marriage contract.

1593 (23rd March). Sasine of Jonet Evison, one of the four daughters of the deceased Duncan Evison, in one-fourth of his property in Culross. Inquest for service as heiress held before John Blaw and Robert Masterton, bailies of Culross. Among witnesses to sasine, John Blaw of Westkirk, probably same as Bailie John Blaw.

1595 (9th Oct.). Sasine of James Blaw, in tenement in Culross, as heir of his father James Blaw of Castlehill. Among witnesses, James Blaw and Robert Blaw, bailies of Culross.

1618 (26th Feb.). Sasine of Alan Blaw, son of the deceased James Blaw of Castlehill. Edward Blaw, one of the bailies of Culross mentioned in deed. Among witnesses, Robert Blaw, burgess of Culross.

1665 (2nd Aug.). Charter granted by William Henderson, son of Thomas Henderson, in [illegible] hills, in favour of Barbara Blaw, daughter of Alan Blaw of Castlehill, his future spouse, of tenement of houses and two acres of land lying in Nether Hawhill, in the barony of Clackmannan, in liferent, in implement of marriage contract.

From the above and the Register of the Great Seal, I have compiled the following pedigree, supplementary to that given by Mr. Hallen at the reference cited :—

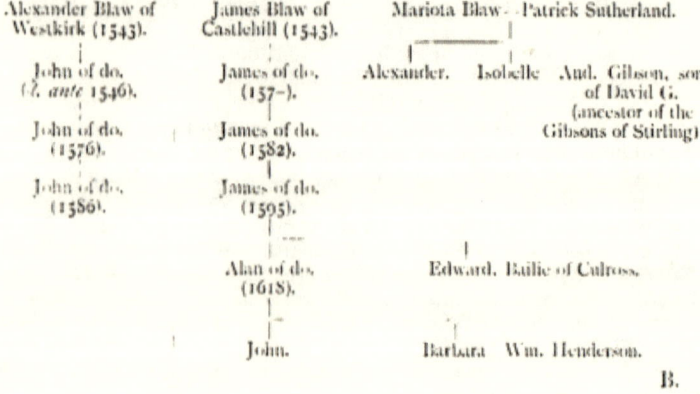

B.

THE MACCULLOCHS OF GLASTULLICH.

The decay and extinction of families of gentle blood has, in no part of the North, been more complete than in Ross-shire, and among the aristocracy of the Earldom of Ross there was no name more respected than that of Macculloch, whose original designation was of 'Plaidis.' Seven generations were so designated until John Macculloch, Provost of Tain, having acquired the lands of Kindeace from the Munroes of Culnald, in 1621, changed his style to that 'of Kindeace.'

A genealogy of the family was included in the 'Earls of Ross and their Descendants,' contributed by the late Mr. Nevile Reid, to *The Scottish Antiquary* (see vol. viii. Ross Index), but unfortunately many errors inadvertently crept into that account, and it is so incomplete that some of those interested have suggested that I might give the accurate pedigree. Than my lamented friend, Mr. Nevile Reid, there could be none more careful, but unfortunately he did not live to see the completion of his great work, and, living so much at his palace at Salerno, he was unable personally to consult such records as would enable him to rectify mistakes in the genealogy.[1]

I. JOHN MACCULLOCH, son of Andrew Macculloch, seventh of Plaids, by his wife Elizabeth, daughter of Alexander Ross of Tarrel, was, as we have already noted, 1st of Kindeace, which he acquired from Andrew Munro, of Culnald, in 1621, and in 1625 he granted part of the lands to his second son Andrew. Six years later he conveyed the remainder of these lands to his eldest son, Thomas. According to *Reid*, he married Janet, daughter of John Ross of Muldarg, but in the *Kalender of Fern* is reference on 7th December 1639, to Margaret Ross, wife of John Macculloch of Kindeace, said to be daughter of 'Walter Ross of Morangie'; while the *Chronicle of the Earls of Ross* makes her daughter of 'Thomas Ross Walterson.' By his wife he had :—

1. Thomas (*see below*) ;
2. Andrew, 1st of Glastullich :
3. Charles, a Surgeon, who married and had a daughter, Anna, who married William Urquhart of Braelangwell—the sasine following on contract of marriage being dated 25th February 1693.

II. THOMAS MACCULLOCH, second of Kindeace. He married Isobel, daughter of James Davidson, Provost of Dundee. After Macculloch's death she married Rev. Hector Munro of Edderton. By her Macculloch had :—

1. James, afterwards third of Kindeace :
2. David, who succeeded as fourth of Kindeace :
3. Alexander, of whom we lose trace after 9th April 1658, when his brother gave him the easter half of Kindeace ;
4. Robert, a merchant in Copenhagen, d. *s.p.*:
(1) Janet married Malcolm Ross of Knockan, to whom David, fourth of Kindeace, conveyed his lands as below :
(2) Abigail, married Thomas Ross, bailie of Tain.

III. JAMES, third of Kindeace, was served heir to his grandfather John, 21st December 1648, and for many years was on the Commission of Supply for Ross. He married, contract dated in 1651, Christian (daughter of Colonel John Munro of Oosdale), who afterwards married David Ross of Pitcalnie. She had a liferent of the lands of Kindeace. James was succeeded by :—

IV. DAVID, his younger brother, who was served heir 1st October 1652.
He had :—

V. DAVID, younger of Kindeace, and Janet, married to Wm. Ross, Lachlanson. In the time of these last two lairds the whole property passed into the hands of Malcolm Ross, who became styled 'of Kindeace.' The succession in the Macculloch family opened to :—

VI. ANDREW, first of Glastullich, second son of John, 1st of Kindeace. This Andrew was Provost of Tain, and had sasine of Glastullich on 20th

---

[1] The substance of the following pedigree I have already contributed to the *North Star* of 16th December 1897.—D. M. R.

June 1650. He took an active part in politics, and represented Tain in Parliament for a number of years. He married, first, Anna, daughter of Rev. James Ferne, minister of Fraserburgh, by whom he had :—

1. John, styled 'eldest son of first marriage' in sasine dated 1st May 1668, and styled 'son and heir of deceased Andrew' on 16th June 1681 ;

2. Mr. Andrew, brother of John, so styled in sasine dated 25th October 1694.

(1) Margaret, married Hugh Rose of Newton, Nairnshire ; on 22nd October 1667 they had sasine of the land of Arturlies ;

(2) Isabel, married (contract dated 30th June 1660), Rev. William Ross of Edderton, her tocher being 2500 merks. She married, secondly, Hugh Ross, writer, Inverness, to whom she brought a dower of 5000 merks.

Andrew married, secondly, Isabel Dunbar, and on 26th May 1651, they had sasine of the lands of Meikle Dallas, in the barony of Westray. He had by her :—

1. Hugh, afterwards of Glastullich ;

2. Charles ; 3. James.

(1) Barbara, married Andrew Macculloch, burgess of Tain, their contract of marriage being dated 4th March 1681.

VII. HUGH MACCULLOCH, second of Glastullich, succeeded as 'eldest son and heir of the second marriage,' to the exclusion of his elder half-brothers. On 29th July 1668, he had sasine on bond of provision by his father. He was twice married, but had no issue by his first wife, whose name is as yet unknown. He married, secondly, Helen, daughter of David Dunbar of Dunphail. Their contract of marriage is dated 3rd July, 1678. He died before 1703, leaving :—

VIII. DAVID, third of Glastullich. He recovered the lands of Glastullich, which were apprised from him by Hugh Ross of Braelangwell. In his contract of marriage with Christain, second daughter of Rorie Macleod of Cambuscarrie, dated at Inverchassly, 30th July 1706, the lady's uncle, Æneas Macleod of Cadboll, became bound to pay as tocher the sum of 3000 merks. Macculloch also became obliged, before the following July, to establish a sufficient title in his own person to the lands of Bellamukie, Glastullich, and others, and grant a formal and valid disposition and life-rent provision of five chaldern of victual to said Christian Macleod, his future spouse, and, on the other part, Macleod of Cadboll obliged himself to pay to Macculloch the tocher at Lammas 1707, about a month after the aforesaid life provision was perfected. It appears that Macculloch could not clear off the encumbrances on his property, and he was obliged to apply to Macleod to hand over 2000 merks of the tocher. Macleod agreed to this, and wrote to George Munro of Newmore, who had not yet paid the 3000 merks, which was the tocher of his sister, Christian Macleod's mother. Munro paid on Glastullich's behalf 2000 merks to George Mackenzie, Bellamukie, whose receipt is dated 3rd February 1707. Mackenzie's claims against Glastullich still amounted to 1500 merks, and Macculloch, being thus involved, tried to get the remaining portion of the tocher from Cadboll, who, notwithstanding the terms of the contract, declared that he was not responsible, and that Macculloch should seek relief from Newmore, who was his wife's near relative. The matter ended in a litigation of thirty years' duration. By his wife Christian Macleod, he had issue :—

1. Hugh, styled eldest son in 1724, but dead before 1735 :
2. Roderick of Glastullich ;
3. Walter, born 19th October 1718. Upon 18th December 1735, his father granted a bond of provision in his favour of 1000 merks, payable on attaining his majority.
4. George, born 28th May 1720. On same date he had a similar bond to above. By his will, dated 15th November 1742, he disponed all his effects to his younger brother, David.
5. David, born 22nd October 1721. He had a bond of provision on same date as his brothers. By his will, dated 9th July 1744, he left all his effects to his brother Walter.
6. Angus ;
(1) Peggy, eldest daughter ; (2) Christian, married David Gray of Newton ; (3) Helen, married William Ross, merchant, Fortrose ; (4) Mary, married Rev. Hugh Rose, of Creich and Tain ; (5) Elizabeth.

IX. Captain RODERICK MACCULLOCH, fourth of Glastullich, succeeded his father. He was a captain in Cromartie's Regiment, and was taken prisoner in Sutherland. He was a man of gigantic appearance, towering head and shoulders above his fellows. His appearance among the rebels as they were marched to their imprisonment in London attracted the attention of a court lady, who, as he passed, unfeelingly called out, 'You tall Scotch rebel, you'll be hanged, sir!' To which salute Macculloch replied with a courtly bow and smile, 'There's deil a doubt o' that, madam.' His bold and manly bearing, and nonchalant reply made such an impression that the lady straightway sought out the Duke of Newcastle, and begged permission to interview a 'giant rebel.' She was refused access, but so persistently did she seek to carry her point that on every occasion she approached the King or his Ministers she begged the life of her giant friend—whose name seems to have been unknown to her. At length, wearied out with her importunity, the King threatened to send her to the Tower, and in an autograph letter, still extant, ordered the Commandant to let her have access, and have the Scottish officers paraded before her. She identified her tall friend, and very soon afterwards Macculloch was set free with a full pardon. What the subsequent fate of the lady we know not. The estate of Glastullich was forfeited, but fortunately through the bonds granted to his brothers, Walter, George, and David, it was preserved to the family through the exertions of Walter, who, although living in India, brought an action of recovery against the King's Advocate, and was successful. Roderick Macculloch married, 1st, in 1752, Margaret, daughter of Gustavus Munro of Culrain. She died in 1756, aged 25, leaving a son, Gustavus, who, in 1757, was served as her heir—but he seems to have died young. In 1766 Roderick made a demand for possession of his wife's effects, and when her trunks were opened they were found to contain a blue cloth riding habit trimmed with gold lace with a white satin waistcoat, a blue cloth skirt, and a scarlet riding great cloak with brass buttons. He married, secondly, Jean, eldest daughter of David Ross of Inverchassly, by whom he had :—
1. David Macculloch, last of Glastullich :
(1) Helen, married Captain Thomas Rose of Bindale, and had Lieutenants Alexander, William, and Roderick (?) of the 93rd Sutherland Highlanders, and three daughters—Isobel, Helen, and Margaret.

X. DAVID, last of Glastullich, a captain in the army. He married Katherine Lawson of Leith, on the 23rd April 1795, and had:—

1. Margaret, born 28th September 1795;
2. Mary; she married, as second wife, 29th October 1819, William Baillie Rose of Rhynie (youngest son of Rev. Hugh Rose and Mary Macculloch), and had:—David Macculloch Rose, late of Rarichie, Lieut.-General William Rose, Hugh Rose. Helen, and Catherine married to Rev. John Baldwin.

David of Glastullich died on 5th November 1802, and on 15th of the same month the Commissary Depute of Ross granted power to James Rose, Depute-Clerk of Session, Edinburgh, and William Baillie Rose of Rhynie, his brother, to act as guardians to the children. From an inventory made in November 1802, it appears there were among the deceased's effects—20 pair of breeches and pantaloons, 4 coats, 11 waistcoats, 2 dressing-gowns, a sword and scabbard.   D. M. R.

WILLIAM ERSKINE, ARCHBISHOP OF GLASGOW

(*Vol.* xii. *pp.* 62, 123).

THERE can be no doubt as to the parentage of Sir William Erskine. Craufurd in his *Peerage* (p. 301, Note *d*) says:—'I have seen a charter in the Publick Rolls to this James Erskine of the lands of Little Sauchy and Katharine Stirling, his spouse, and to their Heirs. They had issue, James Erskine of Balgony, and Mr. William, who got the Parsonage of Campsay upon the Reformation in *Commendam*: he was afterwards promoted to the Commendatory of Paisley, anno 1579, and after that in 1587 made Titular Bishop of Glasgow, though all the while he was a Laick: he afterwards was knighted by King James VI., and left a daughter Janet, married to Sir William Alexander of Menstry, first Earl of Stirling.' Mr. Erskine Scott, in his volume, *The Erskine-Halcro Genealogy* (Table I.), makes William the third son of James Erskine of Little Sauchie, and gives his mother's name as Christian Stirling. The extract from the MS. Calendar of the Register of Deeds furnished to Mr. Hallen by Mr. Maitland Thomson proves that William was the second son. Craufurd is wrong in naming the elder (or eldest) son James instead of Robert.

Sir William Erskine's wife was apparently a cousin of his own. Her name was Joanna Erskine, and in an inscription on a mural tablet erected to her memory and that of her husband by their son-in-law, Lord Stirling, she is described as '*illustri et communi Æreskinorum familia orta.*' Their remains were transferred to the Craigengelt Aisle of Stirling Parish Church when it was acquired as a burial-place by the Earl of Stirling. This aisle was taken down in 1818, and a few years ago I identified some broken pieces of a tombstone in the possession of the present proprietors of the ground on which the aisle was built, as part of the mural tablet above referred to. The entire inscription is printed in Rogers' *House of Alexander*, vol. i. p. 186, and from it Mr. Hallen will see that Lady Stirling was the only daughter of Sir William Erskine. In the same work (p. 38, vol. i.) it is stated on the authority of *The Spottiswoode Miscellany* (vol. i. p. 103), that Alexander Erskine, son of Sir William Erskine, held some office about the Court, and that his grandson, Sir James Erskine obtained

a grant of lands in Ulster, but the authority cited bears that Sir James
Erskine was the eleventh son of Alexander, second son of John, Earl of
Mar, and he could not therefore be a descendant of Sir W. Erskine. I
have not discovered any evidence that the Archbishop left a son.   F.

A FORGOTTEN EPISODE IN THE HISTORY OF
BLACKWOOD'S MAGAZINE.

LOWNDES, who has been followed by other bibliographers, and also by
the late Mrs. Oliphant in her recently published *Life of William Blackwood*, says of the *Scots Magazine*: 'This and the preceding periodical
were driven out of the field soon after the appearance of *Blackwood's
Magazine,*'—1817. By the sequestration of Archibald Constable and Company, John Ballantyne and Company, and Sir Walter Scott, the copyrights
of certain works and periodicals became the property of their creditors,
and constituted the principal assets to be realised. The more important
periodicals whose copyrights were thus suddenly offered for sale were the
Edinburgh Review and the *Scots Magazine*, published by Constable, and
the *Edinburgh Weekly Journal*, published by Ballantyne. The sale of
Scott's copyrights took place on 19th December 1827, but the periodicals
were disposed of immediately after sequestration. It is matter of history
that the *Review* was purchased by Adam Black. Lockhart says the
Edinburgh Weekly Journal was continued to James Ballantyne upon a
moderate salary by the creditors, but this is not in strict accordance with
the terms of an advertisement that appeared in the *Edinburgh Evening
Courant* of 22nd July 1826, which states that 'The proprietors of the
Edinburgh Weekly Journal intimate that it has been purchased by the
person who conducted it for the last nine years.' This person was, of
course, James Ballantyne. Did the *Scots Magazine* obtain a purchaser?
That a flourishing magazine with such a long and historical record should
be allowed to sink into oblivion at a time that may be called the Augustine
age of literature in Edinburgh seems highly improbable. William Blackwood had long been desirous of publishing and editing a periodical.
In 1806, when the *Edinburgh Weekly Journal* was first purchased by
Ballantyne for £1850, Blackwood and Provost Brown of Aberdeen had
jointly offered £20 less. In 1817 Blackwood commenced the publication
of his magazine, whose success was fully assured long before 1826. Can
it be imagined that Blackwood would purchase the copyright of the *Scots
Magazine*? The result of a search, however, revealed the curious fact that
the copyright had been purchased by William Blackwood on 12th July
1826. The price paid does not transpire, but probably Messrs. Blackwood and Sons may refer to their business books and let the amount be
known. In the *Edinburgh Evening Courant* of 27th July 1826 appeared
the following advertisement:—'*Edinburgh Magazine*: a New Series of
the *Scots Magazine*. The Trustee upon the Sequestrated Estate of
Messrs. Archibald Constable and Coy. begs to inform the subscribers to
the above Work that the Publication of it is now discontinued, the copyright having been purchased by Mr. Blackwood—Edinburgh, 12th July
1826.'

This remarkable purchase must have been effected for no other reason than the suppression of the *Scots Magazine*, and possibly he may have attempted to obtain the copyright of the *Edinburgh Review* also. By this diplomatic transaction the triumph of William Blackwood over the rival with whom he had waged a warfare for nearly ten years was complete, but no signs of jubilation appear to have escaped him; and it is doubtful if even his henchmen Lockhart, Hogg, and Wilson were aware of the episode. That it was unknown to the late Mrs. Oliphant may be assumed from the error she commits of consigning the *Scots Magazine* to extinction from other causes 'soon after' the appearance of *Blackwood's Magazine*.

G. W. NIVEN.

GREENOCK.

THE RECORDS OF AN ANTI-BURGHER CONGREGATION.

DUNNIKIER FREE CHURCH has a longer history behind it than most Free Churches. The congregation originated in 1747, the year when the Secession was divided by the Burgess Oath controversy into two Synods, Burgher and Anti-burgher. Dunnikier congregation was the Anti-burgher section of the Kirkcaldy Seceders. It has maintained a continuous existence down to the present time, and in 1852 it joined the Free Church.

Mr. Fairweather, the present incumbent of the church, has compiled an excellent sketch of its history.[1] Naturally the book is of a kind which appeals to a somewhat limited audience. It has, however, an element of general historical interest in the numerous excerpts which it contains from the Kirk-session Records of the old Anti-burgher congregation. These present a vivid picture of Seceder life in a country town a hundred years ago. The Session exercised inquisitorial control over the minutest details of life. The grosser offences, drunkenness and the like, of course receive no mercy. 'Promiscuous dancing' is sternly dealt with. Above all, anything like defection from the testimony is watched with sleepless vigilance. 'Promiscuous hearing,' swearing the Burgess Oath, 'giving countenance' to the Commissary Court at St. Andrews, 'which has a mixed jurisdiction of civil and ecclesiastic joined together, and has its origin in Episcopacy,' are all noted as matters of discipline. On October 24, 1748, John Nicolson acknowledges his sin in being married by a minister of the Established Church, with the further iniquity of 'having a penny wedding.' Perhaps the climax is reached in the following entry, *circa* 1755 (Mr. Fairweather is a little casual about his dates): 'It was reported to the Session that John Collier had *witnessed his brother's being married by a Burgher minister*, and just now offered himself voluntarily to the Session. He was called in, compeared, and was interrogate why he did so? Answered he did it in his simplicity. Was interrogate 2dly if he saw the evil of it as in some measure giving up his profession? Answered he did. Being interrogate 3^{tio} if he resolved in the strength of grace not to do the like afterwards? Answered in the affirmative. He being removed, the Session considering his affair agreed that he be rebuked and admonished before the Session.'

It is not attractive, that old Seceder world. Most people nowadays,

[1] *Memorials of Dunnikier Church, Kirkcaldy; with an Historical Introduction.* By the Rev. William Fairweather, M.A., 1897.

even among its modern representatives, would find its doctrines absurd, its discipline of conduct intolerable. It stood sulkily aloof from the public life of the country. It looked with glum hostility on art, on letters, on all that gives grace and charm to life. But beyond doubt it was a fine school of the sterner virtues (which after all are the important ones), and it developed many of the qualities which have made modern Scotland what she is. One may not share Mr. Fairweather's view that 'cold, colourless imbecility' was the characteristic of the church of Reid and Robertson, or the reverence with which he describes the old Kirkcaldy Anti-burghers as 'those covenanted saints.' But one may cordially indorse his opinion that 'amid whatever limitations of defect it carried on its work, the Secession Church did yeoman service to Christianity in Scotland.'

IRISH TEXTS SOCIETY.

It is proposed to found an Irish Texts Society for the purpose of publishing texts in the Irish language, accompanied by introductions, English translations, and brief notes.

The active co-operation of numerous Irish scholars, among whom may be named Dr. Douglas Hyde, Standish Hayes O'Grady, Tomás ó Flannghaile, and Mr. David Comyn has been secured, and an arrangement has been made with the firm of David Nutt, of 270 and 271 Strand, London, for the publication of the Society's volumes.

There are two classes of readers to whom the Society especially appeals for support; first, the large and increasing number of those who are taking an interest in the language of their native country : and secondly, those who, as philologists, archæologists, etc., are concerned with the scientific aspect of Irish literature. To the former, the publication of Modern texts (1600 A.D. to the present day) is of immediate necessity; to the second, the Middle-Irish texts have a more especial value. As yet only a small part of this great literature, in either of its periods, has been made generally accessible.

With the object of appealing to the first class of students, it is proposed to give the larger place in the Society's scheme to works of the modern class, and the first volume will contain a collection of romantic tales, edited with translation, by Dr. Douglas Hyde.

While directing immediate attention to modern tracts, the Society by no means overlooks the importance of the earlier texts, and it has in view the publication of many of the more important of those that are as yet unedited.

THE LATE SIR WILLIAM FRASER, K.C.B., LL.D.

By Sir William Fraser's death, on Sunday 13th March, Scotland has lost one of its most eminent genealogists and record scholars. Sir William was born in Kincardineshire in 1816; admitted a Solicitor before the Supreme Courts in 1851; Deputy-Keeper of the Sasines, 1852-1880; Deputy-Keeper of the Records, 1880-1892; LL.D. Edinburgh, 1882;

C.B. 1885 ; K.C.B., 1887 ; Reporter for Scotland for some years to the Historical Commission.

In his private capacity he wrote a large number of family histories, a list of which is here added :—

The Stirlings of Keir, and their Family Papers. 1 vol., 1858.
Memorials of the Montgomeries, Earls of Eglinton. 2 vols., 1859.
Memoirs of the Maxwells of Pollok. 2 vols., 1863.
The Maxwell, Herries, and Nithsdale Muniments, 1865.
The Pollok-Maxwell Baronetcy, 1866.
History of the Carnegies, Earls of Southesk, and their Kindred. 2 vols., 1867.
The Red Book of Grandtully. 2 vols., 1868.
The Chiefs of Colquhoun, and their Country. 2 vols., 1869.
The Book of Caerlaverock ; Memoirs of the Maxwells, Earls of Niths-dale, Lords Maxwell and Herries. 2 vols., 1873.
The Chartulary of Colquhoun, 1873.
The Lennox. 2 vols., 1874.
The Chartulary of Pollok-Maxwell, 1875.
The Earls of Cromarty, their Kindred, Country, and Correspondence. 2 vols., 1876.
The Scotts of Buccleuch. 2 vols., 1878.
The Red Book of Menteith. 2 vols., 1880.
The Chiefs of Grant. 3 vols., 1883.
The Douglas Book. 4 vols., 1885.
Memorials of the Family of Wemyss of Wemyss. 3 vols., 1888.
The Earls of Haddington. 2 vols., 1889.
The Melvilles, Earls of Melville ; and the Leslies, Earls of Leven. 3 vols., 1890.
The Sutherland Book. 3 vols., 1892.
The Annandale Book. 2 vols., 1894.
The Elphinstone Book, the last proof of which he is believed to have corrected very shortly before his death. 2 vols., 1898.

These form an imposing and tolerably uniform series of important quartos. How far the Memoirs, which form large parts of them, will stand the test of time remains in some measure to be seen, but they contain many hitherto unprinted charters, and much other valuable information which was previously buried in private charter-chests, and for access to which in these volumes, both antiquaries and historians must ever be thankful.

In addition to these family records, Sir William in 1874 edited the *Registrum Monasterii S. Mariae de Cambuskenneth*, at the request of the Marquis of Bute, by whom the book was presented to the members of the Grampian Club.

All Sir William Fraser's works were of private and limited issue.

QUERIES.

St. Spalding.—In an obligation dated 7th June 1544, one of the terms of payment is St. Spalding's Day, 6th July. Is anything known of this saint? His name is not mentioned in Bishop Forbes' *Kalendars.* The 6th July was St. Palladius Day.   B.

GRAY FAMILY.—I shall be glad to receive information as to the names of the son and grandson of William Gray of Balbunno and Lauriston, who was grandson of Patrick, Lord Gray, who died 1609. (I have omitted to note the number of the Lord as I doubt the accuracy of the existing rotation expressed in the *Peerages*.) The William named died before 1663, I think *circa* 1662, and was succeeded in Balbunno by his great-grandson Andrew Gray designed of Balbunno. Spec. Service (Perth) 11 February 1663. There is another service in the Record of Retours in connection with this William, wherein his eldest son James was served heir to his father, William, in the contiguous property of Lauriston 5 June 1663. This latter person is frequently mentioned *inter alia* in the records of the period in connection with his brother Andrew of Bullion, his father, also designed of Bullion, son of Lord Gray, and his uncle Patrick, the infamous Master of Gray of history. Burke, in his *Landed Gentry*, mentions this family in connection with a daughter and a younger son Charles, but the parochial registers of the parish of Liff, Benvie, and Invergowrie, show that Andrew of Balbunno had other sons and daughters besides those enumerated by Sir Bernard, viz. :—

Helen, bapt. Nov' 6, 1669.   Mary, bapt. May 16, 1677.
John, bapt. Feb. 28, 1673.   Patrick, bapt. March 22, 1679.
Helen, bapt. June 14, 1675.   Charles, bapt. Sept. 20, 1681.

The following is the descent :—

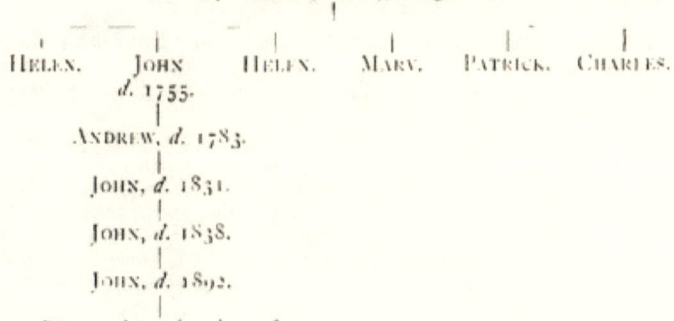

PATRICK, LORD GRAY, *d.* 1609.
|
ANDREW GRAY of Bullion, *d.* 1604.
|
WILLIAM GRAY of Lauriston and Bulbunno, *d.* 1662.
|
ANDREW GRAY of Balbunno (great-grandson), served heir to William (Willielmi, *abavi*), 1663.

HELEN.   JOHN   HELEN.   MARY.   PATRICK.   CHARLES.
           d. 1755.
           |
    ANDREW, *d.* 1783.
           |
    JOHN, *d.* 1831.
           |
    JOHN, *d.* 1838.
           |
    JOHN, *d.* 1892.
           |
PETER, the writer hereof.

PETER GRAY,
of Southfield, Auchtermuchty, Fife.

HON. JOHN JOHNSTONE.—I have consulted Sir William Fraser's Book of the Johnstones for some information about John Johnstone, brother to William, first Marquis of Annandale, but though one might reasonably expect to gain, in this way, some information regarding him, I can find very little. He was born in 1665, and in 1702 had a grant from his brother of the £10 lands of Stapleton in Dumfriess-shire. These lands reverted to his brother's estate on the death of John Johnstone without lawful issue.

I cannot find the date of his death nor that of his will, but he was alive in 1715, in which year he secretly aided the Jacobite rising, as I read elsewhere.

Perhaps some of your readers can tell me when he died, if he was ever married, and whether he left issue.

F. A. J.

LONDON.

DUNCAN CAMPBELL (Lord Ormelie), eldest son of the first Earl of Breadalbane. We find Lord Saltoun (in his own book) objecting to John, a young brother of Duncan, using the titles while Duncan had a son alive. That son was believed to have been baptized, married, and died in the Parish of Aberdour (near Fraserburgh).

Is it true that he, Lord Ormelie, travelled about in disguise, and signed himself a *traveller*, a *caird*?

Can you tell me when and where he died? I will feel grateful for any information regarding him.

G.

JOHN GRAHAM OF KILBRIDE (see vol. xi. p. 108, vol. xii. pp. 33, 36. 129).—Is it certain that the second John, son of Malise, was legitimate? Why are he and his brother Walter described as 'sones carnall' in the renunciation of 25th February 1494? (*Notes on the Priory of Inschmahome*, by the Rev. William Macgregor, Stirling, p. 71.—*Notes and Queries*, 2nd January 1897, p. 9.) Is there any deed in existence in which they are called lawful sons? The charter to Walter of the Lake of Lochton, etc., 8th December 1485 (*Reg. Mag. Sig.*), describe him as 'son' only.

John Graham of Kilbride was certainly alive 19th October 1478, when he appears as baillie for Malise (Inst. of Sasine produced from Montrose Charter Chest, 21st July 1871. Printed in *Minutes of Evidence, House of Lords, Airth Peerage Case*, p. 39).

The Act of Council, 22nd June 1492, contains two erasures, the second of which applies to the word 'apperand' after 'Alex' Grahame' and before 'are.' Two errors having been made in the entry and erased, it is not an unlikely supposition that a third, the words 'and are' after 'Johne Grahame ye sone' also occurred, and was forgotten to be erased by the writer. (A facsimile of the entry showing the erasures is printed in the *Airth Minutes of Evidence*, p. 22.) R. BARCLAY ALLARDICE.

ROLLAND—Arms, a fess chequy *or* and *vert*, between three crescents *or*, two and one, on a field *sable*. Rouland 1528 as in Stodart's *Scottish Arms*, plate 96, from Sir James Balfour's MSS. Any information as to ownership would oblige. W. B.

REPLIES.

TUSTIMAS.—Your correspondent gives the day of the Fair of Tustimas as the fourth Tuesday of November O.S. Against the 28th November on the Dunfermline Kalendar (see Forbes's *Kalendars*) is marked 'Natale sancti Sosthenis discipuli apostolorum . . .' I have not found this saint in the Kalendar of Ferne (*Forbes*, p. 67) a Kalendar more likely, I should suppose, to be observed in Caithness, and against the identification of Tusti with Sosthenes it may be urged that the fair being fixed according to the Old Style would apparently fall at the date of the New Statistical Account, twelve days later than its date according to the Church Kalendar. This would transfer it into the first week of December, New Style, or thereabout. If, however, as is probable, the fair was named before the introduction of the New Style, it would probably have retained its name though its date ceased to tally with the Kalendar of the Church. The feast of St. Thomas, whose name seems quite as likely to have been buried in this peculiar word, does not arrive till 21st December. J.

DUMBARTON PROTOCOL BOOKS.— My experience is the same as that of A. W. G. B. In the *Red Book of Menteith* (vol. i. p. 523) Sir W. Fraser gives an extract from the 'Protocol Book of John Graham, 1529-1542,' which book is stated in a note to be in the Town Clerk's Office, Stirling. It is not there, however, and I am told it may have been lent out to Sir W. Fraser. If this be the case, the obvious inference is that by some oversight it has not been returned, and the Dumbarton Protocol Books may be in the same position. The respective Town Clerks should be asked to see that the registers for which they are responsible are duly replaced. B.

DONOTE.—I find I have transcribed this name Donoce, but queried it with a (?). I suspect it is a clerical error for Dorote (Dorothy). B.

JOHN GRAHAM OF KILLEARN, 1716.--The Justice of Peace Court-Book for Stirlingshire, 1689-1720, shows that on 5th June, 1688, John Graham of Killearn accepted office as J.P. This would indicate his recent succession to the estate. John Graham, yr. of Killearn, is in list of subscribers to Mackenzie's *Lives*, 1722. B.

HOUSTON OF CREICH. 'Spernit Humum' may find an answer to his query (see p. 42) in Mr. D. Murray Rose's communications to the *Scottish Antiquary*, iv. 140-2, and vi. 94-6. Other references to Houstons will be found in ii. 150, iii. 63, 159, iv. 93, 136, and v. 189. ED.

JOHN GRAHAM OF KILBRIDE.—In a letter by Mr. Walter M. Graham Easton, in your January issue, he says :—' John of Kilbride was beneath the sod, drowned, or witched away, etc., before 19th April 1471, when his brother Patrick of Gartrenich (father of second Earl) was son and heir of his father.'

In an entry in *Stirling Sasine Register*, dated 23rd October 1476, 'Malise, Earl of Menteith, sound in mind and body, for good deeds done to him by his dearest spouse, Lady Jonet, Countess of Menteith, gave and bestowed' (certain family plate and personal jewels) *for her lifetime,* and 'same day bestowed (the fee of) the foresaid jewells on John

Graham, his SON NATURAL, for his good deeds and services,' also giving
him sasine of a carucate of land called '*Le Akyr*,' in the barony of
Port and shire of Perth.

While not conversant with the dispute, or having read anything but
Mr. Easton's letter, this appears to settle one point in that controversy,
viz. that Malise, first Earl of Menteith, *had an illegitimate son, John
Graham.*

In a Stirling protocol book a *Patrick* of Menteith is a disputer with
his mother, *Elene Lochaw*, in January 1479-80, and interdict is applied
for against her selling her own annual rents and tenements in Stirling,
he being 'her son and apparent heir,' for her subsistence.   He offers her
board and lodging in John Menteith of Rathow's house.   J. S. F.

MACGREGOR OF GLENGYLE (see vol. xii. p. 136).--Mr. Easton might
refer to Burke for 1849 (vol. iii. Suppl. p. 214, 215) where the pedigree
is given with considerable fulness down to the time of the late laird, James,
twelfth from Dugald Ciar Mòr, who died on 26th January 1897, aged 79
years, and with whom the direct line terminated.   In a memorandum I
have on the family, I find this James noted as being the great-grandson
of Gregor Glune Dhu (1688-1777), whereas, according to Burke, he was
great-great-grandson.   The discrepancy I have not yet elucidated.
                                                                J. L.

12th February 1898.

NOTICES OF BOOKS.

Early Fortifications of Scotland: Motes, Camps, and Forts (The Rhind
   Lectures for 1894), by David Christison, M.D., F.R.C.P.E., Secretary
   of the Society of Antiquaries of Scotland.   William Blackwood and
   Sons. 1898. Fcap. quarto, pp. xxii + 386, 379 plans and illustrations,
   and 3 maps. Price 21s. net.

IF genius be the 'faculty for taking infinite pains,' we see no reason against
placing this book in the category of its products.

Thirteen summers of well-directed personal investigation in the field,
succeeded, during the winters, by equally concentrated and discriminating
research into charters, maps, and books, have given Dr. Christison a claim
to be considered something more than a first essayist in a department of
archæology, which, as he himself admits, is 'so extensive and, from its
very nature, necessarily so vague.'

To zeal and untiring patience in ascertaining primal sources for his
statements the author brings the added charm of a clear and graceful
literary style.   The Lectures of 1894 were good; this volume is better.
It runs to 386 pages, contains over 130 illustrations reproduced from
careful pen and ink drawings by zinco-photography (many of them full-
page), a complete bibliography of the subject, a copious index, and three
large maps showing the distribution of the structures examined.   The
       so far as we notice, are the only defective part of the book; and
       not as maps, but as paper, being in that respect too flimsy for use.

That there have been many other observers, who from time to time
have described British Forts, is evident from the fact that the Bibliography
      130 separate papers, the results in which Dr. Christison has,

however, for the first time collated, sifted, and re-arranged for the purpose of this volume. But, with the exception of Miss Maclagan's *Hill-Forts*, Sir W. Chambers' *Peeblesshire Accounts*, Rev. J. K. Hewison's work on *Bute*, Mr. F. R. Coles' *Survey of the Stewartry*, and Mr. John Smith's *Survey of Ayrshire*, no large section of the country has been examined. Dr. Christison has 'pioneered' the rest of Scotland in this branch of antiquarian lore. One point of great importance, let us add, this volume gives effect to: the more exact and truthful contour of the structures shown in these illustrations, as compared with the older style (*à la* Grose *e.g.*) when hasty sketch-views were worked up at home and the very angles of a mote or fort compressed to suit the page! Throughout the book, truthfulness, in verbal description as well as in drawings, is prominent. As a double record, appealing, thus, to both optical and mental perception, this work is a body of facts, unobtainable elsewhere.

It is natural that Dr. Christison should mainly apply himself to the structural features of the Early Fortifications. That he could also appreciate the archaeological evidence of relics obtained in these structures would also doubtless be certain—if only their secrets had been revealed by excavation. With great justice does the author enter a protest against the too prevalent ambition for exploring in foreign countries to the neglect of our own.

Starting, in part I. with a definition of the term 'mote.' Dr. Christison leads up with a brief review of notices of several in England, Wales, and Ireland, to an account of Scottish Motes, their very unequal distribution, centred chiefly in Kirkcudbrightshire, etc. That they were the immediate precursors of the Norman Castles is the general conclusion upon their probable period. Detailed descriptions follow, culminating with that of the Mote of Urr, 'probably one of the finest specimens in any country.' A chapter, etymologically valuable, on such words as *Burgh, Birren, Burrian*, with four tables showing their occurence in districts, concludes this section. The Second Part, on Rectilinear Works, contains an examination into General Roy's theories regarding Roman Camps, a technical description of Birrens and Ardoch (copiously illustrated), of so-called Roman Camps in Clydesdale, Strathearn, and East Perth, and of other rectangular works not called Roman, with a chapter and tables on the occurrence of *Chesters* as a place-name.

By far the greater portion of the book is devoted to the Forts proper: 'the despised works of one of the few races that succeeded in keeping at bay the proud conquerors of the world.'

Their comital distribution, the nature of their sites, their elevation, their constructive materials, the question of vitrifaction, their ground plans, and all their minor features are most carefully and exhaustively examined. The difficult topic of their characteristics in different districts is then treated of. Burghead has a brief notice, the Caterthuns a very full one, and the remarkable Fort on Culter Water called Cow Castle, has due attention drawn to its peculiarities.

The Chesters near Drem, Kaimes Hill, or Dalmahoy, Edinshall, and Addistonlee near Hawick are among the best illustrated of all the Forts. Chapters XI. and XII. treat of the relation of place-names to the Forts in which it will be matter of surprise to most readers to find so many Rottenrows in addition to the one in Hyde Park. Lists of all the important roots, as *e.g.* Car, Dun, Rath, Lis, etc., are given. In a summary

of the relics hitherto obtained in Forts while under excavation, there is
but the one admission to make, that, with the exception of Dùnbuie, not
one has been excavated in an exhaustive manner; and in short the
results in this direction are as yet too meagre to permit of any sound
conclusions upon the period of their use. Some observations upon
enclosures not fortified and upon Hill-Terraces, such as those at Romanno,
and a concluding chapter giving general results bring to a close this
volume, which, by its style, its scientific method, and its thoroughness,
should recommend itself to all who cherish a true interest in gaining light
upon one of the little studied phases of the ancient national life.

*The History of Scotland from Agricola's Invasion to the extinction of the last
Jacobite Insurrection*, by John Hill Burton. New edition in eight
volumes. Blackwood and Sons. 1897. 8vo, vol. vi. pp. x+426,
vol. vii. pp. x+469, vol. viii. pp. x+556+100 (index). Price 3s. 6d.
each.

Volume vi., the first of the three volumes noted above, begins with a
retrospect of the period between 1603 and 1615—a period, the treatment
of which had been commenced in the last chapters of vol. v. Tytler
accompanies King James the Sixth to London, sees him ascend the
English throne, and there leaves him, and retraces his steps to Scotland.
At our last sight of the historian, as we close his book, he is standing in
the middle of the road by Seton Castle in a fit of gloomy sentimentalism,
pointing to a stone where King James, on his way south, sat while the
funeral of a representative of ancient Scottish nobility passed out of sight
in its sad procession to the place of graves. It was an omen or it was
nothing. In Burton, on the other hand, Scotland still continues to have a
history. Careless of the sentiment of the thing, he narrates how King
Jamie played the part of King of England, how he invented the word
'Great Britain,' how his son, Prince Henry, tried to teach the English the
game of golf, and how hungry Scots flocked over the Border southward.
Burton may not be always accurate, and may be at times too sparing of
his dates to make it easy to check him. Partisans may convict him here
and there of wrong conclusions, but they do not convict him of being a
partisan. His language is often strong, but never violent. As he leads us
on through the times of Covenanting struggles, details the intrigues which
procured the union of the kingdoms, and marshals the elements which
produced the Jacobite risings and their defeat, he displays a panorama of
Scottish history which is full of picturesque incident and illustrations of
the times, and the main features of which remain indelible in the memory
of his reader. The index to the history, which occupies a hundred pages
at the end of volume viii., is a very material addition to the value of the
work as a book of reference.

The Highlands of Scotland in 1750. From Manuscript 104, The King's
Library, British Museum, with an Introduction by Andrew Lang.
William Blackwood and Sons, Edinburgh and London. 1898. 8vo,
pp. xlvi+169. Price 5s.

The latter half of the eighteenth century is in some ways the most interesting and the most critical period of Scottish history. During those
fifty years the history of old Scotland—the impoverished, turbulent Scotland

of the fighting clans and the heritable jurisdictions—came to an end; the Union was for the first time got into working order; and the history of modern industrial and agricultural Scotland began. The MS. which Mr. Lang has edited is a valuable addition to our materials for the history of the transition.

The MS., which is anonymous, is conjectured by Mr. Lang to be the work of one Bruce, a Government official, who in 1749 was employed to survey the forfeited and other estates in the Highlands. The author gives in considerable detail an account of his travels between the Pentland Firth and the Point of Ardnamurchan, thence back to Inverness, then round the East Coast, and across to Argyllshire. He adds 'some General Observations concerning the Late Rebellion and the Dispositions of the People of Scotland,' and makes some suggestions as to 'the most likely means to Civilise the Barbarous Highlanders and improve their Country.' Of course he sees everything from an English, Whig, and Protestant point of view, for which due allowance has to be made. Still, he gives us much valuable information as to the condition of the people, and not a few interesting scraps of clan history and tradition. Like other Lowland observers, he saw little of the 'good old times which tradition beholds in the distance behind Culloden.' His picture of the golden patriarchal age of the Highlands contains plenty of tyrannical and grasping chiefs, and of poverty-stricken people, whose numbers far exceeded the means of subsistence, and who lived in ignorance, dirt, and destitution, on cattle-theft and blackmail. At the same time, he notes many changes for the better. For example, the M'Raes in Kintail 'within these twenty years were little better than Heathens in their Principles, and almost as unclean as Hottentots in their way of Living; but whilst Seaforth's Estate was in the Hands of the Government, about the year 1726, a Large Parish here. where there had been no Minister for many years (nor would they suffer any of the Established Clergy) was divided into two, and Ministers and Schools were planted in them, which has made a Surprizing Alteration in the People, even in point of Common Civility, Decency, and Cleanliness.'

Naturally Bruce's estimate of the character of different clans depended a good deal on their political colour. Thus the M'Kays, who 'of old were reckoned the most Barbarous and Wicked of all the Clans,' are described as being 'the most religious of all the Tribes that dwell among the mountains, South or North. . . . The M'Kays abhor Thieving.' (Lord Reay was a good Whig.) The Monroes, again, are 'well affected, Honest, Industrious, and Religious People. Those who call them Enthusiastical, Revengefull, and Lazy, do not know them or are highly prejudiced against them.' On the other hand, the Camerons are 'a Lazy, Silent, Sly, and Enterprising People,' and Knoydart, in the Macdonald country, is 'a perfect Den of Thieves and Robbers.' It need scarcely be said that the Campbells get an excellent character.

The author's own observations and suggestions are less interesting than his facts, but they show both knowledge and common-sense, and some of them have been justified by history.

Mr. Lang contributes a readable preface and some verses on Culloden. He has been fortunate in obtaining some valuable notes from Mr. William Mackay, author of *Urquhart and Glenmoriston.* The book would be much the better of an index.

The Hunterian: An Account of the Roman Stones in the Hunterian Museum, University of Glasgow, by James Macdonald, M.A., LL.D., F.S.A. Scot., with Prefatory Note by John Young, M.D., Professor of Natural History in the University, and Keeper of the Hunterian Museum. Glasgow: T. and R. Annan and Sons. 1897. Quarto, 100 pp., 45 illustrations and map. 15s. net.

SPECIAL interest attaches to this work, inasmuch as it combines the results of a critical examination of Scoto-Roman epigraphy by several of our foremost Romano-British scholars and antiquaries with the best examples of recent photographic art, in the interpretation of an important section of Roman Legionary Tablets and Altars.

Originally conceived by Dr. John Young, the recording and illustration of the historical stones discovered from time to time on the line of the great Antonine Wall (or Pius Vallum) has now been efficiently carried out by Dr. Macdonald, whose position, as the Rhind Lecturer on the Roman Occupation of North Britain, enhances the value of any treatise on a subject which he has made so peculiarly his own. This has been done, as he himself readily admits, with the hearty co-operation not only of Mr. Haverfield of Christchurch, Oxford, but also of Mr. Bosanquet of Cambridge, who has contributed Notes of definite value and importance upon a fine Roman Bronze Jug found at Sadlerhead in Lanarkshire. The volume contains photogravures of this Jug and of all the forty-five carved, sculptured, or inscribed stones, or fragments of stones, unearthed during the lengthy period throughout which the attention of archæologists has been directed towards the Forth and Clyde Wall—a period beginning with the end of the sixteenth century, when Timothy Pont inspected it and embracing further inspection and description by Gordon of Straloch, Camden, Sibbald, Alexander Gordon, Horsley, Roy, and Robert Stuart. Brief Prefaces by Dr. Young and the author are followed by an Introduction, dealing, first, with the origin of the Roman Room in the Hunterian Museum ; next describing, but all too briefly, the Vallum itself ; thirdly, classifying the stones in the Roman Room. These, the author throws into three groups : Commemorative Slabs, Altars, and Sepulchral Stones. The body of the work then begins with a full description, with necessary references to the older authorities, of the various Inscribed Stones, taking Chapel Hill, on the extreme west, as the starting-point, and so working eastwards to Castlecary, 'the last of the Vallum Forts represented in the Roman Room, and the twelfth in order from west to east.'

The sepulchral slab, inscribed 'DIS MANIBVS AMMONIVS,' for so long doubtfully attributed to the Station at Ardoch, is now on the best authority certainly assigned to that great Roman site. In the second section, the uninscribed Stones are treated of ; nine in number, the majority sadly defaced, and none presenting features of special interest.

In a work manifestly intended to be both popular and satisfactory to the critical—if such an ideal be possible—we cannot but note one point upon which the text of the volume throws no light. To the enquiring student, one of the first points calling for elucidation in connection with the remarkable series of Distance Tablets (i.e., the Inscribed Stones which record that a certain amount of the Vallum was made by this, that and the other Cohort), is : for what lineal measure does the letter P stand on these stones? Dr. Macdonald on p. 7 says : 'It will be seen from the notices of the Vallum Stones that many of them record the number of *paces or feet*,' [italics ours], etc.; and, throughout the descriptions the same alternative phrase is used. Dr. Hübner is credited, farther down on the same page, with the opinion that the P stands for *pedes* and not for *passus*; but into the grounds for this opinion, neither Dr. Macdonald nor Mr. Haverfield seems to have examined. That Hübner's opinion is at any rate very near the mark is surely ascertainable enough by the following simple process of reasoning. The Roman *passus* consisted of 5 *pedes*, the *pes* being a small fraction less than our 'foot' of 12 inches. Measuring the distance on Roy's accurate plan of the Vallum between, say, Duntocher and Balmuildie, we find it is a little over 6 miles Roman measure. Adding up the sums of the measures of work recorded on the ten or twelve stones hitherto discovered in this piece of the Vallum, we find the total to be 46,613 P. In a Roman mile there were 7500 *pedes*; in 6¼ miles therefore there are 46.875 *pedes*. The results of these two measurements, therefore, tally pretty closely. Even if this admittedly rough and ready calculation does not meet the demand for exactitude, it surely at any rate proves that the initial P stood for either the actual *pes* or for something less, certainly for no greater measure, and most certainly not for *passus*, which, if intended, would extend the Vallum for over 195 miles! Even on the supposition that more stones remain as yet underground in this strip of the Vallum, the validity of this calculation is not touched; such a discovery would only prove that the initial P really meant a rather shorter measure still than what we understand by the Roman 'foot.' It is interesting, in this connection, to note that the old Scottish mile was computed, at least up to 1711, in paces of five feet each.

Again, the ascription of the Vallum to Antonine is not readily made clear, from the lack of a brief summary, which should have stated the number of stones inscribed to deities or personages. As it happens, Antoninus Pius is commemorated on quite sixteen of these—but the reader has to ascertain this for himself.

The map on the frontispiece lacks a scale, which is a rather serious want, for the reason that no ordinary maps show the exact line of the Vallum, and, as the names of stations on the line of wall are also not to be found in everyday atlases, the student is now and then at a loss for special localities. The index might have been considerably fuller; no names of *e.g.* scholars or antiquarians, whose descriptions or opinions are embodied in the volume, being entered. The photogravures themselves are excellent, and with the equally excellent typography and paper should be treasured by all interested in the history of Romano-Scotic history and antiquities.

Extracts from the Records of the Kirk-Session of Elgin, 1584-1779; *with a brief Record of the Readers, Ministers, and Bishops,* 1567-1897, *by* Wm. Cramond, LL.D., F.S.A.Scot., Schoolmaster of Cullen. Elgin: *Courant and Courier* Office. 1897. 8vo, pp. i+350. Price 1s. 6d.

This volume, which states itself to be a reprint from the columns of the *Elgin Courant and Courier*, concerns a parish which, as Dr. Cramond rightly says in his preface, was of more than ordinary extent, containing a large burghal and a considerable rural population. The business of the Kirk-Session of such a parish was of a very varied character. The success

sive Session-clerks of the parish of Elgin were, fortunately, men possessed
of exceptional qualifications for their office. It thus happens that the
Minutes of the Elgin Kirk-Session are in several respects the most valuable now extant for the illustration of the social and religious life of the
country in the seventeenth and eighteenth centuries. From so miscellaneous a feast as the extracts from the records of such a court, it is
impossible within reasonable space to present anything representative.
The contrasts among the characters of the items of its administration,
registered in quick succession by its clerks, may be illustrated by the
extracts from the Minutes of 1745. Sandwiched between observances
of fasts on account of the war with Spain and France and the rebellion at
home, is the appointment of a day for administration of the sacrament of
the Lord's Supper, 'if the troubles hinder not,' and a grant of £1, 10s.
to 'help to carry Isobel Glass to the Royal Infirmary, Edinburgh.' The
list of ministers goes considerably beyond that in Scott's *Fasti.* The
volume evinces much patient labour on the part of Dr. Cramond, who
has made of it a valuable addition to his already extensive and useful
series of extracts from parish records.

INDEX

Printed by T. and A. CONSTABLE, Printers to Her Majesty
at the Edinburgh University Press